The First Law of Fate

Felix M. Temple

Clink
Street

London | New York

First published by Clink Street Publishing, 2020
© Stephen Mason, 2020
The author asserts his moral right under the Copyright, Designs and
Patents Act 1988 to be identified as the author of this work.

978-1-913136-86-4 Paperback
978-1-913136-87-1 Ebook

The author thanks Betsy Wing for giving him permission to quote two
lines from the poem by Édouard Glissant, 'Vertige des Temps Froids'
'Cold Weather Fever', from *Black Salt*, Betsy Wing, translator (Ann
Arbor: University of Michigan Press, 1998), a translation of his collection Le sel noir, *Le sang rivé, Boises* (1983).

By the same author

The World's a Minefield

CONTENTS

1

L'addition

He could not imagine it at the time, but the impeccably dressed man that struck up a conversation with him would inevitably lead to his disgrace and death. That was, if he made the wrong decision.

The final item before the interval was the clarinet quintet *Recalling a Serenade* by Paweł Szymański.

'You know,' the man said, as they waited to order refreshments, 'that last piece of music was commissioned by the Kuhmo Chamber Music Festival in 1996. Kari Kriikku played the clarinet with the Silesian String Quartet.'

'I was not aware,' he replied. From his accent, demeanour and quality of the clothes he was wearing, the person that spoke to him was clearly a member of a noble family of the *ancien régime*. 'It was interesting,' he continued the exchange, 'but I came to listen to Ravel, Debussy, and Poulenc, not the Pole.'

'Our French composers are, naturally, wonderful. You say the music by the composer from Poland was interesting. It *is* thought provoking, and it was the first time I heard it. The composer has written a modern piece with references to classical structure – very clever. Did I detect a reference to Sergei Prokofiev's *Classical Symphony*? Maybe. I like the pizzicato. It sounds like rain falling; or, even though it might be a rather fanciful association, like stars twinkling.' The younger man was obviously not interested in discussing the music, so the older man announced who he was. 'But let me introduce myself, I am Guerin.'

They had been watching him for a while. The older man insisted on buying them both a glass of wine. He directed the conversation to politics and the state of the nation. The younger man engaged enthusiastically, outlining his belief that the wrong people were in control of the state apparatus.

As the second half of the concert was about to begin, Guerin told him that he liked the passion the younger man had revealed. 'You are one of us,' he said, 'perhaps you want to know more?'

'Yes, I am passionate about my country. It needs to change.'

'I'm pleased. We will be in touch.'

Some weeks later, during high summer, he was invited to stay at the Château de Canon, in Mézidon-Canon in the commune of Mézidon Vallée d'Auge, rented for a weekend by Guerin and a small number of select grandees. They subtly interrogated him over meals and during the events they organized to pass the time of day. Before lunchtime aperitif on the Sunday, Guerin suggested he joined him for a walk in the grounds of the Château. They walked through the French style garden with its grand symmetrical paths and geometrical flowerbeds, the ornamental lake reflecting the eighteenth-century façade; admired the ten walled gardens before venturing into the English style romantic garden, occasionally discovering glimpses of the *fabriques* – small whimsical constructions so much in vogue at the time when the garden was planned – and little waterfalls fed with water from the river Laizon, which crosses the park, acting to highlight the overall enchantment of the gardens.

'You know of the Twelve Peers of Charlemagne's court?'

'Of course.'

'Then you are aware that they were known as paladins.'

'Yes.'

'You have met a few of us this weekend. You are well educated, a person of taste, and you are discerning. We are mindful that your family is both ancient and noble, from Armagnac.'

He was flattered.

'Then you shall become a paladin?'

'Yes. What you are doing is the future. It is our only hope for France.'

'We are glad you agree with us. We will invest you this afternoon.'

At the investiture, they explained that they were members of the *groupe pour la France*. The organization stood for the France of tradition and control by the educated nobles of ancient lineage. The membership and work it carried out had to be secret to emasculate what they imagined were the worst excesses of elected politicians. He agreed to their purpose. At the end of the ceremony he was told that henceforth he would be known as Guillaume.

After the last of the party left, Guerin took him to the railway station. He suggested they take afternoon tea at the Hôtel de la Gare in the village, because he wanted to introduce somebody to him. They were to work together. Michael Cocke was waiting for them.

His sense of self-importance and condescension to those he perceived to be his intellectual and social inferiors never left him. Some months later he realised that during the epiphany he experienced in the seconds it took to pass the Rubicon between life and death, his judgment had been pathetically inadequate. He had made the wrong choice.

*

The Ministre des Armées placed the plain white cup and saucer on the table.

'So you see, Minister, it isn't good. Our plans for "l'addition" appear to be known to the Russians.'

The Minister raised an eyebrow.

'But we can't be certain.'

François finished his brief introduction to the problem. He stood up in the nondescript plain white walled room and walked to the side table for a cup before filling it with coffee. The Minister scrutinized his movements, his greying head of luxuriant hair giving him the air of a star of chanson. She knew he was slightly younger than Bernard Lavilliers. He had worn well over the years, staying relatively slim, a respectable physique covered by a dark blue business-like suit with a distinctive silk woven Charvet tie to balance the vision, following the dictum of George "Beau" Brummell that clothes should never attract attention; that dressing is the art of not being too fashionable. She remained silent.

Calixte Lavigne, Director of the Direction Générale de la Sécurité Extérieure turned to his subordinates, one responsible for Security Intelligence and the other for Strategy.

'Jean-Frédéric, inform the Minister of our detailed knowledge to date from your perspective of Security Intelligence, if you please.'

The Director leaned back in his chair, clasping his hands over his ample stomach, flesh protruding through the gaps in his white shirt, the buttons stretched under tension, his plain blue tie drifting to one side. The youngest man in the room reached forward in his chair, placing both arms on the table and earnestly clasping them in supplication.

'As we know, Minister, the capacité de renseignement électromagnétique spatiale version secrète,' pedantically, he unnecessarily used the full name of the system, 'is financially protected, and we have continued to develop the program. As expected, we have the usual problems with such a project. They are normal.'

Forever illustrating his intellectual credentials, Jean-Frédéric Esparbès de Lussan used the rhetorical trick of rephrasing the instruction. He underplayed the seriousness of the situation. In his early forties, he had an elongated head with short black hair on top of a tall slim frame. He was ambitious, using his family and political connections to further his career. An énarque, he considered the L'École Nationale d'Administration had failed to recognize his obvious talents. He was graded in the lower half of his cohort the year he finished at the establishment, which meant he did not gain the prestige he believed he was worth. He carried the air of the haute bourgeoisie and the superiority of cerebral self-assurance. When the opportunity arose, he spoke assertively and at length. He often failed to understand that there were times when the game of scoring points was not always appropriate. The old fashioned cut of his suit served to hide his undeveloped body; in black, power black, it was set off with a dark ordinary grey tie against a power white shirt.

'From a strategic point of view,' Stéphanie Beauharnais interrupted, her hands communicating her message as her watch glinted in the sunlight, 'this could be a disaster for France. If our plans get in the hands of the Russians, they will know that we have included a secret program in the satellite. And if our allies are made aware of this program, they will not be pleased. We can expect the Russians, if they are aware of "l'addition", to leak the program when they see a suitable opportunity to humiliate France.'

Wearing a knee-length sleeveless V neck dress in light blue, highlighting the curves of her slender body, finished off with a contrasting silk scarf tied around her well defined neck, Stéphanie Beauharnais did not want to jeopardize her position before the Director, but she spoke out. She knew he was under pressure to deal with this most delicate of issues, and internally de Lussan was not helping. Often mistaken by older men as strikingly similar to a young Catherine Deneuve, Stéphanie took her job and the protection of France seriously. She was aware that the DGSE was highly regarded in the international intelligence community, and intended to continue to play her part in maintaining that reputation.

François passed the time of day with the Minister's chauffeur and security escort as they walked around, looking, admiring and discussing the beauty of his Citroën DS 19 Convertible, designed by Flaminio Bertoni and André Lefèbvre. The chauffer noticed the Minister approaching with the Director. He and the security escort thanked François and walked smartly back to the ministerial vehicle. The Minister turned to the Director at a sufficient distance from them to speak to him without being overheard. She shook his hand and thanked him for his time. She then perused the scene. The chauffer had the engine running and the other man stood at the open door, waiting for her. She walked towards the security escort, the physicality of his muscular frame tightly confined in his black suit. She indicated that she was going to speak with François. He closed the door and the chauffeur switched the engine off.

Eleanor de Beauchamp walked up to François, who had just lit a Gitanes Brunes cigarette as he stood by his Cabriolet d'Usine. She initiated the conversation with a compliment.

'So beautiful, Monsieur Duhamel. My outfit contrasts delightfully.'

'Naturally,' François acknowledged her observation.

He looked directly into her eyes. A woman in her late fifites, the Minister looked as exquisite and regal as her name suggested. Her shoulder-length strawberry blonde hair fell gracefully over a perfectly fitted jacket of a two-piece suit. Her brown eyes appraised his clean-shaven face. He noted a look of enquiry, reached for the packet of cigarettes, and offered it. She accepted, taking a cigarette with an elegant movement of her fingers and thumb; her unpolished nails a tribute to the skill of the manicurist. She did not wear any rings. He waited for her to put the cigarette between her lips before striking a match, watching the movement of her mouth, how her lips rounded on the circular object, carefully, caressing the paper.

'We shouldn't,' he said as they inhaled, each turning their head to exhale to one side.

'I know, but I have slowed down.'

'So have I. I intend to give up, but...' he did not finish.

She looked at the cigarette. 'Now owned by Imperial Tobacco, the British.'

'Yes, but we are the more powerful.' His eyes twinkled, searching for familiarity in a face looked after by years of care.

'But they don't know that.'

'Yes, delicious, is it not?'

She laughed with him. 'How old is this delightful car? It's flawless, and perfect for today. Such a colour.'

'They called the colour "ambre doré". It's from 1961. My father bought it as a surprise for my mother. He saved long and hard.' François knew he had almost said too much about the cost. She appreciated his honesty.

'I'm returning to the Ministry.' She dropped the cigarette and stamped on it with a low-heeled shoe. 'Where are you intending to go now?'

'Wherever you wish,' he offered, following her example with his cigarette.

'Then drive me.' The Minister turned to her security escort. 'Monsieur Fairneau, I will travel with Monsieur Duhamel to the Ministry. Please follow.'

The tone of her voice brooked no opposition. The security escort returned to the official car and moved to sit in the front passenger seat. The chauffer started the vehicle.

The Minister wanted to have a private conversation that was not going to be overheard. François opened the car door for her. She entered gracefully, the sitting position causing her skirt to ride up sufficiently to show a pair of smooth slightly tanned legs. Armed guards opened the dazzling white gates, permitting the cavalcade to enter the Boulevard Mortier.

Back in his office, the Director observed what was happening discreetly.

'You know Stéphanie Beauharnais?' the Minister asked, as her hair flowed in the wind and bright sunshine of late summer.

'Yes. She had her thirtieth birthday last week. Very beautiful. Very intelligent. A patriot.'

'She has an unusual background.'

'Yes. She graduated from the École Nationale des Chartes. She has a first-class grasp of history. Then she did something extraordinary. She went to the English University of York to study for a Master's degree in medieval history.'

'That is rare. She seems to be highly motivated.'

'Yes, she is a pleasure to be with.'

François briefly looked at the Minister. She smiled. He returned his gaze to the road, enjoying the moment. He continued. 'Her dissertation was very interesting. It was about the marriage of Aliénor d'Aquitaine to the English king Henry II.' François knew the Minister's family had lands in Nouvelle-Aquitaine.

'I am intrigued by her watch. It's a Patek Philippe Calatrava.'

'Yes, it's an understated timeless classic. So beautiful. It's from 1932. Her grandfather gave it to her. She wears it to subdue men.'

Eleanor de Beauchamp liked what she heard. She changed

the subject. 'And how is your report? The Du.
cooperating?'

'Yes, but you understand there are, shall we say, problems.'

'Yes, we must deal with those, but it's not impossible. It's
necessary to find a way around them.'

'I agree.'

The Minister took up the discussion they had with the
Director. 'The evidence about "l'addition", what do you have?'

'We are analysing it. It might be the British.'

'Really?' Eleanor de Beauchamp expressed surprise.

'But this is not certain. It could be an attempt to give the
impression that it's a particular nation. We have to be fair, but
more importantly we have to know.'

'I cannot afford to be wrong about this,' the Minister confided. 'The President is, shall we say...' she paused.

'Forthright? Imperial? Impatient?' François quickly interrupted to spare her appearing to be disloyal.

'How much longer do you think your report will take?'

'A few days, perhaps a week.'

'I need it soon. A meeting with our allies in NATO is
planned, and confidential discussions are going to take place.'

They reached the hôtel de Brienne. The security escort had
rung ahead, and as they approached, guards opened the two
tall turquoise doors. François drove into the courtyard and
stopped the car in front of the entrance. Having switched the
ignition off, the hydraulics slowly lowered the chassis. They
sat in the car. The Minister asked him, 'You live in the 9th
arrondissement?'

'Yes, just off the rue des Martyrs. I have a modest flat with
an unremarkable view. We have our parent's home in Rouen.'

'Do you go to La Trinité?'

'Yes, for concerts.'

'You will have to take me.'

François got out of the car and walked around the rear to

open the passenger door. As he did so, the Minister moved the rear view mirror to tidy her hair before removing a small 15ml vial in gold from her handbag, deftly spraying the Fragonard perfume under each ear. A *fonctionnaire* walked down the steps, waiting at a discreet distance until she had finished before opening the door for her. François reached the other side. As she shook his hand and thanked him for the ride, he breathed in her day perfume, Ile d'Amour before telling her, sotto voce, 'You take me back to my holidays and our small garden by the sea, full of the scent of summer flowers.' He continued, reciting the first line of 'Parfum exotique' *'Quand, les deux yeux fermés, en un soir chaud d'automne* – When I lie with both eyes closed on a warm autumn evening.' Her face radiated unanticipated pleasure and palpable delight. 'Baudelaire also spoke of men who are lean and virile in the second stanza: *Des hommes dont le corps est mince et vigoureux.*' Their eyes expressed a mutual understanding of intimacy. Contemplating the car, she then surprised him. 'Roland Barthes was right about the déesse. He said it was the very essence of petit-bourgeois advancement. Perhaps. But it is far more; it is the epitome of brilliance and style.'

*

Charles recalled Pete's skill. He had heard part of a conversation at the shoot. More importantly, he remembered one of his contacts.

'Charles.' The Permanent Under Secretary greeted Sir Charles Beresford, the fourteenth baronet, with his usual assurance as the telephone line connected.

'Hello Francis. You've just managed to catch me before I switch off.' Sir Charles looked at his guests, who nodded to indicate they did not mind the interruption.

'I was hoping to. Peter's just rung. He's come from the glamour of the annual bash. Apparently Lev Gumilyov has been taken up. I thought you'd like to know. It might have ramifications.'

'You mean that old chestnut *passionarnost*?'

'Yes. They've provided a translation of the speech. It'll be a few hours before it goes live on the internet.'

'Is that all? There must have been more to interest me, otherwise you wouldn't have rung.' His friend was loquacious. On this occasion Sir Charles would have preferred not to have been interrupted, but continued patiently with the conversation.

'The meaning of that word *is* vague. He means moving forward and embracing change. It's the usual stuff about reconstruction and strengthening, and it's in the process of being completed.'

'Well, at least they've achieved something.'

'Ha ha ha! very droll. You mean *they say* they've achieved something?' Sir Francis Pelham, a previous ambassador to the Russian Federation, exposed his cynicism. 'Anyway, they're now going to build a rich and prosperous Russia.'

'About time.'

'Yes, they need it, despite my being so disparaging. The interesting snippet that most people will miss is the need for what he called "inner energy".'

'I take it the message is "inner energy and expansion"?'

'Yes, and one other comment. He said that we live in an increasingly unequal world – what's new? – and that the competition is going to be fierce – what's new again? But it could be telling us what to expect. Anyway, that's enough from me. Have a good shoot. You're at Houghton, aren't you? David told me when I spoke with him last night.'

'Yes. It's a small shoot with a few friends. They always look after you.'

'Indeed. Have a good lunch.' Sir Francis Pelham, KCMG abruptly took his leave, as was his manner. Sir Charles turned to his guests as he switched off his device. 'Thanks for bearing with me. It wasn't that important, but nevertheless an interesting start to the day.'

'*Passionarnost* was a big thing for Gumilyov,' Pete followed up, having heard Sir Charles mention it.

Sir Charles looked slightly bemused and surprised about Pete's knowledge of a well known but odd twentieth-century Russian. 'You know about him?'

'He was the son of the great Anna Akhmatova and Nickolay Gumilyov. He wasn't very nice to his mother. He seems to have blamed her personally for his periods of imprisonment.' Jim chipped in. 'And a crackpot. They only listened to him because he said what they wanted to hear.'

Sir Charles knew he had been put in his place, and smiled at his guests. They enjoyed his reaction. They were interrupted when Robert, the head keeper, aged fifty, 5 foot 8 in height, and replete in a well-worn Norfolk jacket and plus twos in brown herringbone called out to the group of six visitors, his manner projecting an assured air of competence.

'Good morning your ladyship, gentlemen,' he surveyed the group with his vivid blue eyes. He spoke in his local accent with an air of authority, well practised as he was in dealing with a variety of people from different social backgrounds, a thick crop of wavy light brown hair atop a ruddy face accustomed to, and shaped by, the weather. He quickly reminded them of the safety measures, using humour to emphasise the need to be careful.

Robert knew four of the Guns, but although Sir Charles had vouchsafed for them, the brothers from North London were an unknown quantity, although their guns were superb, the best makes, a Holland & Holland Royal Sidelock and a Watson Brothers 20 bore side by side. Michael Louca made guns that were a work of art and supreme craftsmanship. Robert admired him for this. Their sense of dress was perfect for the occasion. Jim demonstrated his competence during the course of the day, but Pete was altogether another matter. He was a cracking marksman, a member of the elite. As the day wore on, the twins endeared themselves to the other Guns and beaters for their gentlemanly sportsmanship. Robert took note. The quality of their guns matched the precision of their shooting.

Lunch was located on a prominence overlooking the gentle landscape between the edge of a copse and a field. A flowing Beardsleyesque arabesque line divided the scene between the heavy frost of the previous night, contained within the shadow of the trees, and the grass exposed to the sunlight. Charles had the opportunity to share his taste for beer at lunch, aware of the discriminating palate of his guests. He had sent some bottles of Trappist Westvleteren 8 Blond and two bottles of 12 to Houghton in advance. There was a sufficient quantity to enable the other Guns, the keepers and beaters to have a modest share in the tasting. The 12, dark-brown bordering on red gold in colour with a deep flavour of malt, tasted as the bouquet promised, with sweet overtones that lingered on the palate. For some, the 8 perfectly complemented the cold Roman Seafood Tart, Melton Mowbray Pork Pie and, in keeping with tradition at Houghton, some of Colonel Austin's bacon and marmalade sandwiches – a useful haversack ration that, as the Colonel used to say, was both filling and sustaining.

The group got to know the men from Finsbury Park. Complimented on his accuracy, Pete explained modestly that it was probably because he was a plasterer, always looking at the line ahead, judging the accuracy of getting the finish right. Lady Anne Bourchier became excited when he explained about polished plastering, plastering with lime, and the Venetian plastering techniques. She was even more interested when he admitted being on the Conservation Register. Sir Charles picked up the conversation when Pete talked about his work abroad for an Emir in the Gulf, explaining that his pair of guns was a gift from him.

The brothers endeared themselves to a number of the Guns, and after taking the advice of the shoot captain, they discreetly dispensed tips to the shoot staff and the keepers at the end of the day, posting letters of thanks to Sir Charles and their host a week later. Such courtesy surprised the recipients – unused as they were to mixing outside their own social circles and previously not having appreciated that people from a much lower social class also had good manners.

At the end of the shoot, Sir Charles left his guests in the capable hands of the head keeper, who took them for a stroll around the gardens, in particular to experience his favourite sculpture, James Turrell's *Skyspace Seldom Seen*. Entering the big square box on stilts, the only window a square opening to the sky, sitting on the slightly reclining seat with its back to the wall, they observed the rotation of the earth and the movement of the clouds in the wind, the rays of the sun splashing against the upper white and lower boarded wall, casting a square of bright light that moved imperceptibly, sometimes breaking up as clouds crossed the sun. 'Amazing,' was Pete's immediate astonished response.

Charles decided to use Pete as a discreet way of contacting somebody close to the Arabs with sufficient power to authorise suitable actions, and fast.

*

Walter G. Causey III insisted that Marie-Anne Ouellette enter the Office of the Secretary of State for Foreign and

Commonwealth Affairs before him. They walked through the double mahogany doors into the tall room. Before them sat the Principal Secretary of State, Marmaduke St John, the two Emeralite desk lamps located on each side of his desk switched on, as was the central light hanging from the ceiling, a large circular inverted dome of glass hiding the bulbs, with eight smaller lights encircling the centre globe. St John stood up and walked swiftly towards the ambassador of the United States to the Court of St James's as he and the Deputy Chief of Mission reached a point adjacent to the tall mirror encased in a golden frame, located on the wall between two sets of windows. The two tall men, each fully aware of their respective status and power, looked each other in the eye and shook hands, the room a cocoon for authority, their images indifferently reflected in the mirror. The Minister of State for Europe and the Americas, Reginald Winterbottom, entered the room behind the ambassador. A young woman followed him, pushing a trolley with a teapot, coffee pot, carafe of water, an assortment of glasses, floral bone china cups, saucers and milk jugs. She was ignored as she carried out her duties, placing a plate of biscuits on the highly polished low coffee table.

The pleasantries swiftly over, Reginald Winterbottom took on the role of offering refreshments, whispering gently into the ear of the woman that brought the trolley into the room. He quickly glanced to watch her walk out, his eyes avariciously appraising her disappearing slim frame, her short jet-black hair carefully shaped and unruffled, her white blouse tightly tucked into a black pencil skirt that hugged the shape of her hips and legs. Marie-Anne Ouellette detected Winterbottom's momentary assessment, averting her eyes sufficiently quickly not to have her observation noticed.

'Thank you for having me come over so suddenly,' the US ambassador opened the exchange once they had made themselves as comfortable as possible in the upholstered chairs, the feet of wood sturdy under the weight of the sitter, with wooden arm rests beautifully carved, but uncomfortable on the elbows.

'Not at all, ambassador.' Marmaduke St John put his cup and saucer on the table. 'You know that part of Reginald's remit is defence and international security, and, given your comments over the phone, I thought it would be appropriate for him to join us.'

'Yeah, I know. You're an oil man, aren't you?' The ambassador stated with the confidence of a man used to directing and controlling others.

'Yes, I've been around the industry, ambassador. I understand you're in land and building,' Reginald Winterbottom replied noncommittally but fully aware of the ambassador's background.

'So, what can we do for you, ambassador?' Marmaduke St John opened cautiously, knowing this was going to be a difficult discussion.

An hour previously, the Secretary of State had been hurriedly summoned to 10 Downing Street. The President of the United States of America had made a telephone call to the Prime Minister during the course of the morning, threatening serious repercussions unless the British found out who their double agent was. Marmaduke St John arrived to find that Sir Charles Beresford, Chief of the Secret Intelligence Service, and Margaret Edmonstone, the Director of Government Communications Headquarters, had already spent some time with the Prime Minister. As they left the room at the end of the meeting, the three passed through a small antechamber. It was at this point that St John turned to face Sir Charles. The usual suave composure he put on for public display had dropped and his expression was now one of self-righteous pomposity and anger. He stopped and briefly looked at Sir Charles, struggling to control his temper, his throat fast constricting because of his rising blood pressure. Both men squared up to each other, height for height. The patrician Marmaduke St John with his thin grey hair and finely tailored suit hated the aristocratic background and connections of the equally smartly dressed baronet. 'Get this dammed little runt and do it quickly, or I'll have your hide, Charlie,' he blurted out before striding off in a fit of pique, not waiting for a reply.

'What on earth was that all about, Charles?' Margaret asked, standing eye to eye with Sir Charles.

'I was his fag at school. He didn't like me much, and hated me even more when I led the rebellion against him and his ilk.'

'Did you succeed?'

'Yes. Exceedingly well, I have to say. We were in luck. The timing was right. He's had it in for me ever since. Our paths have taken different courses, so we haven't had to communicate much since.'

'He's obviously born a grudge for a long time.'

'Yes, but this time it's going to cost him.' The composure that Sir Charles normally radiated changed to one of serious determination.

'What about his position? He might be in a top job, but the PM was incredibly dismissive of him just now.'

'Well, as we now know, the PM is under intense pressure from the Americans – that is, at least from the President. We'll see how far that goes after we've talked to the people that actually run the country.' They exchanged the glances of people with inside knowledge. Sir Charles continued to answer her question. 'He's far from safe. He might have been in politics for a long time, but at his age he'd usually have been put out to fallow in the Upper House. Providing, that is, he remained a faithful party serf. The PM is now at the mercy of his little clique after the disaster of the snap election. It's a small group, but they have the backing of most of the media that thinks it matters, so he had to have a senior role to keep him – and his accomplices – quiet. There's another thing, and it's more important. The party nomenklatura is nervous of him. He might lead a rebellion. He's haughty enough to think he'll win a challenge, even though his political career – if you can call it that – has been a dismal failure until recently. Anyway, what I've got for him is something different. He's not expecting it.'

'This double agent you've got,' Walter G. Causey III continued his opening gambit. 'You've gotta find him, and find him fast.' He spoke with the brusque tone he was familiar with when dealing with people he considered to be his inferiors.

'Let me assure you, ambassador, we consider this allegation very seriously, especially concerning a valued and long-standing ally.' Marmaduke St John approached the forceful directness adopted by the ambassador with his usual public persona of glossing over the issue. He had anticipated the ambassador would take an aggressive stance. The President had nominated him shortly after he had been inaugurated, and the Senate had duly confirmed the appointment. The two men had had a long history of mutual business interests.

'See here, Mr Secretary,' the ambassador used the form of address adopted in the United States to refer to St John by the post he held. 'It's looking pretty darn bad for the British right now. You've got a double agent, and that's a danger to the security of the United States. Unless you find him and deal with him, we're going to have to re-think this so-called "special relationship". And that's direct from the President.'

'We are aware of the problem, ambassador. I'm reliably informed that the Chief of MI6 is personally working on this right now, and although you say it's a male, it isn't certain.' The

Secretary of State answered the statement in an attempt to placate the antagonism clearly articulated by the ambassador.

'So what? I've got Homeland Security and the National Security Agency both in my home town, and they're breathing heavily down my neck right now.'

'Yes, but it doesn't help that you haven't given us anything to go on, ambassador.'

Marie-Anne Ouellette, the Deputy Chief of Mission, took the opportunity to interject and reinforce the importance of the issue at an official level. 'Mr St John,' pronouncing 'St' as 'saint', 'you've got the signals station in Cyprus. Naturally, the NSA values this source of information. But there comes a time when the US will stop trusting an unreliable partner. A whole bunch of stuff is coming up for renewal, and we don't mess on security.'

Reginald Winterbottom responded aggressively. 'Are you telling us that you have something else that's as good as RAF Troödos and Ayios Nikolaos Station?'

The Deputy Chief of Mission maintained a dignified posture. She then took her time. Pushing back her curly black hair with one hand of her long, elegant fingers, her princess-length string of 13mm natural seawater pearls in warm cream rocked gently against her neck, the lustre glistening under the central light. Having gained the full attention of the men around her, she proceeded to cross one leg over the other, sit back in her chair and reply with assurance. 'That's for us to know, not for you to ask. You're buying Chinese technology. We don't like that. This is serious, and so are we.'

Marmaduke St John handed Reginald Winterbottom a tulip glass of sherry. The colour of a *sfusato amalfitano* lemon basking in the light of a bright sun blazing against a blue sky, the condensation on the glass heightened their anticipation. Sitting opposite each other in the upholstered chairs, they inhaled the clean bouquet before raising their glasses: 'Chin chin,' they said simultaneously. The almond-sharp dry taste unwrapped briskly in the mouth. Stylish, savoury, with a distinctly nutty flavour, the fresh intensity of the wine gave out a pleasant feeling of warmth, elevating the experience that served to enhance the pleasure of expectation, although both men warmed the sherry by failing to hold the stem.

'Super, don't you think, Reggie? It's muy seco-extra dry.'

'As always, so good. I love it.'

'Well, Reggie, what do you think? Heavy handed or what?'

'Arrogant pipsqueaks in my view,' Reginald offered his opinion. 'They haven't got any evidence of a double agent, and didn't offer any, even after you pressed them. They've got a cheek, with their operatives in China all found and killed a while back because of a double agent in the CIA.'

'Yes, he's just like many of his breed: used to telling people what to do and getting angry if they don't do it. Just like the new lot, totally unsuited to diplomacy or politics. They seem to think it just happens.'

'What does Beresford think?'

'He doesn't know what they're on about, but he's moved understandably quickly. He's set up a team to assess every possible officer in MI6 that might be a risk.'

'Threatening to remove their people from the satellite tracking station at Troödos is a bluff.'

'Is it?'

'Yes, they haven't got anything near as good, even though they've extended their empire in Central Asia.'

'What about the Chinese technology? They might be right. We've discussed it enough.'

'Perhaps, but GCHQ has given us the assurance that they've been over it thoroughly. It's better quality and cheaper than any of the American stuff. Anyway, either we have the Americans putting back doors in, or the Chinese.'

'Reggie, they must have something to be able to accuse us of having a double agent. I know a whisper on some nutty conspiracy theory website is sometimes enough to get people without intelligence to take the rants of others seriously. What we need to know is where this comes from. Let's try the q.t. You're over in Washington in the next day or so, aren't you?'

'Yes.'

'Sound our friends out discreetly. Be careful, though. We don't want word getting back to the ambassador or his boss.'

As they drove back to the embassy, Marie-Anne Ouellette told the ambassador about her observation.

'You think he's straying?' the ambassador asked.

'He's married. It looked to me as if there's more to their relationship than him just whispering discreetly to her before she left the room. She's Spanish or Italian, I'd guess, early twenties. Very attractive.'

'Maybe she's a sleeper,' the ambassador mused. A smile cracked his craggy face as he became amused at his play on the word.

'Maybe she is. I'll follow her up. There could be something there that we don't like.'

'Or we can use.'

*

The cool of the air-conditioned building was appreciated, even if the walk from the bus stop was short. A covered walkway provided shade from the heat of the morning sunlight. The trees added a welcome colour with their shades of green, softening the unrelenting lines of architectural angularity.

'Good morning, and welcome to the Singapore Space Symposium.' The man who spoke to her smiled. 'If you'll let me have your name, I'll find your badge,' he continued.

'Thanks,' Helen responded to his welcome. 'But if I give you my name, I'll need another one,' she said with a look of mischief.

The man laughed, his face radiating the unexpected pleasure he experienced at the joke. 'OK. Very good,' he chuckled with a good-humoured laugh, 'so now I've got to treat you to a Singapore speciality. We'll go for a coffee and buttered kaya toast later.'

'That sounds great, and I'll tell you my name. It's Helen Curlie.'

'I'm Lee Yihong. My English name is Stewart, so call me by my English name if you like.'

'I'm pleased to meet you, Yihong, I'll stay with the name your parents gave you.'

'Oh, they gave me both, so I don't mind.'

'Crikey. I suppose you've got a nickname as well.'

'Yes, but I'm not going to tell you that. Here's your badge and pack. I see you're a project consultant. What about?'

'I've been asked to investigate satellite technology.'

'What aspect?'

'I don't know. I'm here to learn. Your conference looked like a good place to start to meet people after I've read up on the basics.'

'It's great you've come. You'll find some helpful people around. It's only one day, although we're having a private session with a number of invited guests tomorrow afternoon. I'll catch up with you later.'

'Thanks very much. I'll leave and let you collect some more names. You've got a little queue now.'

He laughed again and turned his attention to the next in line. Helen walked into the School of Electrical and Electronic Engineering, located near the Satellite Research Centre. The content of the symposium at Nanyang Technological University was highly technical. Speakers included academics who were active in developing satellite technology as part of a university programme, and commercial entities offering glimpses into their current work whose main purpose for attending was to see what others were doing, identify opportunities and possible new recruits. In addition, there were a few consultants, both employed and self-employed, looking for any opportunities or openings that might take them out of penury.

At lunch, Helen found herself with a small, mixed group of men and women leaving the last session and continuing a discussion about cryptography and the need to provide for the security of communications between satellites and the ground, and how to prevent a satellite from being taken over by an unauthorized person or organization, allowing them to intervene to stop water flowing or wreck havoc on power generators. The group split variously into pairs and threes to navigate the busy thoroughfare towards the room where lunch was served.

A man Helen took to be in his forties worked his way around the group as they left the hall. His intention was to join her and another woman, slightly shorter, with short black hair, wearing a simple dress in pale green silk and plain beige flat shoes. Helen was explaining how the Australians intended to expand their satellite industry, the politicians having finally accepted the importance of satellites for military communications.

'What are their plans?' the woman asked Helen.

'Oh, it's all in the open, no secrets,' Helen answered. 'The government want to improve the imagery you can now get from satellites, and their space situational awareness, whatever that is.'

The man took the opportunity to interject at this point. 'I can tell you what that is. It's having the technology to know where objects are that orbit the earth. The aim is to avoid collisions, like when Kosmos-2251 collided with Iridium 33 in 2009. That was massive. It was at hypervelocity.'

Helen turned her heard to him to ask, 'what's "hypervelocity"?'

'An amazing speed. Both satellites were travelling at about 7.5 kilometres per second. That's 16,170 miles an hour. The combined velocity on impact was 10 kilometres per second, 22,369 miles an hour.'

'*Really?* That was fast. You'll have to tell me more. How do you remember the exact numbers?'

'It sounds better if you say the collision was 36,000 thousand kilometres per hour.'

Helen and the woman she was talking to then continued with their original conversation. 'What your government wants to do sounds interesting. We do a lot of that sort of work. Maybe we can help?' They joined the queue for lunch. Motionless, Helen watched her companion get out a small box from her handbag to remove a card. She held it out in both hands, the English side facing Helen. She took it with both hands and read the inscription. 'Zhuge Xiùyīng,' Helen read out. 'Your name is very good. You are an outstanding beauty, and you're elegant and brave. Well, you are very beautiful, and I have been admiring your dress. I'll have to find out if you're brave, though.'

'Oh? How did you know the meaning of my name?'

'My best friend and I used to play guess the meaning of names at school. Her family left China in 1949. I'm several generations Australian from an English girl exiled for being convicted of stealing.'

'Ah, so you know a lot of history maybe.'

'Not as much as I should. Do you have an English name as well?'

'Yes. Alice. My mother said I should have this name, because it's supposed to mean noble.' By this time, they had moved to the point where they needed to pick up a plate. 'Please, you go first.' Helen had manoeuvred herself behind Xiùyīng to ensure they did not hesitate over etiquette.

As they moved off to find a table, a man approached Xiùyīng whom she clearly recognized, smartly dressed in black shoes, black trousers and an open-neck white shirt. He spoke to her. She apologized to Helen, indicating she was being invited to another discussion, but that they would meet up later in the day.

Helen found herself alone with the man who had followed her and her Chinese companion. She could see that he was keen to speak to her. He was of middling height with receding hair that was cut short to hide the extent of his baldness. He had a furtive, aloof air about him that seemed to be founded on his own innate sense of self worth, with a conviction that his values were standard. Helen watched his eyes. As he spoke, he looked at her, but his eyes constantly moved, watching other people around the room, at the laptop she had taken out of her bag, and at his own Smartphone. He spoke to her about cryptography and the companies across Europe and Turkey that he helped, and highlighted his credentials as a programmer and how he was in a position to advise with his extensive network of contacts, suggesting that some people he knew were from top secret agencies. He filled Helen with facts and figures, personalities and gossip. He needed her to understand how well connected he was.

There came a time when he wanted to give her his contact details. Having agreed that Helen could power her laptop up and sign on without being impolite, he began to encourage her to let him insert a USB into one of the ports on her computer.

'It's great Wi-Fi around here,' Helen said, having connected to it earlier in their exchange.

'Yes, I'm impressed. It's a good signal. Where shall I put the USB?' He asked.

'Oh,' Helen sounded worried, 'they told me not to connect anything to the computer.'

'You work with some smart people. I can send you an email.'

'All right,' Helen feigned ignorance, 'maybe that'll be all right.'

Helen gave him an email address and watched him type and send an email to her. It arrived in her in-box. He became exasperated when she said she would click on it and read it later. Suddenly losing interest in her, he gave an excuse, and walked off to introduce himself to somebody else that had caught his eye.

The next morning the telephone rang in Helen's hotel room. 'Hi, it's Stewart, I promised to take you for a coffee. Do you have time this morning?'

'Yes, sure, that would be great. Where do we go?'

'It's the Far East Square branch in China Street, number 18, called Ya Kun Kaya Toast. Do you want me to come over to meet you, or shall we meet there?'

'Let's meet there. I won't be long.'

Helen finished packing. She left her suitcase with the hotel after checking out. Lee Yihong had arrived before Helen. When she got there, he ordered for them both.

'Aren't these old buildings lovely? The colours are great.' Helen said to Yihong immediately they sat down.

'Well,' said Yihong, 'you wouldn't have wanted to come here a hundred years ago. This street used to be notorious for its gambling dens. It was also a meeting place for some of the secret societies. We're lucky to have it, because the area has now been preserved.'

'I suppose the real estate value must be significant.'

'Yes, but what's the price for retaining a little bit of the past? It took some persuading to keep this area from the rapacious developers. We'll never understand the lives of the people that lived here. The colonial buildings don't tell us what life was really like, especially now they're pristine and in better condition than they've ever been, but we need to be reminded.'

'Yes, a Martiniquais acquaintance has taught me that the past is not what we think we know, and oral culture is as important as physical objects. I looked you up last night. I see you're a professor at the Satellite Research Centre. Have you been in Singapore long?'

'Ah, well, where shall I begin? I'm a Peranakan Chinese. We're also called Straits-born Chinese. My family have lived in this area for over 300 years. We call ourselves Baba-Nonya.'

'Oh, right. I'm learning another lesson.' Helen looked into his dark brown eyes. He was her height, smartly dressed in blue trousers, black shoes and a white shirt, his straight black hair an old fashioned short back and sides. Helen detected a softness in his eyes. She already knew he had a great sense of humour. *He's a really nice person* Helen thought as he explained his work. He admired her slim athletic figure, her brunette hair ending just above her shoulders.

'I'm in the world of quantum computing. We're in the vanguard with colleagues from the University of Strathclyde in Scotland. We created and measured pairs of correlated photons on an orbiting satellite.'

'You'll have to tell me more about this. You've just said something that is meaningless to me.' Helen said as she shrugged.

'Have you got time? When's your flight?'

'Oh, I've got plenty of time. I'm flying to Abu Dhabi later this evening. I don't need to get to the airport until six tonight.'

'In that case, have you been to see the gardens by the bay?'

'No. What are they?'

'OK, so we have to go. Let me call my director to see if she'll agree to me skipping the meeting this afternoon.' Yihong took his Smartphone out of his pocket. 'Excuse me while I give her a ring.' He stood up and wandered towards the door as he made the call. He returned a few minutes later.

'I'm in luck. They don't mind me taking the afternoon off. That means you're in luck as well, unless you are already fed up with my company.'

Helen reacted quickly. 'Oh no, it's really nice being with you, Yihong.' She was very pleased to be with him.

'Great,' Yihong enthused. 'Let's go. I want to take you around. It's a fantastic sight, really wonderful. But I've just thought. Are you all right with the temperature and humidity? The forecast doesn't include rain today.'

'Look, I'm from Brisbane! We get this heat as well. It's like being at home in the summer.'

Yihong's concern eased at her reply. 'Ah, well, that's good,' he said, and led the way.

Yihong refrained from speaking more about his work until after they had visited the gardens, viewing the separate conservatories, outside walks and supertree grove. The heat and humidity ensured they strolled gently around the area, taking in the brilliance of the concept, illustrating how technology had been used with careful architectural design to bring the natural world closer to people. Helen found the vertical gardens amazing, as she enjoyed the splendid views of the OCBC Skyway, occasionally exclaiming 'awesome' – a phrase that normally annoyed Yihong when used so much out of context, but perfect for the views, scents and virtuosity of the design they were walking into and through. A bond began to form between them as they discovered a joint enthusiasm for design, horticulture and tropical plants.

Yihong took Helen for a late lunch to try Peranakan food, where he continued to outline the latest advances in quantum cryptography. 'A light lunch, please Yihong, because I'll be fed well on the flight. I hope you don't mind.'

'Sure, we'll try a mix of small dishes.'

After ordering, Yihong continued with his train of thought. 'So you see, particles can act as if they are in two places at once. This is important, because traditional methods to encrypt data can be overcome.'

'Oh,' Helen quickly interrupted him. 'So that means no current method of encrypting data is safe, even the cryptographic systems of spies and the military?'

'You've got it.'

'That's serious.'

'Yes, but quantum computing can improve things. You have to have two keys, one to encrypt and one to decrypt a message. This means you have to exchange a pair of keys between the parties. There is another way of doing it, called public key cryptography, but the intelligence agencies and the military tend not to use that method. They leave it to the commercial world. For better security, you really need to give unique keys to each party, so they are the only ones to have the keys.'

'I presume you can't do that safely over the internet?'

'No. You need to deliver them by hand.'

'Physically?'

'Yes.'

'So that means there are spies and military personnel circumnavigating the globe delivering new keys in person?'

'Yes, and diplomats.'

'So much for doing everything electronically!'

'Yes, I agree. Anyway, to solve this problem and make encryption safer, it will be helpful if we stopped distributing the keys physically. If we can make it work, we can distribute the keys using quantum key distribution. This is where you use a quantum communication to provide a shared key between two parties without a third party learning anything about the key.'

Helen interjected. 'Do you mean even if the third party can intercept the communications between the two parties?'

'Yes. If the person intercepting the communication tries

to learn information about the key, it will fail, and the two parties will know somebody is intercepting their communications. It's because a photon can act as if it's in two places at once, so if you entangle two photons, they can be sent anywhere and remain entangled. If you look at one of them and change it, you also change the other one. This happens simultaneously, however far apart they are.'

'That's neat. I suppose there's more to this than your explanation.'

Yihong laughed. 'Yes, of course.' He let the time shared with Helen take him further than he would normally do so in social discourse with a person of the opposite sex that he had only recently met. 'You're the most delightful company.'

'Thank you, Yihong, the feeling's mutual.' He was embarrassed, but welcomed Helen's response. He briefly continued to tell Helen about the most recent experiments, how the Chinese had taken the theory to the next stage by beaming entangled pairs of photons from a satellite to three ground stations across China. This was a significant leap forward, because previous attempts to transmit photons had been restricted to very short distances. The Chinese had proved that the concept could work.

'What's interesting about the Chinese,' Yihong continued, 'is that they have teamed up with the Austrian Academy of Sciences. This is because the Austrian proposals to develop quantum computing were engulfed in bureaucracy at the European Space Agency.'

'Stupid Europeans,' Helen offered her opinion.

'Yes, really stupid. But as you can imagine, others have taken this seriously. The Canadians, Germans and Americans are all working hard on this.'

'Are you?'

'Oh, yes, of course.'

'But tell me, why should all this be of interest? Why is it really important?'

'Because the technology we use every day is increasingly being connected via satellites. Think of it – television, telephone, navigation systems, weather, banking, search and rescue, checking fuel pipelines – even motor vehicles. You begin to understand?'

'Yes, I begin to understand. It's massive. And I suppose an enemy, by taking over a satellite, could disrupt another country.'

'You've got it.'

Helen had to consider travelling to the airport. She looked at her watch. 'That's something. But you know, I've got to go now, Yihong. The food – it's good. I don't have a sense of place, though. It was delicious, but you'll have to tell me more about the influences of the region. I get Chinese, Malaysian and Indonesian tastes. Is that right?'

'Yes, then with a unique Singaporean twist. We'll have to try some tutored tasting. Maybe next time you're here?' Yihong escorted her to the hotel, asking for her forgiveness for leaving without waiting for the taxi, because he had duties to attend to. Before taking his leave, he introduced Helen to a more secure email provider by which they could encrypt their communications. They promised that this would be the first of many meetings together.

*

'So, what's the position, Quinton?'

The Head of Intelligence Analysis looked at Sir Charles Beresford and Margaret Edmonstone. He had accompanied the Director of GCHQ on the journey to London. Quinton Myerscough was methodical. He did not tolerate short cuts. Thoroughgoing, meticulous, pedantic, fastidious, insisting on the examination of every item of evidence in a detailed, forensic manner, they had chosen him precisely because of these qualities that he possessed.

'Well, since we found the Australian document and got them on board to work with us, we've been very busy. As you might expect, whoever it is, they use the Tor onion routing network. No surprises there. We'll be pleased when the Americans stop funding it. We're monitoring the Deep Web by joining in over a series of relays. We can then examine the data passing through each of the nodes. We know the website, but we need to trace the users to try and identify the perpetrator. The problem is, no matter how many resources we put into this, every time our man's Tor browser connects, it creates a circuit by choosing an entry guard from one of thousands that are available. We can't control them all. We have a better chance of spotting him when he's logged on if we monitor more entry guards, but the reality is we can't do it because we haven't got enough resources. Even if we had, we'd have to do it for days and nights on end, because there hasn't been any change to the site for a week.'

Sir Charles summed up the position. 'Thanks. So this is the picture. We've got a site on the Deep Web that is virtually invisible and is not visited – or rarely visited. There are three very interesting documents posted that we are, of course, delighted to have obtained. We have the Australian document, classified as Top Secret with a dissemination limiting marker of Sensitive: Cabinet. This deals with the decision taken by the cabinet to counter regional defence imbalances. The Americans are pressing them hard to do something on this. The minutes of the cabinet discussion would be of great interest to our US colleagues. The second is a United States Top Secret Sensitive Compartmented Information document analysing information from their own intelligence sources regarding the attempts by Russia and China to build anti-satellite systems. Most of the sources are highly sensitive, as we would expect, and they have helpfully included the methods, analytical process and the names of the people they used to reach their conclusions. What's not surprising, given the financial implications for the future budget that the President must be considering right now, is that it's also Very Restricted Knowledge. Before we consider the French document, have you got any comments, Margaret, given that you've kindly coordinated this?'

'So far we've looked for links between all of those mentioned in the US document and the agents we know about in Russia and China. We're not surprised about the range of information or the analysis, but I think we've come up with a lead. I discussed this with Quinton on our way to London. Quinton, do you want to tell Charles what your people found before I go on?'

'Yes, if you like. Our monitoring activities have taken us to another website on the open internet that might be linked to the source of the documents. It's like an old-fashioned bulletin board with names of contacts, position and company name. You can only get into it with a password. Once we found it, we asked one of our trusted contractors to join it once they found out how to be invited. We used the password issued to them to gain entry. We have to be careful, because we don't know how sophisticated the administrator is. Our interest lies in the names and companies of those listed. They're all linked to the satellite industry.'

Margaret continued. 'They might be linked, but we agree that it doesn't follow. An analysis of the companies points to contractors and sub-contractors in big satellite projects across the globe. It could be a club. Interestingly, they're all men. Not a single woman, even though there are women at the same level of responsibility that could be on the list if it was a sort of network of like-minded people. Anyway, we're monitoring it through our contractor. He's working on a project for a number of Arab nations.'

Sir Charles interrupted. 'How many companies are represented?'

'Not that many, Charles, only eighteen. It's run by a consultant, a one-man band.'

'Really?'

'Yes.'

'How odd.'

'We agree. He's an unusual character. English father, Welsh mother. Farmers. Born in Belo Horizonte, Mias Gerais state in Brazil. Goes by the name of Michael Cocke.'

'That's where Thea Haberfeld was born,' Charles offered, countering their looks of surprise by continuing, 'my daughter reminds me regularly that women form half of the population, and are often ignored. She's recently found out about her.'

'Oh, right. Well, she's right, of course. Anyway, back to the subject. He's a native English speaker. Close to fluency in Portuguese. Passing command of Russian. Parents shipped him to prep school in England, then minor public school. Bright enough for university, but dropped out when he got into programming and IT. Your people are trying to piece together how he got where he is.'

Margaret set out the facts quickly, succinctly.

'Intriguing. He's working on the periphery. That's clever, if he's up to no good.'

'Let's look at the French document next, then we can go back to that question.' Margaret continued. 'The French document has two markings, Très Secret Défense and Spécial-France, so not only it is seriously secret, but even more so because only French citizens are permitted to possess and read it. It refers to their plans for their latest satellite project. As we know, it's their first operational space-based signal intelligence system, with three satellites that are intended to detect, locate and identify electromagnetic signals on the ground by enemy radio communications systems and radar. They're also aiming to achieve early warning of ballistic missiles. The prime contractors are the usual suspects, under the management of Direction générale de l'armement. The interesting bit is the additional stuff they've included. They've called it "l'addition". It's split into two parts. The first is a program that monitors every communication that's relayed by satellite that originates in France and French overseas territories. The second part is related to the European Union project for a satellite system to rival the Americans. We've put a lot of money into this project. It seems as if they intend to put a back door into the system, so they'll have a way in to the most confidential parts at any time. If it works, they'll have access to some pretty secret stuff. It's supposed to be a joint project, but not as far as the French are concerned. As you can appreciate, if we and our other allies had been made aware of this, they would never have included it.'

Sir Charles commented on the last point made by Margaret. 'Yes, indeed. Although I don't blame them for trying. Nobody will be happy with this. Do we know if they know we've got this document?'

'No.'

'Do we know if they know that somebody else might have this document?'

'No.'

Sir Charles turned to Quinton. 'Quinton, I presume you've not got anything on who might be viewing this Deep Web site, other than this chap you're monitoring?'

'No, but we're actively watching it.'

'Margaret, what's the geographic distribution of companies on this list?'

'America, France, UK, Italy, Russia, Turkey, United Arab Emirates and China. Some are overseas offices of a parent company.'

'Some list.' Sir Charles went quiet, then continued. 'We might be out of the EU project soon. We've got contingency plans in place, but it's going to cost a significant amount of money, and it will take far longer than we'd like. On the other matter, can we prevent calls being monitored by the proposed program?'

There was a knock on the door. 'Enter,' Sir Charles boomed out. A woman opened the door and walked in with a tray of refreshments.

'Ah, thank you, Jean, that's much appreciated.' He looked at his watch. 'Spot on time.' The three stood up to help themselves to tea or coffee. Jean retired as quickly as she entered.

'Interesting,' Sir Charles mused, sitting back in his chair, cup and saucer in hand. 'The Americans say we've got a double agent. We're fairly certain we haven't, but we're looking into this. We can't be complacent. On the other hand, why do they think that? They obviously know something we don't, but won't tell us what, unless it's just a rabbit. And we seem to know something the French don't. By the way, how did we know about this website?'

'Well,' Quinton's face relaxed, showing a glimmer of delight and fun. 'I can answer that one. It's my daughter and her friends. It's been a mix of serendipity and intelligent thinking. She's at the Department of Aeronautics and Astronautics at Massachusetts Institute of Technology doing her doctorate. She and some of the alumni from the Kettering Group decided to see if they could find any top secret documents about satellites on the Deep Web. As we know, the Pentagon once dreamed of dominance in space, but recent developments have put an end to that absurd fantasy. My daughter and her friends thought this must mean that there's a lot of espionage going on with regard to this technology, and wanted to know if it's true. They thought they'd see if there was any evidence of spying and, if so, whether it was available if you looked for it.'

'Is this part of her doctorate?' Sir Charles asked.

'No, they're doing it for fun.'

'Right, well, very good. It seems as if some of their results are proving to be helpful.'

'Yes. They found the website with the documents first. The one with the names came later through an obscure link between the two in the website metadata.'

'So the link was a mistake?'

'Yes, undoubtedly. Sometimes it's just the sort of the break we get. We always look for human weakness.'

'Do any Americans know about this?'

'Not that we're aware.'

'Good. Have you told the Australians about this independent contractor?'

'No,' Margaret responded. 'But I was going to suggest we do. I think we need their cooperation, and they're in a difficult position with this document being disclosed right now. They also need to know where the leak is.'

'I agree. Will you get in touch with them when we've finished?'

'Yes, of course.'

'Have we analysed the American document in any detail yet?'

'I've got my people working on that. We're going through the contacts, sources and the other people mentioned. I'll get back to you on that as soon as we've finished.'

'Thanks. One last thing. Let's talk discreetly to as many of those people listed on the website as possible. We want to know what this Cocke is like.'

*

'Sasha,' Colonel Zinovy Khodzhaminasov addressed Captain Alexandra Milyukov, an officer in the Main Intelligence Directorate. 'We have an interesting situation developing.' He had a gravelly baritone voice, using the diminutive of her name. Having read her file, he wanted to find out her response to this familiarity by somebody she did not know.

Head of Aerospace Defence Command, a unit of the Main Directorate of the General Staff of the Russian Armed Forces, Colonel Khodzhaminasov was in Paris, attending the International Conference on Satellite Communication and Technology. They sat in a room on the top floor of the Brezhnevian era embassy of the Russian Federation, looking over the Avenue Chantemesse. Designed by the Hungarian émigré George Vari, it was finished in 1978. A substantial building, its height tempered by tall horizontal square columns, it is of greater interest than many built during the same period.

Alexandra had expected his use of the familiar. Very good-looking, clearly fit for his age, he had a strong comforting manly voice, similar to the late Dmitri Hvorostovsky – such a great singer, she liked his rendition of Тёмная ночь – 'Dark is the night', although she preferred Mark Naumovich Bernes, who sang it in the film *Dva boitsa* – (Two Soldiers). *He's only eight years older than me*, she thought. When she had arrived in the building that morning, the porters had told her that he had been to the gym. At 40 he was young to fill such a senior post. She had been busy finding out about him through her networks. He was single, and clearly fitted into the current regime.

The Colonel had arrived the previous day. The ambassador had told her personally that she was to meet him. The subject matter was secret.

Captain Alexandra Milyukov sat attentively, looking at the Colonel's slim face, monumental swept back natural brown hair, medium-thick eyebrows framing oval shaped eyes, straight nose, lips that were neither too full nor too thin, with a soft, clean-shaven jaw-line. *She looks so good in that dress – it must be silk – the colours she's chosen compliment the late summer sun*, Zinovy Khodzhaminasov thought as he appraised Alexandra's light chestnut brown hair cut just above the shoulder line set against a fine light brown tan glowing with energy. Her eyebrows were carefully shaped, framing deep brown eyes. He was aware that they were concentrated on him.

Alexandra took the opportunity to offer the Colonel another cup of tea. He liked Russian Caravan blend from China, served traditionally. She took his porcelain tulip cobalt net cup and saucer, designed by Anna Yatskevich of the Imperial Lomonosov Porcelain Manufactory, partly filled it with the strong tea, then handed it back. He topped the cup up with his preference for hot water from the samovar before using the silver tongs to take a thin slice of lemon from the plate and place it in the liquid. At the same time, he helped himself to another tea cake. Alexandra filled her cup, and occasionally ate minute portions of the apple pie she had on her plate.

'We've recently tested a hypersonic missile. It was ahead of schedule. That is very pleasing. The booster has got solid fuel engines, so it accelerates to supersonic speed, and with the scramjet motor at the second stage, it will accelerate to hypersonic speeds. Once it's operational, we will have an advantage over the navies of the world – at least until they catch up. It travels so fast, no anti-satellite system can catch it.'

This was new to Alexandra Milyukov. 'So the British are stupid to think their new aircraft carriers are worth building.'

'Yes. One missile is enough to sink the biggest ship. And the Americans don't like *istrebitel sputnikov*, our new anti-satellite weapons programme. They've always tried to control the world in their own image, but they're not going to restrain us. They claim they don't want to make space a military sphere, but what they say and what they do are not compatible. They send up new satellites that have secret payloads, yet they complain when we do the same.'

Zinovy Khodzhaminasov stopped speaking. He had become impassioned. It was time to calm down. Alexandra listened, liked and understood his rage. The Colonel stood up and began pacing the room.

'Right, let us begin to understand what is happening. What I am going to tell you is of the utmost secrecy. We have identified you as the most appropriate officer in Paris to be involved with this project. You have demonstrated circumspection in the past. That is a highly desirable characteristic.'

He looked out of the window at the central avenue, a little patch of grass bisecting the road, a small area with a slide and other items for children, and benches positioned on the outside looking in, the area devoid of grass. 'What is that area outside? Do you know anything about it? It looks as if there's a statue or something out there.'

'It's called the Jardin Claude Debussy. The statue is a monument to the great composer.'

He turned to look at Alexandra and walked around the room to avoid being seen from the road. She imagined his well built frame under the lightweight grey suit jacket.

'Do you like his music?'

'Yes, he thought of music as a metaphor in the context of nature. It's all about movement. He was very innovative, but he was also inspired by our great masters.'

'Yes, he was influenced by The Five.' Alexandra was impressed with his knowledge. They switched topic with verve. 'And he influenced many others,' continued Alexandra, 'including Igor Stravinsky.' She examined his demeanour as she mentioned Stravinsky. This was her test for him. She wanted to know what his reaction would be.

'Stravinsky was a truly Russian composer, but Dmitri Shostakovich was the greatest composer of the twentieth century.'

'Oh yes, I agree.' He had passed her test at the mention of

Dmitri Shostakovich. He observed the animation in her eyes. 'The *Leningrad* is sublime and patriotic. It's authentic. The best are his quartets. For me, the most moving of all is his last, the fifteenth.' With these words, he understood that she had times of melancholy, but she also knew: it has to be.

Zinovy Khodzhaminasov looked at Alexandra closely. She was aware that she was under scrutiny. She had a strong personality, formed by the ravages of recent history and the travails of her parents, desperately struggling to come to terms with the upheavals that came with what appeared to be the strange death of communism. At university, she had begun to understand that communism was forever going to be a utopian dream, but for her the alternatives of unchecked private enterprise and destructive rentier capitalism were even worse. She had learnt from an older historian, whose career in the university had been obstructed because her views were not considered compatible with the new wave of ideas. She taught that we have to be inquisitive, to question, not only perceptions of facts and opinions about facts, but our own beliefs, our understanding of the world and our preconceived thoughts. In particular, we have to see through those that write history, to know their parents, where they went to school, university, their understanding of their place in society, their politics, their prejudices and weaknesses, otherwise we will never know how to evaluate their work and trust it – especially the men. Reality is unpleasant. Put another way, as she used to say, the reality that you think you know is not the reality that might be, or the reality that others want you to think is the reality. Alexandra would not demean her sense of worth by compromising to fit in with the prevailing wind. Zinovy Khodzhaminasov liked what he saw and what he heard, especially her independence. He began to trust her because of it. He returned to the purpose of the meeting.

'We have an interesting scenario. The French think we

know what they are doing with "l'addition". We do know what they're doing, and they think the British might have leaked it to us. They haven't, of course, but we've, let us say, nudged them to consider that that is a possibility.' Alexandra raised her eyebrows in amusement. 'We have a source that specialises in satellite systems. He seems to have a contact inside the DGSE. He's also managed to make the Americans think the British have a double agent in MI6.'

Alexandra interposed at this point. 'With the present political climate in America and Europe, nobody much likes the British these days. They must be in a very weak position.'

'Yes. It's our intention to make people think this. The conference I'm attending will be full of agents from across the world. We don't want you near it. We want to know how much the French know about our agent and his contacts in their organization. There is an officer by the name of François Duhamel who is carrying out an investigation at present. It's intensely secret. Only the office of the President, the Ministère des Armées and the Director of the DGSE know what he's doing.'

'And us.' Alexandra did not ask how the Russians knew. She was not that imprudent.

'Yes, and us. I want you to find out what he knows. You report to me, no one else. Your immediate superior and the ambassador have been briefed and told to provide you with any support you need.'

As they stood to leave the room, Zinovy Khodzhaminasov turned to Alexandra and looked into her eyes. 'By the way, do you like tea the old way? Perhaps I've imposed my will on you.'

'You have not forced your will on me. I, too, like tea the old way, as well as the new way. It reminds me of my grandmother and of visiting her. I have fond memories of her biscuits, the pancakes she cooked specially, and her preserves. She made them all.' Then she smiled at a memory. He was intrigued. She continued. 'It reminds me of a little romance in the second chapter of Eugene Onegin. The samovar is a blessed invention. Dunya pours the tea. It ends *Приди в чертог ко мне златой!* Come to me in my golden chamber, love!'

He was pleased and amused with her literary reference. 'But that time has not gone.'

'No, it hasn't. I do all these things with my mother in our dacha.'

'It's our duty to preserve our culture.'

'Yes,' Alexandra continued passionately. 'Culture isn't things or books or architecture – those are only what come out of us. We mustn't be a nation of consumers like the West. It's our relationships that are important, like friendship, trust, patriotism and mutual suffering.'

'And love.'

They had begun to eat salt together.

Colonel Khodzhaminasov's immediate impression was that the reports in her file were accurate. He agreed that Captain Milyukov was clearly loyal and highly unlikely to be duped by the West.

*

Colonel Commandant Xú Delun of the Aerospace Systems Department, part of the People's Liberation Army Strategic Support Force, listened to Major Zhuge Xiùyīng. When she finished, she took hold of the purple-brown Yixing landscape teapot and refilled the Colonel's cup with his favourite afternoon tea, dragon pearl jasmine from Fujian Province. Young green tea leaves, rolled by hand with layers of fresh jasmine blossoms, their fragrant oil absorbed by the leaf of the tea, unfurled in the infusion. The tea gave a light and aromatic brew of subtle flavour.

'Thank you,' Xú Delun said, looking at Major Zhuge. Before he could say any more, there was a knock on the door. 'Come in,' he said in a tone of someone used to controlling others. As a young Chief Sergeant third class entered the room, the Colonel beckoned Major Zhuge to fill her own cup with tea. The sergeant handed the Colonel a white folder, standing to attention as the Colonel opened it to review the contents. 'Yes, good. Thank you,' he said to the sergeant. 'That is perfect. You may go.' The Sergeant nodded his head in a slight bow, turned and left the room. Colonel Commandant Xú Delun reviewed the text typed on the single piece of white paper carefully in silence. He simultaneously sat back and moved his chair slightly away from his desk. 'You know, we have done very well with satellite technology over the past few years.'

'Yes, Colonel. It has been very good.' Major Zhuge sought to follow his train of thought, not sure of his reaction to her report.

'We were successful in a rendezvous between two of the Shi Jian satellites that were in elliptical low earth orbits some time ago. It's a complex operation between two orbiting satellites. The Russians were the first to report on that triumph, but nobody knew what we were doing.'

'Most pleasing.'

'Yes. We know what they are thinking, but they don't know what we were doing, or what we are thinking.' The colonel took a sip of tea. 'More recently, we have achieved something even more spectacular with the Micius satellite experiment, which is part of the Quantum experiments at Space Scale. We generated pairs of entangled photons, and then distributed one of each to three ground stations, two on the Tibetan Plateau at Delingha and Ürümqi, and the other at Lijiang. Once we have mastered this, it will allow us to transmit a secure cryptographic key that can be used to encrypt and decrypt messages to ground stations.'

'And any attempt to listen in to messages sent this way will be immediately detectable.' Major Zhuge noticed the colonel had relaxed and appeared to encourage a discussion.

'Quite. And of course, it means that our communications will be totally secure.'

'But there are others working on this.'

'Oh, indeed. People at the Max Planck Institute for the Science of Light have collaborated with commercial companies to measure the quantum states of light signals that were transmitted from a geostationary communication satellite 38,000 kilometres from earth. They're confident that a communications network based on satellite technology that cannot be broken will be possible within a few years.'

'Their system does not rely on the entanglement of protons. It's different to our approach.'

'You are correct. This will happen. Some think it must be for everybody, some of us think it should only be for the state.'

'The position of the Americans is interesting.'

'I agree. They do not like it when we don't write academic reports about our work, but their silence on this is exceptionally loud. We know they have the capability to develop such technology, but they have suddenly stopped publishing papers.'

Colonel Commandant Xú Delun looked out of the window of the air conditioned room into the night sky. 'Major, your work is very impressive.' He took up the folder. 'This report indicates that the company Helen Curlie says she works for actually provides her with a good alibi. It's genuine. That you noticed that man sought to insert a USB into her computer was well observed. And you took a good photograph of him – very helpful. It seems as if he is a wanted man.'

'By the Australians?'

'Yes, and the British.'

'Ah.'

'You seem to have uncovered an interesting new espionage ring that we were not aware of.'

'Ah.'

'And you have an image that they can connect to a documented person. The Australians are very pleased.'

'They know about me?'

'Yes. We have discussed this at the highest level. We were directed to get in contact with officers in the Australian Secret Intelligence Service at the High Commission. We have decided to show a willingness to work with the Australians. They want to get close to us, and we see this as an opportunity to show that we are adaptable in the modern world. It will be useful for us to be close allies with the Australians.'

'But on our terms?'

'Perhaps, but we must demonstrate a commitment to act as partners that can be trusted. Besides which, we want to know about this man and what he is doing. We want to know if he has any of our secrets.'

'Perhaps he might have other secrets that we would like to know about?'

'Indeed.' Colonel Commandant Xú Delun had been told by various sources that Major Zhuge Xiùyīng was intelligent and highly perceptive. He decided to watch her closely. 'We will go to the Australian High Commission tomorrow morning to speak with our counterparts and be briefed. We have just under twenty-four hours, because Helen Curlie is leaving for Europe tomorrow evening.'

'Is it dangerous to meet with them on their territory? They will take our photographs and record our conversation.'

'Yes, that is possible. But they already know both of us, and they have good photographs already. They have assured us at the highest level that they will not record our discussion. This is for a good reason. They prefer it to be an oral dialogue with no recording. It is safer for both of us. We will agree a written text of our joint action in both languages. We will put them to the test.'

'We will have to trust them.'

'Yes. We have to trust in the absence of knowledge. As Confucius said, if your words are loyal and trustworthy and your conduct sincere and respectful, though you be in distant barbarian states, you will be effective.'

Colonel Commandant Xú Delun stood up and removed his jacket from a hanger placed on the coat rack next to the side of the door. Major Zhuge also stood up. As he put on his jacket, he said, 'Now we need to relax. Do you know of the Xiu Hai Lou Collection?'

'No, Sir.'

'It's a private collection of Chinese painting and calligraphy, and it's in Singapore. The National Gallery is open late tonight, and my wife and I are going to visit a special exhibition from this collection. Please come with us. We will go for a meal after.'

'Thank you. That will be delightful.' Zhuge Xiùyīng gave a slight bow; she had begun to extend her *guānxi* relationships.

*

The taxi arrived shortly after Yihong left Helen. To Helen's surprise, Zhuge Xiùyīng was sitting in the back. Xiùyīng got out of the taxi to speak to Helen.

'I expect you're surprised I'm here.'

'Yes,' Helen said with a slightly harsh tone to her voice.

'Can I explain?'

'Go on.'

'Can I invite you to switch your safe machine on?'

'Why?'

'It will help with this sudden turn of events.'

'Very well.' Helen powered up the Australian Secret

Intelligence Service device that had been issued to her, and entered her password.

'If you go online to see your emails, an explanation will be given.' Helen did as she was asked. Xiùyīng was insistent, but her polite manner encouraged Helen not to think ill of her. 'I won't look at the screen, but here is another card for you.' She held out a plastic card with her two hands. It was an identity card with her photograph in uniform on one side. Helen did not understand the Mandarin characters. 'I know you don't understand the characters, but please read the email from your immediate superior,' Xiùyīng continued. Helen noticed a recently sent encrypted email from her manager. She decrypted it, and an image of Xiùyīng appeared in the body of the email. Having swiftly read the contents, she asked Xiùyīng if she would retire to the taxi while she made a telephone call. As Xiùyīng walked back to the taxi, Helen rang the safe number.

'Boss, its Helen.'

'G'day Helen. How you doing? How's Singapore?'

'Great. Look, I've been asked to get into a taxi with a woman claiming to be from the People's Liberation Army Strategic Support Force. She told me to log on. I've got your email. Well, it looks as if it's from you, telling me she's an officer in the space mission of the PLA.'

'Yeah, that's right. It's all fine. I've been waiting for you to ring to check. Things have moved on swiftly over the past few hours. Have a chat with her. Don't tell her too much at this stage; you'll need to build a rapport with her. Stay with information at Level 2. She'll have the same concerns. It's perfectly all right.'

'OK. I'll go along. I suppose this means we're working with the PLA?'

'On this one, yes. It's getting bigger. You'll be briefed and updated when you get to Europe. By the way, you're upgraded to business class.'

'Oh my, very nice.'

'You'll be travelling with your new colleague. We've got you sitting together away from the other passengers. You'll need to agree how to work with her.'

Helen shared the taxi with Xiùyīng to the airport. As they were driven, Helen told her about the gardens by the bay. When they had settled into the business lounge, Helen took the opportunity to say, 'Xiùyīng, is that a PLA taxi?'

Xiùyīng merely smiled and changed the subject. 'I knew you were not who you said you were when it looked as if you were going to let that leech insert his USB into your laptop.'

'Yes, of course.'

'You approached the problem by making him realise you knew what you were doing, but you let him send you the email – although you didn't open it. He probably thought you were stupid, just like most men think all women are stupid.'

'Thanks for that. I didn't want to make it too easy for him. But let's be honest, even though people are told it's fundamental for security not to let other people attach things to your computer, they still do it.'

'I suppose the laptop was just for him? He was a creep.'

Helen cited the two lines of the poem 'Beware the Man'. She continued, 'let's talk about it on the flight and enjoy the champagne. Here's to us.'

'That sounds very good. I'm guessing that the poet is a woman?'

'Yes. Stevie Smith.'

They chinked their glasses.

*

Étienne du Parquet groaned inwardly. He had taken the job because it was interesting. He had also aimed to increase his knowledge and skills, which he had succeeded in doing, but now the directors of the company were causing difficulties. Specialists in providing cryptographic systems for satellites, together with other products aimed at the military, the company had developed quickly during the time he had been with them. It was successful because of the exceptional technical workforce. This eventually caused problems of production and the relationship with the state. A Turkish company that also provided cryptographic systems for satellites had approached the investors.

The majority backers of the German company liked the offer that had been made. Unless the Strategic Surveillance Command or the Federal Intelligence Service expressed an objection to the sale, it seemed to the employees as if the Turks were going to buy a venture with good profits and excellent contracts. Many feared for their future when the proposed changes were announced very late on Friday afternoon.

Étienne was not alone in his dismay at the news. Shortly after the brief talk given by the Chief Executive Officer, the meeting broke up. People wandered around in small groups, closing systems, logging out and preparing for the end of the day. A colleague he was close to passed him briefly, and casually suggested to him that they finish, mentioning in a whisper the name of a beer keller located slightly out of the Saxon town. Another colleague close by simultaneously heard the suggestion. The three nodded in assent to the joint plan. They left the office separately.

Gebhard, Denk and Étienne sat at a small table in a tiny bay window. Gebhard opened the conversation. 'Denk, you're a Turk, and Étienne, you're from Martinique. Yet you've both taken to our German beer. I like that.'

Smiles all round. The three chinked glasses: '*Prost*'.

Gebhard continued. 'Denk, do you know anything about these possible buyers?'

'Not yet. Give me time. But I don't like it.'

Étienne had enjoyed affairs with both individually, each drifting away from the other amicably. Intimate relations apart, Denk and Gebhard were good at their job. He began, 'I don't suppose we could start something ourselves? Our own company and reap the benefits of owning our own labour?'

'Étienne, I like you. I fell for you because of your French accent – a Martiniquais who speaks German with a French accent, so sexy. I also like you, Denk. We work well together. Things haven't always worked out as we've wanted in some ways...' they all knew what he referred to '... but it could work.'

'But?' Denk asked.

'Yes, but. We would have to join the shark-infested sea of corruption, bribery, vice and unpleasant realpolitik. Not only that; we're just technicians. We need other skills.' He stopped to take a drink. 'Look, let's not be too pessimistic. How much money have you got?'

Étienne indicated his savings amounted to a little over €50,000. Denk proffered a slightly higher sum.

'I've got somewhere between you both. The question is, do we have enough to last for, say six months?'

Étienne continued. 'It's a problem. I've been thinking about it, but...'

Denk changed the subject before Étienne finished. 'I'll try to find out about the Turkish company, but I'm going to start looking to move. There are some opportunities coming up. There's a small conference taking place in Belgium.' He took out his Smartphone, his thumb swishing up and down on the screen until he found what he was looking for. 'Here we are, Quantum Cryptography, two days, residential at the Hôtel Jean de Bohême in Durbuy, Belgium.' He showed Gebhard and Étienne the screen.

'There are some good names there,' Gebhard commented.

'It might be worth going to. It's an expanding field. It's becoming reality.'

Étienne asked. 'Are you going, Denk?'

'No. I thought about it, but I have relatives over at the same time. I'm looking after them. Anyway, I prefer Germany. It's my home now.'

'What do you think, Gebhard?' Étienne looked at him.

'Tempting. I'm with somebody at the moment: I'm not sure if he'll be happy with me if I go off to Belgium for two or three days right now.'

'That good, eh? Is he the one?' Étienne and Denk both gently teased him. Étienne looked at his device. 'Let's see where this Durbuy is.' He looked it up. 'It's south of Liège. Not easy to get to. It looks as if it's in a forest.'

'It's in the Condroz and part of the Ardenne. It must be a nice little place. You can go hiking and things.'

'Very sweet, you might find somebody there.'

Gebhard and Denk now ribbed Étienne. They had both fallen for his strong masculine oblong face, oh-so balanced cheekbones, jawline and chin, his straight medium-thick eyebrows curved at the ends, and his physique. Denk could not look into his dark brown eyes without the poetry of Enderûnlu Fâzıl singing in his mind.

Étienne paid the fare and got out of the taxi. Remaining in his seat, the driver opened the boot to allow Étienne to remove his bag. The grey stone façade of the Hôtel Jean de Bohême presented a formidable presence in the Place aux foires, the apparent gloominess enhanced by the overcast nature of the low grey cloud. The hill to the left gave the main block, rising to three levels, an appearance of great height. He walked through the cars parked in the front, and the tables set outside with outdoor umbrellas, patio gas heaters providing heat and light in the damp air. The reception was staffed with a man and a woman, both young, who had a smile through-out the day for new visitors, welcoming them to a pleasant and comfortable hotel. Late in booking the event, he had no choice other than to take a suite. He was told that the hotel was shortly to have a new name, Le Sanglier Bas, and they hoped he did not mind. 'Not at all, it looks very nice, and I'm sure the old and the new will mean the same excellent service. A friend told me he'd stayed here in 2008 and thought highly of the hotel and food,' he replied. The young man rushed to take his suitcase and led him to the room, to the amusement of his colleague, who noticed Helen in the bar area, who in turn was looking out at the reception area. The two women exchanged knowing glances and enjoyed a smile of a moment shared that only they witnessed. When inside the suite, Étienne felt the luxury, convincing himself all was well in all possible worlds as the receptionist eagerly showed him around, his eyes transfixed by Étienne's good looks and commanding physical presence.

The time for dinner approached. Étienne walked into the long bar leading to the restaurant between people sitting on bar stools and those around the small tables near the window. A strong Australian accent spoke out, 'Well hi, gorgeous.' He recognised Helen's voice.

'Hello, it's good to see you,' he looked squarely at her, trying to conceal his embarrassment for failing to remember her name.

'It's Helen, Étienne,' Helen knew he had a problem remembering her name. Later she thought that perhaps he had difficulty remembering the names of all the women he met.

'Ah, yes, I remember. It is a pleasure to see you again.'

He held out his hand to her. Helen took his hand, but insisted on kissing him on the cheeks. He looked at her glass. 'Champagne?'

'Yes, I'm just finishing it. Why don't you join me? Are you staying?'

'Yes, I've just arrived.'

'For the conference?'

'Yes.'

'So have I.'

'Oh, right,' he looked at the barman as he was hovering close to them, waiting for an order. 'Another glass?'

'No, really, but you order and maybe we'll have dinner together. I've booked a table. We can share.'

'Yes, let's do that.' He turned to the barman. 'I'll have the same as the lady, please.'

'Certainly, Sir,' the barman removed a stopper to the bottle and filled a flute.

Étienne thanked him as he handed over the glass and refreshed the bowl of assorted nuts.

They walked the short distance to Le Sanglier des Ardennes restaurant. Over a luxurious dinner of the menu gastronomique devised by Wout Bru, the matching wines, good food and candlelight loosened their tongues. Reminiscing about their previous meeting, Étienne confirmed he never wanted to be a spy. They discussed where they were in life, their loves and lovers, the barrier broken when Helen in her Australian forthrightness commented on the noticeable attraction of the male receptionist towards him that she was able to observe from her bar stool, and his obvious delight in the attentive behaviour of the very good looking young man.

*

On holiday before meeting her sister for her forthcoming wedding, Katharine decided to take a few days savouring the food, wine, fashion and art that Milan had to offer. During the afternoon she wandered between shops and art galleries. When in Princi her device buzzed. Wrapped up against the slight wind, eating a light lunch outside the branch at Largo La Foppa was good for watching the world go by. Trees softening the harsh reality of straight lines, traffic travelling into and away from the six converging roads, it was fun to be observing the quality of driving, viewing the daily ballet of fashion, motor scooters whizzing in and out and parking; young men and women with lovers; friends, acquaintances, women together, men together, elderly women dressed in quiet understated outfits taking miniature dogs for slow walks, the full tapestry of apparently settled lives on show.

A message popped up. Margaret Edmonstone had written 'Please get in touch asap.' Having finished her lunch, Katharine decided to indulge in a *caffè corretto* at the bar before going back to the flat she rented. She rang Margaret on her safe device.

Margaret picked up at once. 'Hello Katharine, film star in Milan.'

'Hello Margaret.'

'I expect you can't move for all the luvvies that surround you.'

'If only. Father might have named me after Katharine Hepburn, but I didn't inherit her beauty. Anyway, what is it?'

'Operation Araneum.'

'Really? Anything new?'

'Yes, that's why I've bothered you. We've got another top secret document.'

'From the same source?'

'Yes.'

'How intriguing.'

'Yes. Our usual contact from the Agenzia Informazioni e Sicurezza Esterna is rushing to Milan to meet you and one of the big players in satellite technology.'

'It's that serious?'

'Yes. I'll send you an address after we've finished talking. We wondered if you wouldn't mind taking time off to have a meeting. I don't think we can do anything, but we'd like to find out what they know. It seems that they think we've acquired something they want to keep secret, but we don't know what it is or what they know.'

'So the new document is Italian?'

'Perhaps it's best for you to remain ignorant of that at this stage.'

'Yes, fine.'

'Anyway, can you make it? It's in a couple of hours and it's in the north of the city.'

'Yes, go ahead. I planned to see Giorgio Armani's fashion designs this afternoon.'

'Oh, right, well you might have time. I'll send you the address. Our contact has promised to be there before you, so you'll know him. We feel you're protected with this arrangement.'

'That's all right. I'll leave my tracker on until I'm sure I'm safe.'

'Thanks. I was going to suggest it. Can you find out more and keep them sweet? Bye!' Margaret Edmonstone signed off abruptly without waiting for a reply, as was her habit.

It was going to take slightly longer than anticipated. Katharine decided to visit the fashion collection on another day. Situated at a crossroads, the main entrance to the squat three-storey building had the appearance of being on the diagonal. A bland unremarkable structure, it sat with the other commonplace buildings in the area of north Milan. External panels of small mosaics in light blue and white scattered randomly helped the aesthetics when set against the blue cloudless sky, with steel supports covered with stone, the windows on the ground and first floors covered with external horizontal bars, and an additional deterrence provided by the cameras dotted around the walls at first floor level.

Giovanni Crespi was waiting for Katharine at the entrance to the building.

'Lovely to see you,' Giovanni said as he kissed Katharine on both cheeks. 'It is very good of you to take time to see us from your holiday.'

'Oh, that's all right. I was told it was urgent. Where have you travelled from? It must have been difficult for you.'

'Actually, not far – from Turin.'

'You must need refreshments.'

'Yes, but that's organized. Please come with me.'

He led the way up two floors and along a corridor. A stylish suit in light grey covered his tall, slim frame, which was topped with a mop of unruly black curly hair. His appearance gave the impression of a man who was constantly dishevelled, a dangerous assumption on first meeting that many made to their cost. Giovanni Crespi was a senior officer in the Agenzia Informazioni e Sicurezza Esterna, empowered to ensure the Italian intelligence services operated professionally and to the highest standards. A few years previously it was agreed that SIS and AISE would repair previously damaged relations. The new leadership in the security services in Britain did not want the embarrassment of not only appearing to treat, but actually treating, agencies other than the Five Eyes, with distain. The change was to emphasise competent cooperation where it was justified. Katharine was the first liaison officer at the highest level, and it had begun to have some success in this respect.

Giovanni knocked on a door: a woman's voice called out *'entrare'*. They entered into an everyday working room at the back of the building, the windows looking out to the car park on another side of the building and some garages. Seraphina Visconti stood up from her desk and shook Giovanni's hand, and then Katharine's as they were introduced. Walking to a small round table with three chairs, she busied herself with offering refreshments set out on a tray. Tall, with straight black hair just above her shoulders, an oval face with pencil sharp eyebrows, Seraphina Visconti was every inch a member of a Milanese aristocratic family. Giovanni had taken the trouble to explain who she was to Katharine as they walked to her room, in the same way that he had also explained to Seraphina that Katharine was from a family of the minor English aristocracy. He took longer to explain the English social structure to Seraphina, reminding her that for a more nuanced overview she really ought to ask her English guest for a better explanation if she had the time.

Giovanni began. 'Katharine, let me explain that Seraphina is head of research here, and she is closely involved with the projects across the European Union and Italy in satellite technology. Seraphina will not tell you herself, but she was awarded a doctorate in spectrograph instrument development from the Department of Physics at the University of Oxford after taking her Master's degree in astrophysics and cosmology at the Università di Bologna.'

'A woman after my own heart. You must tell me more.'

'I will, if you wish to know, but later.' Seraphina responded in a business-like manner as she offered a small plate of wafer thin biscuits around.

Giovanni continued. 'You know how integrated the various industries are?'

'Yes. Most projects are awarded to consortia. Our problem is that the weakest link is the sub-contractors.'

Seraphina Visconti immediately liked what she heard from Katherine. She moved slightly forward in her seat, took her hands off her glass, and enthused at the sentiment expressed by Katharine. 'You are correct. This is the most significant problem. Secrets are easily leaked, even though the contracts are drawn up clearly and explicitly to ensure everybody secures their systems.' She expressed herself with authority.

Giovanni followed on from the comment by Seraphina. 'So, this leads me to the problem. You don't mind me being blunt and coming to our predicament immediately, Katharine? You British like this approach.'

'No, of course not. Anyway, *aperitivo* is not far away, and I need to change.' The uneasy introductory ambiance immediately changed as they all laughed. 'Ah, that is good. Giovanni, you must take our guest to your favourite bar after our meeting.'

'I'm sorry, Seraphina, I have to go back to Rome when we have finished. There is too much pressure.'

'Oh well, Katharine, I shall take you if you like. Now to business.'

Giovanni began. 'Here is the problem. We are given to believe that a report that we classify as *segretissimo*, top secret, has been revealed. We don't know how, but we believe it's by somebody in Britain.'

'Are you able to tell me what the document is? I'll understand if you can't.'

'Plans for a future satellite and new forms of encryption. I have to tell you this in the spirit of being frank. We need your cooperation. If the content is made public it will be highly damaging to Italy.'

'Thanks. What about how it's been leaked?'

'I know this might come as a surprise, but we think it might be the British. To be honest, some evidence suggests the British. Actually, we don't even know if it has been revealed. We wanted to contact you immediately we had a suspicion. We don't want to make it seem as if we're panicking. We're just trying to do the British thing and be pragmatic.'

'I understand. Can you let us have the evidence you've got to help us find out what might have happened?'

'Not yet. As you were in Italy, Sir Charles thought it might be worth meeting in person if you didn't mind. We want to cooperate on this. It is of the utmost secrecy, and we don't want our other national partners to know about this.'

'This is part of a contract across a number of countries?'

'Yes.'

Katharine now knew the contract they were referring to. They did not know the extent of her knowledge. 'I understand your reticence. When might you be in a position to let us know more?'

'A day or so, but we need to know from you what you know and whether you have this report.'

'Well, to answer your question, I don't know. When they asked me to come to meet you, they wouldn't tell me anything. You can't blame them.'

'Yes, I understand. Seraphina, you are coordinating the contractors. What have you done so far?'

'I don't want them to think something is wrong, otherwise rumours will take over from truth. I have invoked a clause in the contract for everyone taking part in the project to submit all their systems, including all devices, to an audit.'

'That's useful. Is it to be with the usual organization?'

'Yes. It's convenient. They were expecting such an audit in the next few months anyway, so nobody is surprised.'

'Good. Then we cannot take this any further at present. Katharine, I am sorry for taking you away from your holiday in Milan.'

'Oh, don't worry; I've been enjoying the break. I was going to Armani Silos this afternoon, but it's been much more fun to see you again.'

'Ah, well don't worry,' Seraphina replied. 'We'll go together if you have the time. I'll ask him to see if we can go when it is closed.'

Katharine expressed a little surprise that Seraphina knew

the great man. 'That's kind of you, Seraphina. One last thing, Giovanni, who else knows about this?'

'My immediate superior, Seraphina and me – and now you Brits. We want to keep it quiet. We don't want to cause complications if there is in fact no problem.'

Katharine always enjoyed an *aperitivo* in Caffè Cova. She took pleasure in the repartee with the baristas in their characteristic white jackets, white shirts and black bow ties, one roughly her age, the other a younger man in his thirties who had made the house Campari cocktail for her. They served the exquisitely dressed pre-dinner crowd speedily with aplomb, the display of petit sandwiches, nuts, minute puff pastries set out on the counter, constantly replenished. Women not so youthful adorned with the glamour of fashionable chunky gold jewellery, younger women having flirted with daring clothes that revealed fabulous figures and sensual lines, more mature men in perfect suits or casual trousers and jackets, ties and gold watches catching the eye, younger men having painstakingly dressed in chic jeans and down-at-heel jackets, the first two or three buttons of their shirts nonchalantly open. A glamorous couple joined in with the witticisms passing between Katharine and the baristas.

Seraphina Visconti had managed to tuck the Maserati into a small space outside the entrance, a little of the rear hanging over the pedestrian crossing. As she got out and closed the door, heads turned in the Via Montenapoleone. Men began to take photographs. One in particular had professional equipment with him, taking rapid artistic shots of Seraphina and the car. Seraphina blew a kiss to him. He smiled and nodded in thanks.

Seraphina had changed from her day dress into smart, dark blue slacks, flat driving shoes in blue, white blouse, brightly coloured silk scarf tied around her neck, no jewellery, with the application of rose lipstick Nuits de Young to finish her ensemble. She said hello to the cashier sitting at the till, reaching over to give her two kisses. The older of the baristas was already making the house Campari cocktail for her. As she approached the crowd, she threw kisses to some of her lesser known acquaintances, greeting Katharine before apologising to say a quick hello to her closer friends.

'Thank you for suggesting Cova, Katharine. I haven't been for a while.'

'I like Cova. It's so elegant, so friendly. It was good to meet you this afternoon.'

'Yes, it's lovely, but I must take you to other places next time. I'm so glad they wanted to have the discussion. It's been such a pleasure to meet you. To think you were in Milan and we would never have met if they hadn't wanted to see somebody from...'

Katharine quickly interjected: 'Yes, from England, and here I am.'

The barista handed over her drink. '*Grazi*, Lamberto' said Seraphina, raising her glass to him and then to Katharine, by which time the younger man had handed Katharine a second Campari. Looking quite taken aback, she decided it was not gracious to refuse, so she accepted the drink, thanking him.

They chinked their glasses. '*Saluti*,' they said together.

'You are quite the *fashionista*, Katharine.'

'Now really, Seraphina. You are joking.'

'No, seriously, your twin set, roll neck jumper and pearls have gone down well in here. Let me tell you, there are one or two present who will be reassessing their wardrobes tonight, and two designers are looking you over carefully. You're already setting a trend. You'll come with me next year for fashion week, then we will see.'

Katharine offered a smile of the worldly wise in response. Seraphina took the hint. 'So why are you here in Italy?'

'My sister is to be married.'

'Oh, how pleasing! Is she younger or older than you?'

'Younger by a few years. We are both spinsters of the parish, I'm afraid.'

'Oh, don't worry. I know I'm young, but I've no intention of finding a man yet.'

'Well, it's taken her years, and it came unexpectedly.'

'But she is marrying here, in Milan?'

'No, in Reggio Emilia. Her husband to be helps run a café in London. He travels between England and Italy. He's such a nice man. I'm travelling down tomorrow.'

'Oh, so it's even more fortunate that we met today. Where are you going to eat? What are your plans for this evening?'

'Well, I thought of a concert, then dinner somewhere.'

'Do you like jazz?'

'Why, yes.'

'OK, then we can go to the Spirit de Milan after here.' Seraphina took over. 'It's in a building called Cristallerie Livellara in the Via Bovisasca a little to the north. We'll drive. My uncle let me borrow his beautiful little Berlinetta when he knew where I was coming to Cova. They have some young Italian groups tonight, and the restaurant is good. I know them. I think you will like it. Shall we go?'

'Yes, super.' Katharine was thrilled to be invited to join a young glamorous woman for an impromptu evening.

'Good, so now I must introduce you to my friends here, then we will get you a new outfit for the jazz.'

*

Sarah was in the large first floor room facing the Viale Antonio Allegeri, across the green from the Teatro Municipale. The white shutters were secured against the pink wall. Luigi opened the windows for her, the summer gradually sliding away before the ladies of Reggio Emilia donned their furs. A bus glided by, stopped and passengers entered and left; people entered the shop below or went about town on their errands. She sat at the Fazioli grand piano, the smallest they made, the quality of the sound a sheer delight, which was so beautiful to play.

Sarah sat in silence. For the first time she felt excited for the future. She moulded her life by being different to her sister, to wider family and friends. Schools and university seemed far away. They were previous chapters of her life, fitting into a world framed by others, now long ago. Music was a great comfort, as well as independence and fierce self-sufficiency. She had to do it her way or not at all. But this led to her being at a distance to others. Sometimes, maybe she had too much self-control. She now realised that meeting Luigi had opened a new vista, a different way of understanding. Feeling love for somebody changed her and revived her life. They had both lost weight. She had become more animated. Sexual intimacy opened a new vibrancy, the sensual pleasures of the body shared with the strength of feeling that accompanies total commitment to another.

In silence, she waited. She listened.

Composure.

Tranquillity.

Those expecting their bus paid attention. It came to her. She played the symphonic poem by Franz Liszt, *Les préludes*. Some removed their earplugs from portable devices to enter the sensory magnificence of the physical world, the music expressing love, storm and calm. It was his path to composition, Franz had told Eduard Liszt in a letter. As her exquisite playing reached the end, the music concluding gently, reaching its rolling finale, the wood floor creaked slightly. A young woman entered the room.

Sarah turned her head towards the sound. The woman looked unsuccessfully for the music score.

'*Buongiorno*, hello, I hope I have used the right words,' Sarah said.

'Hello, yes, that's right,' the woman said as she walked the short distance to Sarah.

'It's a lovely day out there.'

'Yes. I'm Vittoria.'

'Ah, how lovely, come and sit next to me, Vittoria.' Sarah moved along the seat to make room. Vittoria sat, perplexed, as if Sarah could not see her. Sarah continued. 'My dear Vittoria, it's so good that you've come. May I touch your head?'

'Yes, of course.' Vittoria answered quizzically to the unusual request.

'Thank you.'

Sarah put her hands on top of her head. 'Your hair is so soft and luxuriant, and it goes to your shoulder, oh, how lovely.' She then passed her hands gently down across and over her forehead and cheeks. 'Oh, my dear, such lovely smooth skin. My old middle-aged fingers feel so refreshed. Why, Vittoria, you're crying. What's wrong? Why the tears?'

At this moment, Vittoria sobbed uncontrollably, burying her head into Sarah's body, as a child to her mother. Sarah put her arms around her, one hand holding her head in compassion.

When composed, Vittoria told Sarah about her mother's illness and death not so long ago; how she had scolded her father for finding another woman. She now realised that she had been so mercilessly unfair to her father. Meeting Sarah for the first time was a shock not having previously known that she was blind, for her father had enthused about the wonderful woman he had met, yet she had rejected the woman praised by her father in the pain of the memory of her mother, and was now utterly ashamed for subjecting her father to the indignity of her ignorant, inconsiderate intolerance.

'I have wronged you, Sarah, for which I am so sorry.'

'You have not wronged me, my dear Vittoria. I did not know you were so upset. It's your father that has understood the depth of your grief for your dear mama. It is he that you think you have wronged. But you must know that your papa loves you and your brother most dearly. He has told me so much about you all.'

'Oh, Sarah, what am I to do?'

'You are to go and see your papa. You will not need to explain. You only need to kiss his cheek. There is no forgiveness, only love.'

As Vittoria got up from the stool, she opened her handbag to take out a handkerchief to wipe her face.

'But before you go, let's enjoy this time together. We've only just met. I detect you have good soprano voice, just waiting to be trained. Do you know *Le nozze di Figaro*?'

'Why yes, of course' Vittoria said with enthusiasm. 'What can I say? Mozart was – he was such an inspired composer.'

'Yes, he was, but he isn't dead. Like all composers, they live on in their music, having broken free from circumstance. I remember at school when silly young girls, who always know better at fifteen...'

Vittoria quickly interjected 'Yes, of course they know better – we all did, they all do!'

Sarah continued, amused at her comments. 'Yes. They used to say they didn't like dead composers. I was always annoyed with them, because this was so superficial and ignorant. But it was me. I was the odd one out. But we know better. Do you know the part of Susanna?'

'Yes. I know the part. I learnt it a few years ago.'

'Before the death of your dear mama?'

'Yes.'

'Well, Susanna might be a servant, but she's the equal of everybody in the opera. She's an intelligent woman.'

'Yes, Mozart introduced brainy women into opera. It was the first time. To think that men used to think that women didn't have any intellect or capacity for rational thought, or that they couldn't manage their lives for themselves.'

'Well, yes, but that cerebral male incapacity is still with us today.'

'Oh yes, Sarah, how right you are. I agree with what you say.'

'Good. How about the aria that Susanna sings to seduce the Count? It's a serenade really. Just think, a woman – no, a lowly servant woman – singing a love serenade to a man – a Count no less. Unheard of! She's behaving like a man. Delightful, isn't it? Are you ready? Act 4 Scene 10. Let's be delicate. You have some high notes towards the end, and you need to be prepared.'

Sarah began to play the introduction. Vittoria began hesitantly, clearly, '*Deh, viene, non tarder, o gioia bella/vieni ove amore per goder t'appella.*' Come, my beloved, no more delay/ Come, the moment will not stay. Sarah lead the tempo on the piano, enabling Vittoria to develop confidence as she sang about the moon, lilting brook, the breeze, grass, flowers and beguiling nature, and ending with subtle intensity. '*Vieni, ben mio, tra queste piante ascose/ti vo' la fronte incoronar di rose.*' Come, beloved our pleasure-ground/With roses let your head be crowned.

A driver had stopped her bus at the stop outside the house just before they began the recital. She switched the engine off because they were slightly early. As the music began and Vittoria sang, those in the bus sat in silence. There was a buzz in the air. The driver, in her mid-thirties, exclaimed: 'It's Vittoria, she's singing again!' Applause rippled through the bus and the street. Within minutes the town was overflowing with the news that brought joy to the hearts of many.

Katharine followed Sarah, stylishly dressed anew by the women of the family and gaily walking arm-in-arm with Vittoria, with children hanging on to their hands, arms and dresses through the double height hall towards the sounds of laughter, chatter and clinking of glasses, the timbre of voices dissipating with the change of acoustics when walking towards the windows from those outside spilling on to the terrace, the lawn, small groups, larger clusters, couples hand-in-hand walking around the clipped topiary through the garden under trees and around bushes. Friends blessed the couple by providing and hosting the wedding lunch at their seventeenth-century villa under a blue sky of late summer, with formal beds for the last of the roses, a modest sun adorning tables linked together covered with vintage linen white table cloths crisp fold lines providing straight square shadows, pleated white napkins, heavy silver cutlery glasses for water and wine, bottles of the very pale ruby-red Lambrusco di Sorbara given by another friend in wine coolers, vases abundant with seasonal flowers interspersed by silver candelabra with white candles yet to be lit along the terrace doors opening from the library, men and women waiting on the guests of family and friends, multi-coloured against the restrained weathered exterior.

Unexpectedly Katherine felt lonely; there was something missing. Close to her sister, she was also dedicated to her work. The loss of the man she loved so early in her life acted as a restraint; relationships were reserved, closed, and efficient. Life continued formally, correctly, having fun detached from emotion. Now, however, she experienced a hollowness. Sarah had found love. She was now no longer part of her. Living with her lover, companion and now her husband, Katherine was now apart, on her own, no longer to fall back on Sarah when she needed her emotional support. Sarah had been so giving. Katherine understood. Now her sister was receiving so much more after the isolation endured over so many years. Loneliness, Katherine began to appreciate, must have been normal for Sarah for so long. But she had not appreciated this.

As she entered the grand reception room, the host and hostess paid attention to her as she was introduced by Luigi and she felt at ease, knowing how Sarah had found not only a companion and lover but a circle of friends and family that had taken her as one of their own. Satisfied for her sister, lightened by a release of negativity, sustained emotionally by the warmth of generosity pervading the occasion, she began to ease into another chapter of her life. She knew her hosts would not be remotely surprised when, towards the end of the afternoon as the meal came gradually to an end, Sarah visited the kitchen to thank all those responsible for the preparation of the food, and for waiting and serving in her fast improving Italian.

After passing into the library, a tall, elegant woman, roughly the same age as Katherine, came up to her. 'You must be Katherine.'

'Yes, hello.'

'Sarah has told us all about you. She is such a sweet woman, your sister. I am Maria Thérèsa.'

'I'm pleased to meet you.' They shook hands. 'I will miss not popping in to see her.'

'Of course. But they will live in London and Reggio, so you'll have the opportunity to visit when they're here.'

'Yes,' Katherine's face lit up. 'How lovely it will be.'

'Now, you must have a prosecco. But Sarah tells us you like champagne.'

'Oh, prosecco is super,' Katherine did not want to elaborate on the memory of champagne, so personal to her and her beloved Bronisław.

Maria Thérèsa was dressed in muted dark blue, a subtle study in emphasizing the curves of her body without extravagance, a scarf of subtle autumn colours carefully tied around her neck, with a pair of diamond earrings discreetly hidden beneath her shoulder-length black hair to finish the ensemble. She caught the eye of a young man carrying a silver tray of glasses across the room. He made his way over, well groomed, ravishingly black curly hair sitting just above the collar of his white shirt, full dark eyebrows, chic stubble, dark brown eyes erotically caressing beauty. He nodded slightly in deference to the woman and addressed her as 'Marchesa' as he presented the tray to the women.

'Thank you, Marco. Dear Marco,' she continued as she slipped her black crocodile handbag from her shoulder, 'will you take this for me please? I don't need it. Perhaps you will put it somewhere for me?'

'Yes, Aunt, of course. I will look after it.'

Each took a glass from the tray. 'One of my nephews,' she explained as he walked to the end of the room to find a place for the handbag. 'He wanted to help with the reception before we sat for dinner.' She changed the subject. 'Tell me what you think of this prosecco? I like it, but I would say that, wouldn't I? The makers are good friends. This is their gift to the couple. They tell me it has been difficult to make. I think they have succeeded. But you tell me.'

'Oh, that is kind.' Katherine put the glass to her nose. 'Well, I detect mineral and citrus. It's most delightful, but I've never seen prosecco served in glasses like these.'

The Marchesa answered the statement with the confidence and assurance of her aristocratic background. 'Those who serve it in narrow flutes are ignorant. We have a wide bowl for this most precious of wines because the wine demands it.'

The Conegliano Valdobbiadene Prosecco Superiore was superb on the palate; cool but not cold, a concentration of fruit with a taste that lingered on a soft dry finish. 'Really lovely, Maria Thérèsa; it's delicious. You shall have to visit me when you next come to England. We must get to know each other.'

'I am glad you like it,' replied Maria Thérèsa. 'Now come with me to the garden. We should appreciate the gentle blue sky and watch the young people make love and the children play before the struggles of their youth take over.'

As they walked through the room and out on to the terrace and lawn, Maria Thérèsa continued. 'Katherine, you are, let me say, disheartened. No, no, do not think I am presumptuous,' she responded with firmness to Katherine's entreaties. 'I see it in your eyes. You are losing a sister, but as we know, you will, it is hoped, gain another family. You and I, we have had the best years of our lives. There is no going back. We have to live with the past, and this affects how we live in the present. We have had our personal experiences, some desperate, some perfect. We have witnessed the vanity of politicians and men making life difficult through wars and terror.'

They looked across the garden. Neat box hedges enclosed the terrace. A worn gravel path led out to the park, roses lining the way, providing a splash of colour, their scent in the air. They watched the couples and parents with young children. Walking, playing, running through the landscape, serendipitously planted with the columnar *cupressus sempervirens* tall, upright and elegant; *prunus cerasus* Morello for the spring flowers, autumn fruit and evergreen colour; a young black poplar; a mature pedunculate oak in the distance; lemon trees carefully placed to gain maximum advantage of the sunlight, interspersed with an occasional olive tree.

'All these young people around us will have similar experiences. They are affected by the decisions made by previous generations and now our generation as well, just as much as our lives were influenced by the decisions made by our fathers, our grandfathers and those further back in time.'

Maria Thérèsa turned to face Katherine. The voice of

authority changed. It was reflective, mellow, and sad. 'Yes, my life and my family were transformed by the decisions of my father. He made disastrous choices that have affected us, and will continue to affect generations of our family. So painful. I see a deep hurt written in your eyes, perhaps of a different kind. You and me, we have seen unpleasantness and pain, destruction and killing. We have witnessed these events as spectators and as participants. Yet, you know, we must try to make amends for the past. Often people fail to understand that their decisions affect many millions of people across generations.'

'Or maybe they don't care.'

'Yes, or they deliberately want to affect the future in their own image. Looking at all those around us today, here in this garden and beautiful villa, you would think, would you not, how charming. They all live such enchanted lives. And that is true. For some of these young men and women and families, they live magical lives of privilege. But behind each person there are problems, difficulties, burdens that we do not see. Poetry and novels are made of this stuff of life, of the wrongs and unfairness. Sometimes they are righted, sometimes they are not. Of emotions, dreadful things, and breath-taking experiences. We have to accept all this. This life of ours is not a rehearsal.'

She stopped speaking. The women stood surveying the festive scene.

'You know,' Maria Thérèsa continued, 'I do not mean to be unkind.'

'No, I understand. I appreciate your thoughts. I have been very quiet. I've seen Sarah's happiness today. You are right, it's time I began to live life anew.'

'Yes, Katherine. I hope we shall be good friends.'

*

Henry Bravington-Hartley courteously ushered Owain Davis into the soundproofed room overlooking the western inner courtyard in the building at Albert Embankment in Lambeth. He offered him refreshments.

Owain Davis knew that this apparently shy, late middle-aged man was an eminent Arabist, and it had been announced that he was shortly to retire to take up a professorship at the University of Edinburgh. He was also aware that the man was highly regarded in the Service. Conceit in assuming they were capable of appraising a person through first impressions caused many to misjudge him. His slight, thin frame, dated black suit and soft dark brown eyes were often perceived to be signs that he was ineffectual. This failure of insight, however, would be promptly and discomfortingly reversed when subject to his incisive intelligence.

'You've been briefed by GCHQ, I understand.'

'Yes, Mr Bravington-Hartley. They took me through what they know.'

'Will you rehearse the brief for me, please?'

'Yes, Sir. This is as of last night. Three documents, all considered top secret or above have been uploaded to a website on the Deep Web. There seem to be two websites that are linked. One has the documents, the other looks like a user group of like-minded people. The user group covers a number of companies across a range of countries, all of them dealing with satellite technology, especially military and intelligence technologies. The names and companies are mostly sub-contractors to main contractors for a number of highly sensitive projects that are presently being developed.'

Owain had been told before he left Cheltenham that Henry Bravington-Hartley preferred officers to display a commitment to accuracy and brevity in discussing the known facts. He continued, noting that the other man was listening intently.

'The three documents are interesting.'

'Indeed, Mr Davis, they are exceedingly interesting.'

'Yes, Sir,' Owain smiled at the interjection, pleased that his understatement had been noted. 'There's a French document that provides the details of two secret modules. One allows them to monitor communications relayed by satellite that originate in France and French overseas territories. They have also decided to put a back door into the European Union satellite plans to rival the Americans. What's striking is that this is so secret that if it became public knowledge, it would cause the fall of the present government.'

'Indeed. It illustrates that the French are taking a somewhat independent approach to the future, almost in defiance of their allies. However, we don't blame them. That's our unofficial internal opinion, of course. It's not to be broadcast unless you get the go-ahead from me or the Chief.'

'Yes, Sir. Thank you. The second document is from the United States. The content isn't surprising. It's more of a briefing document analysing the attempts by Russia and China to build anti-satellite systems. What's most useful to us are their sources. Some contacts and agents are new to us. No doubt they would be embarrassed, but not overwhelmed or wildly infuriated, if they knew we had a copy.'

'I agree, although it depends on who in the US knew we had a copy. Some would use our knowledge of the document as an excuse to undermine us as much as they could, even if it was only through the medium of the media.'

'Yes, conspiracy theorists would probably reach the conclusion that we are the cunning enemy. The Italian document, which has been uploaded recently, is also very interesting. The Italians are part of a European-wide project undertaking a satellite programme for a consortium of Arab nations. This text tells us that they are doing some extraordinary additional work in secret for the project. They are intending to increase the capacity to listen in to communications passing over the systems they authorize in their own jurisdiction. But more importantly, across a number of other – shall we say – opposition states across the Gulf. In fact, this is probably the most dangerous document of the three. If it became public knowledge, the consequences could be grave.'

Henry Bravington-Hartley offered to re-fill Owain's cup. He accepted. 'Thank you, Sir.'

'All right, so we have an interesting number of documents at our disposal to use – or not – as we deem fit. Now comes the difficult part. First of all, we don't really know who's behind these leaks. We've been given a lead. The Australians are working with the Chinese, or we thought they were. I'll come on to that later. There's an IT consultant who's been going around the world for a few years now, sniffing at all the leading, and some minor, conferences dealing with satellite systems, especially military systems.'

He took a sip of tea and passed over a piece of paper to Owain.

'As you'll notice from this brief, he's a little odd. He's single, a native English speaker, is almost fluent in Portuguese and has a reasonable grasp of Russian. He seems to be technically competent, but doesn't do people. That doesn't surprise me, but he's got an ability to get others to do things for him. He seems to have convinced a number of people in the satellite industry that the little group he's set up – the one you mentioned – is a highly selective networking opportunity.'

'May I ask a question, Sir?'

'Yes, by all means.'

'Do we know anything about any of the people on this list?'

'Yes. I was coming to that.'

'Oh, sorry Sir,'

'Not at all, Davis, it shows you're listening. Some are ordinary, run-of-the-mill employees that have probably fallen for his subterfuge that it's a select networking group. I think it fair to say that some of the people on this list have gained out of it, because they seem to have used their contacts to move into better paid jobs. We cannot discount the possibility that some of those on the list might be working for Russia and the United States. No surprises there. The reason the Australians and Chinese have joined forces on this one is because, between them, they're pretty sure they've identified a rogue agent, and it's the man we've done the work on. We have an image, taken by the Chinese agent in Singapore recently.'

Henry showed Owain the photograph of a man sitting at a table. Plump, rounded head, short thin brown straight hair, greying going bald, thin lips. Ordinary white shirt sporting a bland blue-black striped tie. Podgy in appearance.

'He looks like a lot of people in the IT world, almost anonymous.'

'Yes. He no doubt dresses this way intentionally.' Henry Bravington-Hartley continued. 'The Australians will be able to confirm their suspicions about his activities when you meet them. We think he's the person behind this user group. It seems as if he also runs the other website and might be responsible for uploading the documents. Another problem is that we don't know how he's obtaining these documents, and we don't know what purpose he has in mind.'

Owain began to understand that he was expected to enter the dialogue as an equal. He asked his next question. 'Do we know if anybody else knows about the website?'

'No, and we don't know if the French or US are aware that these documents are available. We know the Italians have a suspicion their document has been leaked, but they aren't sure it has been revealed, and we don't know why they think it might have been uncovered. I presume they have good reason to think that, otherwise they wouldn't have approached us.'

'Do we know if anybody knows we've got these documents?'

'No. You're going to meet the English sub-contractor tomorrow. They might shed a light on this. They might even give us a lot more. They told us about the laptop they were using when they met this chap.' He looked at his watch. 'Somebody from GCHQ is with the sub-contractor now.'

'That's very useful.'

'Yes, it is.' Henry Bravington-Hartley then began to summarize their knowledge. 'So, this is our present position. We've stumbled upon a website that has, to date, uploaded three highly secret documents from three of our allies, the US, France and Italy. We've been given an insight into a number of American sources we weren't aware of, the expansion of French interception capabilities, and an exceedingly interesting development in the Gulf. We don't know who obtained these documents, how they obtained them, or what link this consultant has with either or both websites. We don't know if any of our allies know we have these documents – indeed, we don't even know if they know they've been obtained, and we don't know if they know the websites exists.'

'Mr Bravington-Hartley, you have mentioned the Chinese. What part do they play?'

'Yes, that's an interesting question. The Chinese have made some significant advances in quantum key distribution recently. You know about this?'

'No, Sir.'

'All right, I'll get you briefed on this later today. It shouldn't surprise you that GCHQ has been working on quantum cryptography for some time now. So have the Chinese. A number of university departments from around the world are also working on it. This is important, because if it can be made to work, it will ensure our communications remain private. Interestingly, the Chinese have been fairly open about their work in this area, and, even more intriguingly, the Americans have stopped publishing on this topic completely. A while ago the Chinese decided it was worth attending as many conferences on satellites and associated technologies as possible. They've been sending agents to symposiums, and it was an officer in Singapore that noticed our man attempted to insert a USB into somebody's computer at the conference. This led her to take his photograph. The computer in question was given to Helen Curlie, an officer in the Australian Secret Intelligence Service. She was sent to Singapore partly because they want to improve their own technology. She was given the task of identifying this man. Curlie persuaded him that it was not good security to allow somebody to insert a USB into her computer, and encouraged him to send her an email, which they knew would have a payload. She clicked on the email later. That has allowed the Australians to monitor his surveillance of her device to see what he did with the access he had gained. I understand you met her during the hiatus.'

'Oh yes, I remember. I met her briefly.'

'The Australians gave her a clean laptop. They wanted to find out about this chap. What we don't know is whether the Australians knew about him and wanted to get hold of him, and if they did, why.'

Henry stopped at this point. He looked at Owain. Owain was thinking.

'I suppose the Australians and Chinese know more about him than we do?'

'Possibly. We don't know if they know about the websites.'

'Right. Excuse me Sir, but you haven't discussed the Russians yet.'

'Correct. Of course the Russians are active in this particular field. It's also possible that this chap is working for the Russians, but that's mere supposition on my part. We're working on his background, how he lives his life, and his financial affairs.'

'Do we know if he's found any of our secrets?'

'No, but there's no sign that he has. That said, we're open to the possibility that he has breached our security, or is trying to. Have you any other questions?'

'Not at present, Sir, other than the meeting tomorrow.'

'Yes, they know you're visiting. They know who you are. We clearly want to know the usual who, what, why, where, when. If they agree, I'd like you to obtain the computer for analysis. I'd prefer they agreed, but we can get an order if it's necessary. I don't see why they'll refuse, because they're pretty good at cooperating with us. After that, you'll be off to Belgium. The sub-contractor you're going to visit tomorrow have found out that our suspect is going to a conference on Quantum Cryptography in Durbuy. Helen Curlie will also be there. You'll link up with her and cooperate on this particular issue.'

'What about the Chinese?'

'Apparently Curlie and the Chinese officer travelled on the same flight to Europe. Both agencies agreed to work together on this one. When they arrived, they inevitably missed each other in the process of finding their luggage on the carousel. That's where it stopped. Curlie hasn't seen or had word from the Chinese officer since. At present, we're leaving that to the Australians to follow up, but it adds complexity to the situation. You might find out more when you meet Curlie.'

'Thank you, Sir.'

'There's one more thing. For some reason unknown to us, the Americans think there's a double agent in the service. They won't tell us why they think this, or what their suspicions are. The allegation has come from a highly unreliable quarter, but politically we've got to treat it seriously.' Bravington-Hartley fell silent for a moment. 'You've recently been through Developed Vetting. We both know it's an intrusive process. This work is highly sensitive, with a lot of top secret information, and we're in a very weak position. This means we want you to have one further interview this afternoon. I'm not responsible for undertaking it. However, there's an aspect to your life that will come up in the interview. I expect you know what's I'm getting at.'

'Probably, Sir.'

'You're in your late thirties and single, good looking and very eligible. You live on your own. Very wise, in my view.'

'Yes, Sir. I've found it difficult to keep a mortgage going, but I was lucky with the market when I bought. Life is much better now.'

'Good. But we both know that secrets are exposed because of human weakness. You seem pretty strong, and your finances are in good shape, but your status as a single man stands out.'

'Yes Sir. I know. I keep myself to myself.'

'Why? You have friends and family. Is it your sexuality?'

'Yes Sir, but you must know that.'

'We do, and you're open about it, which is necessary, but also appreciated and understood. We know a person becomes a double agent for a variety of reasons. To reassure you, we don't think you are. We don't doubt your loyalty. What I want you to understand is that you're vulnerable. You've never admitted to any affairs.'

'That's right, Sir. It's because I haven't had any. I don't want to put my employment at risk.'

'Have you met anybody?'

'No, not romantically. I haven't yet met somebody that I've wanted to live with for the rest of my life.'

'I hope you do one day.'

'Thank you, Sir.'

'Forgive this intrusion into your private life. As you might expect, we're investigating the American allegations. We know a secret isn't a secret once you tell somebody, but we trust you not to repeat this. If you're asked about this particular issue this afternoon, you must of course mention that I have made you aware of the problem.'

'Yes, Sir.'

'So, let me sum up. The facts as we understand them beg more questions than answers. I think of this as a puzzle to be unpicked. I just hope that we aren't a target, but, and more importantly, we need to understand what's happening to defend ourselves against the accusations of others – mainly our allies, would you believe.'

The driver of the taxi drove his vehicle through an open barrier into a small car park before a low 1960s two-storey flat-roofed nondescript functional building off Gunnels Wood Road. He parked near the flag poles. A national flag wilted alongside a company flag limp against the windless, overcast grey sky. A tall, slight man over fifty with greying hair, wearing brown shoes, corduroy trousers in rust and a stone coloured moleskin shirt bounced out of the door as Owain got out of the front passenger side, having paid the fare.

'You must be Owain Davies.'

'Yes.'

'How do you do? I'm Peter. Was the journey all right?'

'Yes, thanks. Stevenage looks like one of those postwar new towns. This light industrial area even looks like a nice place to work.'

'That's a polite description. The locals didn't like it, but in 1946 it was decided that there'd be a new town here. Although they said the old town would remain, they knocked down the town hall.'

'There must have been a lot of ill feeling.'

'Yes, but there we are.' He looked around and thought. 'You know, maybe you're right. It's not a bad place to be working. We've got good roads, plenty of grass verges, trees, shrubs, and flowers. Maybe I'll appreciate being here more.

It takes a visitor to make you appreciate things. Anyway, come in.'

They entered the building. Peter walked them to the kitchen, a dreary affair that had been renovated twenty years previously. 'Tea or coffee?'

Owain hesitated. Peter knew what was coming. He'd seen it before with coffee people. 'You're a coffee person, aren't you?' Peter said as he proceeded to fill the lower chamber of the vacuum coffee maker with water before placing it on the electric hob. He took a packet out of the refrigerator and filled the upper chamber with three spoonfuls of ground coffee.

'I call it butler blend. It's got three different types of bean. I grind it up at home and bring it in.'

'I'm betting that butler blend is a joke.'

'It's a way of thinking about another person and their predicament. About somebody who is confronted every day with an arrogance and superiority that is assumed to be a right. But it's a job, and the weak can't be choosey.'

As they waited, they chatted over what the company was doing, the visit the previous day by a person from GCHQ, and the links the company had on various projects across a number of continents. Once the water entered the top chamber, Peter turned the heat down to let it brew for two minutes, and removed the top chamber when the water had fully drained.

Owain was impressed. 'Physics in action. Pretty good. Now all we need to do is taste it to see if it's worth the effort.'

'Good coffee is always worth the time it takes, like everything.' Peter handed Owain a milk jug. Peter noticed the look on Owain's face. He answered the query. 'Full fat. Nothing taken out.'

'Ah, great.' With this exchange, the men began to connect because of a shared sense of the apparently mundane things that were worth making an effort about.

'Do you take sugar?'

'No thanks.'

'Fine, let's go then.'

Peter took the coffee and two mugs. Owain followed him into a back room used for meetings.

'Yes, very good. Now I know what you mean,' Owain said as he tried the coffee. 'I'll have to switch methods.'

'Good idea. Out of the dismal kitchen of a dull office block comes excellent coffee. Glad to be educating your taste buds. Now, down to business.'

'Yes, what's the position?'

'I presume you've been briefed about the projects we're involved with?'

'Yes.'

'I won't bore you with any more details on that, then. For what it's worth, here's the laptop. As you can see, it's a standard windows machine, nothing fancy. We don't let people take insecure devices out with them, and I expect you've already been told we're pretty good at this side of security.'

'Yes. Reasonable.'

Peter laughed. 'So we're all right?'

Owain smiled. 'Well yes, better than most. Do many sub-contractors ignore security or are there particular ones that are worse than others?'

'Over the years I've noticed some that are terrible. I'm told that some security agencies have tried to improve what their people do and don't do, but there are a number of countries that continue to have serious problems. We're not perfect in the UK, but I'd like to think we're better than most.'

'Thanks. This helps me get a feel for what happens.'

'Let me tell you about this machine. I took it to a conference recently as an experiment. I wanted to see how people reacted to seeing me with a machine.'

'Why?'

'Because I'm known never to carry one around. We'd also heard rumours about a maverick attending conferences and trying to insert a USB into machines to exchange contact details. Look, I don't know if they told you, but I'm ex-Royal Signals, and we were taught to treat security with respect. Anyway, that apart, as you can see, this machine looks as if it's a working device. We put some basic stuff on it, such as a few emails and files that were routine, nothing confidential. The usual sort of stuff we'd expect to see if we were looking at one of our competitors' machines.'

'So you didn't have a virtual private network connection?'

'No. We kept it straightforward. I decided to act the simpleton if I was ever approached.'

'You were buttonholed, I presume?'

'Yes. It was a bloke – the same one that I was shown yesterday by your lady from GCHQ. Earlier this year I attended a conference on satellite technologies and encryption. He seemed very switched on, very focused. He'd done his homework. He knew the projects we were working on and our other partners. He said he was in a position to connect us with a better encryption product. I acted a bit dumb, although I gave him the impression that I was a bit concerned about security if I agreed to let him insert the USB stick.'

'But you eventually let him?'

'Yes. I hope I hadn't made him too suspicious. Interestingly, he left me very quickly once he'd finished. He didn't even take my business card.'

'So he's not as smart as he thinks he might be.'

'Perhaps, or he's acting. Having met him, I think he's got some sort of attention deficit disorder. He couldn't keep eye contact. That might be one of his weaknesses.'

'What have you done with the laptop since?'

'Nothing. I alerted my contacts with your people about it, but there was too much going on with another terrorist attack for anybody to think this was something worth following up. To be fair, they were probably right. All we had was a clean laptop with some software code inserted into it by somebody we didn't know. I followed him up. He styles himself as a consultant. We didn't have time to find out what he put on the machine. You know how it is; suddenly something happens that changes everyone's focus. But then we were approached a day or so ago about it. I told the same story to the lady from GCHQ, but she was called up on another urgent matter. You must be hard pressed.'

'We are, but I'm here because something of supreme national importance has hit us, and we need to work on it as a matter of priority.'

'And this might help?'

'Yes. Have you switched it on since he inserted the USB?'

'No. Do you want to find out more?'

'Yes, but we could do with switching it on in a clean environment. We want to be free of wireless connections and any outside interference.'

'Agreed. We've got just the place in the other building. Let's go.'

'It's a key logger. It's been written to track everything typed on the keyboard. No surprise there.' Owain commented.

'Yes, but is there more? If there's a kernel based program as well, then that's more serious, as you know. Depending on the program, it could let the intruder obtain root access, then they would have almost complete control over what passes into and out of the machine.'

'The key logger might be deliberate. It could be a decoy, making you think that once you've got rid of it, everything is all right with the machine.'

'You know what M. S. Balasubramanian says?'

'No, who's he?'

'He's also known as Snake Shyam. He says: *You have to be careful about human beings, not snakes.*'

'He knows a lot about snakes, then.'

'He does. The problem is, we haven't got the facilities here to test the system.'

'That's a pity, but I haven't got much time. I'll talk to my people about what to do. I've got a plan formulating. I'll test it out on them. You said you know a little bit about this consultant?'

'Yes.'

'Do you know anybody in this country that might know more about him?'

'Not in this country,' Peter said with a wry smile over his face. 'But in Scotland.'

'Amusing, I like it.'

'Yes. From your accent, you're Welsh.'

'Yes, of course.'

'You're named after Owain Glyndŵr I presume?' Peter asked as if he knew the answer.

'Yes, Welsh mother and seafaring father, a lascar they call him. My mother insisted on Owain, and when my father realised the importance of this to her, he agreed, and gave me a second name, Karamchand.'

'Ah, so you have one foot in the oppression of Wales and the other in India.'

'That's about right.'

'He was the last native Welshman to hold the title Tywysog Cymru.'

'Yes, and not a single Welshman or woman betrayed him.'

'I know.'

'You know a lot.'

'I know so much that I realize I know so little.'

'That's the conundrum, of course.'

'It is, but the digital world has changed that forever.'

'Yes, it has,' Owain replied, 'perhaps most people don't want to know anyway. Maybe whispers, innuendo and gossip have always taken second place to facts.'

'Possibly, but those with knowledge of the facts remain in control. Power has always lied, or omitted to being forthright, and will always do so.'

'Yes, but the great writer Miguel de Cervantes wrote in *Don Quixote* that *porque la verdad adelgaza y no quiebra, y siempre anda sobre la mentira como el aceite sobre el agua* – the truth always emerges the same way that oil rises to the top of water.'

'All right,' Peter chuckled, 'I agree with that, and the problem is that it's cheap to lie in the short term. If everyone stops listening to avoid being manipulated, then we'll face serious consequences. My point is that it's no longer about truth, but saying that the truth doesn't have any consequences. That's what's destructive. If it isn't challenged effectively, life might become impossible. Think of Jheronimus van Aken.'

Owain looked puzzled.

'Hieronymus Bosch to most of us.'

'Ah, got you.'

'Look at his paintings to see what life might become, or maybe how it is. But only the few notice. Anyway, let me tell you about this couple who might be able to help you in Scotland. They're about 120 miles north of Edinburgh on the west coast. I can ring them now. They're a repository of knowledge. There's little they don't know about the industry. If you've got the time, you ought to visit them immediately if they're free, because they don't tend to talk over the phone. They're very discreet.'

'Good idea. Go ahead.'

Peter rang the office. The answerphone indicated both were out, but to contact them on their mobile telephones. No alternative numbers were given. Peter then rang another number.

It was engaged, so he tried another. Veronica answered. Apparently she was on her way back to Scotland, having visited their accountant in Letchworth Garden City. She was staying outside Edinburgh overnight before returning home and to the office. Owain was welcome to meet her there.

'That's all arranged, then.'

'Thanks, Peter. I'd like to continue with our chat one day.'

'You're welcome. Any time. Now, let me drive you to the station. You can take the next train to Edinburgh. You'll need to change once you get to Waverly.'

Veronica was waiting for him at North Queensferry, and insisted on taking him around the museum in the station. As small as the museum was, Owain agreed that it was worth spending time in looking over the past and the development of the railway. It had affected all walks of life. They then walked down the steep hill to the Ferrybridge Hotel. As the scene unfolded, the sight caught his breath.

'This is astonishing. I've never been here before. I've never seen these bridges.'

'It is, isn't it?'

'Three bridges. They're magnificent.'

'It was worth the travel just to see this, wasn't it?'

'Yes. The light. It's so beautiful, calm, soft, as if there was peace in the world.'

'If only. It can get really tough here. They had real difficulties with the first road bridge, and as you might know, the second rail bridge replaced a previous bridge that collapsed.'

'It's a privilege to be here. The lights are fantastic. What a view.'

'It is indeed.'

They arrived outside the entrance. Veronica turned to him. 'I took the liberty of ordering a meal for you. These people are friends. The chef is very good. He's going to make a seafood risotto for us this evening. You'll find it's the equal of any trattoria in Italy. It's a bit late, which is why I ordered, because you said you didn't have any dietary problems. Is that all right?'

'Yes, thanks, that's really nice of you.'

'And a white wine?'

'Yes, but not too much. I've got to get back tonight.'

'Oh, you won't be getting back tonight, unless you want to go on the sleeper. And you came up from Stevenage, didn't you? You won't be stopping there at night on the way down.'

'Thanks for letting me know. Then I'll have to stay somewhere.'

'Yes, I've thought of that. A friend of ours has a spare room in Edinburgh in the New Town. He said he'd put you up for the night if you like.'

'What can I say? You're overwhelming me with kindness.'

'Nae bother at aw, as we say in Scotland. So a white wine it is.'

Veronica and her husband had an admirable insider's knowledge of the industry. Over an outstanding risotto and a bottle of well-balanced Orvieto Classico Superiore Castagnolo by Nicolo Barberani, she gave Owain a more detailed briefing of the consultant in question, one Michael Cocke.

Later that evening Owain was sitting with his host in a grand ground floor room in London Street, the heavy curtains having secured the room to the world, the far end the shape of an oval with two doors either side, one a mere foil to the other for the sake of symmetry. His host, Archibald, an elderly gentleman with a literary pedigree, asked if he minded a dram of malt before retiring for the night. He produced a bottle.

'Let's try a new whisky. This is Abhainn Dearg, it's a single malt from the Isle of Lewis. They're a new independent distillery. We should give them a try. It'll be a pleasure to open this bottle and taste it with another palate.'

Grateful and dazed by the kindness he had received, this was going to be too much.

'Archibald, I'm sorry, but I think I'm at my limit. My alcohol intake this evening has begun to work its magic. I've got to be very unfriendly and decline. I hope you don't take offence.'

'No, none taken, Owain. Let's leave it for your next visit.'

'That's a deal.' Owain felt relieved. Archibald had not been offended. Owain did not want to think he was snubbing such welcoming hospitality.

In the soft light of two small side lamps, dwarfed by the tall room, they continued to talk into the night of suffering and the general pointlessness of war, and of some of the poetry in response: of Hedd Wyn who won the Eisteddiford y Gandair Ddu in 1917 – the chair, fittingly enough, made by Eugeen Vanfleteren, the refugee furniture maker from Mechelen and his students; the sheer genius of David Jones and the poignancy of his memoir *In Parenthesis*; and discussing whether poets should or could change anything, or maybe whether they should refrain from helping to make things happen, and whether poetry was rightly the inward thoughts expressed to the world.

As they were about to retire for the night, Archibald ended on an optimistic happy note, reading Edwin Morgan's 'Strawberries'. 'Isn't that a lovely poem? It's a shared experience, time taken in love. The beauty of the description is marvellous.'

In the morning, as Owain stepped outside, he looked up and down the grand, massively long terrace with the imposing sandstone façade. He had been puzzled, because it looked as if Archibald had a house with three stories, but he only occupied the ground floor and basement. Archibald explained. 'Ah, well now, let's look carefully at the outside of the house. You see the three grand doors with windows between each?'

'Yes.'

'Now look closely at the middle door, the one to our right. Look up, into the windows.'

Owain stretched his head, trying to imagine what he should be looking at. 'I'm not too sure, Archibald.'

'Can you see the stairs in the first floor?'

'Ah, yes, so I can.'

'Well, that's the stairs going to the flats above us, do you see?'

'Now I see, yes. So this terrace, as grand as it looks, is really a mix of what we call houses and flats?'

'Yes, but made to look as if it's a row of grand houses.'

'Amazing.'

'Sly, I'd say. And if you walk around the area closely, you won't find many mews buildings for horses and carriages. That meant the area was a mix of the wealthy and newly emerging bourgeois. That's not so bad; I can live with that. So the lesson is to always look closely; we humans constantly deceive, even with our architecture.'

He then gave Owain a copy of *The Living Mountain*. 'Owain,' Archibald said to him, 'you like walking. I'm glad. Now read Nan Shepherd on your way to the big smoke, and you'll be transformed. When you've got the time, come back, and we'll follow some of her footsteps. What do you say?'

'With pleasure, Archibald. It's been such a delight to meet you. Thank you; thank very much.'

*

'She is to be humiliated,' Colonel Ding said to the two male guards. 'Strip her and put the *qípáo* on her.' She pointed to the plain white lightweight semi-transparent summer cotton garment draped over the bed. She then left. 'I will be back,' she stated with authority.

When Zhuge Xiùyīng woke, she found herself lying on a metal-framed bed, bolted to the floor, the mattress strapped to the frame to prevent it being moved. The space comprised three nine-foot high breeze block walls open to the room above, the fourth side a line of black rusting bars and a door, also made of bars. A single light above the space provided a sparse weak yellow illumination. Two men watched her through the bars. They stood up as she stirred. She was in need of the lavatory. She told them. They looked at each another. One took a key from a table located adjacent to the barred door. He opened it and bid her leave. As she did so, the other grasped her neck from behind and forced an arm up her back. Xiùyīng stifled a scream. He force-marched her to a single toilet, located in a space fully exposed to the room. He maintained his grip around her throat. She began to anticipate what the future held while in captivity. Deciding to act with as much dignity as the circumstances allowed, she silently completed her ablutions. Thereafter, both men took an arm each, forced it up her back, marching and pushing her into the cage. She looked around the room, into the void above her, and out into the black space beyond the bars, topped with rusty barbed wire. She noticed the monitors for close circuit television located in four locations and various angles. Lights positioned for various viewpoints, switched off. Quiet, but not silent. An occasional vehicle passed backwards and forwards in the distance. The two short male guards were dressed in commonplace grey overalls and light rubber-soled canvas shoes. They were competent. They knew how to handle a body. Major Zhuge Xiùyīng turned her back to the bars, sat on the floor and waited. *They saw me naked. How shameful.*

The men had a meal. One took a nap on a military camp bed.

The bell rang.

Both men rushed to the side door leading to the street. One

opened a small window overlooking the gate. He indicated to his fellow guard to unlock and open the door.

Colonel Ding entered the building. She was wearing black casual clothes, a shirt, jacket, and trousers. Acknowledging the guards, she directed them to push a set of heavy internal doors located in a metal channel across the void, creating a sound-proof space. All three then put on their goggles. One of the guards switched on a 1,000 watt metal halide floodlight that hung over the void of the enclosure.

'Major Zhuge Xiùyīng' rapped out the Colonel in a hard high pitched shriek.

Zhuge Xiùyīng remained sitting in front of the wall, her back to the bars. She put her hands over her eyes. The Colonel nodded to the guards. One got ready to open the door of the enclosure, unlocking and opening it in a swift well practised movement, the well oiled hinges silent in their action. Within seconds, Zhuge Xiùyīng had been grabbed by both men and pulled around, forced to her feet.

'Bring her out here,' Colonel Ding ordered. 'Sit her here.' Xiùyīng was placed on an interrogation chair, her feet locked into metal circles, the gate at the front secured into place, hands forced into metal restraints on the front gate, her body strapped tightly down.

Zhuge Xiùyīng knew the Party preferred to discipline recalcitrant cadres in private. Matters that were considered necessary for corrective action were those that happened to be in vogue at any period in time. Now it appeared to be her turn. As she had been forced into the car at the airport, a lower ranking member of the Central Commission for Discipline Inspection informed her that she was under investigation, and that they were working with the Bureau of International Cooperation. The *shuanggui* disciplinary system had begun. She knew that unless a well-wisher released her or she succeeding in escaping, she would inevitably compromise her self-esteem by confessing to whatever they were looking for. The tiger chair was very painful. The harsh lights were extinguished. Two new lights directed at each side of her face were switched on. She could not see beyond the intensity of the black.

'Major Zhuge Xiùyīng,' the Colonel repeated. 'You are to be interrogated because of corruption and violations of the Party rules.'

Zhuge Xiùyīng knew that people had been subject to beatings; being made to stand or sit in uncomfortable positions for hours or days; strapped, as she was, in positions for long periods that caused permanent damage to the body and subject to cold, heat, hunger; insulted, deprived of sleep, food, water; and beaten. There would be no contact with the outside world, her family, her department hierarchy, least of all a lawyer. Zhuge Xiùyīng knew that there were rules, but in reality there were no rules. Political reliability, understanding the law, an aptitude for strong work, appropriately trained – these official written requisites did not matter. What she had to discover was the reason for being taken into custody. What purpose did they have? Was the Colonel wanting to advance her career – the guards did not matter, they were dispensable – or was she under pressure to fulfil a quota? This was not a joint investigation. She knew she was in grave danger.

'You are working with the Australian Secret Intelligence Service?' The Colonel began questioning Zhuge Xiùyīng.

I was not told whether this was secret or not. They did not tell me the authority under which I was required to work with the Australians. If I agree, she will have a fact confirmed that she might not know about. She could be deceiving me about her state of knowledge. If I acknowledge the truth of this, I might be putting the lives of others at risk. I don't know who this Colonel is. She could be a traitor. I don't know if she has the authority. I don't know if she wants to destroy me, or Colonel Commandant Xú Delun, or both of us. This might be a test. I don't know.

Colonel Ding was impatient for an answer. 'Remaining silent is not recommended. Tell me. Who told you to work with the Australians?' she shouted.

If I respond, she'll want more. If I don't tell her what she wants, will she stop? If I don't know answers, will she stop, or will she continue the pain? If I don't say anything, she'll make it worse.

'Stubborn, are we? Well, we'll see about that. You're a *hanjian*, nothing but a traitor, and I'm going to find out more for the Party. Traitors are filth.'

She turned to the guards. 'Leave her in this. I'll be back.'

Colonel Ding stamped her feet as she rushed with annoyance to the door to be let out. She motioned both guards to follow her. 'Put all the lights on. Shine one directly in her face. Make sure she can't avoid the light. No toilet breaks. No water. No food. Leave her like this until I come back.'

Both men nodded in acquiescence. After locking the door, they switched on a supplementary mobile light, focused on the front of her body. One of the men pushed back her hair with a bandage to ensure, when she lowered her head, her hair did not fall in front of her eyes. To avoid the intensity of the burning luminosity, they left the main room to sit in the space between the outer door and sound-proof folding doors.

Zhuge Xiùyīng closed her eyes.

So it began.

Now was the time of her struggle, both physical and mental. She did not know how she would respond. They could continue with different types of torture for days, weeks, and months. Each part of her body would be subject to excruciating pain; it would be distorted, pressured, expanded, crushed to make her bend to their will.

Confucius, I follow your path. I try. I will improve. My personal behaviour must seek to be impeccable. In my essence of being human, a proper human being, I must continue to cultivate myself through self-creation. To be righteous and to do good. This I have tried all my life, but in my own way. I honour my mother and my father and my ancestors. I have acted properly in my life. I have endeavoured to act with propriety. I have done what I am required. I know what is right and fair. Many do not follow the master in this. If I could get out of this, I'd kill them all. But that means I fail. I will not be compassionate. I am not benevolent. I have failed for thinking this. But then I have to be true to my weakness that makes me fail.

I have to accept my failing. Our friendship at university. She was so delightful, beautiful, and wonderful to be with. We could not be together. Our intimacy is forbidden. To love was to be. I have remained true to her. I have failed. But I must try. I must try to be moral, to be worthy. I am in contempt. But what should I do for myself? How am I to be true and not be in contempt?

The heat and light saturated her skin, penetrated her closed eyelids into the burning retina and optic nerve. Her ankles imprisoned, feet unable to move, hands trapped before her, body tightly strapped down causing her back to bend forward, the intense pain excruciating and without end, a constant torment.

How long?

The occasional passer-by walked along the Quai de Mariemont in Sint-Jans-Molenbeek, seeing but not processing the flow of the canal confined between concrete banks; looking at but not taking in the ubiquitous small industrial buildings, in plain brick, concrete, supporting light industry and all other things hidden behind flaking wooden doors and metal shutters.

*

'There are several events this evening, Sir.' The secretary to the ambassador placed a file on his desk in the Embassy of the

People's Republic of China in the Kingdom of Belgium. The heads of the political section and the senior military attaché were in attendance, as usual. The secretary continued. 'The Australians have sent an invitation to all diplomatic missions to attend a private viewing of an exhibition of an Aboriginal artist. The Danish sent out a late invitation this morning, for which they apologize. They are hosting an informal event of the Zangger Committee, and the Deputy Prime Minister of Belgium is holding a meeting of the United Nations Truce Supervision Organization at the Federal Public Service of Foreign Affairs.'

Kung Mu spoke. 'It is correct that the political section ought to attend the meeting with the Belgians?'

'Yes, Sir, we must know what the Russian intentions are in the Arab world.'

'Good. You will report as usual.'

'Yes, Sir.'

He turned to Colonel Ding. 'It is unusual for the Zangger Committee to meet outside Vienna.'

'Yes, Sir, but I think it will be important for me to attend. The position of nuclear weapons and those developing them is crucial to the defence of our country.' The ambassador signified his agreement. 'Yes, please attend. I will go to the Australian Embassy.' He turned to his secretary. 'Please find out if they agree that my wife may accompany me. If they do, please contact my wife for me. I will speak with her. It might be good for our relations to attend together.' He turned to the head of the political section. 'Do you agree?'

'Yes, Sir, the Australians want to get closer to us, and your interest in art will be appreciated.'

The ambassador and his wife arrived slightly early at the Australian Embassy and Mission to the European Union and NATO in the Avenue des Arts. They were keen to view the display. Two short, slightly plump figures, they dressed conservatively. He wore a business suit, nondescript tie and white shirt, his wife a plain two-piece grey assemblage with a matching blouse. The curator of the exhibition was delighted to find a couple exhibiting an interest in the exhibition. She noticed their gaze as they focused on the shape, colour and decorative features of the internal décor, eyes dancing as they sought out the pictures without frames.

'We are very pleased to have got agreement for this small exhibition, ambassador. It's entirely the work of Craig Allen Charles. From his father, he has Yorta Yorta heritage, and Mhutti Mhutti tradition on his mother's side. His great grandparents raised him, and told him many stories, and the children did lots of drawing. He has always been concerned with the spirit of Aboriginal people, and how tough they have had to be in responding to the white man. He pays tribute to his family, his ancestors and his country.'

'Ah,' the ambassador and his wife gave an indication of interest, 'like in China.'

'Yes. This is a series about the birth of his son. Let us look at this picture. It's called *Birth Place*. You can see he includes a margin of gold leaf to the left of the painting. This is to signify his respect for his elders and traditional owners, but it's also to venerate the country he paints, such as the Murray River. This river runs through Latje Latje country. He identifies with this area very powerfully. The white dots are part of the journey through life, and the cracks in the red of the earth are the power of the sun, evaporating the water.'

Kung Mu and his wife were very attentive. They looked at each other as the curator explained. The ambassador's wife commented, almost involuntarily. 'The twists and turns of life run unevenly.' Her eyes met with her husband. They exchanged a burning moment of their shared knowledge of the past. Of the painful challenges, decades ago; of insults;

degradation; physical pain; lack of food; humiliation; the reality of fear. Rehabilitation did not erase the memories. Distance did not diminish the mists of time. Unknown to anybody, they had a rare ink-and-gouache landscape painting by Mu Xin. They knew the dangers of taking action without thinking. They knew the suffering it caused.

As the ambassadors and artistic elite began to fill the room, the Australian Head of Mission, Patricia Thetford, took the opportunity to have a word with Kung Mu. Discreetly, the curator took a step to one side.

'Ambassador, I am so delighted you and your wife are enjoying this small exhibition of ours.'

'Thank you, yes we are,' he acknowledged her interest, a glass of wine in his hand.

'May I take this opportunity to ask for a discreet meeting?'

'A meeting?'

'An important discussion in private of the utmost national importance to you and China.' The ambassador looked at his wife. 'Well, yes, if you think it is necessary.' The curator stepped forward. She spoke to the Head of Mission. 'Please accept my apologies, ambassador, but I wondered if Mr Kung and his wife might like to view some of the other paintings we have in the embassy?'

'That is kind of you,' the Head of Mission took up the suggestion. 'Might you take Mrs Kung while the ambassador and I have a word?' Kung Mu began to understand the need for tact, and nodded to his wife to accompany the curator, who offered to take his glass. He gave up the wine and followed Patricia Thetford discreetly to another room. As he entered, two men stood. He was greeted by somebody he knew, General Yuan Ah, one of the deputy chiefs of the Joint Staff Department of the Central Military Commission. The other was Colonel Phillip Rockox of the External Intelligence and Security Division of the Belgian General Information and Security Service, dressed in civilian clothes. After being introduced to Colonel Rockox, the four sat down around a circular table.

Patricia Thetford began. 'Ambassador, we were relieved when you and you wife agreed to attend this exhibition. We will have as short a meeting as we can, because of the problems you might face if you were missed from our reception. Let me assure you that this room is sound proof and we are not recording the conversation. If you wish me to write a note to this effect, I will do so, but once you understand why we are here, perhaps you might agree with General Yuan Ah that a record of this meeting is neither necessary nor desirable. General, do you wish to outline the position to the ambassador?'

General Yuan Ah opened the discussion. 'Yes, thank you ambassador. Kung Mu, I will be brief because time is short, and we will meet later. We have been informed that an officer of the Central Commission for Discipline Inspection was waiting at Brussels airport to take one of our officers into custody. This occurred about thirty-six hours ago. No one has seen our officer since. She was on a secret mission, working with our Australian colleagues. The assignment was agreed at the highest political level and incredibly secret.'

'Ah. A woman officer.'

'Colonel Ding is responsible to the Central Commission for Discipline Inspection here in Belgium.'

'Yes.'

'She has not reported to you about this?'

'No.'

'Ah. In that case I will not let you know about any other information at present. We do not want to put you in a position of additional knowledge. The matter is far too delicate. We do not want anybody at the embassy to know of our meeting or of our concerns.'

Kung Mu and General Yuan Ah were well acquainted. The

ambassador understood the General was being tactful. 'Of course. I understand.'

'Colonel Rockox is dealing with this in Belgium. The State Security Service is supporting him. The Belgian government has agreed to give us all the help we need, but they insist that only they recover our agent. We concur with this. We have no wish for China to be seen to be operating in a foreign country, even with the agreement of the domestic government. Colonel Rockox, will you kindly inform the ambassador of your plans?'

'Thank you General. Ambassador, we have had intelligence from one of our allies that might help us locate your agent. Once General Yuan alerted us to the problem, we decided to watch Colonel Ding. Unfortunately, this has only just begun.'

'If she suspects...' the ambassador began. 'Yes Sir, if she has any suspicion, she will not lead us to the place where your officer is held – that is, if she is in Belgium.'

'How long do you think it will take?'

'I am hopeful that we will find her soon. You will understand that we could not do anything until General Yuan informed us. Perhaps you can also appreciate that we did not involve you with the political discussions for fear of alerting members of staff at the embassy. Wagging tongues might have put Colonel Ding on notice that we suspected her of abducting the agent.'

General Yuan continued the briefing. 'Colonel Rockox and his team are searching all the relevant surveillance recordings from the airport. When they find the vehicle that was used, they will check all the cameras that recorded the vehicle as it was driven from the airport. We are busy looking at Colonel Ding, her family, friends and acquaintances to try and understand what her motive is, if she is responsible.'

'The suspicion is on her?' The ambassador asked.

'At the moment, it is. You know the Central Commission

for Discipline Inspection is highly secretive. It is probable that they have our officer.'

'Unless a foreign power took her? Or she has absconded?'

'We have thought of both of these as possibilities, ambassador. We are carrying out a thorough check on the officer as well as Colonel Ding.'

'Very well. What happens now?'

The General answered the question by setting out his decision. 'We will help Colonel Rockox as much as we can. I will visit you tomorrow officially, because we know that I cannot remain in Belgium without a courtesy visit to see you. If we are fortunate, we will have found the officer.'

'If not?'

'Then you and I will have to decide what further action, if any, we must consider.'

Patricia Thetford interrupted at this point. 'Gentlemen, I fear we must end the meeting now. If we stay away from the reception much longer, we are in danger of being missed.'

'Yes, you are right, ambassador,' the General replied and they all stood up. General Yuan and Colonel Rockox quickly shook the hands of both ambassadors.

'Please, ambassador,' Patricia Thetford said. 'Will you kindly follow me? We will leave through another door and meet your wife and the curator. You can see our other paintings and then return with your wife to the reception together. I will return by another way.'

Before following the ambassador, Kung Mu faced General Yuan and Colonel Rockox, and slightly tilted his head forward. 'Thank you for keeping me informed. Let us wish that your efforts reach a satisfactory conclusion.'

General Yuan and Colonel Rockox sat with Major George Isgrove, the Australian military attaché, in the temporary operations room in one of the blocks of the GISS in the rue d'Evere. Colonel Rockox summed up the position. 'We have identified the vehicle that was sent to the airport to collect Major Zhuge Xiùyīng.' He walked over to a large screen and touched the surface to bring up an image from a number of monitors placed around the arrivals pick-up point. 'They had diplomatic plates, and were permitted to go through the security barriers, General. Looking at these less than perfect images, might you think that this could be an official vehicle from the embassy?'

'Yes, possibly. I am waiting to get confirmation from China as to how many vehicles they have, and who might be able to requisition one for the purpose of collecting a visiting dignitary.'

'Well, Sir, we have also managed to follow the direction of travel across the city. Their route took them around the periphery, on the N290,' he opened a new window to show a map of Brussels with the route outlined in bright red. 'And then drove down the rue de Bonne. The images end there, but we know the embassy vehicle was back on a main road within minutes, because we have recorded it travelling as swiftly as the traffic would allow back to the embassy on the other side of the city.'

'So they could have put the Major into another vehicle and driven further,' the General began, 'or the driver might have reached the destination.'

'Yes, Sir. We have split the area into sectors. It's full of light industries, with a mix of modern and older buildings, mostly for industry; some are houses. I have sent our people out in teams to go over this triangular area between the Rue Nicolas Doyen,' he pointed the street on the map, 'and the N8, which runs along one side, to where it meets the Quai de Mariemont, here.'

'What are they attempting to do?'

'We are trying to establish whether there are any buildings

that are empty. We are also carrying out checks with those premises that are in use. We are asking the occupiers if they have noticed any strange movements over the past few days. In addition, we are investigating the utilities, water, gas and electricity to find out if patterns of use have changed. I've also requested internet service providers and mobile telephone operators in our jurisdiction to inform us if there is any activity that might give us an indication as to where she might be held. We started this afternoon, so it might be a little early to say for sure if we are wasting our time.'

'I understand. Your help is most appreciated. You have been very efficient. I thank you for this. What about our internet service providers? It will help if they cooperate with you?'

'Yes, Sir. Can you make the arrangements?'

'I will obtain a suitable contact and introduce them to you.'

'Thank you, General.'

General Yuan turned to speak to Major George Isgrove. 'Major, your government and intelligence service have been very helpful.'

'We have tried, General. Unfortunately, our respective officers did not exchange email addresses or telephone numbers, although if Major Zhuge Xiùyīng is in captivity, it's probable that all of her personal effects and devices have been seized.'

'You are possibly correct. I am waiting to receive information from China about Colonel Ding, such as her background, family, acquaintances and service record. Colonel Rockox, I anticipate that we cannot do very much more at present.'

'No, Sir. If you do not consider it to be inappropriate, our Assistant Chief of Staff Intelligence and Security has asked if you will join her for dinner this evening.' The General pondered for a moment. It was important to thank those at the highest level for the cooperation they had received over this most sensitive matter. 'Thank you, I will be pleased to meet the Assistant Chief.'

*

'Switch the lights off,' the Colonel demanded. The contrast caused Major Zhuge Xiùyīng to experience sudden absolute darkness.

My back stooped so much, the pain gouging through my back, over my shoulders, down into my arms and hands. My legs forced against the chair, throbbing in the back of the muscles, pressed into the seat, so numb and excruciating at the same time, my bottom raw, sore, wet from urine out of my body. Mortifying. The smell. So degrading.

'Well, Major, have you had sufficient? Now we will have a chat.' The short portly woman stood over Zhuge Xiùyīng's head, a single dull light shone from one side. 'You travelled business class. Who paid for it? Why are you here? What is your mission? Who is paying you? What business do you have here? Is it your uncle?' The last question slipped out unwittingly, unwanted. It was a mistake. She had given Xiùyīng a glimpse of the motivation for kidnapping and incarcerating her.

Ah, so is that what she wants? My uncle. Not me. This is not the Party. I am not here because I have transgressed. It is for another reason. This is corruption.

The Colonel was getting angry. No longer exuding the cool exterior of command, but signalling annoyance. It was not going to plan. The situation was getting out of hand. This had not been considered. 'The Party does not wish to discipline for minor offences,' the Colonel sought to distance herself from the last question, 'and if you cooperate, then these things can be resolved.' The timetable had slipped. Colonel Ding was under intense pressure.

Out of the silence at the end of her comment, she heard a click. A weapon. Two lights were switched on simultaneously. The area in front of the barred enclosure was suddenly bathed in light from naked bulbs suspended from the ceiling. Four figures, their heads covered with balaclavas, each pointed a SCAR-H CQC rifle with a 330 mm barrel at her. Two moved rapidly to overcome the Colonel, gag her mouth, force her hands behind her back, attach handcuffs and quickly march her out between the wall of the cage and the rear of the building from whence they came. At this moment, a loud bang was heard in the front, and men entered into the small space between the outer doors and the sound proof barrier. The two guards were swiftly overcome. A Cantonese speaker was ushered in to find out from the guards where the keys for the tiger chair were located. Neither wished to speak, until both were subject to a powerful knee in the groin with a promise of far more pain. One guard weakened. They were then bundled into a waiting unmarked van.

Once in possession of the keys, one of the rescuers freed Zhuge Xiùyīng. She could not move, and kept on saying, 'Thank you, thank you, thank you so much.' Two of the liberators uncovered their heads. Both were women, their hair falling over their unadorned uniform. They took hold of Zhuge Xiùyīng's body, lifted and placed her gently into a folding wheelchair, brought in by another of the rescue party. In undertaking their duties, they reassured Zhuge Xiùyīng with gentle soft voices. 'That's all right, please do not worry. We're here to help.'

Very late that night, Colonel Ding sat in a windowless room at the airport. She heard the key turn. General Yuan Ah strode in, having changed into his uniform. She stood up, a look of concentrated fear etched into her face.

'You are a disgrace to your colleagues and the honour of China.'

She did not speak.

'You will be taken back to China on the next flight. You are under arrest. You will be interrogated upon your return. The National Congress of the Party has decided to end *shuang-gui*. The Party anticipates that from this decision, those who transgress will provide all necessary assistance to the officers invested with the authority to investigate matters brought to their attention. It is no longer expected that physical means of encouragement will be necessary. You are now under detention. You will be expected to cooperate fully. It will be in your interests to do so. In the West, the legal system permits judges to decide that if you do not offer explanations to facts that require clarification, it follows that your failure to provide an account of your actions means you accept the truth of what is put forward. Our system is changing.'

2

Istrebitel sputnikov

François sits back in his angular comfortable 1960s armchair designed by Geneviève Dangles and Christian Defrance for Burov. He looks at the garden through the double doors into the enclosed centre of the apartment block, the sky a nautical twilight.

I'm too old for this. I should have retired when my post was eliminated as the new wave began, and my responsibilities were dispersed. But enough. It's now only a short time before I finish and receive my pension. Then – well, then I have freedom.

Two sparrows flitting, hopping, flying short distances between branches as if dancing, playing a game of children's tag, or fun between lovers.

Freedom. Freedom from what? The work, not life. Staying in the job was easier. The terms were not advantageous to leave. Silly, some said. Others thought they were just trying to get rid of the old. I was a supernumerary. Somebody didn't want me. But now I'm in the centre. I'm no longer on the periphery. Something is wrong. Now I have nothing to lose if I don't succeed.

All the birds suddenly fly in a group. A breeze catches the highest lightest branches of the trees, wavering gently; waning sunlight sparkles in the movement; leaves flutter to the ground.

This is important. For France, and for me. The Minister for

Europe and Foreign Affairs overhears something said by the ambassador of the Russian Federation. It's a noisy room. It might be a mistake. The ambassador was speaking to a company executive from a French satellite company. Was it serious? Did they intend the conversation to be overheard? The executive reports it to us anyway. They say the British know about "l'addition". That must mean the Russians also know. But they don't use it against us. Why? Do they really know? If they know, how do they know? Do they just know of it, but don't have copies of the documents? If so, how? Do the British know? Why have they told us the British know? If the British know, do they have a copy of the documents? Do we have a double agent? Or maybe our systems have been penetrated. I have a suspect, but he's untouchable unless I have hard evidence. He's uncooperative. Like a worm, he has worked his way into the confidence of men at the highest levels. To deal with him I must have both a strong case and political patronage – no, it must be more than that. Formidable support will be essential. Those who are mighty will crush me and those that I serve. But I am far from achieving this. The proof is not there, only supposition based on circumstantial evidence. I need more. Time is not with me. Perhaps I should have retired. This dilemma would then be with someone else. But similar problems will always arise. Now is not the time to go, but after I have gone it will be different.

François's thoughts are interrupted. In a cloudless twilight purple sky, the moon shines a bright pale yellow.

Such an enchanting scene. I saw the moon like that on a pair of screens. Now, where was the exhibition? He gets up from the chair and walks a short distance into the entrance area to a bookcase in the alcove. *Here it is.* He finds the catalogue and returns to be seated. *Ah yes, at the British Museum in London. Matazō Kayama. A pair of a byobu, fourfold screens, 'Weeping Cherry Blossoms', painted in 1988.* He looks through the book, unfolding the double photographs. Some have stuck together.

Care is needed to open the pages, his fingers slip between the gaps and gently strains against the adhesive nature of the finish. He eases the edges of the pages open. *Beautiful, so sensitive. I have never forgotten those screens. So few colours, yet so many in the imagination. The branches of the tree supported by poles – the poles are always integral to the experience in Japanese gardens, the sky in gradations of gold, the land covered in grass, short small gold lines breaking the bulk of the colour, silver dust covering the ground of fallen blossom.* He looked out at the night sky. *What would Sei Shōnagon say?*

Lost in thought as the black night engulfs his picture, he is framed by the open doors. He shivers. The cold air reminds him that the doors are open.

I know. She'd say 'especially delightful', I'm sure. In Japan, they'll soon be getting together for tsukimi, *moon-viewing parties.*

There is a clear double-tap, followed by a single tap on the door.

'Charles? Is that you?' François stands up, places the book on the table and moves some CD cases. He quickly closes the casement windows and opens the door to his apartment. Charles enters. They embrace.

'My friend, how did you come in? I didn't hear the intercom.'

'I didn't use it, François. Your concierge let me in. She's lovely. I wanted to say hello to her.'

'Well, here you are. It's good to see you; so unexpected.' François closed the door. 'Come in, come in. Look at me. I'm in my scruffy at home clothes. Let me tidy up. This is not how I should be for my guests.'

'Apologies. It's unfair of me to surprise you like this.' Charles handed a brown paper bag to François.

'Cold. It's at the right temperature', he said as he lifted the bottle of Pineau des Charentes from the bag. 'And Château d'Orignac. Thank you, Charles. Will you be the host and prepare our glasses as I change?'

'Of course. It's the least I can do when surprising a friend out of his reverie.'

They both looked at the recordings scattered across the white nineteenth-century chateau dining table at the head of the room, Villeneuve oak rattan back chairs tucked under, an oil painting by Bernard Buffet from 1958 entitled *Nature morte à la cafetière bleue* on the wall, the blue of the elongated coffee jug dominating the black of the background, the yellow of the lemon highlighting the dark green of the pears. Scattered CDs of music by international stars littered the table: Jacques Brel *Ne me quitte pas* singing of beauty in the rhythm of a poet; Charles Trenet *La Mer* about the people of Paris; Monique Andrée Serf under her stage name Barbara *L'aigle noir*, so intellectual, moving, sophisticated; Serge Gainsbourg *La Javansaise* written for Juliette Gréco, sexual, provocative; the singer and songwriter Françoise Hardy *Tout les garcons et les filles* about the loneliness of a woman without a love; Georges Brassens *Les copains d'abord* about friendship, living life's lessons through song. Irony, sentimental, spirited emotions of words; chanson, poetry.

'Nostalgia, Charles, nostalgia. You know how it is sometimes.' François shrugged his shoulders as he opened the door to a bedroom. Charles noticed the Verlys opalescent art deco glass ashtray, deep with cigarette stubs.

'Ah,' François nodded, his eyes tired, head slightly bowed.

Charles took up the heavy object. 'Be off, my friend, be off,' he spoke urgently to François, walking into the kitchen, busying himself with finding the glasses and placing ice cubes at the bottom of an ice bucket attached to a circular plate with two circles of holes cut in a fleur-de-lis pattern raised on three scroll legs that sat inside the ice bucket to allow the cubes to melt below; opening and pouring the aperitif, placing all on a tray and taking it through into the main room; cleaning and replacing the ashtray. François returned in smart fashionably brown trousers and a textured cashmere roll-neck jumper in stone.

'Thank you, Charles for a most enjoyable start to the evening.' He noticed the clean crystal, nodded in thanks and motioned Charles to be seated.

François passed a glass to Charles. They toasted each other, the rich amber colour of the wine offering tints of gold in the subdued light of the two small table lamps. Each enjoyed the complexity of an elegant wine with an authoritative aromatic nose, restrained hints of ripe yellow fruits, honey, raisins, spice, flowers and oranges. Full, rich, satisfyingly sweet, refreshingly harmonious, intense, distinguished. Such a delight.

'So,' began François.

'Yes,' replied Charles.

'Well?' François asked.

'You know, François. We've been friends for a long time.'

'We have, but there's a purpose to your visit.' François wanted to cut to the chase.

'Yes, of course. But after we've retired, it will be different.'

'Ah yes, after we've retired, then there is no more guessing about the actions of others. But for now?'

'For now, I came to Paris for a few days. There's the conference on satellite technology.'

'Yes. We're watching it.'

'So are we, as you know. Well, we all are, of course. It must be both fun and a difficulty for the DGSC.'

'Yes. We try our best to find out what we can, and track everybody that comes.'

'Of course. But François, you're not yourself. You look worse than I've ever seen you. What's wrong?'

François sighed, looking into his glass. He caught Charles's eye. He remained unspoken. His face drawn, hair a touch tousled. Charles stood up, walked over to the doors and closed the curtains, returning to the settee.

'Has the flat been checked for surveillance devices recently?'

'Yes. Last week. Nothing.'

'How about the block? Is there a flat opposite that might be used to eavesdrop?'

'Unlikely. I'm the only one in this part, so they don't think I'm much of a risk. If there were more officers here, then they would be more concerned.'

'All right. Let's work on the assumption we can't be heard or recorded.'

Both men were silent for a while. Neither could prevent themselves from appraising the room for possible listening devices, even though they knew it was a futile exercise, given that those that were placed with care by the most expert of fixers could not be found without suitable technology.

'We have some serious problems, Charles.' François began.

'I know.'

François raised his eyebrows.

Charles continued, 'I'm not sure if I can help, but there seems to be some misinformation going the rounds that's putting us in a bad light.'

'You mean the British?'

'Yes.'

'I know, but I don't know where it's coming from.'

'You have an important brief.'

François's eyes expressed surprise. 'Yes, but it's extremely secret.'

'I know. Only you, the President, the Ministère des Armées and the Director of the DGSE know about it.'

'And you.'

'And the Russians.'

François let out a long low breath, closing his eyes. 'This is serious.'

'Yes, but remember, it's the office of the President that knows, not just him.'

'I know. Can you tell me what you know?'

'Yes, but I need your help.'

'Between the two of us?'

'Yes, strictly between the two of us, as before.'

'We can do that.'

'I agree. In the circumstances, I think it's the best we can do.'

'Where shall we begin?'

'By filling our glasses.' Charles took the bottle out of the late nineteenth century English silver plate ice bucket made to look like a barrel with three hoops, the handle sitting on the top to one side, and filled their glasses to one third full.

'Let me begin. We became aware of "l'addition" recently.'

'Oh. It's worse than I thought.'

'Probably. It's an interesting development. As you can imagine, on a personal level, I don't blame you for developing it.'

'But if it gets out.'

'The government will fall.'

'Yes, and the repercussions will continue.'

'Agreed. The fallout could be catastrophic. Constitutionally, the government will be in serious breach of the law.'

'How did you find out?'

'Let's come to that later. Now, you're doing a special report on a possible double agent because you think the Russians know about "l'addition".'

'Yes, partly.'

'What's your deadline?'

'I don't have one, but the pressure is on to produce it before the next ministerial meeting at NATO. Space security is on the agenda.'

'That makes sense. Your minister needs to know the extent of the problem. It will help shape her position.'

'Yes, but we must also find out who the double agent is.'

'If you have one.'

'If we have one.'

'It could be a leak.'

'Yes. I've tried to investigate thoroughly.'

'But you've been, let us say, frustrated, perhaps obstructed?'

'Yes. You know the usual problems with powerful people.'

'You mean people who think they are powerful, and remain powerful until they're exposed. But François, you are looking so stressed. There must be more to it for you.'

'You know I had the opportunity to leave.'

'Yes. You use the word opportunity as a euphemism.'

'Yes, maybe. Well, I should have taken it.'

'But it was on bad terms. You couldn't possibly have left with any honour.'

'I know, and you were so kind to ensure they partially failed.'

'And Bruce.'

'Yes, and Bruce. The roving job has proved interesting, but there are those that don't trust me. My bond with you and Bruce is such that they are always suspicious. They prefer I didn't have such a rapport.'

'Maybe it's not that they don't trust you, but they don't believe that you're on their side. They know you'll do a first-class job, and that might be to their detriment.'

'Perhaps. One or two at the top politically want me removed.'

'And some in the DGSE?'

'Yes, one in particular.'

'This report is very important for you and your reputation.'

'And for France.'

'I agree. It's also important for us. We need to help you as much as we can.'

'But not officially or through formal channels.'

'No. Your report has got,' Charles paused, 'to point the finger decisively.'

'And with irrefutable evidence.'

'Yes. Who do you trust?'

'The Director of the DGSE.'

'And?'

'The Minister.'

'And?'

Silence. They both took a sip of the of Pineau des Charentes. Charles continued. 'So, we know the problem.'

'Yes, but how to deal with it. Can you tell me your source?'

'Not yet.'

'Soon?'

'I hope.'

François wanted Charles to be slightly more explicit. 'What's your timetable?'

'The next forty-eight hours.'

'Right, that's very helpful, really useful. Excellent. What can I do?'

'Not much. I don't need details. That would be asking too much, and we don't need to work that way. Just names.'

'All of them?'

'No. Just those you have good reason to suspect, but you can't get at, or where you think if you secured more detailed background information, the suspects would be likely to find out where you're looking. You might be missing some important facts, such as background, financial affairs, liaisons, interests, ambitions, bank balances. All of this might lead you to make links that are helpful to your investigation.'

'I've had difficulties with some of this because I don't have much back-up, and I'm not part of a department.'

'So you've been given an important job to do, but not the political backing?'

'Yes, not full political backing.'

Sir Charles expressed a thought. 'Somebody is out to make you fail.'

'I've reached that conclusion.'

'Recently?'

'Yes, today.'

'It's a coincidence, but it might be fortunate that I came up to surprise you this evening.'

'It is, my friend.'

'We have to work fast. My visiting you shouldn't give rise to any suspicion if they find out.'

'I'm not so sure. It looked to me today as if the knives had been sharpened and were ready for filleting.'

'We'll have to meet again. I think we can make sure they don't suspect anything next time we meet. If I was followed, your enemies will know I'm here.'

'I wouldn't know if you were followed, but it might be bad if they knew.'

Charles thought. 'Let's be open about meeting. It's the only way. Of the two people you trust, is it worth letting them know what we'll do?'

François deliberated. He stood up and walked around the back of the chair and around the dining room table, casting his eyes over the painting. His short walk took him back to his chair. 'Not the Director. I think it's better he was not involved. We need to protect him and his position. Maybe you should approach him when you think the time is right.'

'I understand. Agreed.'

'Maybe the Minister.'

'How well do you know her?'

'Not well. We've recently met.'

'What do you think?'

'Well, on a personal level, she's a really nice woman.'

Charles looked at François. His eyes sparkled. 'Oh, very good. Perhaps more appealing than nice? Or even attractive?'

François smiled and continued. 'Well, maybe. But as a politician, she's an outsider. Possibly she was appointed for several reasons. Female. Well connected. First time in a senior position. Useful for the appearance of equality. Doesn't have a wide political base. Easy to sideline.'

'Or dismiss.'

'Yes, or "release" as they say. They might have appointed her because they think she's a "yes-woman".'

'Is she?'

'I don't think so.'

'Nor do I. We agree on our assessment.'

'Yes.'

'You might need a strong advocate in the next few days.'

'I know.'

François began to relax. Despair giving way to optimism. No longer not knowing what to do or what approach to take, who to trust, or what the future held.

'If the wrong people find out,' Charles continued his train of thought, 'both of us will be in difficulties.'

'Yes, but what's the alternative? Timing is everything.'

'In this case, I agree, timing is all. I wouldn't have suggested our working together if we didn't have an excellent chance of succeeding.'

'This was a surprise visit, Charles?'

'Yes, just the two of us. I didn't want to alert you.'

'Because of what you know?'

'Yes. I wanted to find out more before we make any moves. That is, if we decide to do anything. I had to establish what you knew. Relationships between allies can be strained unnecessarily. It's imperative to avoid precipitate actions by politicians.'

'How shall we proceed? Anonymous phones, our codes, or as you said earlier, in the open?'

At that moment, there was a knock on the door. They looked at each other. Charles out of interest. François more circumspect, uneasy, enquiring.

'I wonder,' François said as he walked to the door.

'Minister,' he expressed surprise, 'please come in.' The minister's face conveyed an interest in his use of the English language.

Charles stood up as the minister entered the room. François introduced them. 'Madam de Beauchamp, this is Sir Charles Beresford. Charles, this is Madam Eleanor de Beauchamp, our minister.' Charles waited for the minister to speak.

'I am pleased to meet you, Sir Charles.'

'I am pleased to meet you, Madam de Beauchamp. Is it to be le ministère or la ministère?'

'As you wish,' she said with amusement.

'Very well, le ministère,' Sir Charles responded. Eleanor de Beauchamp understood the nuances noted by Charles – of gender, power and culture. Knowing his friend as he did, François smiled.

'It is somewhat unusual for me to meet the Chief of the British Secret Intelligence Service in the apartment of one of my most trusted officers, Sir Charles.'

'Indeed, Minister. Meeting in an official capacity might be considered to be more appropriate.'

François motioned the minister to sit in a chair and went into the kitchen for a glass, returning and filling it to the appropriate level.

'But then,' the minster continued as she made herself comfortable in the chair, 'it might also be questioned as to why a minister visits an officer without an appointment or invitation in his apartment on her own.' François handed the minister the glass before returning to his chair. She thanked him.

'That I do not comment on, Minister,' Charles continued, 'and I take no view on such a visit.'

'You both go back a long way,' said the minister, opening a new thread of conversation. François followed the lead of the minister. 'Yes, we have a long relationship, Minister.'

'And friendship,' added Charles. They were impressed with the control she had of her brief. As the host, François lifted his glass and led the salutation, 'à votre santé'.

'This is excellent' the minister observed, holding the glass at eye level to look at the colour.

'It's a gift from Charles. You know how the English insist on importing only the best.'

Eleanor de Beauchamp laughed. 'Very good, Monsieur Duhamel.' She liked the joke, crossing one leg over the other.

'It's an unexpected pleasure for you to visit, Minister,' François gave her an opportunity to offer an explanation for calling.

'Thank you. The working day has ended, and I was able to visit discreetly. Your concierge let me in. She has tact.'

'A human is so much more than the function that software code is increasingly made to serve, especially to gain access to buildings and rooms these days. Although a person might not be honest or is sometimes unreliable, we should always be careful of trusting software code to open doors.'

'Indeed, Sir Charles. If you have no knowledge, you have to trust. Too many people believe the machine. Software is rarely challenged. So unintelligent.'

'Your car?' Charles asked.

'Parked near a local restaurant. My security guard has positioned himself in a location that controls access to the entrance without being conspicuous.' The minister knew it was incumbent on her to explain why she called in to see François. She had to do so in a way that did not give away her real purpose.

Charles eased her embarrassment. He decided to take the initiative. 'François has had two surprise visitors this evening, Minister. He was not expecting me, either.'

'Ah.'

'I am over for a short period on official business, and will call in tomorrow to visit Monsieur Lavigne. We have become aware of certain matters that are highly significant to France. If they were revealed beyond their present circle of knowledge, the facts will prove to be highly damaging to the French state.'

'Without knowing the precise details, Sir Charles, you appear to be well informed,' the minister cautiously observed.

'Charles is always well informed, Minister,' François contributed to the exchange.

'So it seems.'

'Thank you, François. I'm informed as well as can be expected.' Eleanor de Beauchamp was entertained at his use of the classic English understatement. Sir Charles continued. 'It's the reason for my visit to François. Matters are very difficult at present, and François and I have discussed them frankly.'

'Yes, Minister, on the basis of our mutual respect for each other.'

'And loyalty?' the minister asked.

Sir Charles assuaged the minister's concern. 'As you will have surmised, Minister, we have a long relationship that is recorded by both our Services. The evidence is that we have always acted honourably.'

'I know, but I have to ask the question.'

'Naturally, especially because of the coincidence of us meeting this evening in such circumstances. You're correct, of course. The political responsibility is immense. The situation we find ourselves in – or perhaps more accurately that François finds himself in – is highly sensitive.'

At this moment the minister interrupted Charles, 'Your interests, or that of Great Britain?'

'Mine.'

'Personally?'

'No, for the Service I have the honour to lead, and because of my friendship for François. He is in danger. He needs my help.'

'I know.'

'A grave injustice might befall an innocent and praiseworthy officer of the DGSE.'

'And your friend?'

'Yes, and my very good friend. I'm of the opinion, although this will not be shared with many people, that it's not in the interests of the United Kingdom to stand to one side and refuse to help our ally in circumstances where France might face serious international and regional consequences if matters get out of hand.'

'And are not dealt with appropriately?'

'Yes.'

François interposed. 'Minister, we reached the decision to inform you – only you – of our working together.'

'A decision? Not a request to collaborate?'

'Yes.'

'What about any actions you take and the results?'

Sir Charles joined in. 'From your perspective, Minister, it's appropriate to ensure you can plausibly deny the consequences of any actions we might determine. That is, if they become public knowledge. The question is how much you want to know.' A studied silence enveloped the room after Sir Charles's remark. The three exchanged glances of understanding, of a tentative confidence.

Madam de Beauchamp ended the pause in the conversation. 'The situation is delicate. We are all compromised by this discussion. I have to trust the bond between you. I am in a sensitive position. I have to be tactful. When I agreed to be minister, I was flattered. I am aware of the nuances you face, Monsieur Duhamel.'

Within seconds of each other, the secure devices of all three vibrated. Each looked at their screen. As the minster got out of the chair, François recognized her need to be able to answer the telephone in private, and directed her to the second bedroom: discreet, quiet, tidy. Charles walked into the kitchen. François paced around the room, to and from the front door and the casement windows leading on to the balcony, the length of the dining table. Minutes later, they reassembled. The minister began. 'The pressure has changed. I expect you have both had a similar message. It seems as if there's been a terrorist outrage. Some shooting in a suburb. Maybe a bomb.'

'Yes,' François agreed. 'Was it the same for you Charles?'

'Yes.'

Madam de Beauchamp continued, taking control of what she needed to do. 'The police are trying to understand what is happening, or if it is finished. The press got there quite quickly.'

'All right. It's safe for us to be here now, but I expect you will both be needed shortly.'

'Yes, Charles, but not immediately. My people don't want me there yet, because it's in the hands of the police and the Groupe d'intervention de la gendarmerie Nationale. They asked me if it was appropriate for you to go there now, Minister. I suggested not. I thought it was too dangerous and too early.'

'Yes, the office of the President agrees with you. The President wants to speak with me again later. He will make an announcement first. He wishes me to appear on a late news update on France Télévisions, maybe at eleven tonight.'

'I'll have to go, François,' Charles finished sending a short message.

'Of course.' François looked at Eleanor de Beauchamp. 'Minister, we will both need to be briefed later, and you will have to discuss matters with the President before you appear on the news update.' He looked at his watch, a colourful Black

Storm tourbillon by Alain Silberstein. 'We have two or three hours. We could go back to the ministry and order a meal. Our problem is that it will be closed, and we will have to wait some time before people manage to get back into the office.'

Sir Charles made a suggestion. 'François, I booked a table for two at your local favourite restaurant. Why don't you both go for a meal? It might not be discreet, but it will ensure we three are not seen together. You can both be in public snatching a meal in a little corner. Minister, you are with a senior official having travelled to his apartment to discuss the situation. You have not gone to the incident because you have been requested to stay away for your own safety. The minister of the interior meets you both there. He has a police escort. You are all seen discussing the issue before going to the location when it is safe and appropriate.'

François looked at the minister. 'There are worse scenarios.'

'A bright journalist might follow the police cars to the destination. They see you all in the restaurant. They enter to ask if they can ask some questions.' Charles turned to François, 'Your minister asks you to make some comments, but outside, because she is on the telephone. You offer appropriate answers, indicating the minister visited you as one of her senior officers in the DGSE because the Director was already at the scene.' François and the minister looked at each other, uncertain, hesitating. Sir Charles continued. 'It would put your enemies on notice, François. You are now close to power. Suddenly they have to be careful. It will give me time to search for the evidence you need to help ensure those responsible are apprehended.'

Eleanor de Beauchamp expressed amusement, 'Sir Charles, how Machiavellian. I would not have thought of this. It might work.'

François looked worried. 'But some might think that having a meal in a local restaurant close to my apartment was evidence of a romantic attachment. They might get the wrong impression.'

Charles looked at them both. His face expressed a bemused confidence in the energy between the minister and his friend. Eleanor de Beauchamp knew immediately what Charles had observed in their joint body language. Then François realised. He interrupted his train of thought, 'ah...' unable to continue.

Charles broke the moment of reality. 'Look, you are both at home. I am an outsider. I have a more nuanced view of what is happening. I am not as close as you are to events. Your French journalists are so secret, so wishing to know insider information, but not to publish it. Even if some reporters did think that you two sitting together in a restaurant was worthy of being published in a gossip column, this attack is the focus. The adrenalin for the action sweeps them up.' They smiled as they realised that Charles was probably correct.

'Let me leave first. I'll find an alternative way out of the building. I need to leave discreetly,' Charles began to be practical. 'François, let us be in touch tomorrow. We can meet in the open now. It will be expected. Your enemies cannot be seen to be against you, not for now.' François walked Charles the short distance to the door. Sir Charles took the hand of the minister and wished her goodnight.

'Before I go, I took the liberty of booking the table in your name, François. I thought it might be difficult if I used my name.'

'Thank you, Charles. Until tomorrow. I will wait for you to get in touch. I'll get the information to you later tonight.'

'Thanks. We'll need it to start the searches. *Au revoir.*'

*

It is evening at the Westin Bonaventure Hotel, the mid 1970s grain store with windows and views by John C.

Portman Jr. in South Figueroa Street, central Los Angeles. The time is 21.45 on the upper level above the lobby. A Maker's Mark with ice is closely contained in a cut glass tumbler, which in turn rests on a low smoked glass table. There is a humdrum low chatter. An indifferent black grand piano, burnished, not highly polished, with an elegant slim woman at the keyboard. Bleached blonde hair partly tied with a black lace knot, a fringe over her forehead, carefully falling either side of the neck to flow down over a becoming cleavage. A black brassier under a black lace top with a black lace pencil skirt over a white lining, black high heel patent leather shoes, bare legs. Lipstick a light rouge, eyebrows and eyes highlighted. Making up a dramatic appearance, with a three-strand string of artificial pearls in a neat row, single pearl earrings, and bracelets on the right wrist in diamanté and on the left wrist in plain silver. She plays a tango with passion, precision, and with an air of excitement, enough for two couples to want to dance to, ending with a brief pause before playing a recognizable extract from Bach's Goldberg Variations, and then on to the opening of the popular piano concerto in A minor composed by the young Edvard Grieg during his stay at Søllerød. It is played with assurance from memory, demonstrating skill and talent, which is unrecognized, though maybe the initiated might think it was respectable, but perhaps not excellent enough.

His secure device rang. 'Hi there, BW,' the cheery voice of the Deputy Director of the Central Intelligence Agency spoke to the Director of the Directorate of Analysis, 'how ya doing?' he continued in his North Carolina dialect.

'Hi, Bart,' Bruce answered the question, an amused nuance to his voice, knowing that Bartholomew Ridens almost knew no time limits, 'just enjoying a Cuban pianist and a glass of the best before turning in.'

'Well, I'll be darned young fella,' the Deputy Director

laughed, 'as if I didn't know what you might be up to. You just be careful with that Cuban, now.'

'Well, she's a real treat, Bart.'

'Pretty?'

'Sure is, and plays well.' At that moment Dorothy and two of her friends walked up to join him. 'Bart, Dorothy has just arrived. Is it urgent?'

'Too right, Bruce. We've got some high-jinks going on here in DC.'

'It is on TV?'

'No, we're grateful for that. It's all under wraps. I'll need your people to work on this with intelligence and foreign affairs. I'm just ringing to ask if you'll come in and see me first thing when you get back.'

'Sure thing, Bart. I'll let my deputies know.'

'Bring Myra along. She's covering the UK, isn't she?'

'Yes, the best. We've had some interesting stuff from the London embassy.'

'Tell you what, go in as usual, brief your deputies and come over with Myra as soon as you can. Let me know when you're on your way.'

'Done deal, Bart.'

'You go and have a good night now, and I'll want to know from Dorothy how talented that girl on the piano is.'

'OK. She's not done yet. I'll ask Dorothy to let you know.'

'Hey, yeah, that's great. Next week when you all come over for dinner.'

The head of Section Myra Gaines and Bruce Waller walked towards the office of the Deputy Director in the building at McClean, Virginia.

'Nice news, Mr Waller, the British failed to get a judge on the International Court of Justice for the first time.'

'Yeah, any influence Great Britain had is rapidly evaporating.'

'They're not much now.'

'No, but listen to this.' Bruce stopped before the Memorial Wall. He took out his personal device and moved his thumb across the screen. 'Here we are,' he found the recording he was looking for, then leapt forward 20 minutes and 30 seconds. They listened. 'On top of all this came the great French catastrophe. The French Army collapsed, and the French nation was dashed into utter and, as it has so far proved, irretrievable confusion. ... When I warned them that Britain would fight on alone whatever they did, their generals told their Prime Minister and his divided Cabinet, "In three weeks England will have her neck wrung like a chicken." Some chicken; some neck.'

The Director of the Directorate of Analysis looked at his Head of Section. 'You know this?'

'No, Sir, but it's the British Prime Minister, Winston Churchill. I can tell his voice.'

'You're sure right. It's Sir Winston Churchill. It's his speech to the Senate and House of Commons of the Canadian Parliament on December 30, 1941, after visiting the US.'

Myra Gaines stood transfixed. Naturally she knew of the British wartime Prime Minister. What amazed her was that her Director should have known about a speech he gave during the war. She had not appreciated the amount of extensive travelling the Prime Minister had undertaken during his period as a war leader. Her bright blue eyes and long blonde hair reflected back from the window in the bright sunlight of the autumn day, her mouth a little open in awe.

Bruce continued. 'We could say so much for the French. They were easily defeated in 1940. But were they? No. The allies fought well, but they were overwhelmed. There was a great loss of life. The German military had the superior skill.' He stopped for a moment. 'Then the French couldn't keep Vietnam after seven years of fighting and a lot of US financial support.'

'Well, Sir, when Pierre Mendès-France became President of the Council of Ministers in France, he didn't waste any time. He negotiated a withdrawal from Indochina. He took a bold decision, but the right hated him for it, even though nobody in France wanted to continue with the fight. And we didn't do so well in Vietnam, either.'

'OK Myra, you're right. We have to beware of the falsifications. We should never have been there. Our presence was based on the false premise that if one country collapsed to communism, the rest would fall like a pack of cards. So wrong. So many brave US servicemen killed; so many Vietnamese killed. So many innocent people killed all around. That was an unnecessary political catastrophe, and the future President, Nixon, committing treason to help his being elected, and Kennedy had the US stay in Vietnam because if he hadn't done so, he said he wouldn't be re-elected. I know you've got an effective hold on contemporary events in Great Britain, but remember this, Myra. Great Britain stood alone from the fall of France until the Japanese bombed Pearl harbour.'

'Ah, but Mr Waller, Great Britain had an empire. It had the colonies, the Dominions, the Polish, the Free French and the Greeks. It wasn't all that alone.' Bruce laughed. 'Well, you're right there, Myra. Thank you for reminding me, and if we think about it more, it wasn't a war to save Great Britain.'

'That's correct, Sir. It was a war to uphold the territorial integrity of Poland, and Mr Ghandi and his fellow Indians couldn't have cared less about the Poles. They just wanted independence.'

'Sure, Myra, but if the Brits hadn't succeeded, life would be different right now. For the past few decades the British have had lousy leadership, and you're right; their influence is diminishing and will continue to decline. But don't underestimate them. That's a mistake. They're still our allies, and right at this moment, I think we'll be glad they're on our side.'

'Thank you, Sir. I'll have to do some more studying.'

'Well, we all need to do that. But right now, we've got to see how we can deal with our own house. Let's get right over to the Deputy Director shall we?'

'Sure, Sir. What a pleasure it is to be with you, Sir, I'm always learning.'

Before they continued to the office, Bruce briefly stood at the Memorial and remembered. Then he confided in her, 'Myra, let me tell you now, we appointed you because you were right for the job. There were some who thought you were far too young and inexperienced, but you had one thing that no other candidate had – and that was a willingness to listen and learn. For us in the Agency, that's more important than anything. We value that. Loyalty, conscientiousness and courage are important, but you've gotta have an open mind. You've always gotta be curious.'

Bartholomew Ridens stood up when his secretary ushered Bruce and Myra into his office. 'Hi, you guys.' He shook Bruce firmly by the hand and stopped Bruce by saying to Myra, 'Hi, Myra, it's nice to see you. I know Bruce was just about to introduce us, but he knows me. You don't mind there, Bruce?'

'No, for sure, Bart. We've worked too long together for me to be offended.'

Bartholomew Ridens had occasionally worked with Bruce on operations. He knew Bruce to be bookish, but he was calm under stress, which is just what a team needed at difficult moments. His unassuming manner meant his work was sometimes ignored, but people always felt reassured when they were assigned to work with him.

'That's the spirit. Let's take a quick walk to get some coffee, shall we?' He led them out of the office, letting his secretary know in passing where they were going and gently thanking her for offering to take the order.

There was a kitchen at the end of the corridor. 'Hi Mary-Ann, how're doing?' said Bartholomew.

'Well, hello Mr Ridens, I'm doing just fine, Sir. Angelina ain't not call me.'

'I haven't seen you to say hello today Mary-Ann, so I thought we'd come down and put our order in.'

'Well Sir, I know your order. How about you, Mr Waller? Yours as usual?'

'Sure is, Mary-Ann. I don't know how you do it. Let me introduce Myra to you. Mary-Ann's a permanent fixture here.'

The women said hello to each other. Myra took Mary-Ann's hand in hers, and felt an overwhelming sense of warm-heartedness and goodness in her hand-shake. She looked into Mary-Ann's eyes and saw wisdom and pain, love and forgiveness, a sister, wife, a mother who had no option other than to live her life in the slot society had forced her into, with her tight curly hair greying against the beauty of her black skin.

'It sure is real nice to meet you, Myra. You're a lovely young lady. You do the Agency well now,' said Mary-Ann.

'Thank you, Mary-Ann, I'm honoured to have met you. I'll work hard at that.' Myra then indicated her preferred choice of coffee.

'Heck, Bruce, you know Mary-Ann has seen some things and had some experiences coming up from Mississippi and all that,' the Deputy Director followed up, 'and not all good, to the shame of the Agency. But we're trying, aren't we Mary-Ann?'

'Well, Mr Ridens, you've made some changes, and I thank the Lord.'

'Amen to that,' the Deputy Director replied, continuing, 'now, we'll be off back to the office. Is that all right?'

'Yes Sir, Mr Ridens. I'll be along.'

'Thanks Mary-Ann. You keep safe now.'

The party returned to the Deputy Director's room. Bruce began, 'Bart, I thought we had a meeting with the other Directors.'

'Yeah, we did, Bruce, but we've had a new Twitter storm. It's caused another crisis.'

'Oh, right. We must have missed it.'

'Yeah, well, you'll catch up. I reckon we'll have to change our working patterns if this keeps going for the entire duration of the current Presidency.'

Myra was about to take her device out of her handbag, but noticing that neither man had a Smartphone on the table, she quickly realised it had to stay where it was.

'Now Bruce,' the Deputy Director began, 'you know we haven't always seen eye-to-eye, but we've worked together.'

'Yes Bart, you're right. We haven't always agreed, but I have a high regard for your job. You know that.'

'I sure do, Bruce.' Bartholomew stopped talking with a knock on the door. Angelina opened the door and let May-Ann in with the tray.

'Thank you Angelina, thanks Mary-Ann, we really appreciate this. Hey, cookies as well. You know I'm trying to lose weight, and now you're putting temptation in my way.'

Mary-Ann smiled. 'Well, Mr Ridens, you ain't got no will power, you know. It's only right your guests should try some cookies with their coffee.' As with the French language, double negatives were perfectly correct, and Mary-Ann never stopped communicating thus to remind people of where she came from and who she was.

'Gosh, Mary-Ann, you're testing me. And Bruce here is going to tell you if I slip.'

'I sure am, Bart, so you've got a carrot and a stick.'

'OK. Well, thanks again Mary-Ann,' he said as Angelina closed the door.

'Please, Bruce, Myra, you've gotta try a cookie, otherwise

it'll be noticed they haven't been touched.' As Bruce and Myra took a cookie each, the Deputy Director began.

'Bruce, we all know it's the President that personally appoints this post. And we all know that can have consequences. But you know and I know that Major General William J. Donovan's first principle was to be an independent agency. That's dead-on, and don't let anybody think the Director or I am gonna change that.' Myra remained silent, waiting, watching the dynamics between the two men. Bruce paid attention. Bartholomew Ridens continued. 'And I can tell you that I'm highly honoured that the President himself selected me for this position.'

Bruce interjected. 'Bart, in all seriousness, and I've not told you this man-to-man, but I feel the decision to appoint you was just about his smartest move. And that's serious. That's not hogwash.'

'Well, thank you Bruce. I really appreciate that.'

'You're welcome, Bart. We're working for the Agency to protect the state. It's best we work together.'

'OK, thanks Bruce. Now let's get down to the problem. This summer the US Coast Guard Navigation Center received a report that a ship was not where the Master thought it was. This occurred in the Black Sea. Their GPS was out by 25 nautical miles, and twenty other vessels were affected.'

'Yeah, I remember. Are you thinking what I'm thinking?'

'Sure am, you've guessed it. The Russians have developed some decent technology.'

'That means...' Bruce began. 'Yep, that means,' the Deputy Director interrupted to finish the sequence of thought that Bruce began, 'that our surface naval warships, missile systems and drones could all be redundant, useless, just when we might need them for real. North Korea has been using this technology against us for years.' They sat in silence, recognizing the enormity of the realization.

'Gee,' Bruce said slowly, the word drawn out. Bruce Waller was not known to use swear words often.

'Yeah, and a lot of more bad words,' the Deputy Director sounded disconsolate.

'OK. So where are we at the moment?'

'That's what we've gotta consider. It's real. The Global Positioning System can be fed incorrect data as well as being jammed. We can detect the jamming of signals, but signals that trick the software, that's a much more insidious threat. The hardware and software is easy to get, and it doesn't need much power. All you need is a transmitter rated one watt on the top of a hill or in a plane or a drone, and you can fool everything as far as the horizon. The list goes on increasing. Thieves use jammers to steal automobiles. They block the signals to satellites used to locate stolen autos. It affects everyday life. Opening and closing doors on railroad passenger cars, disrupting banking systems, by-passing road tolls, undermining electricity grids. The catalogue goes on.'

'You know what, Bart, I need another coffee.'

'Yeah, right Bruce. I'll ask Mary-Ann. I could do with another as well.'

The news mesmerized Myra. Entranced in learning about the extraordinary reality that lay behind everyday life, she stepped out of her reverie. 'Hey. Let me go do that.' She got out of her chair, put the empty cups on the tray and left the room.

'She's a girl, Bruce, just beginning to learn.'

'Yes Bart. She's got what it takes. This is just what she needs for the next stage of her life and career.'

'I agree. That's why I asked you if she could come along. Hey, I've got to go to the john, see ya in a minute.'

Myra returned with more coffee at the moment the Deputy Director re-entered the room. He opened the door to allow her to walk in first.

'Thanks Myra. Right, OK,' Bartholomew Ridens began to take up the thread of his thoughts with the second coffee, reaching out and taking a cookie, 'I shouldn't, but here goes.' He watched Bruce as he took a bite. 'Sorry!'

Bruce laughed. 'You go ahead, Bart. I'll join you.'

'As I was saying, this is serious. Our military know the problem. Of course they do. We need to find out in detail what the Russians are doing, their plans, capabilities and the extent to which they can prevent attacks. Also the Chinese. We know the Iranians likely used this method to down our drone a few years back, and maybe caused the naval patrol craft to enter into Iranian waters recently.'

'Yeah, that's a big job, Bart.'

'Sure is, Bruce. But it's for the long term. We've got an immediate problem we need to deal with.'

'Oh?'

'Yeah. Now, before I go any further, what I'm gonna tell you is between these walls. Nobody else is to know. Got it?' he looked at Bruce and Myra each in turn. 'Phones in the box.'

'Sure, Bart.' Bruce knew some things had to be treated as close secrets until the final analysis could be shared. He had already switched his device off, but he knew this might not prevent a determined third party switching it on and activating the microphone to listen in. They placed their devices in a lead lined box and the Deputy Director closed the lid. Myra wondered what was next.

'It's the Brits,' the Deputy Director began.

Bruce raised his eyebrows, slowly greying at the same pace as the hair on his head. The desk job meant he had began to add weight to his tall frame, but recently he had begun to take action to change his lifestyle, improve his fitness and slim down. His actions had begun to work. When he sat up in his chair, Myra took notice.

'OK. Interesting. I'm listening.' Bruce leaned forward slightly to concentrate.

'The President thinks they've got a double agent. That's why it's the Brits.'

'Uh-huh.'

'And he believes the Brits are responsible for revealing information about his financial affairs.'

'Right. Bart, I don't suppose there's some evidence to go on? We all know we might have double agents in the Service. Nobody is immune from that.'

'Too right, Bruce. But it's the usual thing. We're just told to find the double agent. No evidence.'

'OK.'

'But there's more. We've been thinking about Global Navigation Space Systems. No surprises there, I hear you say. Agreed. But we're working on the technical stuff and how to adapt our military strategy. This is a multi-disciplinary project. But here's the problem. We've had our agents crawl over Russia to identify jamming devices. Some are pretty easy to see. Some are much more discreet. They've been listed in a report with the locations, buildings and physical settings. On its own, it's nothing special, but there's a separate file with a list of all the agents we've used to compile the report. There's a problem. We've had what seems like an unauthorized intrusion.'

'Virtual?'

'Yeah. It was highly targeted. We're guessing that copies of both reports were downloaded.'

'Anything else? Just these reports?'

'Other stuff, but you're not authorized to know.'

'OK, fair enough, Bart. This could be bad.'

'Yeah.'

'Do we know when this happened?'

'We found out over the weekend.'

'What about alerting the sleepers?'

'We're on to that. It'll take time.'

'It will. But it doesn't mean the documents have found their way to the Russkies.'

'That's right. We've got some high-flyers inside Russia, and we don't want them exposed. We're watching the FSB, G.R. and FSO to see if they move. They know we know about their anti-satellite weapons programme. They call it "istrebitel sputnikov", and they know we're trying to find out more. If they've got these files, they can take countermeasures and detain our informers on the ground.'

'It'll be bloody.'

'Yeah. They'll be killed. It could work itself into a serious incident. You can see why this is important.'

'Yeah. We need to do some thinking, and quick.'

At this point Myra decided to risk a question. 'Sir, may I ask a question?'

'Sure, go ahead, Myra, anything you like,' the Deputy Director's countenance opened up.

'This might sound silly,' she began.

'No question is trivial, Myra, even the most basic of questions. There's no such thing as a stupid question. Only a thoughtless answer. You just go ahead and ask.'

'Do we know how the attack took place?'

'It might not have been an attack.' Bruce and Myra exchanged glances. The Deputy Director continued. 'It might have been one of our agents.' The three looked at each other. Each reached for their mug to finish their coffee. At this point the Deputy Director's secretary buzzed the intercom. He stood up and walked over to his desk.

'Hi, Angelina.'

'Hi Mr Ridens, I have the IT Director to see you, Sir.'

'OK, ask him to come in. Thank you Angelina.'

Tall and thin, tension written across his face, the IT

Director, dressed in a blue jacket and beige trousers entered the room cautiously, as if he was unsure of the reception he might be given.

'Caleb, come in, come in. Nice to see ya. You've got some news, I hope?'

'Yes, Sir, I've just come from the Director.'

'Great, great. Now you just come over and join us here at the table. How about a coffee?'

'Thank you, Mr Ridens, but I've just had one.'

The Deputy Director introduced Myra to the IT Director. Bruce and Caleb knew each other and briefly shook hands. Caleb Baugh was not sure how to begin. The Deputy Director understood his reservation.

'Caleb, we know the intrusion is secret. I've briefed Bruce and Myra as far as they need to know. The only thing we're interested in is how it occurred.'

'Thank you, Mr Ridens. Well, an authorized username and password was used.'

Bruce interrupted. 'So likely it's one of our agents?'

'Maybe. But the internet protocol address was hidden. We searched it back over the Tor network to a French connection. This points to someone without authority knowing information they shouldn't know.'

'Caleb, do we know precisely where?' the Deputy Director asked. Caleb looked uneasy. 'I'm asking, because it looks like Bruce is flying to Europe tonight, and Myra will be acting as his back-up for further research from here on in.'

'We can't be certain. If you believe the location data, it was Paris.'

Bruce stood up. 'OK, there's a satellite conference on in Paris in the next few days. Everybody will be there – the industry and just about every security agency in the world. We've got agents covering it, but they'll be busy. Bart, you're right, I'll go pack a bag.'

The Deputy Director looked at Bruce. 'Haven't you've got a buddy there in the DGSE?'

'Yes. I'll get in touch with him.'

'See what ya can do,' Bartholomew Ridens drawled, 'and you be careful with those Parisians, Bruce.' He cracked a smile.

*

Dr Utku Köprülü, the Director of the External Operations Directorate of the National Intelligence Organization, studied Boran Avcı carefully. He finished his coffee. The accompanying glass of water was untouched. Two brushed aluminium flag poles stood either side of his desk, one with the flag of Turkey carefully arranged, the other with the emblem of the organization. He exuded a calm, measured self-assurance. He had confidence in himself, the history of his family, and his links within the hierarchy of the state.

'We have called on your help,' he began to outline the purpose of the meeting, 'because I am informed by my friends in the Gendarmerie General Command that your department in the Gendarmerie Intelligence and Counter-Terrorism might be able to help us.' Boran Avcı knew he was not expected to respond to this statement. The Director continued. 'What I have to say to you is of the utmost secrecy, that is *çok gizli* – top secret. I have been informed that you are cleared for such information.'

'I am, doctor bey.'

The Director was pleased he responded formally. 'For your information, it has come to our attention that a very sensitive document might have been obtained by the British.' Boran Avcı raised his thick black eyebrows. He concentrated his dark brown eyes on the Director.

'We have a synthetic aperture radar reconnaissance and

surveillance satellite system under development. This system is publicly known, but there are certain aspects of the program that are highly sensitive. We regard the additional, highly secret, programs as being essential to the security of the state.' The Director spoke softly, with determination. The formality of his black suit, black tie and white shirt commanded the utmost respect. Respect for him personally; respect for the status of his family; and respect for his position.

'The Informatics and Information Security Research Centre,' he continued, 'wrote a top secret report for the most senior people in government. It was an exercise in setting out the future – the future that we are planning and presently putting into operation. If our allies were to find out the content of this paper, it would put us into...' he paused, raising his elbows on the table and bringing the fingers and thumbs of both hands together, '...extreme difficulties. We are a sovereign nation and can do as we please, but some countries will misinterpret the plans we are putting into effect, as they so often do.'

'I understand, doctor bey.'

'Good. My people have traced a possible disclosure of this document through a computer owned by an Italian contractor. You know that working with other nations is burdened with difficulty, and the weakest security is when lower grade employees of sub-contractors and independent workers are engaged to take part in projects. Security tends to be weaker with inferiors. If the document has been leaked, we think that this might have occurred through this supplier.'

'Doctor bey, may I ask a question?'

'Certainly.'

'How can the British have the document if it has been acquired through an Italian computer?'

'That is an appropriate question, Boran Avcı. There a go-between in the satellite sector that occasionally sells intelligence to one of our commercial legal entities. The legal entity in question is close to us for reasons of state security. It is a useful conduit for us to know what is going on at arm's length. So far, this intermediary has been accurate. He has informed us that the computer of the Italian sub-contractor is not secure. We do not know if the document has been leaked and, if it has been, whether the British have a copy.'

'Doctor bey, what do you want of me?'

The Director looked closely at Boran Avcı. He perceived a man who wanted to impress. The clothes he wore – the second rate dark blue well-worn shiny suit, the cheap patterned tie, albeit in subtle, subdued colours, the regulation haircut, clean shaven face – made the Director believe that the man before him sought promotion, enhancement of his lowly social position, advancement perhaps politically as well as professionally.

'We need to know if the document is in the hands of the British. We also want to know if we can rely on the information this informant supplies. If we cannot, then we will have to reconsider whether our confidence in him is misplaced.'

'And that means, doctor bey?'

'And that means we – MİT – have a duty to ensure that he is dealt with appropriately.'

'Yes, doctor bey.'

'Everything must be discreet.'

Both men were familiar with the need not to be precise. Fastidiousness about purpose, means and ends were dangerous. The implicit acknowledgment of what was required sufficed for their objective.

Boran Avcı left the Director and drove through the Ankara traffic from Çankaya to the definitive monument of the Second National Architectural Movement. He walked across the kilim patterns of the Ceremonial Plaza, designed by Emin Onat and Ahmet Orhan Arda, in the final resting place of

Mustafa Kemal Atatürk. He stood surrounded, enwrapped within the memory of the founder of the modern state. He felt safe, secure, enveloped in the wisdom of significance and certainty. He was determined to follow his example. Outsiders were not going to undermine his nation. *They know nothing. They just wanted to use and weaken my country, our way of life and faith.* When he began to realize that they were always attacking, he decided to volunteer. Physically strong, his personality traits were quickly identified. He was encouraged to join the Gendarmerie, subsequently demonstrating the capacity to act ruthlessly when requested. For him, it was necessary to be tough. His physical strength improved with training, as did his knowledge of how to use his body for the deadliest of purposes. His trainers discovered that it was not necessary to reinforce his mental outlook. He was perfect.

After paying his respects at the sarcophagus in the Hall of Honour, Boran Avcı proceeded on his way.

*

Abdülkadir Turgut sat in the conference room. The opening speaker introduced the topic of quantum cryptography before the specialized talks that followed. Turgut was not listening. He knew nothing about the subject, or had any wish to. He wanted to identify Étienne du Parquet. He had a photograph. Once he knew Étienne was present, he aimed to establish whether his device was switched on and connected to the Wi-Fi station he had set up in the room, imitating but by-passing the hotel Wi-Fi, and to attempt to monitor it. As was usual, over half of those attending were not mentally in Durbuy. Their fixation was directing them to concentrate on the other, the trivial, or the mundane, looking, endlessly scrolling and perhaps interacting with what might be on their computer, Smartphone or other device to hand.

Michael Cocke, his face immobile, short cut hair thinning on top of his skull, surveyed the space, observing faces and demeanours. His black leather computer holdall was closed beside the chair he was sitting on. An unopened notebook in black was placed on the small writing tablet arm attached to the chair. Standing out from the other participants by wearing a dark blue suit, white shirt and dark striped tie, his demeanour was aloof, distant, disdaining. He was aware of Abdülkadir Turgut, an officer of the Ministry of Interior Undersecretariat of Public Order and Security, the KDGM, but Turgut did not know who he was. Cocke did not know why he was at this event, but that did not interfere with his scheme. The most recent of his projects had been carefully planned, and was reaching the final stages. The Turkish would undertake what he regarded as the disreputable – but necessary – side of his business, and he would be recognized as the agent that provided them with the benefits. All seemed most satisfactory.

Helen gently opened the door into the conference room. Holding forty people with comfort, they faced the speaker in the distance. Helen offered a sheepish smile as the speaker moved her eyes regularly over the attendees as she spoke. Glancing around the room for seats, Helen noticed Michael Cocke's back with his distinctive head. She had the presence of mind to nudge Étienne, immediately behind her, point to her device as if to say they had forgotten something, and they left the room together, quickly closing the door.

'Étienne, I know you're here to learn about this stuff,' Helen whispered a few steps from the door, 'but the guy that approached me in Singapore is in there.'

'So?' questioned Étienne in a hushed voice.

'We're watching him. He's dangerous.'

'You mean he's passing secrets?'

'Well, sort of,' Helen began, 'can I ask...' before Étienne interrupted her.

'No.' Étienne spoke with a slight tone of annoyance. 'I'm not a spy, Helen. I like you very much, and you're great company, but I'm not part of your world, and I don't want any more to do with it.'

'Yes, I'm sorry. Really sorry. Sometimes I assume too much. It's just that he's up to no good, and we need to find out who he talks to.'

'Look, if I happen to see him speaking to someone, I'll let you know. But that's it. Right?'

Helen looked relieved. 'Thanks. I'm expecting somebody from the UK to be here, but things are happening so quickly. I don't know where they might be. Please do me a favour, though.'

'What?'

'Let's exchange contact details. Here's my personal email address and telephone number. Will you keep in touch?'

'Yes, of course. I'd like us to remain friends.'

The swap completed, they entered the conference room a second time, gliding into spare seats with the minimum of fuss.

A coffee break followed the end of the talk given by the opening speaker. Owain Davis remembered Helen when they had met during the disruption. 'Be careful, too many of these delicious petit fours don't help with the weight,' Owain commented to Helen, standing behind her, watching as she looked over the tantalising display of sweet and savoury delicacies.

'Oh,' Helen turned to face Owain. 'How lovely to see you.'

'Yes, it's been a while.' Owain smiled. 'How are you?'

'Hey, I'm fine. It's really good to see you. We need to catch up.'

'Yes, that'd be great.' He looked at Étienne, who took a

coffee and walked over to the table. 'Hi,' Owain said to him, looking into his eyes.

'Hello,' Étienne looked into Owain's eyes. Before he could continue, Helen interrupted. 'This is Étienne,' hurriedly trying to recall Owain's name. They shook hands.

'I'm Owain, nice to meet you. Don't worry, Helen, we only met briefly.'

'I know, but sorry.' They laughed in an attempt to move away from Helen's embarrassment. 'It's fine. Life's too short and we can't remember everyone we meet. Do you two know each other?'

'Yes,' Étienne answered the question. 'We met in France, then Barcelona.'

'That was also during the time we were under attack. We didn't know whether the forces of disruption would succeed.' Helen explained.

'Right. I understand. That was an interesting period. But we survived.'

'Yes, it was, let me say, scary.'

'You were involved as well, Étienne?'

'I was.'

'Maybe you can tell me more some time.'

'Yes. How long are you staying?'

'That depends. Certainly tonight. Perhaps we can meet up for dinner or something?'

Helen stood by, watching, observing the manifestations of desire as Étienne and Owain quickly embraced the dance of the newly attracted. At this point, Michael Cocke joined the group, saying hello to Helen. She introduced him to Étienne and Owain. By only giving their first names, both knew it was for them to introduce themselves and their reason for attending the event. Not only was Michael Cocke unaware that Owain possessed the laptop he was monitoring, but he also did not know that Abdülkadir Turgut was trying to identify

Étienne du Parquet. Detecting the computer was one thing. Establishing whether the device was in the possession of the person he thought had control of it was another.

Étienne felt safe. He made his excuses to leave the group and began to introduce himself to other attendees, catching the eye of the opening speaker as she managed to break away from a small group of men. With a number of important commercial companies represented at the event, he wanted to ensure his time was well spent. Something special had also happened to him. He had unexpectedly met a strikingly good-looking man that he wanted to meet again.

Helen and Owain remained in the conference room for the sake of appearances. After lunch, they took advantage of the usual thinning out of those attending, finding something more interesting or more important to do, rather than sit through yet more presentations. Owain left the room to stroll through the town to Le Parc des Topiaires. Helen followed him a short time later.

'It's warm for the time of the year.'

'Yes. I like early autumn. Have I been followed?'

'Not that I noticed. The laptop. Have you got it with you?'

'Yes, in the bag. I've switched it off.'

'Let's walk around the gardens and enjoy the colours for a while, just in case.'

'Good idea. Do you like gardening?' They spoke of flowers, fruit, vegetables and weeds – plants growing in the wrong place – and how to deal with creatures that would eat every leaf and juicy strawberry and the problems of preventing potato blight.

'We've got a lot in common. I used to help my father as a child. I have a small garden right now where I live in London. I find it relaxing to help out when I go back.'

'My garden in Brisbane is a bit of a mess. I leave it to my mother. One day, I'll take more control.'

They sat in silence for a short time.

'We know they can switch the laptop on at any time remotely. Can anybody listen in to our conversation through the laptop case?'

'No. I've put it in a faraday bag.' Unknown to Helen, he had two laptop computers in the holdall. When he arrived in Brussels on Eurostar, he was handed the Italian computer. A plan had been formed. He had switched both computers on when he was in the conference room.

'It doesn't seem as if he's followed you.'

'Yes. But what if he only wants to know where we've gone?'

'I've been thinking about that. Do you know if he suspects who you are working for?'

'I don't know, but the Chinese were impressed that my credentials stood up to scrutiny,' Helen noted.

'Cocke doesn't know me, other than we've just been introduced.'

'And the way you're dressed, you could easily be a geek.'

'Thanks. I've tried hard to get this look. You flatterer...' Owain smiled.

'All right, let's guess he's assuming we went out for a chat about opportunities or technology.'

'Agreed. We'll take the risk. Anyway, he might be with that Turk.'

'Oh?' Helen raised her eyebrows.

'You know how quickly things have moved in the past twenty-four hours.'

'No, tell me about it.'

'We know the Turk. His name is Abdülkadir Turgut. He's an officer in the Gendarmerie General Command. We've come across him before. He specialises in commercial espionage. I can't quite make out why he's here yet.'

'Uum..., maybe I'm beginning to figure that one out.'

'Well?'

'Maybe he's after Étienne. We had dinner together last night. Apparently he works for a German company, and the investors are discussing a possible take-over by a Turkish company specialising in cryptographic systems for satellites. They were told the news recently, and he's decided to move.'

'That makes sense. The Turks are strong in this area. They take care to make sure they can't be undermined too easily, but the German authorities will have the final say over any acquisition or take over if it involves state security.'

'What do you think they might want of Étienne?'

'I don't have enough information on that one. I'll follow it up with my people. Anyway, I was given some background about Cocke before I left. We need to swap knowledge. Do you want to start?'

'Sure.' Helen began. 'He acts as a middle man. He doesn't have any loyalty to a particular country. They think he's got a compulsion to be up there with power, but prefers to keep a low profile.'

'Yes, but we've found him.'

'Yes. It seems as if he's been successful; that is, until now. He prefers to be unobtrusive, but likes to be considered as somebody that can be relied upon. He sells information discreetly.'

'So it seems. We've found out how he manages the money. He's got an arrangement with a London bank. He gets paid through intermediaries – all legitimate – then insists the bank uses a complex mechanism to move the funds. He's got accounts in a number of countries. He uses well established lawyers specialising in legal ways of transferring funds, and we've discovered that he's contemplating buying citizenship in one or two countries.'

'He's done well if he's managed this without being noticed. I can tell you he's bonzer.' Owain looked puzzled. 'Oh right, that's Australian English. First rate, I think you'd say in English,' Helen explained.

'Thanks.' They laughed.

'Anyway,' Helen continued, 'he knows technology. He's got a back door into the laptop I've got with me. He wanted to insert a USB into it when I was in Singapore, but I told him that was against our security policy. I suggested he send me an email instead. He wasn't happy, but he sent me an email when we were together, and I clicked on it later. It had a keylogger attached, which we'd anticipated. Our people are monitoring it in real time. He's smart. He knows how to manipulate people.'

'It'll be interesting to know what he's doing with my computer. Our people are doing the same. Apparently he found satellite technology when he was working as a contractor a few years ago. He could see the future, especially the ability to manipulate data to make significant changes, like changing the course of ships and closing down satellite systems.'

'That's serious.'

'Yes. A lot of everyday life is now online. Too much for my liking. Politicians have let it happen, but the reality that everyday life can be seriously affected has only just begun to be appreciated, especially with the attacks we've seen.'

'I'm beginning to understand. That's why this cryptography stuff is so important. Without strong cryptography, we haven't got a chance of keeping secrets secret.'

'Something like that. And if the cryptography isn't implemented properly, it's just as bad. That's a big deal as well.'

'Now I understand the Turks being interested in the German company.'

'So do I. I'm beginning to wonder how safe Étienne might be. What was it between you two?'

'I'll let him tell you, but whatever he says, he's what you English call a gentleman.'

Owain looked at her with a condescending smile. Helen looked puzzled. 'I don't care what the English might call him. I'm Welsh.'

Boran Avcı parked his hire car in a spare slot on the rue du Comte Théodule d'Ursel. Owain and Helen were returning to the hotel where the conference was being held. Owain identified the muscled figure, wearing a black leather bomber jacket covering a well-developed torso, exposing the tight rounded shape of his backside and powerful thighs for all to see, a massive stainless steel watch strapped to his left wrist. His back to the watchers, Boran Avcı walked purposefully into the Place aux Foires. He was clearly going into the hotel.

'Do you mind if we take a walk over to that car, Helen?'

'What?'

'We'll walk by that car that's just parked. I'd like us to record the make, model and registration number.'

'OK. I presume you've got your reasons.'

'Yes. I want to check it with our Belgian colleagues.'

They walked down the narrow space and to the vehicle. They turned to each other to appear as if they were exchanging information on their Smartphones. Each took a photograph of the car and noted the registration number. Owain sent the details to his Belgian counterpart.

'That man that just got out...' Owain began.

'Yes, gorgeously beefy. I saw.' They exchanged smiles. She knew him. He knew she knew. He switched to being serious. 'Well, if he's who I think he is, he's dangerous. He doesn't know me, but I'm guessing he's after you or me.'

'Or Étienne. How do you know him?'

'Images I've seen.' Helen looked at him sceptically.

'I remember these things,' he stated, and continued with some urgency in his voice, 'or he might be after all three of us.

That's why we've got to reassess the situation, *now*. Let's hope my opposite number responds quickly.'

*

François sipped his tea.

'I chose a TGV that had spare seats, so she could buy a ticket and travel with me on the same train. I wanted to make sure she did not misplace me.'

'François, you are so charming, and so helpful.' Katharine was amused. The garden of the Hôtel La Mirande was abuzz with insect life and bees busy gathering the last nectar of the year in the late summer sun under a dappled light blue sky.

'She followed you to the conference at the university?'

'Yes. She enrolled.'

'I intend to go back shortly to attend the last talk. It sounded vaguely interesting.'

'The law of space does not interest me that much.'

'I have to say it's not quite as scintillating as concentrating on *Opus Anglicanum*, but probably more important.'

'Yes, maybe you are correct.'

'I also want to assess how she responds when she's in what she perceives as a hostile environment. I'll tackle her at the reception at the end of the day.'

'You are wily, Katharine. Sometimes you beat the French at their own game.'

'Does she know you're staying here?'

'The chair of the conference asked me that question when I arrived. She was just behind me, so I'm assuming she knows.' François changed the subject. 'Thank you for helping me. It is welcome.'

'Oh, that's no problem, as you well know.' They exchanged smiles, of a profound comradeship bound by the intensity of shared memories of stress, enjoyment and sadness. 'Anyway,'

Katherine continued, 'I had great fun in Milan after my sister's wedding.'

'Oh yes, I sent her my apologies. I couldn't attend.'

'Our family turned out. It was delightful. She is very happy. She understood why you couldn't come. She said she was used to us always having something urgent to do in the national interest. I think she doesn't care any more.' Katherine carried on. 'Charles asked if I didn't mind coming to Avignon. How could I possibly refuse? There's a concert on while I'm here. It's a perfect ending to my holiday – together with helping out, of course. But first, what was the incident last night? It cannot have affected you much if you were able to leave this morning.'

'There was a lot of excitement, but I was not needed. It was useful for me to be seen with the minister in public last night. Things are moving. I might need to return tonight.'

'Do you want to brief me here, or shall we take a slow walk to the university?'

'Let us take a promenade. It will be interesting to know where my Russian agent is. I would hate her to miss me. She is very attractive.'

Leaving the hotel with a nod to the receptionist in thanks, they were content for the presentation on satellite technology to take place in their absence. They strolled through the smaller, narrow empty streets at a leisurely pace: rue Banasterie, rue Bertrand, rue des Infirmières, rue Pascs. Occasionally one of them would move out of the roadway to walk in front of or behind the other inside the bollards to allow vehicles to pass, as they continued their conversation.

François had noticed, and could not refrain from commenting. 'Katherine, you have changed. Pardon me, but I have noticed. You, your demeanour, your clothes – so chic. So very Italian.'

'Oh, really?' Katherine was unusually unsure of how to respond. The attention he paid her was unfamiliar. Katherine had begun to be taught by her Italian ladies that the most important rule was to know your body. After that, it was necessary to be very careful to make things easy, clear and simple, never mix more than two colours, and to pay attention to the quality of the fabric.

'Well, with Sarah now being married, I have met some younger women, and things seem to have happened.'

'You will find somebody, I know.' François alluded to the past. 'Trust in your future.'

'If only. Well, maybe.'

'Yes. I hope so. But now to business.'

'Yes,' Katherine smiled. 'A good idea. Tell me.'

'Your people have provided me with some very helpful information. It means my dossier cannot be ignored now. The strength is in the corroborating evidence. That was important. I am here to speak with somebody that can add some intelligence to my dossier. It is better to do it physically. I hope it will corner our man and a few others.'

'I agree. What can I do?'

'I wondered if Charles might be able to help out in some further way when I realised I was being followed. It seems as if I'm now a target, perhaps for the Russians, but I am not sure why.'

'Do they know what you're doing?'

'Yes, Charles told me.'

'And others might know?'

'Yes.'

'But everybody is keeping their knowledge secret?'

'Of course. Maybe we all want to know if we have a double agent, and if so, who it might be.'

'So your suspect, if you have one, could be working for a minor player?'

'Yes.'

'And you don't know?'

François turned his face to look at Katherine. 'Maybe nobody knows,' he raised his eyebrows to pose a question he could not answer.

'Perhaps they're not working for a state.'

'I have begun to think that this is a possibility.'

'What's the evidence in broad terms?'

'Of a double agent?'

'Yes, or of a traitor selling secrets. Don't tell me anything you shouldn't.'

'No, of course not. We have traced a leak to a particular laptop. The computer is at this conference. We know the owner. It's the company that has sponsored the event. They are a significant sub-contractor, working on one of the satellite programs. The lady in possession of the laptop is one of the in-house lawyers.'

'So she's got a good reason to be here?'

'Yes. The device is available for anybody that needs it.'

'But it's not safe.'

'No, not any longer. Somebody managed to put a root kit on it, so a third party has full administrator access.'

'You're monitoring it?'

'Yes. There's little on it now with any value, but we don't want to alert the third party that we know, so we are putting information on the device every now and again. The information is innocuous, but sufficient to satisfy the interloper. We hope.'

'Do you have a suspect?'

'Your people helped to substantiate my opinion of who it is. If I'm right, it's serious for us, but I do not know if he will be brought to justice.'

'He's close to power?' Katherine asked.

'Yes, very close. He has a number of connections above his station in life. He appears to be sufficiently useful to the grand Monseigneurs, so much so that the suspect will probably be protected. I do not know how far the grand men will go to defend their pet, though. They have been very clever.'

'But not sufficiently adroit to prevent exposure.'

'That's what I need to do. My reputation is being attacked and my position undermined. I need to unmask the culprit and make sure the political will is in place to reach a satisfactory conclusion.'

'What do you want of me?'

'Well, not much really. Charles thought you might like to come over to help out. He knows you hate missing out on the action.'

'You know I like to know what's going on if I can, and if I can take part.'

'It's the Russian agent. I have not alerted anybody internally that I am being followed, because I do not want to let my suspect know, especially if they are working for the Russians.'

'Does anybody else know about the Russian?'

'No.'

'You'd like me to find out whatever our Russian colleague is doing and what she wants?'

'If you can. They might know about my dossier, but not know whom I suspect. They might just be trying to find out if any of their agents are in the frame, and if so, how close we are to them.'

'Or they might have other interests, and what you're doing is a minor but important part of whey they are doing.'

'Correct.'

They had arrived at the gate leading into L'université d'avignon et des pays de vaucluse. Long regular oblique shadows cast by tall, slim trees divided the light and dark of the rectangular lawns laid out along the length of the former L'hôpital Sainte-Marthe d'Avignon beside the eighteenth-century façade.

*

'Do you feel you are recovered?' General Yuan Ah asked in the car after the briefing.

'Yes, Sir. Thank you for helping me, Sir.' Major Zhuge Xiùyīng was hesitant. She had never been in the presence of such a senior officer before.

'Please relax, Major. Before you continue with your task of getting back in touch with the Australian officer, we shall have what the English call afternoon tea.'

An embassy chauffeur drove them to Bloomsbury, to the London Review Cake Shop. It was mid-afternoon, just before the modest space filled up with connoisseurs who knew one of the few places to go to for quality tea. The General led the way through the bookshop. The table nearest the plate glass window was free. He sat with his back to the wall. He indicated that Major Zhuge Xiùyīng was to sit in the chair opposite him.

'Yes, Sir, thank you Sir.' She walked behind him and sat in the hard composite chair. To her surprise, the chair was quite comfortable. The General asked her to look at the menu of teas. The list was impressive. He suggested she might want to try the Earl Grey tea. She accepted, in deference. He ordered tea and scones. It was clear that the lady who took his order knew him. He whispered additional instructions, to which she nodded in assent.

'This has real bergamot in it,' the General said as he introduced the tea to her when it arrived on the table. 'You have the option of drinking it with milk or a slice of lemon.'

She looked at him in disbelief.

'Ah yes, our English friends developed peculiar tastes when they controlled India. However, I have acquired a liking for this particular blend, and it actually goes well with a very small amount of milk. You will try it?'

'Yes, Sir, thank you Sir.' Major Zhuge Xiùyīng remained

in a state of shock in the presence of such a senior person, and being taken out of the embassy to a tea shop in London. He poured tea into a cup seated on a saucer, and then added a slight amount of milk before passing it to her.

'Please try. Be honest. Do not tell me you like it because I have given it to you or because I like it. I don't like obsequiousness.'

Major Zhuge Xiùyīng held the saucer with one hand and raised the cup to her mouth. She took a minute sip of the liquid to test the heat. It was acceptable. She took a second sip. She rolled the tea in her mouth, feeling the mix of tea, bergamot and milk.

'Yes, Sir. It is interesting.'

The General laughed out loud. The hard surfaces, the chairs, tables, wood floor and hard walls helped the sounds of hilarity bounce around the room. Two people sitting on separate tables looked in their direction, and the two members of female staff on duty turned and smiled.

'Please accept my apologies, Major, but when the English say the word interesting, they mean something like, well yes, it is something that I might take into account, but probably will ignore. And if it relates to food or drink, it usually means they do not like it.'

'Ah,' Major Zhuge Xiùyīng commented, 'it is a distinction I had not realised.' Major Xiùyīng realised she was learning about an English figure of speech.

'Indeed, but you will find out these cultural nuances.' The General changed the subject after encouraging the Major to join him with eating a scone, strawberry jam and clotted cream. She waited for him to begin the ceremony, not knowing what to do or how the various items were to be prepared before being eaten. As she did so, she noticed the security escort enter the café and collect a tray containing tea for himself and the chauffeur.

'We are pleased you were rescued before you were tortured beyond endurance. The Australians and Belgians worked hard to discover where you had been taken and to rescue you. We have thanked them. You will be given the opportunity to thank those involved from China at a later date. As for Colonel Ding, she is now in China. She is under investigation. The Party has decided to end *shuanggui*. She will be dealt with under the new regime. I understand you began to have a suspicion about her motives for imprisoning you when it became clear she wanted to put pressure on your uncle.'

'Yes, Sir. One of my uncles is responsible for working with Chile to extract lithium for batteries in the Atacama Desert.' The General interrupted her. 'We know. We have others working in Argentina. We have to control as many resources as we can. We have to stop the Americans and Saudis. They are in danger of taking the market over and creating a monopoly. Lithium is relatively scarce, and we will need a significant amount of it in the very near future.'

Major Zhuge Xiùyīng remained silent. She was used to men taking over conversations and undermining her thoughts and work. The General continued. 'It appears that Colonel Ding's family have misjudged the flow of the wind. They had strong ties to the world of aluminium, which is important strategically. We are watching the Russians with their plans for aluminium. Colonel Ding was pressurized by her family to find out what your uncle was doing. What she did was wrong. She abused her power. Her family continued to give lavish banquets. They failed to understand that the Party intended to make changes. They misconstrued the words of the Party – that the change affected the tigers *and* the flies. They did not grasp that the change also applied to them. We know that many think they can continue along the old way, but that is no longer an option. The words of the Party have begun to be made into actions. Your uncle understands this. He has been a loyal citizen. We have interests in extracting raw materials, but we must not be associated with the consequences of the corruption that has taken place and is now the subject of murderous dispute. Both your uncle and father have been cautiously negotiating around the chaos in the South American states.'

Major Zhuge Xiùyīng realised the importance of the comment made by the General. This was directed at her personally. He was making a tacit observation that she was in her post partly because they considered that her extended family were trustworthy. This meant that she could also be relied upon, although she had to continue to demonstrate her personal allegiance to the Party and the Service by her actions. General Yuan Ah wanted to move on. 'Colonel Commandant Xú Delun tells me that you like art.'

'Yes, Sir. Perhaps art, like music and inventing, is what we do as a species.'

'Maybe. I will think about what you have said.' He stood up and issued a command. 'Come with me. There is a painting I wish you to see.'

Having paid the bill, the General led the way out of the shop. The security escort, having previously returned the tray with the empty cups, opened the door for him. He indicated to Major Zhuge Xiùyīng to enter the car before he got in. As they drove to Trafalgar Square, Major Zhuge Xiùyīng looked puzzled.

'Major, you are thinking something.'

'Yes Sir.'

'Tell me, what is it?'

'Well, Sir, I thank you for taking me to an English tea shop, but was it not insecure?'

'You ask a good question, Major. When I am in the United Kingdom, they follow me everywhere. At first I was annoyed. But then I thought well, we follow the British everywhere at home, so I should not be offended if they do the same to me.'

'Ah.'

'The ambassador told me about some of the best places for tea in London, and he introduced me to this particular place. I have a fondness for the English tea ritual now. Also, the woman that has been following us needed to have a drink, so it is only appropriate for us to allow her to have refreshment, don't you think?'

'Yes, Sir, I understand.'

'Also, there might be some people that understand Cantonese in the tea shop, but the probability is that we were alone, so what we had to say remained between us.'

'Unless they were recording our discussion, Sir.'

The General expressed amusement. 'Yes, you think about everything. They might record conversations in that shop, but technology now allows them to intercept our communications more effectively. They used to have recording devices in restaurants in London. Ah! We are here. Let us go into the National Gallery.'

Slightly stout, carefully cut short silver hair, dressed in a well cut dark grey suit with a white shirt and matching dark colourless tie, the General led Major Zhuge Xiùyīng with a proprietorial air through the throngs of tourists up the outside stairs into the classical portico and into the building. Once in the Central Hall, he turned to show her the view into the distance. From this vantage point, they could see the outstanding and definitive portrait of *Whistlejacket* by William Stubbs. It dominated the far end. He asked what she thought of the painting they could see at the end of the corridors of rooms.

'It's truly remarkable. From here, it is a breathtaking sight. So powerful a horse.'

'Yes, The Englishman Stubbs was perhaps one of the best painters of horses who ever lived. I particularly like this painting. But that is not what we have come to see. Let us walk to that room.'

They took a straight course to room 34. It was her first visit to a major art gallery in Europe, and Major Zhuge Xiùyīng was, to some extent, disconcerted in having to simply scan the paintings she saw as they walked to their destination, through the rooms relating to Spain and Venice, Canaletto and Guardi, British portraits of the mid-eighteenth century, Hogarth, and into Great Britain 1750–1850. The General stopped opposite the painting he had purposely taken her to see.

'This painting is called *Rain, Steam, and Speed – The Great Western Railway*. It is by a famous English painter called Turner. You might know of him? Have you seen any of his paintings before? His full name was Joseph Mallord William Turner.'

'I have seen some of them in reproductions, Sir. Never have I been so close to an original.'

'What do you see?'

Zhuge Xiùyīng looked at the painting. A locomotive hauling carriages, off centre, travelling towards the viewer. It will pass to the right. Two bridges span a river. The scene is richly fuzzy with greens and browns and blues, of weather, and movement. Two people sit in a small boat in the river, one with a black umbrella. They might be fishing. The locomotive pulls carriages at a speed faster than any man or animal can ever achieve.

She was entranced by the image she was looking at. The sounds of people moving around the gallery, the height of the rooms giving off an echo effect did not disturb her. 'Beauty. The colours of the landscape are blurred, they go into and are part of the distance. The sky is a force of nature. The clouds skim across the scene, like rain or fog or maybe both. The man-made machine rushes through the countryside, its crude hot furnace alight to the senses. We are watching it. It is going to pass us. It is the fastest thing on earth. This painting – this painting is a representation of the new; everything is out of focus except the funnel; it illustrates velocity, and of spectacular progress.'

'You speak poetically. You have introduced me to a different perspective. That is of benefit to me. I like that. But there are other aspects we must consider. Look at the figures near the river. There is no spatial relation to the train and bridge. These items have their own perspective, as if they are not connected to the country that surrounds them.'

'Yes, I see. Maybe he wanted to illustrate comparative size.'

'Perhaps, but Turner was a professor of perspective, so he knew what he was doing. But we have to consider this more carefully. From the painting itself, we can think about what the painter wanted to achieve, what we see in the painting, and whether the artist is objectively correct in portraying the scene and the artefacts. Then there is another aspect. How others write about this painting, some of whom claim to be experts.'

Zhuge Xiùyīng felt bolder in the presence of the senior man as their discussion continued. 'But does art always have to be viewed in this way?'

'No, of course not. But we must remember that the artist is always responding to their environment, even if they do not do so consciously. In this case, Turner is deliberately reacting to the dramatic changes that are taking place. Lu Xun was just one of a number of writers who wrote excellent literature that challenged the ancient ways of living.'

'He was right.' Zhuge Xiùyīng expressed her opinion in a forthright manner.

'Of course. But let us consider the commentators. Some assert that this train is travelling to Charing Cross, which is a railway station a *li* or so to the south of where we are now standing. But this is not correct. The railway line is the Great Western, as the painter indicates in the title. This rail line terminated at Paddington station, some way to the north west of us. This tells us that apparently intelligent people can and do get basic things wrong. Then there are the problems with the interpretation of the location, the precise bridges in the painting, and even the figure on the right. Is he ploughing the field with two horses, or is he carrying a shotgun, out with his dogs?'

'There is so much to interpret in such a painting. I understand that is why Turner is considered such an important painter.'

'I agree. Good painters express ideas, and Turner is certainly doing that with this painting. Even the firebox is contentious. We see white heat and the bright red of the fire. People agree that this locomotive is a representation of the Firefly class engines. They were designed by Sir Daniel Gooch. They had a domed firebox, and you can see that behind the funnel. But some people suggest that from this view, the painter could not see the firebox. You could say that the painter is illustrating the incandescence from the underside of the boiler. There must be a correct answer to this particular point, but I am not sure if anybody has resolved it. Internally to the painting, there are other questions, but perhaps they are for the painter to manipulate as they see fit.'

'Can you explain, Sir?'

'Well, the chimney is about the right height, but the funnel is thinner than it should be. On these steam engines, it was made with a cap at the top, which seems to be missing. There is also a problem about the smoke. There are only a few puffs of smoke.'

'He might have decided against these things, like he did when painting the *Fighting Temeraire*. In that painting he did not depict the scene accurately.' Zhuge Xiùyīng looked over to the painting she mentioned.

'Yes. With a master such as Turner, it is art, image and

emotion loosely linked to reality. It is the same with this painting. The observer is actually suspended in the air, looking at the train, because the geography does not permit of such a grand view. By the way, did you notice the hare? Turner added it on a varnishing day.'

Zhuge Xiùyīng looked alarmed. She had missed something. The General pointed out a splodge of paint on the rail line in front of the engine.

'Oh, yes, thank you, Sir. Very clever. The hare runs quickly.'

'Yes, but not as quickly as the locomotive, unless the machine is reducing its speed as it reaches a station.'

'This is truly velocity and the domination of life by humans. It's as if the painter is reacting metaphysically to the human condition of forever inventing.'

'Yes. Perhaps he had been thinking about the painting for a long time, and then had the inspiration of adding the hare at the last moment; perhaps as a metaphor for speed. If my suggestion is correct, it was inspired, but we will never know. Does it matter? Perhaps not. Our reaction to this painting is different to the responses of Turner's contemporaries, but in essence, it is about feeling and movement and change. It is also a lesson for us to try to understand everything we can. We must be alert to any traps.'

He touched his device to light up. 'Come, we must go. You have to travel and I have other duties to attend. We will drive you to collect your bag. But you would like to view the impressionists perhaps?' Her face expressed her answer. 'We will go back that way, but we do not have much time. You will have to visit London as a tourist in the future.'

In the car, the General closed the glass partition between them and the chauffeur and escort. 'Major, I took you to see the painting to explain. We have to be wary in the work we do. Not only of the documents or images we see, but who has written them and who is reporting on them. We can obtain a secret document from another power, but we must understand, as we analyse it, that all might not be what it seems. We have to be aware of what we have been told, how the document has come into our possession, what our agent tells us about it and the circumstances in which it was written and found. All along the chain the facts will differ. The report of facts can be magnified, and altered – whether deliberately or inadvertently – and manipulated, and other information deliberately suppressed. The reason, purpose and intention to enhance, misconstrue or misunderstand are manifold. We have to be meticulous before committing ourselves.'

'Yes, Sir, but there comes a time,' Major Zhuge Xiùyīng remarked, 'when we must also make decisions.' She knew this remark might be taken as a slight. In China, those that anticipate problems are highly regarded. It is a virtue to consider an issue comprehensively before choosing what to do.

The General turned his head to look at her. There was a smile on his face. *She will go far.* 'Yes Major. Ultimately, we must make decisions.'

'But the decisions must be made in the knowledge of our own prism.'

'Yes, except we have to know ourselves first. Now I will ask, what do you think of English afternoon tea?'

*

Abdülkadir Turgut left the conference room having identified Étienne. He now needed an opportunity to approach him. It was clear Étienne was going to remain. He noticed Boran Avcı enter the hotel reception area. Neither man knew the other, but Abdülkadir Turgut had received an email within the hour, informing him to expect an officer from MİT to arrive during the afternoon. He was ordered to identify the officer and cooperate with him. As Boran Avcı walked towards the conference room, Abdülkadir Turgut decided to use his intuition.

'Excuse me, Sir. I hope you are well. This is an important conference for our nation, do you think?'

Boran Avcı stopped to look at the tall, slim middle-aged man dressed in the typical uniform of jeans, dull woollen check shirt and brown shoes. He agreed with the statement, also speaking in Turkish.

'Yes, Sir, I am told it is an important conference. You are here for a reason?'

'I am.' Turgut took out a plastic card with his photograph, identifying him as an officer in the KDGM.

Boran Avcı looked at the card. He was suspicious. He had not been informed that officers from other agencies were involved with the project he had been assigned to deal with. He had never been asked to work with others when instructed to carry out a task of this nature.

'I do not have relations with the Ministry of Interior Undersecretariat of Public Order and Security.'

'I can only say that I was informed this morning that an officer from MİT was due.'

Boran Avcı considered this unexpected approach carefully. He was guarded in his response. 'Perhaps we should discuss this development.'

'Yes. I agree. We are both taken by surprise.' Abdülkadir Turgut understood the other man's reserve. 'What do you suggest?' He decided to allow the younger man to take the initiative. Boran Avcı considered for a while. He looked around the busy reception of the hotel and the chairs and tables full of people eating and drinking outside. 'This is not suitable. I have a car. Do you know where we can drive that is discreet and quiet?'

'I drove here yesterday. I discovered a small country road that leads to some woods. It is not far from here.'

'Then let us go.'

Abdülkadir Turgut directed Boran Avcı the short distance south to Clos du Manoir, a lane leading to a few houses.
Boran Avcı parked the vehicle where the road ended and a
track began that led into the wood.

The late afternoon merged into the beginning of the evening.
Helen joined Owain in the small courtyard of the Brasserie
La Ferme au Chêne.

'This is what I've got,' Owain said in a low voice, wary of
being overheard. 'His name is Boran Avcı. He's an officer in
the Gendarmerie Intelligence and Counter-Terrorism. He's
well known and very dangerous. They use him to assassinate
traitors and those that get in their way. He's very good at what
he does. Sometimes he makes it look like an accident or sui-
cide, maybe to give the local police a way out of investigating
things too deeply.'

'Maybe they're like the Russians.'

'Yeah, it's happened to the Americans, such as the death
of Mikhail Yuriyevich Lesin in the Dupont Circle Hotel in
Washington DC. And, as you know, we've also had similar
experiences.' Owain continued after a short pause. 'Anyway,
our Belgian colleagues tell me that they were expecting him.
We now know the name he used on this occasion for the purposes of travel. They ensured he hired a car that was bugged. The
tenor of their conversation is that neither man was expecting
the other. Turgut was told this morning that somebody from
MİT was coming. He assumed it was Avcı. Avcı played hard
and got out of Turgut that he was here to find out what Étienne
was doing. The Turks are watching the most important people
that work for the German company. They have Étienne in their
sights because his work is crucial, apparently. They don't want
him to leave. From a commercial point of view, I can understand
that. We know differently, of course.'

'I don't think he'd want to work for a Turkish company.'

'No.'

'OK, so what is Avcı up to?'

Owain answered Helen's question. 'The Belgians don't know. Avcı wanted to discuss the matter outside the vehicle. They got out and walked for thirty minutes.'

'So Turgut is watching Étienne. I don't understand why he hasn't spoken to him. He must know what he looks like.'

'Maybe he's waiting for the moment.'

'Maybe. Then there's Avcı. He's obviously here for a reason. They wouldn't have let him off the leash unless they had a purpose in mind.'

'Yes. Our people are working on infiltrating his device to see if they can find out more. It could be that he's come to see Cocke.'

'And kill him?' Helen asked.

'Possibly.'

'We don't want that yet.'

'No. We want to know what Cocke's up to and what he's got before we let them dispose of him.'

*

People eagerly left the heat and staleness of the lecture hall. Having sat through the last of the day's presentations and discussions, they were impatient to get out into the late summer sun sitting low on the horizon, a vivid red orange fading into yellow as it merged into the blue of the sky. A temporary gazebo had been erected during the last hour of the conference, and young women and men were waiting with trays of champagne, water and orange juice. The sponsors of the event had decided pre-dinner drinks were a useful method of getting people to speak more freely. Katharine emerged talking with a man of her own age, tall, distinguished, with neat clipped greying hair, wearing a well used chestnut unstructured Donegal jacket in lightweight herringbone tweed, tan corduroy trousers, check shirt and a muted tie, with a pair of fondly worn full brogue gillies on his feet.

They both accepted a glass of champagne as they followed others on to the grass. He took the opportunity to change the technical discussion they were having over evidence from satellites and introduced himself.

'Anyway', he continued, 'my name is Robert, Robert Lynch-Blosse. I'm pleased to meet you.'

'And I'm pleased to meet you, too. I'm Katharine Neville.'

Robert Lynch-Blosse mused for a few seconds. 'That name: isn't it linked to the Duke of Bedford?'

'Why yes.' She was caught unawares. 'We have vague ties to a previous Duke of Bedford in the 1470s.'

'Ah, I thought so. In my spare time I look over the genealogy of ancient English aristocratic families to see how they tie into those who helped to colonise Ireland.' Katharine turned to look at the eighteenth century façade.

'Hmm... well, looking at this frontage, I suppose the eighteenth century style of classicism in Ireland is partly associated with the British – no, perhaps the English.'

Robert Lynch-Blosse laughed. 'I think the link to Britain did mean that architecture might not have been a wholly Irish affair, but we both know that we Irish were not exactly in thrall to the might of the British Empire.'

Katharine liked this man. He was a most intelligent gentleman, urbane and knowledgeable, without hectoring.

'I'm sorry if I have offended you.'

'No, not at all. There is one great thing the English have given us which we have used to our advantage ever since.'

'Oh?'

'The English language. It's not yours any more, and we have helped to make it what it is today.'

Katharine's face visibly expressed relief. In the corner of her eye, she saw the figure of Captain Milyukov, unaccompanied, looking around those gathered on the grass and outside the main entrance on the wide esplanade running along the length of the building. She had missed her as they left the conference hall. Katharine took the opportunity to bring her into their conversation.

'Hello, I hope you have enjoyed the conference?'

'Good afternoon,' Captain Milyukov was polite in return. 'Yes, thank you. It has been most interesting.'

'My name is Katharine and this is Robert.' They each shook hands.

'I am Alexandra. I am pleased to meet you.'

Katharine continued the conversation by changing the topic. 'We were discussing the architecture of this building. Some styles are named after architects, like Andrea Palladio. You are Russian?'

'Yes, from Bryansk.'

Robert continued with the exchange. 'Ah, the city of the lyrical poet Fyodor Ivanovich Tyutchev.'

Alexandra expressed surprise. 'You know of Tyutchev?'

'Yes, of course. If you esteem poetry, you might know of Tyutchev, but I expected you to know of him. Bryansk was occupied by the Germans during the Great Patriotic War.'

Alexandra tried to hide her astonishment at his knowledge and reference to the war fought by the Soviets, carefully not referring to it as the Second World War. She did not understand the distance he was making between Ireland and Great Britain. 'Yes, but the partisans made life very uncomfortable for the Germans, and we had to fight in the east with a terrible loss of life because our allies did not engage the enemy until 1944.'

'Well, I dispute your assumption that the allies didn't support the Russian war effort. To begin with, the Russians entered into an agreement with the Germans that gave them the freedom to conduct their ruthless war. You sold the food, raw materials and oil they needed to invade other countries in Europe and bomb the United Kingdom. Then, when it was obvious the German attack on Russia was imminent, Stalin ignored the warnings from both his own secret service and the allies. You forget that over fifty thousand men lost their lives in the air in carrying out bombing raids across Europe to destroy the ability of the enemy to continue with the war. And remember the men who suffered as they shipped war materials to Russia in the north Atlantic. Think of those who were badly injured and killed in the bitter cold of the sea.' Robert spoke with a convincing, assured manner, deciding to change the subject in an attempt to prevent the conversation becoming inflamed. 'Anyway, I wonder what Tyutchev would think of the world in which we live now.'

Katharine had only met this man during the course of the day, and she did not know anything about him. She remained quiet. She wanted to find out more. Robert was used to asking intrusive questions. 'You know he wrote the poem *14-oe dekabrya 1825* in response to the Decembrists revolt. In it he spoke of the iron winter, and in a later poem, he asks about what will happen after the thaw.'

Alexandra knew he was speaking about present-day life in Russia. 'But life is so different now. The Tsarist regime was successfully toppled, and after 1953 great changes occurred.' She was flustered about his knowledge of the destructive events of the mid-twentieth century and the allusion he was making to the contemporary world. Katharine liked the way Robert had approached the topic, and preferred that he pursue the discussion. She wanted to listen and watch.

'Indeed,' Robert conceded. 'But Tyutchev was a censor in the government and considered it was important to allow opponents of the regime to voice their opinions in open debate. Not everybody agreed with him, of course, but the outlook was more relaxed under Tsar Alexander that it is now. It must be said that life in Russia now is, let us say, difficult for many.'

Katharine was pleasantly interested and amused at Alexandra's discomfort.

Alexandra decided not to become agitated. Here, she thought, were two people that only superficially understood her modern Russia, making a stand in a hostile world. 'Life is difficult for many people in your country, too.' She took this opportunity to establish that Katharine was a single woman living just outside London, and that Robert was a judge in the Court of Appeal in Dublin. This information did not concern the questioner, but enabled Katharine and Robert to gather more information about the other without the necessity of asking intrusive questions.

An imposing figure of a man walked up to the group. Alexandra looked over the blue-eyed, clean-cut American, dressed in a dark suit, white shirt and sombre tie. She approved. Katharine saw him come over and introduced him to the others.

'Good afternoon, Harry, I saw you in the audience and wanted to say hello. Let me introduce you. Alexandra, Robert, meet Harry Eagleburger. Harry is currently with the US embassy in London. He's a lawyer.' They each shook hands with Harry. Robert engaged Harry with a discussion on the legal aspects of the subjects discussed during the day, and others joined their group. Time passed with small talk about the topic of the conference, history, literature, and music. Alexandra hesitated, looking around, trying to locate François. Katharine watched her.

'Are you looking for Monsieur Duhamel, Captain Milyukov?' They stood alone. Alexandra's face indicated her amazement. Katharine knew she did not have the presence to respond. Alexandra exhibited surprise that this woman should know who she was and why she was in Avignon.

They heard a slightly raised voice from the main group. 'Are you certain? You say the law presumes computers are reliable?' The tone of the speaker, a young German lawyer, expressed astonishment. The technologists laughed at the proposition identified with such confidence by Robert. A group of technologists and lawyers had been discussing how evidence from satellites was accepted into legal proceedings.

'Why yes, it's the same in most common law countries,' Robert expanded confidently, 'how else could the state prosecute effectively?'

A Spanish attendee reacted with incredulity. 'In that case, the number of unfair prosecutions and convictions must be – well, must be beyond comprehension.'

On hearing this, Alexandra turned to Robert to articulate her contempt. 'You western countries are so smug about your legal systems. You always boast about how good they are, yet you admit to deliberately ensuring the state prosecutor can use untested evidence to condemn the accused. Why is it that so many supposedly educated people actually believe such stupidity?'

Katharine placed one of her arms under Alexandra's. 'Excellent response, Captain. I agree wholeheartedly with you,' she uttered to Alexandra in an undertone. She intended to educate Robert on this issue next time they met. Alexandra allowed herself to follow the party towards the Collégiale Saint-Didier to attend the concert. As they followed the group, Katharine commented to Harry as he walked by with Robert. 'Charles tells me you're soon to be married. I'm looking forward to the day.'

'Yes,' he blushed, remembering when exactly, where and how he proposed.

*

The first time he saw Cecilia Philadelphia Beresford was after viewing an exhibition in the Barbican in the city of London. She was playing the cello with her fellow musicians, the Bow Belles String Quartet. He heard them playing the tune *Tea for Two*, arranged by Charles Martin. Two floors above the musicians, the music floated up through the empty space, jaunty, fun, delightful, a perfect accompaniment to the April scene under dappled trees in the courtyard, with summer on its way. He walked down to watch and hear them play. The violinists wore blue, the viola player was in brown and the cellist in green, their silk dresses reaching to the floor, with revealing short sleeves and round necks. The cellist had black hair that just touched her neck, ending in curls. Very rosy cheeks, abundant eyebrows and high cheekbones, her dress buttoned at the front, with a big bow tied at the back. Harry saw a fulsome, erotically attractive woman. She captivated him. Vivacious, attractive, full of wit, she sparkled with the joy of life.

As they busied themselves with packing their instruments at the end of the performance, the other three enjoyed the furtive glances she made as they told her they had noticed a dashingly handsome well-built tall young man with his gaze fixated on her. Cecilia had not noticed, being deeply engaged with the music as she always was. As they left with their instruments, Harry approached. He thanked them for a most enjoyable musical afternoon. He wanted to speak directly to Cecilia, but modesty and bashfulness meant he was to attend two of their concerts before he successfully asked her if she wanted to go to an exhibition with him, a mechanism for getting together he found the easiest to adopt.

An acquaintance developed into a romance. Months later she asked him to spend a weekend with her parents in their home deep in the Wiltshire countryside. When he arrived, he was taken aback. Home was a fifteenth-century moated manor house, the weathered Bath stone a light brown. The sunlight threw shadows diagonally across the mottled surface. The original building, erected in the mid to late 1400s, had undergone the usual expansion, change of use and renovation over the centuries. He had not anticipated this. Cecilia had told him to open the front door when he arrived, because the rest of the family would be out. He drove very slowly over the gravel entrance yard, not wishing to damage the vehicle. Cecilia had chosen what he was to wear: brown loafers, sand chinos, a washed out button blue button down shirt. No tie. No jacket. She knew he was in danger of dressing far too formally and wanted him to feel comfortable. *Cecilia*, he thought, as he saw the house, *you said it was your family home. This is ancient. This is terrific. What a place.* Harry could hear Cecilia practising in the Hall with its four bays and original roof timbers as he walked into the stone entrance porch and opened the heavy, studded front door. She was playing a sonata for solo cello. He tiptoed in quietly to stand in the doorway above the minstrel's gallery crossing the hall at one end to watch and listen. He saw her diagonal profile, her left side, her left arm and fingers busy moving along the strings, her body imperceptibly swaying to accommodate the music. She was both in and part of the music, her body an extension of the cello she so carefully looked after. The third movement *allegro molto vivace* of the sonata she was practising by Zoltán Kodály revealed the folk music of Hungary. Harry was entranced with this woman. He was weak with her loveliness. Her hair was made up into a little bun. Wearing a summer dress with a low neck line, he was transfixed by the beauty of her neck.

When she stopped he waited in silence until he knew it was the right moment to step into the hall and wrap his arms around her. Cecilia squealed with delight, put down her cello and reciprocated his warmth and tender kisses as he embraced her. She had liked him from the moment she first noticed him, but uncharacteristically for her, did not gush her enthusiasm too much, not wanting the American to know of her interest in him.

It was early in the afternoon, and after she had taken him to his room to unpack, she insisted he must come with her to pick blackberries, because her father had asked her to make her 'painting pie'. She told him that the blackberries were early this year, which meant they were lucky, continuing the topic by explaining that she had seen the still life *Stilleven met aangebroken pastei* by Willem Claesz Heda. The artist had painted a pie with blackberries and slices of lemon. She had decided to make it herself one day, and it had become a family favourite. They took two old chipped stoneware bowls from the pantry for the fruit. She led the way along the river path, the sun in a bright blue sky as they walked through a cathedral of perennial ryegrass, common reed, bentgrass, swathes of gipsywort, stinging nettles waist high and taller, common hemp nettle with subtle pink hairy flowers – the occasional plant supporting encircling reddish stems of large dodder for the brief length of summer, hedge woundwort, wild angelica, cow parsnip, teasels covered with spiders' webs, red-veined docks, dragon flies and damselflies flying in and out as they brushed against the plants: downy emeralds, common blue and blue-tailed damselflies. Moorhens rummaged along the river bank for snails and insect larvae; a pair of mute swans passed by with a cygnet, a bundle of grey fluff with a pinkish bill gliding by looking out for suitable aquatic plants and grass to eat; pigeons flying between fields; a red kite hovering on the lookout for carrion and worms, and, if the opportunity arose, any small mammals that happened to be moving around; a flock of swallows lining up on the power line, feeding on flying insects and airborne spiders as they flew between bushes and over the water; interrupted, a kestrel took to the air as they walked by, as did two grey herons, who gracefully initiated flight with a gentle bounce of their legs.

'You know, when the hawthorn trees are in full boom in the early summer, we're lucky to have great reed-warblers stay,' Cecelia pointed to a group of reeds along the river. 'Their song is so lovely.'

'You don't say.'

'Oh, Harry, I do like how you say things.'

As they sauntered along the path, he asked her about the sonata she had been playing. She explained it was a tour de force in B minor for solo cello, his opus 8. She was practising to perform it at a recital; it was a very challenging piece to play and technically very demanding. The bowing was difficult and she had to learn to change her technique, explaining both delayed and anticipated shift. She told him how she had to deal with the consequences of *scordare* – interrupting her discussion of the piece as they passed small groups of white and red deadnettles, telling him that those plants were helpful to bees and bumblebees because of their nectar – then continuing her narration as if she had not changed the topic by indicating that it was necessary to alter the standard tuning of the C and G strings by a semitone, and understanding how to adjust her bowing to accommodate *saltato* and *ricochet* strokes. Harry was captivated. He heeded her words with attention and pleasure.

As they walked by, two coots, interrupted, shot across the river into dense undergrowth, with a flurry of black and white pattering noisily over the water. Suddenly she stopped talking and slowed down, putting her finger to her lips to be quiet. They approached a tall hawthorn bush, supporting long arching thorny stems of a bramble, a veritable tangle and perfect to hide in. She stopped again. They listened in silence. They hear whistling, clicking, rattling and other notes, and a chatter inside the dense interweave of branches. She smiled at him in delight.

'It's the starlings and sparrows together. It's like a secret den for the birds. They're the arboreal voices. As we get near, they'll stop until we go,' she whispered. 'Do you know what John Clare wrote?'

'John Clare?'

'An English poet.'

'Oh, right. No. Tell me.'

'I found the poems in the fields/And only wrote them down. Isn't that lovely?'

He looked into her dark brown eyes. 'That's pretty sweet. What a poet.' He was delirious with exhilaration. Here was the girl of his choice. He was walking in the English countryside with the woman he adored. The yellow sun burned brightly. Ragged clouds of *cumulus fractus* were suspended in the blue sky. He was thrilled. She was sharing her life with him along this grassy path of sward, *fully woven for summer/in stuff of limpest green.* This was England. This was his woman. Would she want him as her man?

The picking was glorious. Cecilia, in her forthright chirpy way, was explaining, somewhat teasingly, that he must only pick those blackberries that were ripe. Their drupelets had to have swelled, she said, otherwise the juice of the fruit would not have developed sufficiently, demonstrating the differences with examples as she dropped the not so ripe and ripe berries into his mouth to compare, some warm from the heat of the sun as it landed on his tongue. They finished near a pool of water that was used for bathing.

'It's such a lovely day,' Cecilia suddenly said, looking at the familiar spot, secluded, private, enticing. On home territory, she decided to be her usual spontaneous self. 'Come on,' she began as she put down her blackberries and taking off her clothes, 'let's have a swim.'

Harry was shocked. Abashed, he said, 'I haven't got any swim trunks.'

'So? Neither have I. Last one in's a sissy!' Cecilia removed her summer dress to reveal a nudity he had never seen before. She turned to him, not in the slightest embarrassed. 'Come on, come and join me. It'll be super.' At which she jumped into the water and started to swim. He wanted this woman to be his wife; he had discovered she was everything to him; he loved her sheer exuberance with life; yet he found it difficult to understand her ease as she revelled in the spontaneity of the moment, the sudden change from formality to intimacy. He was her opposite. Taking courage, he took his clothes off, embarrassed at his arousal.

'Oh, how splendid, you've got an erection,' Cecilia shrieked with amusement, ever accurate and never abashed at speaking unequivocally. 'Come on in, don't be nervous, it'll go in this cold water, you'll see.' He jumped into the water.

'Don't you just love the water over all your body? It's such a wonderful feeling of freedom.' Cecilia asked Harry as they played, their naked bodies suspended in the clear water, splashing and racing, holding hands and kissing. Cecilia was doing what came naturally to her; life was to be lived; you take the instant and enjoy it. At this moment, Harry began a journey of stripping bare the anxieties that had gradually developed over his life, one at a time, as defence mechanisms during his experience of childhood and education.

Cecilia swam to the bank and sat on the grass. She looked at him. She knew he was her man. She opened her arms. 'Come and hug me. The sun is so lovely. We'll dry off before we go back.' He heaved his tall, powerfully built body out of the water with a single easy athletic movement. He took the two paces to her, sitting at her side.

'What do you see?' Cecilia asked.

'A most wonderful woman. My woman. A Renoir woman.'

Harry looked at her, his eyes a mist of wonder, exposed, in front of the woman he loved.

Cecilia looked a little sharp. 'Now look here, Harry Eagleburger, I'm not...'

Before she could finish he held the back of her head in one hand and kissed her. He then explained what he meant about her being a Renoir woman. He had not intended that her weight was more than it should be, just that 'he painted such lovely women.'

At that moment she wrapped her arms around his neck and gently pulled him down on top of her, two bodies waiting, eager to be discovered. They kissed, caressed the supple smooth skin of youth – backs, chest, breasts, buttocks, thighs; an erotic exploration of muscle, the late summer sun warm on their flesh, insect life gently disturbed as the passion of intimacy took them on their first passage of discovery, of rapture, of ecstasy, of deeply satisfying shared sexual fulfilment. Physical euphoria, contentment, and happiness followed as they rested together, her head tucked into his arm, breathing on his chest, her body half over his, her thigh across his groin, his arms forming an intimate shield of affection and tenderness; a gentle trust.

Becoming conscious of their surroundings, Cecilia brushed her hand through Harry's hair.

'Harry.'

'Yes, my darling.'

'That was so beautiful. I love you.'

Harry looked into her face. 'I love you too. I love you so much. You're an amazing lover.'

'I'm so glad. So are you. After all this, what shall we do?'

'Do you mean what shall we do now that we've made love?'

'Yes, now we've copulated.'

This was another aspect of Cecilia that he was getting used to – her straight talking. He smiled. He was in love with her and her fierce independence. 'Shall we be married?' She gazed deeply into his blue eyes.

'Cecilia. Will you marry me, or have you just asked me to marry you?'

'Oh, Harry, we've both asked each other. It's just what I wanted. I didn't know when or where or how. Of course I will.'

He was overjoyed. 'Yes, of course I'll marry you. Oh Cecilia.' She had agreed. His life was complete.

'Harry, when did you know you loved me?'

'It's been growing. I can't tell when, but from when I first saw you, I thought you were so lovely.'

'Oh, so adorable. I liked the look of you when they told me you were watching me. It's nice to have a man as tall as me to look at.'

'Well, not so tall.'

'No, but slightly above average, would you think?'

'Maybe.'

'I don't have to look up into your eyes.'

Clouds gently crossed the sky. Insects, bees and butterflies went about their business.

'Harry.'

'Yes?'

'Listen. Listen to the sounds of peace.'

They lay in silence, their hearts beating adoringly to the time of love.

'And contentment.' Harry followed.

'Smell.'

'Yes. Mown grass and the scent of wild flowers.'

Cecilia looked up into the sky. 'Aren't they lovely, all these clouds, so like in the paintings of John Constable.'

'Yes, also like the American painter Charles Harold Davis. He was a great cloud man.'

'I've not seen his paintings. Where was he born?'

'You'll just have to come with me back home, won't you? He was born in Amesbury, Massachusetts. It's a city in Essex County.'

'I'm so looking forward to visiting America.' She stroked the hairs on his chest and sighed in contentment.

'Do you hear that?'

She listened.

'What am I listening to?'

'The grass. It's growing.' He laughed.

'Oh, you sillybilly.' She giggled with him. Blissfully, they did not measure the passing of time.

After a while, Harry sensed Cecilia become matter-of fact. 'You're thinking.'

'How do you know?'

Harry squeezed her body into his. 'I'm getting to know you. We're getting to know each other.'

'You're right. Come on, let's get back. We've got to tell everyone, and I've got a pie to make. Come on, my paramour. How much I love you.' She put both her hands around his neck, preventing him from putting on his pants, and gave him a deep, lasting ardent kiss. 'Now you're my clean-shaven firm-featured American,' she exclaimed.

Harry took control of the fruit. He placed all the blackberries into a single bowl, placing the filled one inside the larger empty bowl. He carried them in one hand as they walked back, hand intimately in hand. Near the house, their arms were entwined around their waists.

Harry discovered that he had met the daughter of Sir Charles and Lady Beresford on his first visit to see her at their London home, and had met them occasionally since. He would not have the opportunity of asking Sir Charles for her hand in marriage. Cecilia announced they were getting married, and when her father asked about getting permission from the father of the bride, she marched to her bedroom, donned her sash of purple white, and green, then promptly stood defiantly before her father, who had anticipated what was coming.

The family and Harry had moved out into the garden as she was rushing to and from her room, and Charles and his son opened two bottles of champagne before joining them. When she found them, her father handed her the first glass. Harry was nonplussed about how this was played out, reminding himself that the English upper classes really did understate and act differently to Americans. He was rapidly discovering that his future wife to be was not only passionate, but had a firmly held understanding of her place in the world.

Charles and Sofie Beresford had carefully watched the development of their daughter's romantic liaison. They wanted to feel secure about the person she had agreed to join her in the intimacy of her life.

The weekend passed, the evenings spent in making music and acting. Cecilia playing the piano to accompany Harry singing *O Mistress Mine* from Twelfth Night, put to gently lilting music by Amy Beach, repeating the second lines of each verse, looking at Cecilia when he sang *Trip not further, pretty sweeting/ Journeys end in lovers meeting.* Her parents enacting a scene they always made up from the English radio comedy series *Round the Horne*, a particular family favourite, Harry was to discover. Betty Marsden played a character called Dame Celia Molestrangler. Dame Celia in turn played yet another character, Fiona. Hugh Paddick played a character called Binkie Huckaback. Binkie in turn played the character of Charles. Cecilia had already made Harry watch the film *Brief Encounter*, one of her favourites, so he could begin to understand the humour he would encounter. She also raved about the music, Sergei Rachmaninoff's second piano concert – so romantic. Sir Charles and Lady Beresford enjoyed making up the dialogue. As always, they had the entire family of all ages falling about with laughter. Harry began to learn the rites of the English gentry, especially those closely connected to the aristocracy.

Later, he asked her about the engagement ring. Cecilia was adamant. 'No, Harry, I don't want an engagement ring. The only thing I want to say to myself is: born, lived, met Harry. I don't need or want anything else. Just you.'

'And your music.'

'All right, and my music.'

*

As the evening descended, the pink sandstone of the Laxmi Niwas Palace, commissioned by Maharajah Sir Ganga Singh Ji and designed during the British ascendancy by Sir Samuel Swinton Jacob in Indo-Saracenic style, looked resplendent in the comfortable heat of the early evening. A background of puffy white clouds filled the scene as high as the eye could see, losing colour in the fading daylight, the electronic lights illuminating the façade and dominant *chhatri* overlooking the front of the palace. Intricate filigree, abundant latticework, marble courtyards and fountains all attested to the quality of the craftsmen who worked on the building.

Henry Bravington-Hartley met Douglas Irani as he got out of the taxi. Climbing the white marble stairs, they entered the central courtyard, the middle covered with lush grass around a marble fountain. The space was surrounded on all sides with three sets of colonnades on the ground floor, and the first and second floors were lit against the darkening blue sky with electric light. They sat at a table, the chairs covered and tied in white linen.

'I'm glad that I can thank you in person at last,' Douglas Irani continued the conversation after their initial introductory chat as they sat down.

Henry Bravington-Hartley thought nothing of it. 'Douglas, we were both in difficult positions. We had to help you once our position had improved.' He referred to the near-catastrophe of the take-over of their respective agencies with the usual understatement that Henry was used to. He continued. 'The Ambassador car was superb, I have to say. It's so fragile that my grandson will have to wait until he is a little older before I give it to him.'

'It's a piece of history.'

'Yes, secret history. Best not written. The painting is stunning.'

'I found a local man to do it. He is very discreet. It's exquisite. He is so skilled. I knew you would know where I was and that I was reasonably safe once you found it.'

'Yes, Agra. There are worse places to hide. The double-tiered crown imperial, *fritillaria imperialis*, carved into the upper cenotaph of Shah Jahan. The image reminded me of the visit we made together with our families. I assumed you were referring to this in particular, because it was a happier time, but also because you were under the protection of the spirit of the great emperor.'

'Yes. I hoped you would understand.'

'I did.'

'And now you are on holiday after retiring?'

'Yes, we are going to Scotland. I have a position there.'

A good-looking young man approached them wearing a white short-sleeved jacket with epaulets and a mandarin collar, and black trousers. He had black hair, neat and short, and was clean shaven with a heavy beard under his brown skin, with attentive dark brown eyes and rich black eyebrows sweeping across his forehead.

'Ah, Dinesh, you have come to ask us what we want to drink?' Douglas questioned him.

'Yes, Sir.'

'Henry,' Douglas said to him and looked at the waiter at the same time, 'this young man is from Jaipur. He's trying to make a living. He's doing very well here, but he hopes to stretch his legs and see the world one day.'

'Hello Dinesh, I hope you succeed with a small part of what you would like to achieve.'

The young man bowed slightly. 'Thank you, Sir.' He stood motionless, watching the Anglo-Indian and the Englishman, who were clearly very close friends.

'We will have two Kingfisher beers and some snacks, thank you.' Douglas ordered for them both. As the waiter left, Douglas continued. 'Thank you for letting us know about the Australians. It might be useful to work with them politically, but that's not for me to decide.'

'They authorized me to get in touch. They intend to expand their satellite industry, especially satellites for military communications. Let's say they're also under some pressure.'

'I can imagine where the pressure is coming from. We need to improve our resources. India signed an implementation agreement with Australia recently. It was between the Indian Space Research Organisation and Geoscience Australia. It's intended that we cooperate in earth observation and satellite navigation. Now is the time to move things on. We created the Integrated Space Cell under the Integrated Defence Services a little while ago, and we are integrating space technology and military operations at last. We have to think about space security rapidly. Our neighbours are well advanced. It will affect how we control our borders, including the coastline. Internal security is high on the agenda as well.'

'You'll need to ensure you have an excellent communicator to liaise with the Australians to prevent misunderstandings.'

'Yes. Apparently they have an experienced woman officer they want appoint as a facilitator from their side.'

Dinesh returned with the beer and a platter containing the

local snack *Bikaneri bhujia*, together with small helpings of *pyaaz pakora*, *aloo pakora*, *paalak pakora*, and *paneer pakora*. He carefully set the table and returned to the bar. Both men waited until he finished, thanking him as he left.

'Excellent.' Henry raised his glass, chinking with Douglas, wishing him good health. 'It was fortunate you were travelling near Bikaner to meet us.'

'Yes, I like to meet people in the outposts once a year. It helps with morale. I have to move on tomorrow, but it's nice to be staying here tonight and having a meal with you and your dear wife.'

'We're glad you could stay.'

'When I knew I was coming, I booked the Swarna Mahal restaurant. The room is dazzling, with the teak roof and the hand painted panels of stone. You'll love it. The food is excellent. But before dinner, there is something I want to give you. Let's go to my room. I need to be discreet.'

They walked to the first floor, along the corridor and turned towards the rear of the building into a corner where his room was located. The porter had already taken his luggage to the room.

'Let's not be long, Henry,' Douglas said as he switched the light on in the tall gloom of the room, with elaborate shutters and filigree surrounding the windows to keep out the harsh summer light and sandstorms. Henry sat on the heavy Victorian chair as Douglas opened a suitcase, then slipped his hand into a secret compartment to reveal an A4 manilla envelope. He gave it to Henry.

'Henry, as you know, the Chinese have a massive launch centre called the Jiuquan Satellite Launch Centre in the Gobi desert in inner Mongolia. It's part of the Dongfeng Aerospace City, or Base 10. They launched the first quantum communication satellite there recently. As part of my work in the Defence Intelligence Agency, I go to Kashmir every now and again.'

'You've been there on this trip?' Henry asked, holding the envelope. It was sealed. Douglas sat on the bed.

'Yes. You know the nomads are not fond of the Han Chinese. We occasionally get them slipping over the border after a long trek. We get to know them, as you can expect. One in particular brings little items of news that sometimes has great value. Occasionally this person brings documents they try to sell to us. We've had one or two very valuable papers from this source. Recently, they brought what is contained in that envelope. It's written in Mandarin. It's marked top secret. You'll find it very useful. It's a bit crumpled, but that's because it has travelled a long way by horse and camel.'

'It's not of interest for you?'

'Yes. I've taken a copy.'

'Why give me the original, if it's genuine?'

'You'll remember the time you gave me something that not only helped our country, but also ensured I got the commendation and resulting promotion?'

'I do, but we all need to do that sometimes. We know it helps both ways.'

'I know, and this time, bearing in mind the nature of what is contained in the document, I thought it would be useful to you. We're following the Paris International Conference on Satellite Communication and Technology, as you probably know. We also know that there are a number of secrets floating around, some of which would be very damaging to the state concerned if they were made public.'

'Yes, something like that,' Henry volunteered without commitment.

'To be frank, we don't care about any of it. The content of this document doesn't affect us. It's useful to know the secrets, but more information sometimes makes analysis more difficult.'

'Yes, too much can cloud the judgment.'

'Precisely.'

'We're at the beginning of our trip. Fortunately, a good friend is joining us tomorrow, so this can get to the embassy and on to the UK to be considered sooner rather than later. It's very helpful that Nal airport is now operational.'

'Yes, because the journey by train is fairly long. You're going to the wildlife sanctuary?'

'Yes, we'll stay at the Gajner Palace. Rajasthan is a lovely state. Anyway, let me leave you to get changed, and we three will have dinner together.'

After the meal, Douglas retired for the night. Henry and his wife decided on a nightcap before returning to their room. They went into the Trophy Bar, which was empty, other than Dinesh, standing behind the beam of mahogany that formed the bar. To one side of the bar was the head of a rhinoceros, and on the other side, the head of a Nepalese bison. Behind and around the room, there were more heads of stuffed dead animals mounted on the walls, all shot for pleasure: leopard, pairs of lionesses, platypuses, boars, deer, tigers, Royal Bengals and coyotes. They engaged in conversation with Dinesh, who was polite, ready to listen, and happy to tell them about how he lived in the hotel hostel and how he wanted to travel to England and make a life there. Before they left, Henry offered him a few words, 'Dinesh, we wish you well in your life. You want to explore the world and lead a better life, and if you do, we hope you achieve the success you want. But beware of the snarling arrogance, self-absorption, insincerity and unkindness that you will discover over and over again. It will not end. Always be positive, but please remember, take heed.'

*

'Well, Charles, isn't this just a wonderful place?' Bruce had a very wide smile on his face. He continued. 'They've given me this room for a few days because it's not being used. The chandelier, isn't it just amazing? I like the green curtains with the gold brocade. Dorothy told me the curtains are made with silk damask and the trimmings are called *passementerie*. Great word. She's thrilled with the photos I've sent her. The view is fantastic.'

Bruce took Charles into the grand reception room in the George C. Marshall Center in the hôtel particular of the hôtel de Talleyrand on the corner of the rue Saint Florentin and the Place de la Concorde, an exceptional example of the architecture of the autocratic Bourbon regime of the eighteenth century.

'Bruce, it's super. And handsomely restored. It's a gem. I've got to hand it to you, your office here in Paris is grander than the pocket-sized space they've let me use at the embassy. The mirrors are impressive. I'd better pay homage to the man with the biggest and grandest office.'

They laughed. Bruce knew Charles was expressing genuine admiration while teasing him simultaneously. Having shared so many experiences together, he had learnt to understand the British sense of irony, of subversiveness, of understatement. Charles knew Bruce understood that this was a compliment.

Both enjoyed the contentment of a surprisingly respectable cup of coffee and each other's company in silence. Their reflections bounced around the room in the full length gilded mirrors, the formality of their suits and ties appropriate for the original purpose of the *grande salle d'audience*. They were quiet. Each was absorbed by their own thoughts, reflecting on why they found themselves in Paris on this occasion.

'You know,' Bruce began in a subdued tone of voice, 'we're not in a good place right now.' Charles remained silent. He knew that Bruce had a lot to say. Experience meant it was best to be patient. He would say it, as he wanted. 'I guess I don't know where to begin, Charles, if that makes sense.' Charles knew what Bruce was going to talk about, and he knew it was embarrassing for him. This was the time to interrupt. 'Bruce, we've been chums for a long time.' He expressed his sympathy by repeating his words. 'Neither of us is in a good place right now.' He paused, before continuing. 'We're friends. We share stuff with each other. We know our countries always come first. That doesn't mean we can't criticize our own Service or country in private, especially when the critique is legitimate.'

'Thanks Charles. I knew you'd understand. You know how it is. OK, our President has told us to find the British spy. We both know there isn't a British spy that's working against the United States. But we've got to respond. The problem is, what's the evidence? We haven't got any. There's no evidence the allegation is correct, and no evidence that proves there isn't a British spy. Those that work in the present administration just assume there is a British spy. They don't need evidence.'

'You're right. We can't prove or disprove something that has no basis in any fact.'

'It's really a political problem.'

'Yes. We need a different angle.'

Bruce noticed Charles had finished his coffee. He topped both cups up, passing the milk jug to Charles. Charles took the initiative. 'One of our ministers is on his way to Washington DC. Between us, he wasn't on the do not appoint list, but we have grave concerns about him. He's got links with some of people in the US we don't trust. He's one of those that believe in the ideology that the state needs to wither away. Of course, such people don't like paying tax, even though they like the idea of the state providing them with security. He and his counterparts in the US don't understand that the Russians are using them to weaken us. We assume your people will be following him when he gets there, but if you had somebody you could trust to watch him, that would be useful.'

'OK, I could do that. Where does he fit in?'

'He's got all the connections that mean something in the present administration. That's why I expect he's on your list. We've been investigating him for some time, and we've come across some interesting and very damaging facts about his activities. I can't tell you any more yet, but what we've got, if it's accurate, is going to help us with this problem.'

Bruce breathed a deep sigh. 'Our difficulty is that we have to deal with somebody that never admits a mistake, and never concedes a weakness. Flattery is helpful, but it doesn't mean you'll be valued – in fact, you can usually expect ingratitude. Any response he'll listen to must have his name on it. That there isn't a British double agent must come from him, or be presented to him from a source he trusts.'

'You're right. I've been thinking about it. That's why we need to concentrate on the politics and unsavoury links. We'll have to work closely on this. We can share what we've got with you personally and one other you trust implicitly. We need to keep the number of people in on this one to the minimum. I don't trust anybody else in your outfit right now. Only you.'

Bruce looked shocked. He was silent for a short time.

'Seriously?'

Charles looked directly into his eyes.

'Yes.'

'Is it really that bad from where're you're sitting?'

'I'm afraid so, Bruce. But that doesn't mean we can't deal with this successfully. You know that. We've got to be careful. We can hope to find the right solution, or something else might come along that makes the allegation wither away as the fantasy it is. It could be either.'

'Thanks for sharing that with me Charles. I appreciate your honesty. Shall we go?' Bruce asked, as he looked at his watch.

'Yes, good idea.'

'I'm over for another problem; that's why I arranged to meet François.'

'Yes, I told him I thought it will be useful. He said he'd asked you if it was all right to contact me about it.'

'Yes. You don't mind?'

'No. We need to act together. If we don't, the ideologues will use every connection they've got to undermine what we're doing.'

They retraced their steps through the rooms to the grand staircase, admiring the gunmetal balustrade and the details in brass. Bruce looked up to the restored ceiling painting by Jean-Simon Berthélemy, *La Force accompagnée de la Prudence portant á l'Immortalité le globe de la France*. Their mood was pessimistic. 'Charles, there's a lot of hubris in that image.' Charles looked up at the painting. 'Yes, everybody does it. We all have men with their excessive self confidence, and historians mislead us by calling them great.'

'Yes. You know, I've never worked out why Alexander III of Macedon is called the great. Why? Why was he great? Because he killed, raped and enslaved so many people? Was it because he destroyed so many buildings and cities?'

'The military genius is revered.'

'I know. The past is distorted into myths to reinforce the dogma of the present. The academics do a great job.'

'And those that control the school syllabus do even better work.'

Charles looked at Bruce as they descended the stone stairs. Bruce liked using irony when he was with Charles. He knew how the English liked to mock.

'To think the name of this building is linked to two great men who were actually quite reasonable.'

'Yes, George C. Marshall is properly remembered in this building, I think. It's said he had a plan, but it wasn't a plan.'

'No, it was a program.'

'Yes. The European Recovery Program.' Charles took a sideways glace at Bruce, his eyes smiling. 'And it worked. It wasn't necessary, but it was a great propaganda move to circulate European capital that was already being released. All to ensure Europeans bought American goods after the 1945 US recession.'

'You've got it. And, more importantly, it was to make sure the US companies got paid in hard currency. Truman was close to the mob, and he knew how to obstruct the Russians after the war, although he didn't do it in a vacuum. Stalin wasn't playing fair. First, he and his acolytes organized the media to change the way Americans thought of the Russians, from being helpful allies to being evil. That didn't take long. Then he ensured the programme was organized in such a way that the Russians would refuse to let their satellite states join.' Bruce in turn let his eyes smile at the reality.

Sir Charles joined in. 'He got the great US capitalist machine moving. You've got to hand it to him. And then we have Talleyrand. Now there's a much maligned character. Well, he remains so with some people. Towards the end of his life he asked whether it was all worth it: the useless agitations, fruitless attempts, tiresome complications, exaggerated emotions, squandered gifts, inspired malevolence, loss of perspective, exhausted tastes – to what end?'

'It feels like that sometimes for me.'

'Yes, but we've got to resist that feeling. What we're doing is important. It's just that only a few people really know what we do.'

'That's the problem. The powerful that know what we do use it to their own advantage.'

'But if they go too far, there are mechanisms to deal with them.' They had reached the bottom of the stairs. Bruce looked into Charles's eyes. 'Darn right, Charles, and we're not gonna let them get us.' Charles let his cheeks break into a smile and the sides of his eyes crimpled. 'Let's see if François has some answers.'

*

The Service booked a room for Owain in the l'Hôtel Le Saint-Amour. Owain had to establish whether Boran Avcı was one of his fellow guests, and, if so, he wanted to know which room he was staying in. The female receptionist beckoned Owain to one side and explained in a soft voice that the manager had briefed them to pay attention to Boran Avcı, and to cooperate with Owain.

'He'll be away for a while later this afternoon.' She continued the conversation aloud, turning to her fellow receptionist, a man younger than her, twenty, just over six foot tall, his white shirt and blue tie uncomfortably restricting his chest and biceps, giving him a wry smile. 'The man you are enquiring about is very good looking,' she continued, looking at the full lips of the male receptionist. He could not hide his anticipation of the enjoyment ahead. Owain watched their interaction.

'We'll be looking after him. He asked me to show him some of the local historic sites.' The two exchanged conspiratorial glances.

Boran Avcı followed her instructions. He parked the car behind the small, low late nineteenth-century barn, locating the side entrance, just where she said it was. He opened the door and smelt the sweet scent of newly mown hay, the bales stacked high into the rusting steel roof trusses. He found himself in a small area lit by a line of bespattered narrow windows in the eves running the length of the building, covered with accretions of cobwebs. The crop had been brought in through the double doors opposite. The space he found himself in was sufficient for a few bales of hay to have been positioned as improvised seating.

He removed his jacket and placed his Smartphone on top. He listened. Suddenly a wall of bales crashed into the gap. There she was. The female receptionist adopted an aggressive pose, her blonde hair tied in a knot. Hands outstretched, silent, expectant. Trained in various forms of hand-to-hand combat, he recognized this most beautiful of women, slender, powerfully feminine, with a strong muscle tone, was probably a devotee of a martial art. He anticipated the hedonism to come. He also realised that he was not going to dominate, as he was used to. This was going to lead to extreme fulfilment. He reacted to her nakedness by stripping off his T-shirt in one quick movement, and throwing it out into the bales. She jumped onto his body. He spread his legs to catch her as she wrapped her strong thighs around his torso. Very shortly he was naked, linked to her in an instinctive exploration of eroticism and carnality, enjoying the application of concentrated strength to the intimate physicality of the sexual act.

During a lull in their activities, the door opened. She was lying on top of him. Turning her head to view the visitor, she then looked into his eyes, raised her eyebrows in an expression of awareness, placed a forefinger over his mouth so as not to ask questions, then extracted herself from him. She stood, her body glistening a provocative sexuality in the dull light, the rays of the sun illuminating the mass of microscopic particles floating in the air. She placed a foot on his chest. He fondled her leg, turning to watch the interloper, who, having quickly closed the door, flung his clothes off. The male receptionist reached over Boran Avcı's body and passed a hand around her neck and held her head close. They kissed, deep and long. She pressed his torso into hers, spreading her hands over the muscular contours of his biceps, shoulders, back, grazing over the supple tension of his skin in pleasure, her fingers lightly stroking the fine hair at the base of his back before caressing the firm cheeks of his buttocks.

Boran Avcı now realised this was planned. But the boy – he was a prize. He had not realized they worked together. For him, it did not matter. The youth had a pleasingly powerfully built body. This was going to be an even match, so much the more pleasurable. Entertained by this unexpected development, he studied their embrace from below, continuing to stroke her calf with his right hand and the young man's calf of hair with his left hand as he observed his body react in anticipation of what was to come.

'*Merci, ma chere*,' he whispered into her ear.

'As we thought. He's a man's man,' she spoke in a low voice. 'Satisfactory for you?'

'He knows how to pleasure a women. Sufficiently adequate, shall we say.' She shrugged her shoulders, her face expressing a playful half smile. 'He's yours now.'

The male receptionist lowered himself down on to Boran Avcı's impatient sweating body. As the men set about gratifying their strong visceral mutual lust, she slipped her dress over her lithe body. Noticing the Smartphone, she picked it up and recorded them playing and tussling. She left, silently closing the door to the muted sounds of shared pleasure.

The receptionists were living through a unique experience in their lives that summer – one that they would never repeat or forget. Having discovered they had equally satisfying hedonistic characteristics, they became people-watchers from the vantage of their position. Careful and discreet, they sought opportunity when it was offered and accepted.

The hotel used RIFD plastic tokens manufactured by a European company to open doors to rooms. He used a device given to him before he left London to manipulate the key data of the hotel on the door entry card. Taking seconds, he now had a card that gave him the highest level of privileges in the hotel computer system. He had a master key to every room in the building.

First, he entered the system via his computer and disabled all the cameras on every floor. He then took the stairs to Boran Avcı's room, putting on a pair of surgeon's gloves as he descended. He slipped in quietly. Owain looked at the laptop computer first. It was connected to the mains, left to charge up. The screen was partly down. The danger was that it was set to record sounds in the room and images of anybody moving within sight of the screen. Owain knew Boran Avcı was not a sophisticated user of technology. The chances were that he did not need to understand computer security as much as the usual officer working in the Gendarmerie Intelligence and Counter-Terrorism. Owain had to make a quick decision. He lifted the screen sufficiently to cover the microphones and camera with small pieces of tape. Moving the touchpad, the screen lit up. It was switched on. It was not protected by a password. Owain quickly inserted a USB into one of the ports. The program automatically initiated and indicated it was active. It then disappeared from the screen. Before leaving, Owain quickly searched the room. Boran Avcı travelled light. A small black battered simulated leather holdall was empty with the exception of a Yavuz 16 pistol concealed in a carefully constructed compartment. He emptied the magazine, pocketing the rounds of ammunition. What few clothes he brought were quickly searched. The bathroom contained nothing of note. Removing the tape from the laptop and carefully replacing the screen to the angle he found it, he listened carefully before deciding it was safe to leave the room.

*

Étienne and the young receptionist from the Hôtel Jean de Bohême returned from the circular walk they had made via Palenge. The hike ended outside the apartment that Michael Cocke had booked for his stay in Durbuy. Cocke was able to slip in and out of the conference hotel and get to and from the Studio Le Vedeur without being noticed. The building was well placed, opposite the bridge, on the corner of rue de la Haie Himbe, the Avenue Louis de Loncin and Fond de Vedeur. He could monitor pedestrians and vehicle traffic over the bridge should he want to, or consider it necessary.

Sitting on the bench looking out on the river Ourthe, Abdülkadir Turgut turned when he heard them talking as they descended the stairs past Cocke's accommodation. He had overheard the two discuss the route they were going to walk before they left the hotel. He sauntered towards the men as they crossed the road to the bridge. They were dressed in hiking boots, shorts, lightweight shirts and carried small knapsacks.

'*Guten tag*,' he said.

Étienne looked at his companion and replied in German, '*Guten tag*' before changing language, 'I do not know you.'

'I know, but I have a word of advice for you.'

Étienne was perplexed. The receptionist watched respectfully. 'You are not German.' Étienne had met many Turks when working and living in Germany, and he assumed that Abdülkadir Turgut was an emigrant Turk.

'No, I am Turkish.' Turgut looked at his watch and decided to be forthright. 'You work for a German company. A group of Turkish investors have decided to buy it. I don't think the Bundesnachrichtendienst or the Militärischer Abschirmdienst will agree to the sale, or if they do, the terms will be onerous, and the Turkish government will not accept them.'

'You are well informed.' Étienne was cautious.

'I was sent to check you out,' Turgut continued.

'So what is your conclusion?'

'I haven't reached a decision. I've been ordered to return home.' Turgut's response was unexpected and forthright.

Étienne felt it was safe to open the discussion. 'Do you know why?'

Abdülkadir Turgut was terrified at what to expect when he returned to Turkey, but was not in a position to disobey the order. 'I cannot answer your question. Life is in turmoil in my country at present. I have to return and assess my own position. I do not know what to expect.'

'Then why approach me? You're work isn't complete, and it doesn't matter that I did not know you or why you were here.'

'I wanted to warn you. The work you are doing is very sensitive. Please be cautious. As the poet Karin Karakaşlı warns, you will be punished if your plan is wrong.' The three stood silent. The river continued to flow, reflected images splintering in the sunlight. 'You know,' Abdülkadir Turgut continued, 'I have begun to understand that the past is always distorted by people in the present for their own purposes. Most people are too simple to realise when they are being manipulated. Karakaşlı continues by reminding us that we are now living through a new truth, the lie, where duplicity has become the new appropriate.'

'Good words, Sir. But most people fail to understand the complexity of the world that we have collectively created, even those with an apparently superior education. Maybe people aren't so stupid. Maybe it's because they cannot do anything to change things, and maybe many people prefer to believe the distortions. Perhaps that is why those that ought to govern rarely put themselves forward. Modern democracies allow for the narcissist, the mediocre, and the loudmouth to dominate. The outriders do their dirty work on the side. Do you know French?'

'No.'

'In translation, the poet Édouard Glissant wrote *And like fancy dress our lies/Are tears mirrored into life*. Thank you for your warning. I have become aware of what are called the GEC Marconi deaths in the UK, and my experience is beginning to tell me to keep away from the defence industry, but it is becoming unavoidable.'

'We know about them. Do you believe the deaths were because of the British state?'

'Religions are belief. People believe because there is no proof. The evidence about the British is compelling. That is, what we know of it. In my experience, I'd say that the British state would carry out such actions; after all, their Special Air Service soldiers were able to kill three members of the IRA during daylight in Gibraltar with impunity.'

A taxi passed along the bridge slowly. Abdülkadir Turgut waved at the driver. 'That's my taxi. I have to collect my bag and then go to the airport.' As an afterthought, he asked, 'Are you two a pair?'

The young receptionist laughed. He looked at Étienne, whose face expressed amusement. He answered. 'No. I wish.' Abdülkadir Turgut got into the front seat of the taxi. After listening to instructions, the driver made a wide turn back into the town. Turgut waved at them as they went by.

'What's all that about Marconi?'

'A number of software programmers died mysterious deaths in the UK in the eighties. They were all linked to the defence industry.'

'I wasn't born then.'

'Well, I was only just growing up,' Étienne hastened to inform his walking partner, 'but people haven't forgotten about them.' The taxi turned the corner out of sight.

'He didn't shake your hand or ask you who Édouard Glissant was.'

'I know, but people like me are used to that.'

Michael Cocke stood back from the window as he watched the taxi go by.

*

Helen chose a table for four in a discreet alcove in La Gargouille in the rue du Rèmoleû at Heyd, a few miles from Durbuy. She ordered an aperitif while she waited. Alice arrived. They exchanged news, Helen expressing her concern for Alice at missing her after arriving at the airport. Alice smoothed over her absence with an explanation that she was briefed in London for other purposes. Helen knew she would never know the truth, but having been recalled from her current assignment, she was not inclined to stretch a relationship. The women discovered a natural mutual interest beyond their roles with their respective agencies. Both knew that this was important for long-term relations between their countries. They also enjoyed each other's company. They had begun to understand each other.

Owain walked out of the hotel to see if he could find a taxi. Unexpectedly, he saw the female receptionist waving to him in the dusk from across the Place aux Foires. He hurried over. She walked between two low buildings, a *brasserie* each side. He followed. She waited for him.

'Did you get what you wanted?'

'Yes, thanks. I don't even know your name to thank you.'

'That's how I like it. I'm leaving at the end of the season. I like to move on.'

'You're an untamed girl.' She frowned, and interrupted him. 'I'm a woman.'

'Sorry.' Owain immediately realised he had lost some respect. 'I should have known better. But there aren't many like you in this world.'

Her face regained composure. 'I'm a free spirit. The last six weeks have been fun. You see a lot of life as a hotel receptionist.'

'So I've deduced. Where are you off to? Is the boy going with you?'

'Nowhere you need to know. He's been a playmate. He'll go his own way back to university. I don't know if we'll stay in touch. Sometimes you don't need to. We've been lucky to have met each other this summer. We can leave it.'

'Well, thanks again. You've really helped me.'

'You're a spy, aren't you?' He was silent. 'It's all right, I know you can't say. Here, I think you'll find a use for this.' She held out Boran Avcı's Smartphone. He took it and placed it into a pocket immediately.

'Now I really don't know what to say.'

'Then don't say anything. I have a feeling about you. You're honest. And chaste, but that will come to an end soon.' Owain looked somewhat astonished. 'Don't be afraid, I won't tell you any more, unless you'd like to know about your future. I have an insight that many don't have. Assessing humans is always risky. We're a tricky, devious, lying group of animals.'

'I know.'

'That's why you've been so careful all your life. But he's not far away from you now. You like the company of women, though.'

Owain looked at this angelic figure of a woman, exuding confidence in her every movement, every word. He answered her statement. 'Yes, I find women more open than most men;' before continuing, 'you're extraordinary. I'd like to get to know you.'

'Maybe one day. Anyway, I know you're up to something important. You can tell who the killers and sadists are. You're different. You need a taxi, don't you?'

'Yes.'

'I'm going to my lodgings. Walk over to La Note d'Or around the corner, and I'll pick you up in five minutes.'

As he left the car, she gave him one further item of information. 'You might like to know that he's leaving the hotel tomorrow morning.' Owain held the door open and looked at her. 'Thanks again. I hope we meet again one day.'

'*Bon voyage*' she said as he closed the door.

She drove into the evening.

Helen heard Owain enter the restaurant. She excused herself and went to find him. Returning, she introduced him to Alice.

'Zhuge Xiùyīng, this is Owain Davis. Owain, this is Captain Zhuge Xiùyīng.'

Zhuge Xiùyīng shook hands with Owain. 'Hello, my name is also Alice. I am happy to meet you.'

'How do you do. I am also happy to meet you, Alice. Helen has introduced your rank. Has she told you about me?'

'Yes. You are a British spy.'

Owain laughed, as did Helen. Alice was pleased that they liked her response. Alice had been briefed to observe. Her superiors wanted to know the links the Australian agent was making – with whom and for what reason. Their knowledge of such relationships might be useful in the future.

'Well,' Helen took over, 'you two have hit it off. That's good. I've booked a table for four. I've asked Étienne if he'd like to join us.'

'He won't be coming.'

'Oh?'

'I've just met him. He's packing to travel back to Germany now the conference has finished.'

'Ah, right.'

'But this gives us the opportunity to plan what we do next.

We've got to work quickly now.' Alice and Helen looked at each other. Owain continued. 'I've been given authority to work with you both on a short-term plan regarding Cocke and Avcı. Have you been told yet? I've only just received instructions.' Helen and Alice quickly looked at their devices. Both confirmed the news. Helen also discovered that she had been recalled on being promoted, not wholly unexpected, and well received. She was instructed to remain to finish this additional part of her mission. They congratulated Helen before discussing and planning the next move.

*

Michael Cocke had noticed Boran Avcı. He caught a passing glimpse of him in the same vehicle as Abdülkadir Turgut. He did not know who Boran Avcı was, who he worked for, or whether he was in government service. His intuition told him that Boran Avcı was in Durbuy for a purpose. It might be to do with him. He speculated that Avcı might well be a violent man. He might have been sent with the purpose of violence. Cocke was in a world where the application of force was normal for those that wanted their own way without giving anything in return. It was a hazard that he was fully aware of, and had studiously and successfully avoided. But unknown to Cocke, Boran Avcı was going to meet him in peace.

*

The digital screen on the bedside clock registered another minute, 02:03. He heard what he was expecting. A click. The handle was slowly lowered from the outside. A white dot glowed in the dark from the laptop located on the desk; a wafer-thin longitudinal block of dull orange light framed the top of the curtains; the bar of light under the door from the corridor widened into an angle. The door was quickly closed. The intruder intended to surprise the occupant, but he in turn was startled as he moved from a bright corridor into the black of the room. Within two seconds, his head was seized, pulled down, and a knee smashed into his groin with great force. He fell, groaning, his hands automatically wanting to protect the area of agonizing pain. Once on the ground, the main lights were switched on and he received a solid hit to a knee. This was sufficient to disable the joint.

Owain quickly tied Avcı's hands with a leather belt. He then fell back onto the bed and wiped his brow. He watched the Turk. Doubled up, Avcı could do nothing other than gurgle moans of serious discomfort as his body began to recover from the beating. The clock continued to measure the passing of time. Owain listened to the ponderous breathing of the Turk as he regained his composure. Owain got up, went to the bathroom, put the end of a small towel under the tap, returned to Avcı, and wiped his face. He then moved his body so that he was sat on the floor, his torso propped against the wall.

'All right, why me?' Owain was instructed to beware of Boran Avcı. He was also to assess what level of confidence, if any, he could be sure of in the Turk for the purpose of cooperation. The Service had no interest in antagonising the Turks. Owain was aware that his actions made Avcı feel deeply humiliated. Avcı's face expressed the disgrace he felt. 'Look, you came to kill me, so I'd like to know why.'

Boran Avcı remained silent.

'All right, let me tell you. You're after a man called Cocke. You want to know if he can be trusted. You've targeted me because I've got the Italian computer. Your colleague, Abdülkadir Turgut, used his skills to identify the device and link me to it. You both assumed that I was Cocke, or if not him, then somebody who obtained Turkish secrets.'

Boran Avcı stubbornly remained silent. He would not look at Owain.

'It doesn't help me if you won't cooperate. I'm trying to understand and help, but if you're rejecting the offer, I can't do anything about it. You've got two options. I call the police and you face the consequences. The other choice is for you to leave the hotel as if nothing has happened. The close circuit television will show you entering my room.' At this point, Owain searched Avcı's pockets for the card he used to gain entry. He retained it. 'If you're not willing to cooperate I'll make the decision.'

Boran Avcı looked contemptuously at Owain. 'The CCTV is dangerous.'

'I can handle that, but it depends.'

'I'll leave. You deal with the CCTV.'

'I'll manage the CCTV when I'm ready, and not before.' Owain freed his hands by removing the belt, allowing Avcı to gradually, painfully, stand up. He opened the door. 'Just to let you know, I'll watch every move you make as you leave. I'll watch you return to your room. Now go. I'll see you tomorrow. We can continue with this conversation when you're in a better mood.' Boran Avcı slowly limped down the corridor, one arm on the wall supporting his body, partly stooping to contain the stinging soreness.

Helen and Alice sat at an outside table to have a morning coffee in Le Grand Café in the Place aux Foires. Shortly after they arrived, Boran Avcı slowly walked by, his halting leaden steps testifying to the damage caused to one of his knees, carrying his holdall towards the car he had hired. Helen called to him. '*Günaydın.*' He turned to the sound. '*Günaydın,*' he politely responded, surprised at hearing his native language in a small town in Belgium spoken with an Australian accent.

'You came to the conference,' Helen offered an opening.

'I was late,' he turned to face them. 'Are you scientists?'

'No, just two girls. You're Turkish, aren't you? Won't you join us for a coffee? Do you know the poet Nâzım Hikmet?' Helen deliberately asked a question weighed down with the history of the modern Turkish state. It was a calculated attempt to get him to be seated. They did not know if he would respond, but decided the night before that it was an opening gambit worth trying. He gazed at them, looked at the big stocky watch on his left wrist, placed his bag to the side of a chair and sat down. A waitress noticed him, and strode over to take his order for a coffee.

'He was a communist.'

'Yes, but he is said to have met Mustafa Kemal Atatürk and he served on the cruiser *Hamidiye*. Isn't the world in which we live ironic? The ship was built by Armstrong Whitworth, a British company, and the ship took part in the war against the British.'

'He did not take part in the war of independence. Some like him.' Boran Avcı adopted a taciturn silence. As the waitress returned with his coffee, Owain walked up.

'Good morning, Helen, Alice. May I join you?'

'Sure,' Helen greeted him. He sat next to Boran Avcı, saying 'Hello,' and receiving a nod in response. Helen continued, 'Owain, this is – ah, we don't know your name.'

'I am Boran Avcı.'

'I know, we've already met,' Owain placed his Smartphone on the table and ordered a coffee from the waitress. 'You are in the Gendarmerie Intelligence and Counter-Terrorism.' Avcı's face expressed bewilderment. He began to stand up, turning to Owain with a thunderously threatening movement of his body. 'Sit down,' Owain instructed him calmly. 'Look behind you. There's a car. You'll hear the doors open shortly.'

Avcı swivelled around. Close to where he was sitting, an imposing federal police Audi A8 had just parked. The two police officers were getting out of the vehicle. They were armed. The waitress waited for them to ask if they wanted something to drink. Nodding an acceptance, they made their order and took the table next to the group of four.

'What is this?' Avcı asked furiously.

'Don't be so overbearing and Turkish,' Owain intentionally added to Avcı's rage. 'They are there at our request. We want to talk to you, but not in anger.'

Alice spoke. 'Calm down, Sir. This is a public place. It is not in your interest to be violent. We wish to apprise you of some facts. You are here to find somebody.' Alice was polite before she continued with a change in tone with strident words of command. 'Put your hands on the table and leave them there.'

Boran Avcı realised this meeting had been planned to the last detail. He wanted to kill all three. But moving to release the pistol he carried in his jacket pocket would mean an instant and forceful reaction by the police. They were watching his hands. He would be shot or arrested or both. By making such a mistake, his employer would disown him. He would be dismissed, perhaps be sentenced to aggravated life imprisonment if and when he ever returned to Turkey in such circumstances. Owain took out a round of ammunition from his pocket and placed it on the table next to Avcı. Avcı's face expressed astonishment. He lifted a hand off the table, took the round and placed it into a jacket pocket, then finished his coffee. He then asked the waitress, who had returned to give the police officers their coffee, for a replenishment. He realised that he had failed to notice that the pistol was lighter than normal. He felt foolish. He was embarrassed. Over the past twelve hours, his professionalism had been tested and was found wanting.

Owain took up the conversation. He did not allude to the events of the early hours of the morning in his room. 'You want to speak to a man that sells state secrets. We have an interest in watching the same man. There are nations other than Turkey that are watching this man. It will not help your people if you find him and,' Owain paused, 'kill him.' Boran Avcı did not like what he was being made to listen to, but knew he had put himself into a position where he had no choice.

'You can assist us,' Helen continued, 'or you can be deported. Which is it to be?' Avcı realised they meant business. 'You are spies.'

'We have a joint interest,' Alice remarked, 'to track this person and ascertain how he has obtained state secrets.' Boran Avcı began to realise that this was a more complex matter than perhaps his managers in Turkey knew, or had told him. These people were offering him a way to find out more. It did not seem as if he had to give anything in return. He was not in a position to argue. He calmed down.

'What do you want of me?' Owain gave him instructions. 'You will travel to Paris. There's an important conference about satellite technology taking place. Some of your colleagues are there. The man you want to speak to, Cocke, is already on his way. You were ordered to meet with him, and so you shall. We'll help you.' Boran Avcı wanted to admit he did not know what Cocke looked like. He did not know who he was pursuing, having been told that somebody from the Italian contract would be at the event in Belgium to identify Cocke, but they were wrong. Alice divined his dilemma. 'You do not know what he looks like, do you?'

Avcı remained silent for a while, and then admitted he did not. 'No.'

Alice swished across the screen of her device. She found his image, holding the screen towards Avcı. 'Is this sufficient?'

'Yes. It is enough for me.'

Owain continued. 'We will get in touch to tell you where he can be found in Paris.'

'You want me to tell you where I go for a hotel?'

'If you wish, but if you don't, we'll know anyway. I'll be waiting for you.'

A taxi stopped near the café. Helen turned to Alice, 'I guess that's our taxi.' Both women stood up. 'Well, it's been interesting meeting you, Mr Avcı. Before we go, one more thing about Nâzım Hikmet. You know he wrote a poem entitled 'Yaşamaya Dair'. He says that living is no joke, and that we must live with great earnestness. Perhaps you'll give those words a thought next time they ask you to undertake a deadly mission.'

'So you think you white Australian people who have killed so many aborigines are saints?' Boran Avcı sneered at the haughty moral tone Helen had adopted. The men remained seated as the women got into the taxi. Owain attracted the attention of the waitress to ask for the bill, indicating he would pay for the group and the police officers. Owain continued by commenting to Avcı. 'Many Turks distort the memory of Nâzım Hikmet.'

'He was scum.'

'He was born under the empire of the Ottomans, and he was later imprisoned for inciting the Turkish armed forces to revolt. The reason was pathetic. Military cadets were reading his epic poem *Şeyh Bedreddin Destanı*, the 'Epic of Shaykh Bedreddin'. It's about a rebellion against the Ottoman Sultan Mehmed I, yet the state hounded him. Just for words.' Boran Avcı looked contemptuously at Owain. 'Where do you come from,' he sneered, 'with your brown skin?' Owain was used to such hatred. 'I'm Welsh by my mum and I'm a citizen of the United Kingdom in her family name. I now have an Indian passport in my dad's name.' The waitress placed a plate with the bill on the table. Owain thanked her. As he took his wallet out, he continued, 'I know racism is endemic in this world. Maybe you might grow up one day.'

Avcı looked menacingly at Owain, who had stood up by now. He quickly took out a roll of euro notes and placed them on the plate before Owain had the opportunity to pay. The police officers remained seated at their table, watching. Owain was not intimidated. He looked towards the police officers. 'If you think I've arranged for the federal police to be here because you think I can't handle myself, you're wrong, as you know. You're a killer, we know that, and you're not going to be deported because you will be cooperating with us. I've got one last thing for you, just in case you decide to tell Dr Utku Köprülü about this meeting and what you will do with us in Paris.'

The information he gave was sufficiently calculated to encourage Avcı not to report this arrangement with his superior. Owain picked up his Smartphone and placed it in his pocket. He then took out Avcı's device. He flicked on to the recording of his activity with the young man late the previous afternoon. Boran Avcı had certainly missed his Smartphone and had looked carefully for it in the barn. He was astounded that this Indian should be in possession of it, and that the woman had recorded his pleasure.

'I expect it was exciting? Here. I'll see you in Paris.' Owain dropped the Smartphone on to the table. He turned to walk towards his hotel, offering one final comment before leaving. 'That is, if you perform to our satisfaction. You can't return to Turkey until you hand the weapon back to your armourer. You'll have to explain to him that you've got to keep it because you've been told to go to Paris. I'll return the rest of your ammunition in Paris.' The police officers nodded to Owain. He returned the acknowledgment. They got up from their chairs to return to the vehicle.

Owain offered a final comment as he left. 'Oh, by the way, the music you have on your device – I listened to some of it: *Türk Müziğinde 75 Büyük Bestekar* – 75 Great Composers in

Turkish Classical Music. It's really good. I'm going to buy it. I'd like to listen to more of the recording later.'

Boran Avcı realised he had seriously compromised himself for the first time on a mission. He knew what the consequences would be if the organization found out. He had no choice. He would have to follow the instructions given to him. By so doing, he persuaded himself that he might gain sufficient additional information to satisfy his superiors and avoid having them know the truth about the position he now found himself in. He intended to have his revenge against the Indian, although he grudgingly respected his final comment about Ottoman music.

In the taxi, Zhuge Xiùyīng asked Helen, 'You know Turkish?'

'Only a little bit. I had a Turkish boyfriend once. He was very romantic, but too' she hesitated. Zhuge Xiùyīng continued for her, '...too mannish, loutish, supercilious?'

'Yes. They think that 50 per cent of the population of the world is only here to satisfy men.'

*

At the end of the day, Stéphanie Beauharnais took the métro Line 1 to Les Sablons. She was meeting her fiancée before going to look at the Daniel Buren exhibition *L'observatoire de la lumière*, and have a drink before dinner on the roof terrace at Frank Gehry's iceberg. The art work covered the static sails of glass with coloured filters, turquoise, different shades of red and green, blue, orange and yellow punctuated, at equal distances from one another, by alternating white and blank stripes perpendicular to the ground.

She walked passed Le Séquoia Café and down rue d'Orléans. Jean-Frédéric Esparbès de Lussan caught sight of her as she turned the corner. He was sitting in the café, his chair facing out towards the street. He was looking at the screen of a laptop computer with Michael Cocke. Cocke sat with his back to the street. They had briefly met at the satellite convention, at Centre des Congrès in Aéroport de Paris-Orly, and had made their way separately to Avenue Charles de Gaulle to find a suitably discreet meeting place away from the hive of scientists, commercial agents and spies. Cocke did not realise that de Lussan suggested the location because he lived nearby. From the angle he was sitting, de Lussan thought he saw Stéphanie's face turn in towards the plate glass window and direct her gaze in their direction. He was agitated. He was certain she recognized him. Although Cocke noticed his attention falter, he did not ask de Lussan about his distraction, since he was anxious to leave. Cocke was not interested in his change of behaviour, because he had finished. He powered down his laptop, closed the screen, placed it into his holdall and nodded goodbye to de Lussan, leaving him to pay the bill. Seated at a discreet table a little distance away, Owain Davis closed his copy of *Le Monde Libertaire*, placed it under his right arm, put the change into the saucer to pay the bill, and discreetly followed Cocke out of the café.

Disoriented, Jean-Frédéric Esparbès de Lussan stood up, forced his left hand into his trouser suit pocket, and shifted through some euro coins to pay the bill, hastily dropping the change he identified into the saucer. He typed a telephone number into his Smartphone with the thumb of his right hand as he walked towards the door. The call was connected as he crossed the rue Charles Lafitte.

'Yeah?' A gruff male voice answered the telephone. He closed a door to shut out the noise from the buzz of machinery.

'It's Guillaume.' He spoke quietly into his device.

'Yeah.' The tone of voice expressed indifference.

'I want a hit.'

'When?'

The petitioner was adamant. 'Now.'

The voice offered a low whistle. 'Where?

'I'm following them. We're in the Boulevard des Sablons walking towards the Bois de Boulogne.'

'That's very public.'

'I want it now.'

'Wait.' The silence continued as he walked into Avenue du Mahatma Gandhi. The voice returned. 'Are you sure?'

'Yes. The target saw me with the broker.'

'That's serious. I need higher authority.'

'Then get it.'

'Wait.' This time the delay was shorter. 'All right. What do you want?'

'Dead or permanently comatose. Make it look like an accident.'

'You're lucky. I've got the best man for the job. He needs a description.'

'Height 1.77, brunette, long hair, slender, grey dress with dark grey top, handbag over shoulder, piercing blue scarf around her neck. Is that enough?'

'That'll do, but there's not enough time for an accident.' The voice continued. 'You must see where she's going. We need to relay that to our man.'

'Yes. I understand. Ah, I see now. She's entering la Fondation Louis Vuitton.'

'Stay there and let me know when she comes out.'

De Lussan was terrified. If she had seen him with Cocke, he was certain that it would not be long before François Duhamel found out. De Lussan had not been able to penetrate the people around Duhamel. Those that knew François Duhamel were intensely loyal towards him. What de Lussan did not appreciate is that although he thought he had taken care not to alert those he spoke to of his interest in what Duhamel was doing, every person he conversed with informed François. De Lussan reported to others in the *groupe pour la France*. He was not aware of precisely what his actual position was in the *groupe*, but they let him assume that he was reasonably senior. He only met high-ranking members, who were well beyond his position on the social scale, although for him, his family name was as ancient and as aristocratic as any of those he was associated with. They usually gave the impression of treating him with the respect of an equal, although the patrician condescension directed towards him was obvious when he was occasionally permitted to meet the grand men of the elite, who exuded the righteousness of authority imbued in them since birth, reinforced throughout adolescence and substantiated in adulthood. He knew that if Duhamel found out about Cocke, his actions could expose the *groupe* to the unwanted attentions of the Direction générale de la sécurité intérieure.

3

Shŏshŏujiàn

The three men sat in comfortable, overstuffed armchairs in a withdrawing room of the Cercle de l'Union interalliée, each with a cup of coffee by their side.

'Great meal, thanks François,' Bruce picked up his cup and took a sip of coffee. 'Indeed, thank you François,' Charles joined Bruce in thanking their host. 'Super lunch.'

'So, gentlemen, we hope we can finish everything tomorrow.' François began the discussion. An officer of the club interrupted him by whispering into his ear, 'Dame Katharine has arrived, Monsieur.'

'*Ah, merci*,' François raised himself out of the chair, 'Katharine has just arrived. Excuse me, I will go and meet her.' François returned with Katharine a few moments later. Charles and Bruce welcomed her. A waiter asked Katharine what she would like to drink.

'Thank you, Gérard, it is nice to see you again. A coffee is fine.'

'Yes, Madam.'

She looked around the room. 'We're fortunate. We're on our own.'

'Yes, Katharine, but it might not be for long,' François replied. 'Thank you for calling in on your way home, Katharine,' François continued, 'we've had a productive discussion,' he looked at Bruce and Charles, 'and we were wondering what your assessment of Captain Milyukov might be.'

At this moment, Gérard brought a tray with a cup and saucer of coffee, a silver sugar bowl, milk jug, and a small plate of chocolates. He placed the items on the table next to Katharine and then retired gracefully from the room. 'I'm beginning to doubt if I'm able to assess people any more,' said Katherine. 'Two women in Italy have recently unnerved me. One, in Milan, sold me an item of glass that I discovered was slightly defective after I unpacked it, and another in Genova sold me another item that was scratched – again, I discovered the damage after I unpacked it. They were both very nice, charming to speak with, and yet both of them must have known what they were doing.'

'But that must happen everywhere,' Bruce hazarded a guess.

'Yes, Bruce, I'll wager you're right, but I hate to be hood-winked. I felt stupid.'

'It's the relationship between our personal traits and the situation we find ourselves in,' Bruce continued. 'At work, we test information all the time. But when we're in different sit-uations, we're susceptible to acting foolishly. It's when we're acting this way that we become thoughtless, and fail to realise what we're doing. We all do it, but maybe you're pretty good most times, Katharine.'

'I suppose I'm tetchy most of the time, Bruce, and that's what makes it more infuriating. Anyway, to answer your ques-tion, François, Captain Milyukov is an interesting woman. It's clear from her file that she has an abiding hatred towards those who pillaged Russia in the transition. She's contemptu-ous of everyone, the Russians and the pirates who joined in with the theft-fest from the rest of the world, although she prefers to emphasise the culpability of outsiders. She has a deep antipathy to the west. She's well read in Russian literature, and has a narrow preference in music, favouring Russian composers of the nineteenth and twentieth century. It's this restricted view of the world that seems to motivate her. I'd say she's very capable, honourable, and loyal to the Russian state, and clearly highly motivated. There's one more thing, though. She's got a good grasp of technology, which I like. She made her feelings known about a rather stupid English legal presumption that I didn't know about – that computers are deemed to be reliable. Would you believe it? It's laughable. Does that accord with your assessment?' Katharine passed the plate of chocolates around.

'Yes, just about. Did you manage to find out why she was following me?' François asked.

'No, but she was clearly unnerved when she couldn't find you.'

'With the current high state of alert, we did not have enough people to monitor her. Do you know if she returned to Paris?'

'After you told me you were stretched, I decided to keep her under observation. I was informed that she caught an early train back to Paris this morning.'

'I expect she will have returned to the embassy.'

'Is that where she's based?'

'Yes. It will be easier to keep track of her movements. Thank you Katharine, it's really appreciated,' François raised his cup to take a drink of coffee before he continued. His mood had changed with the developments. He was more optimistic. 'Charles, your people have been very helpful. I've now got some excellent evidence to help me deal with our problem. I now have ample proof to arrest our suspect. I'd like to catch some of the more senior people, because they cause the nastiest damage, but I haven't got enough evidence to tackle them. The political repercussions would be catastrophic if I tried and failed because the proof wasn't good enough. Bruce's difficulty is different, as you might know, but we think there might be a common link with an outsider.'

Bruce interjected. 'Yes, we're agreed. Our dilemma might be linked to what François is wrapping up. Charles has also given me some stuff about one of his Members of Parliament. He's in Washington DC right now, and I've got him under surveillance. We'll see who he's meeting. If there's a link, we might strike it lucky.'

François looked at his watch. 'Well, I have a report to finish. I haven't got long, and my minister needs it as soon as I can get it to her.'

'Yes, time for action, François. I'd better follow up with what you and Charles have shared with me. I've gotta move fast on a few things.'

They all stood up. François led the way to the main door. Their respective chauffeurs had driven their vehicles to the club. After saying their goodbyes, Bruce and François entered their separate vehicles and were driven off. Charles and Katharine entered the car together. Charles wanted to discuss matters with Katharine as they drove to the Gare du Nord.

*

After thanking the chauffer for collecting them, Charles closed the dividing panel of glass between the driver and rear passengers.

'François is much happier now. It's a little odd, though. He didn't ask me what I thought she was doing, other than that she was following him,' Katharine observed.

'I noticed that. It could be that he knows the Russians are aware of his investigation, but now he's at the end, it doesn't matter any more. He was more concerned about finding out who was responsible for the leak.'

'Possibly. You were very quiet, Charles.'

'I probably said as much as I needed to over lunch. Bruce has an agent in Washington who is working with him. Her name is Myra Gaines. She's in the Office of Russian and European Analysis, and currently covers the UK. Bruce tells me that they are as interested in finding out about the apparent double agent as we are.'

'Why's that? Is he interested from the point of view of the United States or the Agency?'

'They've found out why the President thinks there's a British double agent. It's because there have been leaks about his financial affairs. Evidently they're very damaging. It seems as if somebody the President trusts is feeding him false leads to implicate us.'

'That's not helpful.'

'I agree. It strains the relationship.'

'There's nothing in the press about this.'

'Yet.'

'Ah, so there's a threat to let the media know.'

'Yes. It's not surprising that the President wants to find out who is responsible as soon as possible. The CIA is trying to find the source, and Bruce has given me some leads that we can follow up. They'll be with you and Margaret shortly. It will be helpful if you two can decide who will lead the team on this. I know you're both busy. We need to restrict this investigation to the small group I set up before I left London. Myra Gaines has been instructed to work closely with you and Margaret.'

'This isn't anything about a double agent, is it? It's some previously wronged businessman getting his own back.' Sir Charles turned his head to look at Katharine. 'Precisely. All we need to do is find the needle in the massive haystack of discontent.'

Katharine's face showed her cynical response. 'Yes, of the hundreds, which one?'

'Actually,' Charles continued, 'I don't think we have to look very far. He's close to being identified.'

'I'll wait for your briefing. Does François know whether the Russians have a copy of their document?'

'No, but I'd expect him to think that they did have a copy.'

'Does he know that we've got a copy of their document?'

'Not as far as I'm aware.'

'That's helpful. I presume the Russians intend to make use of the systems the French are installing.'

'Yes. So are we, but we'll wait for the Russians. We want to see how they go about it, so we can take advantage of what the data is and where it goes. We're anticipating it will also help with our cyber defences.'

'What about Bruce? It's helpful for us that there's this diversion going on about the possibility of a double agent. It's straining their resources.'

'I couldn't have organized a better false scent, and it's the President's creation. Bruce has got to get an answer about the double agent, because it's on the President's hourly agenda. We're helping him out on that one, and I'm expecting us to bag one of our own in the process. I'm anticipating we'll get more. As for the American document, Bruce didn't mention it. I expect they don't even imagine that we've got a copy. That suits us, because there are a few names on their list that are supposed to be working only for us.'

'What will we do about them?'

'We don't know if they've been double crossing us to the Americans. I'm not going to take the trouble to find out. We'll dispense with their services. None of them are essential. We've had some good stuff out of them, but we'll terminate the association. I'm forming a plan on that one. There are one or two on the list that are new to us. I'd like to see if we can get them on our side. Our people are working on that now.'

*

Colonel Zinovy Khodzhaminasov stood up when he saw Captain Alexandra Milyukov enter. He beckoned her over to his table in the café Mariage Frères at 13 rue des grands Augustins.

'Alexandra Milyukov, be pleased to meet Semyon Vorontsov,' he introduced a rotund man in his sixties dressed in a blue suit, tieless, brown shoes, with a Quai de l'Ile retrograde annual calendar watch in pink gold visible on his left wrist, the sleeve of his suit having been tailored marginally short to reveal part of the timepiece. He remained sitting as Captain Milyukov shook his hand and replied formally to him, as she did when introduced to Zinaida Volkonskaya, who likewise remained seated, also wearing an ostentatious Vacheron Constantin on her wrist.

Colonel Khodzhaminasov briefly informed Captain Milyukov that Semyon Vorontsov and his wife Zinaida Volkonskaya concentrated on ensuring the mining industry of Russia remained stable. He looked at the empty cups and plates of discarded cakes and asked Semyon Vorontsov if they had time for another tea or other drink. Semyon Vorontsov looked at his Finney Smartphone, swiped through a few links, and decided it was time for them to move on. They got up from their seats. Colonel Khodzhaminasov and Captain Milyukov rapidly stood up immediately they saw the couple begin to move. Semyon Vorontsov thanked Colonel Khodzhaminasov, using the more familiar singular. His wife kissed him on both cheeks. They departed to a waiting car.

In this brief moment, Colonel Khodzhaminasov gave Captain Milyukov a glimpse into part of his world of *sistema*: the personal loyalty, open secrets and unnamed matters that only the cognoscenti were aware.

'Now, I see it is time for something between afternoon tea

and dinner,' he smiled at her. He raised an eye to the waiter, who walked smartly over to take his order. He ordered in French. The waiter removed the debris of the previous repast and returned with a selection of *macarons* and the house champagne brut blanc de noirs. He opened the bottle, poured the wine and wished the couple well and to enjoy the experience. Colonel Khodzhaminasov raised his glass. Captain Milyukov was not quite sure how to respond to this apparent show of decadence, but raised her glass. He clinked his glass on to hers, looking into her eyes as he did so, and they drank the fizzy clear dry liquid.

'You must try these *macarons* with the champagne,' he said, 'especially the rose-flavoured ones, they are delicious together.' Captain Milyukov did as she was bid. To her surprise, the combination was enjoyable, the sweetness of the *macaron* contrasting with the austere taste of the liquid. He watched the enjoyment she encountered as her face gave away her thoughts and reaction. 'Splendid, I am glad you like it,' he was pleased that she overcame her obvious hesitancy.

'Yes, it is pleasant,' she offered, 'I did not expect to experience such a pleasing mix of tastes.'

'So you might be persuaded that this bourgeoisie pastime is to your liking?'

'Perhaps,' she admitted coquettishly.

He laughed. 'I will tell you. It was my grandmother who introduced me to it. Her grandmother had told her about her visit to Paris before the revolution, and the deliciously decadent things she had done. She always wanted to try this before she died. I owe it to her that we are sitting here enjoying this experience in Paris.'

He continued. 'You might be puzzled that I am not worried about you following the Frenchman. It was important when I briefed you, but certain developments have taken place that mean he is less important now. But first, I will tell you a little about Semyon Vorontsov and Zinaida Volkonskaya. They are acting to protect the interests of Russia, especially in bauxite. It needs to be properly controlled in the interests of the state. You are aware that the Americans are trying to make life difficult for Russian mining interests, and that our emphasis has altered in the interests of controlling the raw materials required for satellite technology? But they are also working on improving the mining of palladium. We are one of the few countries that mine it, and vehicle manufacturers across the world need the metal.'

Captain Milyukov looked around to assess the other people in the café.

'You are wondering if our conversation can be overheard?'

'Yes.'

'Maybe it is, but it is unlikely that anybody will speak Russian here.'

'We cannot rule it out.'

'Of course. But the city is full of spies at the moment because of the conference. Two more Russians sitting in a café in a remote location in Paris are hardly likely to attract the attention of the French. They have the bomb incident to deal with.' He observed her closely as he spoke. 'But in deference to your caution, let us enjoy this moment together. Tell me what you like about Paris.'

Leaving a few *macarons* and some of the wine, Colonel Khodzhaminasov paid the bill. He placed thirty euros in the dish as a tip. Alexandra Milyukov knew that even on the colonel's salary, paying for the afternoon tea and their champagne and *macarons*, agreeable as it was, meant he spent a meaningful amount of his monthly income. The tip, unnecessary as it was because of the *service compris,* made the experience even more painful for him. He noticed her eyes. He understood her thoughts. 'We ordinary people have a problem with the oligarchs,' he offered as an explanation, 'they throw money around, and if the rest of us don't do the same, we are disparaged. Semyon Vorontsov visits this café regularly, so I have to be careful.' They walked out of the café, the waiter holding the door open and thanking them as they left.

'Come with me, let us be *flâneurs*. We will walk the streets of Paris. Where are your lodgings?'

Alexandra Milyukov explained she was renting a one-bedroom flat on the fourth floor in a 1970s building on the rue Claude Terrasse.

'Near the embassy? That's convenient. What are your plans for an evening meal?' he looked at her closely. She liked his company. He was very considerate, but he could be impetuous. She recognized he had the usual male tendency to dominate, and thought he probably always got what he wanted. She knew he wanted to get her into a private space. She was unsure. He was her senior, and she did not want intimacy at so early a stage in what appeared to be a blossoming relationship. Reading this in her face, he understood her hesitant silence. 'Let us gather some food on our way. I will cook for you tonight. As we walk, you can tell me what you know about Claude Terrasse. The street must be named after somebody famous.'

She explained that she had discovered that he was a French composer of operettas, who lived between 1867 and 1923. Apparently his brother-in-law was the painter Pierre Bonnard. That was about all she found out. He insisted on buying the raw ingredients for a simple quick meal. She admitted to liking steak. He shopped: a mixed salad, olive oil on finding she had none, cheese and a delicate pastry to finish, and a bottle of red table wine.

She was embarrassed that she had not tidied up after returning from Avignon. There was sufficient wall space for decoration in the living area. He nodded to the reproduction hanging on the wall. He admired the landscape by Boris Fedorovich Borzin from the realism school of Soviet art. 'Borzin was Ukrainian. He died just as the Soviet system collapsed. I don't like all of his work, but this is good.'

He insisted on preparing the meal while she went about making her flat respectable, after which she watched the rhythm of preparation and cooking, helping when he permitted. His actions, deft and well practised – precise when peeling and cutting the potatoes, then lightly boiled, dried and sautéed to perfection. He asked her to open and pour the wine as he thinly sliced the truffle and lay the slices in a warmed pan as the shallots melted in the butter and olive oil before adding a little of the cooking water for want of stock, finally spooning in the cognac and quickly setting light to it. Once the steak was cooked to his satisfaction, he placed the meat over the layer of truffle slices, covered it and let it rest for five minutes, turning it once. He then finished the cognac shallot reduction by slowly adding more butter, incorporating the addition until the sauce was slightly thickened.

Before plating up, Alexandra gave him one of the glasses of wine she had poured. They touched glasses, 'за здоровье,' to your health. He adjusted and dimmed the light. They sat at the small bar looking into the minute kitchen as they took pleasure in the food and wine.

'You enjoy cooking.'

'Yes, but this was simple. The most important thing was to make sure the steak was not overcooked. It's good?'

'Yes, just how I like it, thank you. Such quality. The truffle goes so well. Helping you reminded me of happy days at home with my parents.'

'My father owned a restaurant. I spent many hours working in the kitchen as a child and young man. Washing up, preparing, making sauces, learning to make pastry.' His tone was of the past. 'But...' he began. She interrupted.

'Then he had *reiderstvo*?'

'Yes, by a criminal gang. They took over his business by threatening violence. He'd seen others give up after they were beaten up. He decided his family was more important.'

Having finished his steak, he put his knife and fork down. He filled their glasses. Her question reminded him of an unpleasant time of his life. He began to explain that, as a young man, he had witnessed the rampant chaos inflicted on the country by the failure of the previous Soviet leadership, the American reaction, and rapacious western businessmen. She interrupted. 'I am sorry, I didn't mean to be inquisitive about your private world.'

'No, no, that's all right,' he answered. 'Can I call you Sasha?'

'Yes, of course.' This time she wanted him to be less formal, but before he could respond, she took over. By opening the topic, he caused her to reveal her thoughts. She told him of her loathing of those that took advantage of their country in their hour of need, moving out of a command economy into capitalism. Of economists who were inflexible, unbending until the brittleness of their ideas were shattered like cast iron when put under inappropriate stress, and the arrogant men who liked to think they were good at business, but all they did was steal the future, buying up state coupons from poor people ignorant of the ways and means of what they call private enterprise in the mid-1990s, and selling them at a massive profit shortly after. Deluding themselves, in their privately-paid public school Oxbridge Ivy League style, that what they had done illustrated how good they were as business people. She ended this release of emotion with a final expression of loathing. 'They are contemptuous. They are beasts. We will have our revenge.'

He sat in silence throughout her fiery outpouring. He knew she had passion. He liked her for this. He also realised she was not afraid of telling him not to do something. This woman was his. He wanted her. He knew at this moment that he had met the woman he wanted to share his life with. He poured the last of the wine between their glasses. 'You took the words from me. Your family had a similar experience?' He asked the question, not expecting or needing a reply.

'My father died. He was young. His father, my grandfather, his medals and hardships in the war – he felt they were for nothing.'

'Yes, my father died too. My mother could not deal with the new rules. She also died young.'

He took one of her hands in his. He kissed it. They sat in silence. She took her hand away to take a tissue from the side and wiped the tears. He reached over to hold the back of her head. Without asking, he kissed her. She felt compassion in his hands and mouth. She folded her arms around his shoulders, stroking his back and biceps through his shirt. Their tongues penetrated their bodies, their innermost emotions, and the depths of their being. His body wanted more, so much more, to feel the weight of her body as she lay on him, to caress her back, but this was the wrong time. The kiss ended. He held both her hands. Each knew they were going to be together. Mutual attraction strengthened by bonds of bitter memories. He looked at his watch. 'It's late. I had better go.' She did not stop him. She wanted to have more than just a kiss, but as an equal, as a partner and lover. She recovered her poise. 'This afternoon and evening has been a delightful interlude.'

'Yes, thank you. It has been wonderful. You have been so kind.' She accompanied him to the ground floor. He returned to the voice of authority. 'We will meet tomorrow at the embassy.'

*

A junior official took Major Zhuge Xiùyīng through the corridor and out on to the pale paving stone surround of the Hôtel Montesquiou. Serving as the Chancellery of the Embassy of the People's Republic of China, it was designed by Alexandre-Théodore Brongniart, who survived the revolution and was later chosen by Napoléon Ier to design the Bourse de Paris. Having entered through the black reinforced doors set in the plain sandstone setts of the building facing the rue Monsieur, she was surprised by the revelation of the restored neoclassical building.

She was ushered into a room on the first floor. Major General Xiang Jiangyu, the defence attaché, sat at her desk, the window behind her. As the door opened and she entered, Colonel Commandant Xú Delun turned from looking out of the window. Major General Xiang Jiangyu removed her black-framed Lindberg spectacles, placed them carefully upside down on her desk, stood up and moved her chair back. Mid-height, she was the tallest in the room. Her black hair cut short, no make-up, a smart black two-piece suit adorned her body, her feet occupying a pair of plain flat black shoes of the highest quality. The collar of a white blouse lay over her jacket. She wore a single strand of modest sized freshwater peach pearls.

Colonel Commandant Xú Delun, wearing a dark suit with a sombre tie, effected the introduction. 'Major General Xiang Jiangyu, may I introduce you to Major Zhuge Xiùyīng.' The women shook hands. Major General Xiang Jiangyu bid them join her to sit in the informal part of the office. They sat around a low table and chairs especially designed for the embassy by Derek Chen. Three waiters entered, each with a tray upon which sat a tea cup and a Yixing Zisha *guang qi* tea pot. They were placed before the Major General, who set about placing quantities of White Hair Silver Needle tea into each of the three pots, and added the prepared water given to her by one of the waiters. One waiter stood by as she finished, and, at her nod, passed over an individual tray each to the Colonel and Major. This was conducted in silence.

Major General Xiang Jiangyu initiated the conversation once the waiter left the room. 'I am told you were very brave in Brussels,' she addressed Major Zhuge Xiùyīng. Zhuge Xiùyīng responded, using formal language in addressing a lady of such high rank. 'An unfortunate event occurred that caused me to fail to carry out my mission successfully, Madam.'

'So I have been informed. You recovered well in London. General Yuan Ah tells us that you have an eye for fine art. Colonel Commandant Xú Delun has also discovered your interest.'

'Thank you, Madam. The painters of Europe are interesting to compare to our Chinese heritage.'

'Comparison is interesting, but it is important to appreciate the aesthetic beauty of the art in its own right.'

'I agree, Madam. This building is also to be appreciated.'

'Yes. Both the architect and the person he designed it for survived the revolution. It was built for Anne-Pierre de Montesquiou-Fezensac, the marquis de Montesquiou. After the Third Estate declared itself as the National Assembly, a number of nobles led by Louis Philippe II, Duke of Orléans, including the marquis, joined them on 25 June 1789. He was a close supporter of the Duke, so it was not surprising he followed Louis. However, Louis Philippe did not fare so well. His son followed General Dumouriez, who intended to visit the enemy. Although the Duke was not involved, he was guillotined because of the association with his son. Interestingly, both Dumouriez and the Duke's son survived.'

'There is a lesson for children to learn, Madam.'

'Indeed there is, and for parents of over-zealous children also to take note.' Silence followed. Major General Xiang Jiangyu did not need to explain her meaning. She continued.

'We are here because there has been a serious development. It has caused Colonel Commandant Xú Delun to visit us. I will leave it to him to indicate the problem we now face.'

Colonel Commandant Xú Delun thanked the General. 'A delicate matter has come to our attention. The operating system of our leading telecoms provider is very useful to us. The British have adopted our technology, and we enjoy – shall we say – helpful access to British secrets. Not all secrets, of course, but sufficient to help us. It has provided us with a significant amount of information we would otherwise have had difficulty in obtaining by conventional means.' The Colonel raised his tea cup and took a sip. He continued. 'But we have noticed something of concern. The British system seems to have been closed to us. Our normal sources of data have stopped.'

Major Zhuge Xiùyīng took the opportunity to interject. 'May I ask, Sir?'

'Of course.'

'When did this occur Sir?'

'This week.'

'May I ask another question, Sir?'

'Please.'

'Are any of our officers in the UK at risk?'

'Not as far as we know. They are on alert, although I do not expect the British to carry out any sudden action. The head of MI6 is here, in Paris. It is rare for him to be out of his country at this time of the year. The satellite conference cannot interest him. They have as many spies covering it as any other nation. We are beginning to have a suspicion that one of our own operating companies has breached security.'

Major General Jiangyu spoke at the moment the Colonel came to a natural pause. 'There might be a double agent working for a foreign power.' Each took up their tea cups and enjoyed a drink of tea. The Colonel continued. 'The man you identified in Singapore – the Australians are no longer interested in him. You know the Australian officer has returned to her country?'

Major Zhuge Xiùyīng knew the answer to this statement, posed in the form of a question. 'Yes, Sir. I understand she was promoted.'

'You are correct. She will be acting as a liaison officer for a joint project with the Indian government. We are viewing that carefully.'

Major General Jiangyu took up the conversation. 'The man in Singapore is now here, in Paris.'

'Yes, Madam, I understand.'

'He does not appear to be working for any country. It seems as if he obtains secrets and sells them.' She turned to the Colonel to continue. 'He has been active in Paris. He identified an over-zealous employee of a Chinese software company that does a lot of sub-contracting for one of our biggest and most important information technology companies. This person fell for the trap and let him insert a USB into his laptop.'

'Ah.'

'We do not know whether or not it will prove to be dangerous. The company is aware that a root kit tried to establish itself into the operating system.'

'Do we know if it succeeded, Sir?'

'Perhaps. It has been useful for us to be made aware of the exploit used by this man Cocke. It is now under control.'

The Major General asked a question. 'The British are watching this man?'

'Yes, Madam.'

'You know the British agent?'

'Yes, Madam, but I do not have his contact details.'

'The man Cocke – we understand he has infected other computers.'

'Yes, Madam. He wanted to insert a USB into the Australian officer's laptop in Singapore. She was very clever. She told him it was against security, but suggested to him that he send her an email, which he did. She clicked on the email after he left her. The email contained a payload. This allowed the Australians to monitor how he used the computer.'

The Colonel took the opportunity to provide Major General Jiangyu with the background information he had not had the time to give her earlier. 'The Australians were working closely with the British on what appeared to be a leak. The emphasis has changed for the Australians. We are assuming that the British have found a way of monitoring his cyber activities. If the actions of our stupid contractor gave Cocke sufficient time to download data stored on his laptop before the exploit was found and disabled, it is possible that the British also have this data.'

'That would be very serious, Sir.'

'Yes, Major, you are correct.'

'May I ask, Madam, was the laptop clean? Do we know if it had any data on it?'

'That is a good question, Major. The person lives in France. This means the rules for visiting foreign countries do not apply. The other problem is that it is difficult to impose security on impulsive people that we do not have a direct relationship with.'

'So it is assumed there was data on the device?'

'Yes, and it is possible that there was sufficient time between the root kit initiating and the time it was neutralized for a complete transfer to take place.'

'And twenty-four hours later, we lost our link to the British,' the Colonel informed Major Zhuge Xiùyīng as he filled his tea cup.

'So we are assuming the British have neutralized our back door, Sir?'

'Yes. The laptop is with our people at present. They are analysing it now. We need to establish the extent of the data stored on the laptop and what, if any, was leaked.'

Major General Jiangyu took up the thread. 'The employee had security clearance for technical documents that are very sensitive. Until now, our man has been very useful. Over the last year he has obtained documents from the Russians and Japanese about their quantum computing projects. This has been very valuable for our work in this area.'

'It will be embarrassing for us if either country becomes aware of this, Madam.'

'You are correct. However, it is our opinion that if Cocke has the data, if there was any, he will try to sell it.' The Colonel continued. 'This means that if there was secret or sensitive information on the laptop, and it is in British hands, it is expected that they will only use it themselves. The danger is if Cocke also has the data, and he finds a willing buyer.'

'The Turkish and the Americans will be interested in buying the data, Sir.'

'We agree with you, although he does not appear to work for, or sell to, the British. Our aim now is to gain possession of his laptop, find out where his permanent base is, then seize all of his equipment.'

Major Zhuge Xiùyīng asked. 'Do we know where his permanent home is, Sir?'

'No. We are working on that.'

'May I ask another question, Madam?'

'Of course.'

'What is to be done with Cocke?'

'He is to be eliminated. Our specialist officers have been briefed. Your task is to work with them to get hold of all of the equipment he has in his possession here in Paris.'

'Yes, Madam.'

Colonel Commandant Xú Delun stood up. 'I will take you to meet those you will be working with.'

Major General Jiangyu and Major Zhuge Xiùyīng also rose from their chairs. Major Zhuge Xiùyīng thanked Major General Jiangyu for the tea. They shook hands. As she led the way to open the door, Major General Jiangyu addressed Major Zhuge Xiùyīng. 'When this is finished, you must come with me to visit the Louvre. It is very big, so it is best to identify one aspect of the museum and enjoy it without exhausting yourself and seeing everything and nothing.'

'Thank you, Madam, I will be guided by you. It will be very exciting to visit such an important art collection.'

Colonel Commandant Xú Delun escorted Major Xiùyīng to the entrance. 'Excuse me, Sir, but may I make an observation?'

'Yes, as you wish.'

'The Embassy was owned by the French State?'

'Yes, they sold it in 2008 to some Russian investors. Maybe we might call them speculators. China bought it in 2012.'

'Do you think, Sir, that the Russians might have planted surveillance devices in the fabric before selling it?'

'Our security people thought of that, Major.'

'Very good, Sir. Thank you, Sir.'

*

'Great to see you, Reg.' Selby S. Pennewill stood up from his chair, his mane of greying hair swept back against the tall forehead, his bright blue eyes looking directly into the gaze of the waitress as she led the slightly portly Reginald Winterbottom with his slick black thinning short cut hair into the cool comfortable John Carroll room in 1789 restaurant at 1226 36th St NW, Washington DC. They shook hands. Selby smiled and nodded to the waitress, to whom he had given a $50 tip when he arrived. She retired after filling Reginald Winterbottom's water glass. Both men wore casual jackets and trousers, white shirts and single colour ties.

'Good to see you, too, Selby.'

'Are you over on official business Reg?'

'No, not this time. It's a private trip. But to be blunt, there's something I'd like your help with, if you can.'

'Sure, Reg. We go back a long way. Hey, do you remember when we got into those North Sea deals? We were late, but we got some good money out of the rush to get in there.' At this point, the waitress returned, carrying a tray with two vintage champagne glasses. 'Excuse me, Mr Pennewill, Sir. Two glasses of champagne Brut Réserve by Billecart-Salmon, as you requested. Please enjoy, Sir. The manager asked me to tell you these are on the house, Sir.'

'Well thank you, Susan. Please pass on our thanks, and we'll call in to see the chef as always.'

'Sure Sir, Mr Pennewill. Shall I give you some time to decide what to order? Chef said to let you know she's worked on a special three course for you once she knew you'd booked.'

'What can I say? Reg, are you up for it?'

'I am indeed, Selby. It's always good to eat here at 1789.'

'Then we'll go for the special, Susan.'

'And Mr Kaufman has picked some wines to accompany the different courses by the glass if you'd like, Sir.' The men exchanged glances. 'It's a done deal, Susan, we're in for it.'

'Thank you Mr Pennewill, I'll let chef know.' The waitress left.

Reginald Winterbottom returned to the memory. 'Yes, those were the days, Selby. We were on the frontier then. The government even discarded health and safety, all in the name of experiment. It was worth it.'

'Yeah, great times. You know, I'm slowing down, Reg. I've now got some good people I can trust to run the business.'

Reginald Winterbottom decided to raise the double agent problem immediately. He wanted to get the business over before they talked about money and opportunities. 'We've got a little problem over in London, Selby.'

'OK. Anything I can do to help?'

'You might be able to. But this is on the q.t. Secret. Very strictly secret. I can't afford for this to be revealed.'

'Sure, Reg. You bet.'

'Thanks, Selby. I knew I could trust you. It's very sensitive. Here's the outline. Your ambassador in London tells us that the President thinks there's a British spy acting as a double agent.'

'OK. That could be bad.'

'Yes, it isn't good. We're going over our own people. The President thinks we're leaking details of his financial affairs, although they're not pretty if you ask too many questions.'

'I don't have any time for that double dealing – I'd like to use an expletive, but I won't. Adjectives like exceptionally shabby, unpleasant, worthless, and seedy creature only just begin to indicate my contempt for the man.'

'I know, Selby. I'm with you on that one after he stitched you up.'

'Yes, I don't forget.'

'Nor do I. We've had some great times together, and I did all I could to help you out on that one.'

'You sure did. I'll never forget that, Reg. Together, we can get through adversity. I lost one hundred million bucks thanks to that son of a bitch.'

The waitress arrived with the first course, a foie gras torchon.

'This looks real good, Susan.'

'Thank you, Sir. Let me pour your wine.' The waitress had previously placed a bottle of sauternes into an ice bucket adjacent to their table. She removed the cap, placed and turned the corkscrew neatly into the cork, withdrawing it with one clean smart professional action. 'This is a 2001 Château Rieussec premier Cru, Mr Pennewill. Mr Parker and Mr Martin disagree with their views on this wine, Sir.' She poured a small amount into each glass. As both men swirled the wine and sniffed it, Susan continued, 'Our sommelier takes the view that this is a well balanced wine that will go perfectly with your starter, and hopes you will agree.' Each man lifted their glass to taste the rich golden liquid.

'Susan, please tell Richard that his choice is perfect for me. That is liquid gold of the finest. What do you think, Reg?'

'Superb, Selby, just superb.'

'Thank you Susan.' The waitress retired, asking them to 'enjoy' as she walked from the table. Selby took up the conversation.

'You know, Reg, I've always wanted to get even with what he did to me.'

'I know. I'd want the same.'

'Thank you for that, Reg. I really appreciate you telling me how you feel. Look, there's a problem. This is only between us, right?'

'Right, as I said, strictly between us.'

'No CIA, no MI6?'

'Neither, just the two of us.'

'OK. I'm the one getting his finances leaked out there.'

Reginald Winterbottom looked stunned. Then his face relaxed. He smiled. 'I've got to hand it to you, Selby.'

'Thanks, Reg. But don't you go thinking I'm making it appear as if it's the Brits. No Sir, no way. It's news to me that he thinks it's the Brits doing it.'

'Well, Selby, thanks for sharing that with me. It's appreciated. I can see the problem. Somebody might be influencing him.'

'That might just be the case. You know what he's like.'

'This is the problem then. He's getting his come-uppance for swindling you. Too right. But somehow he's blaming it on us. You've got the leaks under control?'

'Yes, Reg. It's highly circumspect, very careful. I want to attract the attention of the justice department in the hope they might follow it up.'

'That could work.'

'I'm banking on it.'

'It narrows down where we need to look to discover why he thinks it's us.'

'Yeah, I see that. How's your pet boy? He's found some great stuff. He's helped me out a lot.'

'My runner from the *capite censi*? Yes, he's good. I'm glad he's been of use to you. Did you see him when he came over last month?'

'I did. He's got the cutest of lips. So docile. He's the best you've found in a long time. And so good looking.'

'Yes, I've managed to link him up to a girl. It'll be good cover.'

'Oh? What's he say about that?'

'It's too good an opportunity for him. Marrying into two classes above his station in life. I'll also be able to keep control of him.'

'Will I be able to see him in the future?'

'Oh yes, don't worry about that. She keeps him on a tight rein. He's overwhelmed by the elevation. He'll be even more obedient when they're married.'

Selby S. Pennewill changed the subject. 'And how's that new tea lady of yours? I bet she's sweet in bed.'

'I've brought her over on this trip. She's just perfect. Does everything. Just what a man needs.'

At the end of the meal, Reginald Winterbottom thanked his host. 'That was a very good meal, Selby, as always. Thanks for that.'

'My pleasure, Reg. It's always good to spend time with you. Look, on the problem you've got, let me find out where he gets the idea of a double agent from.'

'That'd be great, Selby. We need to get to the bottom of this for internal party reasons, and quickly. Things are looking shaky right now.'

'Sure, Reg.'

*

Margaret Edmonstone and Dame Katharine Neville sat together in a small meeting and conference room in one of the outer offices facing the main building at GCHQ in Cheltenham. The screen was switched on. Margaret Edmonstone accepted the request to connect. The face of Myra Gains appeared, sitting at a desk on her own in a similar room in Washington DC.

'Hi, I'm Myra Gaines. Mr Waller asked me to reach out to you.'

'Hello, Myra, yes, we were expecting you. I'm Margaret Edmonstone, and next to me is Katharine Neville. Katharine knows Bruce very well, as you probably know. Thank you for suggesting we speak now. It happens to be a good time for us because we're in the same office today. How are you?'

'I'm good, thank you.' Margaret and Katharine both grimaced slightly at the response that Myra was 'good'.

Myra noticed their reaction and carried on quickly. 'Where shall I begin?' Myra looked at a sheaf of papers placed before her on the desk.

Margaret continued. 'If you can bring us up to date with reports from Bruce, that will be a good start.'

'OK, thanks. We've been following your MP. He's with a man named Selby S. Pennewill. They're having lunch at the moment. We think they'll be there some time. They're regulars at the restaurant when your MP is in town.'

Margaret and Katharine looked at the clock. It was two o'clock in the afternoon in Washington DC. 'Thank you, Myra, that's helpful.'

'Mr Pennewill is a well-known businessman who runs a lobbying company here in DC. His clients are mainly in energy, and he's beginning to pursue eco-friendly energy companies. Both he and your MP were in the oil industry together in the 1980s and 1990s.'

Katharine retorted quickly, a little sharply. 'Yes, we know they know each other well.' She immediately altered her tone somewhat by asking a more subtle question, with the intention of eliciting more information than Myra was authorized to provide. 'Do you know if they might have a purpose for this particular visit? How long have they been eating?'

Myra was slightly taken aback with the direct questioning. 'Well, Dame Neville, they've been in the restaurant since 12.30.' Bruce had ensured that Myra knew of Katharine's title.

'That means they must be leaving soon. Do you have an agent in the building or are you listening in to their conversation remotely?' Myra was not sure if she should answer the question, but Katherine's forceful personality and direct approach was such that she admitted they were recording the discussion.

'Good. Can you send us the recording?'

'Yes Ma'am, of course Ma'am.' Myra was not sure if this was permitted. She had the technical ability to send it.

'Thank you. While we wait, do we know what the purpose of the visit might be?' Margaret took advantage of Myra's mild sense of anxiety about the material she could share. Margaret and Katharine wanted to gather the porous information, the noise – the details that, on their own might not mean much, but with knowledge of other facts, had the ability to provide a more rounded understanding of the unexplained.

Myra reminded herself that Bruce had asked her to be as cooperative as possible. The limit was not to share material denoted as US eyes only. 'We think your MP is looking to work with Mr Pennewill.'

'Thank you, that's interesting. We'll be frank, Myra,' Margaret ameliorated the tone of her voice to a hushed complicity. 'Is there a young man with them? Good looking, blond hair, tall, slim with a good physique? His name is Nigel Taylor.'

'No, Ma'am. We scrutinize Mr Taylor's movements when he's in DC because he seems sometimes to have access to information that we think is confidential, but we've never found him to have violated any law.' To Margaret's delight, Myra provided more than she was expecting.

Katharine continued the topic. 'He spends time with Mr Pennewill when he's in DC.'

'Yes, Ma'am. They seem to be...' she did not finish her sentence.

'Lovers, yes. We think so too. That means they're susceptible to being compromised.'

'Yes, Ma'am, that's our assessment. But we don't think they're a high risk, given they're not connected to any strategically important industries.'

'That's possible,' Margaret purposely did not ask about the woman that travelled with Reginald Winterbottom.

After terminating the call, Myra went for a coffee. She returned to the office and sat in her booth. It was late afternoon in Europe.

'Hi, Mr Waller.'

'Hi, Myra, how's it going?'

'Fine, Sir. Is it OK to ring?'

'That's all right, Myra, you just fire away.' Myra briefly told him about her conversation with Margaret and Katharine. Bruce noted her voice was taut, exhibiting signs of stress. She explained that she might have given out more information than she ought. She wanted reassurance. 'OK, Myra, thanks for the debrief. Giving them the recording of the conversation was not the best of things to do, but we're on a buddy system this time, and anything we can do to help them, they'll reciprocate, so don't worry about that one.'

'Thank you, Sir, I appreciate your feedback.'

'Don't be too anxious any more, Myra. You've had a masterclass from two of the best women in the business. Don't forget, they're on our side. Learn from this, Myra, and you'll feel much better.'

Margaret and Katharine made an afternoon tea and returned to Margaret's office.

'That was useful.'

'Yes, it was, Margaret. She gave us more than she ought, but I'm sure Bruce will be relaxed. We need the recording of their conversation. It'll tell us why the Minister is with Pennewill.'

'Agreed. Have we got anything on the tea lady and who she's meeting yet?'

'I briefed Washington. I'm waiting to see what they report back.'

*

Jacques de Lalaing was waiting for Stéphanie inside the vast height of the sky and white hall inside the gallery. On meeting, they held hands and kissed twice on each cheek. They anticipated experiencing the shapes, colours and falling light of the installation inside the excitement of the building. After relishing the unexpected juxtaposition of light and shade

244

against form, Jacques surprised Stéphanie. He had booked Le Frank for a dinner high above the gardens, surrounded overhead by floating fish. He wanted them to have a meal by Jean-Louis Nomicos.

At the finish, the waitress brought coffee and a selection of *mignardise* to their table before placing a small box, tied with a ribbon in Bachelor Carnation next to Stéphanie with a smile. Stéphanie was intrigued. Jacques suggested she investigate to satisfy her curiosity. She pulled the bow and lifted the lid to reveal a smaller, slightly worn box inside. She exclaimed 'Oh!' after picking it up and opening the lid. Inside was a ring by Pierre Sterlé, sporting a white diamond set in yellow gold, surrounded by twelve smaller diamonds, each placed in a tear-shaped setting, the entire ensemble encircled by a twisted rope of yellow gold, in turn buttressed by irregular lengths of gold carefully made in the form of a stocking stitch, expanding out of the ring as if they were a sunburst of brilliance from the centre. She quickly moved from where she was sitting and onto his lap, and wrapped her arms around his neck as they kissed. Those nearest to them looked unobtrusively and gave muted shrieks of delight as they watched the couple. Stéphanie made him put it on her finger.

'It's beautiful. How romantic.'

'Will you marry me?' He asked with delight in his eyes, a broad smile on his rugged face.

'Oh, Jacques, of course I will. And will you marry me?'

'If you will have me, my darling.'

He later explained that his grandmother had asked him when he was going to propose to her. She insisted he have the ring, the engagement ring her late husband had given to her. She stipulated that Stéphanie should be the next recipient. She wanted the couple to share the romance that she had shared with her husband throughout their life together. A token of love was now passed to the future generation.

Jean-Frédéric Esparbès de Lussan waited. He received a call.

'He's ready.'

'Thanks. She's still in there.'

'Find out what's happening and ring back.' Reluctantly, de Lussan went into the building. Eventually, he established she was with somebody in the restaurant. 'She's with a man. They're having dinner.' A voice of harsh authority spoke. 'All right. We'll take over from here.' It was not to de Lussan's liking that he was spoken to in such a way.

Dismissed, de Lussan retraced his steps to the rue Deleau, opened the main door into the double width block of flats on the corner with rue Jacques Dulud, walked in and climbed the stairs to the fourth floor. He entered his flat. When he reached the main room they pounced, quickly dispatching him, discarding his lifeless body on the oak parquet floor.

*

'Hi Bruce, nice to see you again,' the Chief of Station in Paris, Juliate E. Page, said as Bruce entered the office, 'we sure do appreciate you coming in, seeing how busy you are right now.'

'That's no problem, Miss Page, we have to work together on this, and it's a pleasure to work with you.' Bruce had briefly met the Chief's mother before she retired, and knew her daughter wanted to continue to be referred as 'Miss', as her mother had always insisted on being addressed.

'It's late. Too late for a coffee. How about a beer?' The Chief had closed the white plastic venetian blinds. The window faced the interior courtyard of the embassy. The LED light of the NJP table lamp shone a gentle diffused glow over a table of files and papers. A blank computer screen was pushed to one side. 'Well, I don't drink on duty, and I know you don't, either, Miss Page, but it's past nine, and as we've both been working all day as if there's no tomorrow...'

The Chief interrupted him at this point, 'Good, Bruce. It's a beer then.' She pressed the intercom. 'Peter, can we have three beers please?' Peter's voice rang clearly over the wires. 'Yes, Miss Page, coming up. The ambassador has just arrived.'

'OK, ask him to come right on in. And you have a beer as well.'

'Yes, Miss Page, thank you.'

The Chief walked around her desk to open the door to welcome the ambassador. The tall, thin imposing and distinguished Tyler J. Longstreet had just entered the anteroom as the Chief opened the door.

'Thanks for coming, Sir.'

'No problem, Juliate. I've managed to tie up the loose ends I had to deal with.'

'Mr Ambassador, have you met Bruce Waller?' The two men shook hands firmly. 'Sure have, Juliate. Hi there, Bruce, nice to see you in Paris. Bart told me you were over on a delicate mission.'

'Nice to see you, Sir. Yes, it's sensitive, Sir. Paris must be great fun for you and your wife, Sir.' The Chief of Station beckoned them both to sit down at the small conference table.

'It is, Bruce. My wife is thoroughly enjoying it, now the children have left home and it's just the two of us and being retired.'

There was a knock on the door. 'Enter,' the Chief called out, and Peter, in a white shirt, dark blue tie and dark blue trousers entered the room bearing a tray with a dish of potato chips, three glasses and three bottles of Murica, an Indian pale ale. 'Mr Ambassador, I thought you'd like to join us for a beer at the end of the day. Your security told me that you had no more engagements after our meeting.'

'Thank you, Juliate, I will. We all need to wind down.'

Peter left the room and quietly closed the door.

'That's a nice beer, thank you Juliate. Are you ready to

bring Bruce up to date with the events we've been told about in the last few hours?'

'Yes, Sir,' at which Juliate E. Page opened a brown leather writing journal notebook at a page marked by a silk yellow bookmark. 'OK, Bruce, we've had a new development on the intelligence that was illegally downloaded. The report dealing with our assessment of the Russian jamming devices is what the Russians would expect us to have prepared. They'll probably have something similar about our abilities in this field. But it's the list of our sleeper agents in Russia that's really serious.'

'Yes, it is. Bart started on that right away.'

'He did, although we've decided to go slow on it so as not to alert the Russians. We've got a hunch that they're not the ones that obtained the document because there's not been any movement from them.'

The ambassador took up the conversation. 'That's right, Juliate, but as we know, they could be waiting to see what our reaction is, and to round up our sleepers and friends once they've got evidence we're approaching them.'

'Yes, Sir, correct. But we've got another problem, Bruce. You weren't told about this in DC, and we're imparting this information to you now on the strict understanding that it doesn't go any further without authorization.'

'Sure, Miss Page.'

'That's all right, Bruce. Call me Juliate.'

'Why, thanks for that, Juliate.'

'You're welcome. Now this is it. We had a whole load of stuff taken. The list is embarrassing. It includes plans of the F-35D, the Patriot missile system, and our plans for anti-satellite weapon systems. Some of our most secret military bases have also been exposed on satellite maps.'

'Phew.' Bruce groaned.

'You've said it. If the countries we sell to get hold of this, we're in it deep.'

'It's a gold mine.'

'Yeah, but at least our guys have established how the attack occurred. First, what the attacker got wasn't all in the same place. But that doesn't help us. We know the biggest problem has always been the way the Department of Defense is made to operate. It's a complex bureaucracy, and it's never had the full complement of employees that are necessary to undertake the role. This means they have to employ contractors, and they aren't always controlled properly. We've discovered that whoever it was penetrated into a number of different databases. They used the same method, and made their way into one after another in quick succession.'

Bruce interrupted. 'Say, Juliate, that means that whoever did this was pretty good and had a whole bunch of technical knowledge.'

'Yes Bruce. They also had a whole load of passwords as well.'

'Gee. Was this state-sponsored or a loner?'

'We don't know. Our people traced the one attack they knew about to Paris. We followed the evidence up locally, but we had no luck. The device connected an hour or so ago for a short time, likely to connect for email. This time it's in Amman in Jordan.'

'Oh my.'

'Yeah, you've got it.'

'That might be serious.'

'Very serious. We've got agents on the ground there, but they've got to tread carefully. The US is *persona non grata* in the region. We haven't got the best of relationships out there right now.'

'Do we know who's behind the device?'

'We do,' Tyler Longstreet joined the discussion, 'it's a member of the royal family. He's a professor of computer science at Cambridge University in England. He's rich and very well connected. He's intelligent, with a world reputation for his work on crypto systems.'

'From what you describe, Sir, he's not the sort to be breaking into sensitive US databases.'

'We agree with you, Bruce,' the ambassador continued, 'our guys have traced it to a university computer that isn't well protected for some reason. We figure it might be a loan device, and he was just given it to use when he was travelling.' The Chief took up the thread. 'He and his department are working on a project with a sub contractor and a US university for the anti-satellite weapon systems. If our enemies get hold of this document, they'll have a good idea on what we're planning.' The ambassador picked the conversation up again. 'And to make matters worse, we lost a load of stuff that shows what we're doing in Saudi Arabia and the United Arab Emirates, and how we're working with Israel.'

'That's a toxic mix, Sir.'

'Sure is, Bruce.'

'So this is where we hope you can help, Bruce,' the Chief began to air her thoughts after taking a drink of beer. 'You're a great buddy with the head of MI6.'

'We go back a long way, Juliate.'

'You do. Over the years, you've done some great work with him and that French agent you know. The Agency has appreciated that personal touch. It's been very effective.'

'Yes, we operate on the basis that we'll help out as much as we can, and sometimes we'll stretch the rules, but the understanding is that our individual national interests always come first.'

'It's worked.'

'Yes.'

'OK, here's the request. We've not got any evidence that this professor knows that his device has been used. That could be because it's a university computer and he hasn't got anything on it that's secret or sensitive. That's our premise. We're assuming he's totally innocent. We need to get our hands on it to conduct a forensic analysis. We want to know if the attacker left any fingerprints behind. We need to find out how they entered the university device and what they took and where they sent it. The head of MI6 is in Paris right now.'

'He sure is, Sir. We've already met once or twice,' Bruce said.

'OK. We were wondering. Can you approach him to find out if he can ask this guy to help us out? It's got to be real tactful, real discreet.' The Chief finished. All three knew this was a delicate issue. They sat in silence. Each took a sip of beer. Bruce spoke. He thought out loud, expressing clear, logical thoughts. 'That's a tall order. We need to see this device, that's for sure. I can't tell Charles why. I'll have to ask a favour. I'll have to open out his goodwill. It'll be a stretch. There's nothing in it for him.'

'Not much,' the ambassador accepted this point, 'except he'll know we've got something up, and he'll get his people to explore the possibilities.'

'Sure, Sir, that's right. You need it real quick?'

'We do,' the Chief answered.

'I'll get on to it now.'

The three stood. 'Thanks, Bruce,' the ambassador shook his hand, 'we appreciate it's going to be difficult. We've got teams working on it right now, but they can't get into a device that's switched off. In the circumstances, this seems to be the only way. The professor is due to visit the States in a couple of weeks, and we could seize the device if he enters with it, but it'll be too late.'

*

The operators at GCHQ traced Boran Avcı to a small hotel located in the rue des Petits-Hôtels in the 10e arrondissement. Owain Davies was detailed to follow Michael Cocke.

A locally based intelligence officer kept Boran Avcı under surveillance.

The maître d'hôtel opened the door to Elizabeth Yearwood, who entered the bistro Aux Lyonnais in the rue Saint-Marc. 'Welcome Elizabeth,' he said as they kissed on each cheek before he took her coat.

'Thank you for finding a table, Michel, you are so kind.'

'That's not a problem, Elizabeth. We are delighted you had time to visit us this evening.'

'I've got another person joining me – oh, he's just arrived.' Elizabeth looked out of the window. Michel turned to greet Owain Davis as he entered the restaurant. Owain and Elizabeth exchanged greetings, and Owain shook Michel's hand upon being introduced to him, 'I am pleased to meet you, Monsieur,' he said as the director of the restaurant accepted his coat and showed them to a table for two on the far side of the small space in the front room of the bistro. He took them to a table adjacent to the white tiles reaching the top of the chairs, with a single layer of green tiles, then a row of tiles decorated with pink roses and green leaves on a white background, with one further line of green tiles fixed above. Owain was dazzled by the room, painted yellow, with tall, bevelled mirrors reaching to the ceiling, a poster the same height between the mirrors, and a panel sporting floral mouldings, the floor tiled in yellow and red, brightly lit by a 1920s art deco plain white spherical ceiling lighting signed by Jean-Claude Novaro from Biot. They sat at an old school oak table with a steel frame, a white cloth across the top with a check pattern of light red and dark red woven down one side, laid with white plates and napkins, silver cutlery, water cups and balloon wine glasses.

Owain, nonplussed, looked anxiously around after being handed the menu. 'This is a bit public, isn't it? Don't you think we should be near where he is?' he spoke in a low voice.

'I agree, but in the circumstances, I hoped you wouldn't mind.'

'All right,' Owain showed signs of being slightly exasperated, 'Let's get on with it.' Before Elizabeth had the opportunity to speak, the sommelier approached with a bottle. 'Mademoiselle Elizabeth,' he began as he poured wine into her glass, 'a little aperitif – on the house.'

Elizabeth laughed and interrupted him 'Oh, Florentin, you shouldn't,' to which he responded as he poured some wine to Owain's glass, 'Mademoiselle Elizabeth, you are so English. Please accept. It's a viognier from Domaine Vallet. I hope you enjoy.' He smiled as he left.

'Come on, relax a little,' Elizabeth sought to appease Owain. They had joined the Service together and were both reaching the stage where their careers would take them from operational matters to managing relationships. Given the recent instructions she was sent, it was obvious that Owain had yet to receive an update. Her face beamed a smile as her dark brown eyes twinkled under swept eyebrows in the light, her skin a beautiful dark brown against the dark grey of her outfit, a pair of practical trousers, white blouse and loose-fitting jacket. They raised their glasses and nodded to each other before trying the wine. 'Perfect,' Elizabeth closed her eyes for a moment as she let the wine affect her body.

'Yes, quite nice,' Owain admitted. 'You sound just like an Englishman,' Elizabeth chuckled in her Barbadian accent. Owain smiled sheepishly. 'Well, maybe we need this. What have you got?' He spoke quietly, under the hubbub, the group of four women on the table next to them clearly deep in animated conversation and oblivious to those around them. 'He's in a small bar just around the corner from the Opéra Comique, in rue de Marivaux. It's full of men. No women.' Elizabeth set out the facts in the same unobtrusive timbre.

'How long?'

'He's been there an hour or so. I've got him on my device. That tracker you installed is very helpful. I assume he doesn't know it's there.'

'No, our people tell me it's impossible to detect. They'll remove it when we've finished. It took me some time to find Cocke. Did they meet?'

'Yes. In the Tuilleries garden.'

'Maybe Cocke wanted the protection of being in public.'

'No doubt. Boran Avcı went back to his hotel, then walked to the bar.'

'Could you hear what they were saying?'

'No. I couldn't get close, and his Smartphone was in his pocket, so I presume we didn't record anything.'

At this moment Michel approached them for an order. Elizabeth saw him. 'Oh, Michel, I'm sorry, we've been talking. Your special sounds wonderful.'

'Yes, I'll go for that, too,' said Owain.

Michel thanked them, and said, 'I'll match it with a wine.'

Owain's safe device beeped. 'Excuse me, Elizabeth.' He quickly read the message. 'I've got to ring in. I'll go outside.'

'I expect it's an update. That's why I'm here, Owain, because of the new instructions I received a little while ago.'

'Right,' he said as he left. He returned shortly. Taking a good mouthful of wine, he briefed Elizabeth. 'As you say, it's my update. We're now stood down. They're monitoring Cocke remotely. Apparently there's an arrangement in the process of being made about Avcı. I'm to hand over something I've got of his. The courier will be with us shortly.'

'It sounds as if something's going on that we don't need to know about.'

'You've got it.' At this moment, Owain's device buzzed again. There was an image of a face, together with a response. 'Excuse me again, I won't be long.' He left the bistro. A tall, well-developed man with a mop of tousled black hair reached the front door as Owain left the restaurant. The image on the screen matched the face in person. As they shook hands, they exchanged comments about the accuracy of clocks and watches that Ahmet Hamdi Tanpınar gave to the narrator in his novel *The Time Regulation Institute*. Owain took out a small bag containing the remaining rounds of ammunition he had removed from Avcı's hotel room. As he handed them over, he offered a comment. 'He made a mistake. We all miscalculate at times. I tried to make him understand. I had to prevent him from killing me.'

'So I am told. You are the first person that has ever stopped him.'

'I had surprise on my side.'

'It appears so. But we will not neglect to be more aware of you now.' He smiled. 'Thank you for this cooperation.'

'I am carrying out my orders. You are welcome.' The man turned, and walked back to the awaiting vehicle. Owain returned to the restaurant. 'Well, that might the last of him.'

'They'll dispose of him?'

'Perhaps. He was employed to kill.' He was silent for a moment, then continued, 'Right, well, let's enjoy the meal. So, how do you know about this place? And why do they know you so well?'

The driver drove the vehicle to the end of rue Favart, turned right, then turned right again into rue de Marivaux. Lamps located above the windows of the shops at ground level provided a dim light to the four-story buildings either side of the street. He stopped the vehicle outside a small bar. Two men got out of the car and walked into the bar. The bar keeper was polishing a glass. A man stood drinking a beer at the bar. The two visitors walked with a purpose into the depths of the room. The change in light deepened into semi darkness. Three men were sat at a table, one of which was Boran Avcı.

On seeing the pair, he half stood up. His initial reaction was to be aggressive. The man who had spoken to Owain opened the package Owain had given him. Without a word, Avcı followed them out.

*

A member of staff wearing black trousers, a maroon silk waistcoat, with a silver triangular motif alternating base to apex, sporting round silver buttons over a white shirt and a jonquil silk tie, opened the door into the Cabinet Vert – the Duff Cooper Library – and announced, after knocking and hearing 'come' through the door, 'Mr Quinton Myerscough, Sir Charles.'

'Ah, thank you, Xhosa,' Sir Charles stood up from the desk and turned towards the door. He shook Quinton's hand.

'Is there anything I can get you, Sir Charles?' Xhosa asked.

'Have you eaten, Quinton?'

'Yes, thank you Sir Charles.'

'Then we'll have a glass of cognac, Xhosa.' He turned to his guest, 'I presume that's fine?'

'Oh yes, thank you Sir Charles.'

'I'll bring it directly, Sir Charles.'

Charles ushered Quinton Myerscough further into the book-filled room, inviting him to sit on one of the green leather, plain high back Queen Anne chairs with their exposed hardwood legs, positioned on each side of the fireplace. Quinton Myerscough placed the saddle tan document case he was carrying next to the club fire fender, the top upholstered in the same colour green leather as the chairs with deep buttons, the structure made of brass. Sir Charles rearranged some papers on the desk.

'Good trip?'

'Yes, thank you, Sir Charles. When it works, the train from St Pancras to the Gare du Nord can't be beaten.'

There was a knock on the door. Sir Charles Beresford turned and opened the door. 'Do come in, Xhosa, thank you.' Xhosa entered with a silver tray with two cognac glasses. He walked to Quinton Myerscough and placed one glass on the table, and, at the request of Sir Charles, permitted him to remove the other glass from the tray. 'His lordship asks me to let you know that this is one of his favourite cognacs, Sir Charles. It's Très Vieille Réserve Grande Champagne. It's made by Jean-Luc Pasquet and is aged for an average of forty-five years. His lordship hopes you will like the somewhat initial forceful sensation on the palate, but in his view it's well balanced, complex, and most enjoyable.'

'Thank you, Xhosa, I'll report back to John tomorrow.' Xhosa smiled and left the room. Charles walked to Quinton Myerscough, touched the bell of his glass, which he had also raised as he stood up from the chair, and said 'Good cheer.'

'Thanks for coming over, Quinton. I need to get back tomorrow. If what you've got is helpful, this visit will prove to have been beneficial.'

'I hope so, Sir Charles. Once you'd discussed it with Monsieur Lavigne, I was able to bring the paper you wanted. I'll give you a verbal report on the rest.'

'Yes, I've begun forming a plan, and, depending on your findings, I might be able to tidy all this up tomorrow. If you can take me through the latest.'

'Right, Sir Charles.' Quinton Myerscough took a sip of cognac and then led Sir Charles through the intelligence they had gathered over the previous forty-eight hours.

'We've been monitoring the laptop from our friends in Stevenage and the Italian device. There's also a Turkish laptop and Smartphone.'

'Two Turkish devices?'

'Yes, Owain Davies managed to put our system on to both.'

'Excellent.'

'Cocke seems to be our man. He's infiltrated each of these devices with a kernel program that gives him root access, and he's got complete control over what passes into and out of the machines. We've monitored what he's been doing. First, the Russians. What we've discovered is that the information ties in with the allegation that we've got a double agent. We know it's nonsense, and it won't surprise you that the Russians have been playing this all along. They've got hold of the President's entire financial history, courtesy of the Internal Revenue Service and the various law firms that he's used over the years. They've got the best information from the law firms.'

'It doesn't surprise me. The lawyers are the weak link, but they don't know it, and neither do most of their clients. Have we got all of this data? It will be useful to have it.'

'No, Sir Charles. We know it exists. We know the Russians have it, and it's probably on Cocke's system somewhere.'

'How did the Russians get it?'

'Cocke sold it to them.'

'Do we have access to the Russian database?'

'We're working on that right now. You're aware of Semyon Vorontsov. He's central to the protection of Russian interests in bauxite and other important raw materials. He's recently visited his regular optician in Moscow. Opticians scan the retina of their patients' eyes by ophthalmic coherence tomography. It's used to obtain high-resolution images of the retina and anterior segment. The machine helps to assess a range of possible problems with the eye, and opticians compare past readings with future scans. The supplier of the instrument stores the images on a server somewhere. It's easy enough to get into these databases and obtain a copy of the image.'

Sir Charles interrupted. 'Yes, it's a useful service, but the opticians have no idea how vulnerable such systems are.'

'Indeed, Sir Charles. Usually the company providing the service makes a few noncommittal and relatively meaningless noises about security. That's normally sufficient for the optician. And it's rare for a customer to ask about security, so nobody cares. As you know, retina scans are now used to open computers instead of passwords. Naturally, we can only use this data if the biometric security system uses identical measurements to the ones we've obtained. I've got a team working on this at the moment. We've found a remote point through which we can obtain access, but we've got to be sure we can get in before attempting it.'

'You think Vorontsov might be controlling the files?'

'Perhaps. He and his wife are deep inside the circle of power. They persuaded a person in the US close to the President to give the impression that his finances were in the process of being leaked.'

'Who is it?'

'His name is Frederick A. Starring. The Russians have him in their grasp. They have some salacious images of him caught in the midst of sexual activity with a very attractive young woman who is not his wife. His business is also in bad shape. It needs refinancing. They made it clear that he could help himself if he made sure the President thought his financial affairs were being exposed by a British agent.'

'Has he or the President seen any of the files the Russians have got?'

'No. It's just innuendo, but it's good enough for the President.'

'Clever and effective. We'll discuss about how to deal with this one later. We have to work out how much to tell Bruce. In the meantime, we need to find out where Cocke's physical base is and to get hold of his devices and storage systems.'

'We're working on that, Sir Charles. He seems to have covered his tracks very well, even in the digital age.'

'Keep me informed of your progress. The Australians seem a bit peripheral now.'

'I agree. They tell me that Cocke hasn't done anything with their computer.'

'Perhaps he thought the opportunity was too good to miss and intended to gain access when it suited.'

'Yes, or if an opportunity arose. As for the list of intelligence sources in the American document, our people on the ground in Russia have not seen movement by any of the Russian agencies that we'd expect to take action. It's our opinion that Cocke obtained the document and intends to sell it to the Russians.'

'Yes, you could be right. We need to make sure it never gets into their hands. The list demonstrates that some of our people are also working for the Americans without our knowledge. We'll deal with them, and I intend to get a small number of others into our fold. What have you done with the website these files were found on?'

'Nothing yet. Just passive monitoring. We can disable it immediately you're ready.' Quinton Myerscough anticipated the next question. 'And Cocke has not entered it for some time.'

'Right.' Sir Charles raised his glass to sip his cognac. 'Nice stuff this. Do we have any feedback from those listed on the website that Cocke runs? I know we can't expect our people to have approached everybody on the list. It will be interesting to know what their appraisal of Cocke is.'

'Yes, Sir Charles. We've had some comments: arrogant, controlling and secretive are repeated, and one person told us that he implied that he had contacts in most hush-hush agencies. He obviously likes to make it appear that he's well-connected.'

'That's no surprise. Thanks.'

'Now, the Turks, Sir Charles.'

'Yes.'

'Up until very recently, Cocke has been trusted by the Turks. He has sold them a great deal of NATO and European

Union materials. It's quite impressive. But they now have reason to believe that he's double-crossing them. This is where the Italians come in. Cocke has unlimited administrator access to the Italian computer. This has enabled him to penetrate the Turkish Informatics and Information Security Research Centre. He has a copy of a top secret report that provides very interesting reading, so our translators tell me.'

'They're working on the translation now?'

'Yes, Sir Charles. There are some far reaching proposals for the future development of satellite systems that, in theory, could affect our cyber security.'

'Do the Turks know we've got a copy?'

'No, but they think we might have a copy, although we don't know why they think that yet. They want to see Cocke to discuss it with him.'

'If they have some good evidence to indicate we have it, he's in for an unpleasant experience. But it's imperative we get to him first.'

'Agreed. Owain Davis has been working on somebody they sent over to identify the person behind the Italian computer. His name is Boran Avcı. He deals with people. He's very effective. So far, Davis has frustrated him and has managed to get our software on to his work computer. We need to decide how Davis deals with him. They're both in Paris. Davis is monitoring Cocke, and we have one of our intelligence officers based in Paris observing the Turk. We instructed them to coordinate their moves and adopt a passive approach. We don't want them to cause a disturbance.' Quinton Myerscough looked at his watch. 'They should be reporting back to London soon.'

'I'd like to know more about this, but we'll have to wait. What about the Chinese? This brings us to the document you've bought. The Chinese are all over Paris for the conference. Even Colonel Commandant Xú Delun is here. It's unusual for him to be in Europe.'

'Yes, Sir Charles, I have a document here to show you, but before I do that, you'll recall our update yesterday. The Chinese had a back door to some of our sub systems. We found this out through an employee of one of their subcontractors. We got into their laptop recently. Cocke managed to add his software to this computer today. We're aware that the Chinese know we've closed their access.'

'We need to be careful about this.'

'Yes, Sir Charles, it was touch and go whether we fixed the code to prevent the leaks. We've become aware that they're planning something. Possibly an attack on the banking system,' at which Quinton Myerscough removed a crumpled script in cream from his document case and reached over to hand it to Sir Charles. He continued as Charles perused the heavy paper, twenty pages stitched together with yellow silk. A number of manuscript comments in mandarin had been added to various paragraphs. 'We're having it translated now, Sir Charles. It's entitled "Shāshǒujiàn". We've been familiar with this process for some time, as you know.' The SIS had long taken it to mean, in the context of Chinese thinking, "anything that ensures or provides for success".

'This was the one that came in the diplomatic bag from India?' Charles asked.

'Yes. It was given to Henry Bravington-Hartley by one of our friends. It's got the stamp of the Jiuquan Satellite Launch Centre. It's top secret. A quick reading indicates that it's an outline of the revised Chinese plans to dominate space. All air sea and ground forces are to be more fully coordinated. If this plan is put into effect, it has the potential to be a serious contender in the future. It might live up to its name.'

'That's if it's implemented competently and fully. There's always the clash between the flawed hubris of the expert planners and their refusal to acknowledge the skills, intelligence and experience of those that have to implement such grand schemes.'

'Of course, there's often a difference between a well thought out plan and its successful execution – between the imperialism of the authoritarians, and how plans can be made to work practically by those on the ground. I imagine that this document won't tell us much more than we already suspect the Chinese plans might be anyway, but we agreed it might be useful for you to have the document in your physical possession. This is a numbered copy, and was issued to a particular person. Our obtaining it is a significant setback for them. It demonstrates that the security measures put in place to keep such documents safe have failed. Revealing this document to them might be useful in relieving any pressure from the Chinese about us finding their back door into our systems. Our response is legitimate, but it has annoyed them.'

'Thank you. This seems to be peripheral to the main events at present, but the threat to our banking system is something we can't ignore. You've alerted the Treasury and Bank of England to the possibility?'

'Yes, as you requested, Sir Charles.'

'Now for the French. François and Monsieur Lavigne have told me how much they appreciate our help with their problem. They now have sufficient evidence to take action and close the case. As for "l'addition", we know what their plans are, and I'd expect them to reconsider what they might do about this now.'

'Probably, Sir Charles.'

Sir Charles glanced at the clock. 'It's late. You're staying at the usual place tonight?'

'Yes, Sir Charles. The embassy kindly indicated they will have a car to take me once we've finished.'

'That's good of them. I'll let you leave. Thanks for coming.'

*

'He was screened to level *secret-défense* twelve months ago.'

'That was before this problem.'

'Yes. He had another four years before it was renewed.' Eleanor de Beauchamp looked at Calixte Lavigne. The minister sat back in her chair. 'Monsieur Duhamel has done excellent work with the help of the British.'

'Yes. His report has tipped the balance. We have all the evidence to act.'

The minister placed her hand over the folder. 'Indeed. Do you have any other recommendations?'

'For the future of security?'

'Yes.'

'May I ask, Minister, if this is...' Eleanor de Beauchamp interrupted him. 'Between us?'

'Yes, Minister.'

'It is.'

'Thank you. I think we ought to use this incident to make it possible for us to obtain surveillance warrants more easily.'

'What about the screening of officers?'

'I have taken the liberty of making some proposals, Minister.' Calixte Lavigne passed a file over the table to her. 'I have taken Monsieur Duhamel into my confidence, Minister. We have known each other for some time. We have worked together on operations, although our careers did not follow the same path. Monsieur Duhamel prefers a collegiate approach when assembling a team to carry out a complex task. He thinks that this type of approach is the more fruitful. It reflects his personality, of course. He has achieved excellent results over the years, as you know. But he is not afraid of using his authority and the full range of disciplinary powers available to him when people fail – especially when they deliberately ignore advice and instructions. He might appear to be more interested in the arts, and his reputation for fairness and success is recognized by most of us in the Direction Générale de la Sécurité Extérieure.'

The minister raised her eyebrows. 'We speak the same language, Monsieur Lavigne. Thank you for the comments about Monsieur Duhamel. I will pursue this agenda as expeditiously as the political landscape permits. We both know I might not be in this ministry long enough, but it is worth trying. The forces of the right are damaging our country.'

'They are too powerful.'

There was an urgent knock on the door.

'Enter,' the minister called out. The minister's secretary entered. 'Minister, Monsieur Lavigne, the operations room ask that you get over there immediately.'

'It is that urgent?'

'Yes Minister.'

François Duhamel was waiting for the Ministre des Armées and the Director of the Direction Générale de la Sécurité Extérieure. Eleanor de Beauchamp entered the room. Her sense of self-possession and control acted to dampen the agitated nature of the atmosphere. She looked around the area. Three men and one woman were controlling screens and communicating with people on the ground. François knew it would not be appropriate to brief the minister and the Director before subordinates. He had arranged for a side room to be opened. They sat at a small round table in a windowless space of modest proportions, the walls scuffed with use. François offered refreshments. They were politely refused.

'There have been dramatic developments, Minister, Monsieur Lavigne.' He did not wait for a response. 'We have found de Lussan dead in his apartment.'

Eleanor de Beauchamp looked annoyed. 'That prevents me from compelling him to face the full force of the law for his part in selling state secrets and attempting to undermine you, Monsieur Duhamel.'

Calixte Lavigne took the opportunity to question François.

'We were intercepting de Lussan's phone. Have you any news on that?'

'Yes. Shall we go to my office?'

Eleanor de Beauchamp ignored the suggestion. 'Inform me immediately we have more news. I will speak to the Prime Minister and President.'

Calixte Lavigne, the Director of the Direction Générale de la Sécurité Extérieure, looked at François Duhamel. They had finished listening to a recording of the telephone conversation initiated by Jean-Frédéric Esparbès de Lussan, having returned to the office as soon as they could when called in as a matter of utmost urgency.

'We have our man' the Director began, looking out of a window into the moody night sky of black heavy clouds illuminated by the artificial light of the metropolis, 'in his own words ordering the death of not only a close colleague, but an honourable servant of the State.'

'And an intelligent and much loved woman.'

'Yes.' The Director looked at the accompanying file. 'It was recorded between 18:35 and 18:50.' Both men registered the time on their watches. 'Just over two hours ago,' François observed. The Director called the Directeur Général of the Police Nationale.

'What do you need, Calixte?' Patrice asked.

'There's going to be an attempt to kill at least one of our officers in the Bois de Boulogne. It looks as if the killer is new to us. We're attempting to establish their identity and who is behind the organization. Our officer, Stéphanie Beauharnais, is with Jacques de Lalaing. He's an officer in the gendarmerie nationale. We have not been able to contact either of them. As you know, we have been cooperating with the police Judiciaire and Procureur de la République on this matter. We need to get some people to the area now. We know de Lalaing has a black Renault Safrane Biturbo Baccara. We are trying to find out the registration number.'

'Do you want noise and lights to get there, or should it be discreet?'

'Hold on.' Calixte looked at François.

'We want to catch the person they've sent to kill. I know it's risky, but I suggest we get people in place quietly.' The Director continued the conversation. 'Let us be careful, Patrice. Our respective operations people need to liaise with each other, so you can ensure the matter is coordinated.'

'I will do that now, Calixte. Are you going over there?'

'Yes, we will drive over. We will park discreetly in Porte Dauphine.'

'Good. We should have everybody in place within the next fifteen minutes. See you.'

Calixte Lavigne stopped the dark grey DS 7 Crossback in front of the police car at the signal of the officer. He and François opened their respective doors, closed them carefully, and hurriedly followed the police escort to the scene.

*

Jacques de Lalaing and Stéphanie Beauharnais stepped out into the cool clear night. They walked arm in arm to his car. Both had switched off their devices hours before, and neither powered them up after the emotion of the evening. He opened the front passenger door for his fiancée. Stéphanie slipped into the space and made herself comfortable in the leather upholstery. Jacques started the V6 engine and edged out into the road, the absence of traffic allowing him to turn the vehicle around so as to drive to the traffic lights, where he was able to steer into Route de la Muette-à-Neuilly, aiming to drive back towards the porte Dauphine. As he drove sedately towards the Allée de Longchamp, he noticed a single bright light in the rear view mirror approaching very quickly. Suddenly, the rear window was shattered by two high velocity rounds.

'Stéphanie,' he called out urgently as he immediately reacted by changing into a lower gear, 'my jacket pocket. Get out the gun.' He pressed his foot on the accelerator to take advantage of the flexibility of the 268 bph power unit. Stéphanie wound down her window and took out his weapon. 'How far behind us?' she asked in a tone of command as she prepared the Heckler & Koch USP45 Tactical pistol.

'It's catching fast. Try to disable the guy driving the motorbike. The shots probably came from a passenger. I can't do much on this road to stop them running alongside. I can't get off it.' Jacques had noticed the small concrete beams dug into the grass verge at regular intervals on both sides of the road to prevent vehicles from parking. He was not able to veer off along a track.

The killer set off another burst of rounds, hitting the rear passenger doors as Jacques used the outstanding road-holding of the vehicle to veer the car across the road and prevent the motorcyclist from getting close enough for an accurate shot.

'Stéphanie, I can't see how I can get you into a good position.' Jacques rang out as the unknown hit man attempted to kill them.

'You're coming up to the junction with Allée de Longchamp.' Stéphanie was matter of fact. 'I can see a blue light in the distance behind the motorcycle. Give me a wide swing at the corner. I'll try then.'

As he neared the junction, the traffic lights changed to green. 'Relief' Jacques said under his breath. He positioned the car in the centre of the road, shouted 'get ready,' and then applied the brakes and handbrake to swerve sideways on. This gave Stéphanie her opportunity. She rotated her body, raised the weapon through the open space and pressed the trigger slightly, letting out two quick rounds. The bullets hit the torso of the motorcyclist. The impact caused him to take one hand from the handlebar. The machine swerved violently. She took the opportunity to fire a further two shots in the direction of the passenger, who dropped the machine gun he was carrying and fell backward as the motorcycle twisted out of control, sliding into and bouncing over the curb, coming to a halt on the grass. By this time, three cars of the Police Nationale had converged on to the scene from different directions. It took seconds for the police officers to seize both assailants, seal the junction to all traffic, and compel those caught up in the mayhem to turn around and attempt their journey via an alternative route.

Immediately Jacques brought the vehicle to a halt, he turned to wrap his arms tightly around Stéphanie. They kissed and hugged each other, Jacques wrapping his hands protectively around Stéphanie's head.

'Are you all right?' Jacques asked.

'Yes, darling, I'm fine thank you. How about you? That was brilliant driving.'

'Darling, it wasn't my driving but your composure. You were so calm.' She smiled as she removed the magazine and rendered the weapon safe. She returned both to Jacques. Stéphanie Beauharnais loved this man sitting next to her, and she liked the thought that he had begun to realise that not only was she attractive and an intelligence officer in the DGSE, but that she also knew how to handle a weapon and remain calm when under stress. Jacques de Lalaing was impressed with himself. This woman had agreed to be his wife. Indeed he was blessed. He began to realise that asking her to marry him was possibly the best decision he had made in his life.

At this moment, the director and François appeared. Both were concerned for the safety of their officer, and were pleased that the motorcyclist and attacker were both dead.

*

'Charles, it's late, but can we meet?'

Sir Charles Beresford looked at the face of the gilded mantel clock, which measured six minutes past eleven o'clock.

'Of course, Bruce. Do you want to come here, or shall we meet elsewhere?'

'I'm not far from the Hôtel de Charost. Shall I call in?'

'Yes. I'll let the night porter know you're on your way.'

'Thanks, buddy.' There was a note of sincere relief in his voice.

Sir Charles arrived in the hall as Bruce entered. The footman took his coat. Charles led Bruce to the first floor and the Salon Vert, adjacent to the Cooper bedroom he had been allocated.

'Charles, what a fancy place.'

'Yes, isn't it? The Duke of Wellington persuaded the British government to buy it from Bonaparte's sister when he was appointed ambassador to France in 1814. Anyway, here we are: the sitting room. Let's talk. Take a seat.'

Bruce fell into one of the overstuffed red sofas. 'Nightcap?' Bruce mused. Charles answered his own question. 'No, I don't think so. Let me order.' He picked up the internal telephone. 'Ah, Ben, may I ask for two of your suggested beverage? No sugar for either. Thank you.' Charles's face expressed the anticipation of future amusement. 'Don't ask, Bruce. Let it be a surprise.'

'OK, I'll do that. Can I come to the point?'

'Of course. Go ahead.'

'This is real delicate, Charles. This is a real personal ask.'

'If I can do anything, I'll do what I can.'

'OK. There's an Arab professor from the University of Cambridge who's a member of the Jordanian royal family – on a branch line – that's got a university computer with him.

He's well respected across the world in his subject. We've had some stuff go walking. It's very serious. We need our guys to go through the device to search for the attacker. It's urgent, but we can't use our people on the ground, because we're seriously out of favour right now.'

'You need a discreet approach to get the computer in for analysis?'

'You've got it.'

At this moment, there was a knock on the door. Sir Charles got up from the opposite sofa and opened one of the doors. The footman thanked Sir Charles and entered with two cups, each with a silver spoon resting in the saucer. He placed one before Bruce, while Sir Charles took the second from the tray and thanked him for bringing the drink. The footman left as modestly as he entered. 'Hot chocolate, Bruce. Just what we both need. Enjoy the taste. It's one of the best.'

'Thanks, Charles, maybe it's what I wanted and I didn't know it' Bruce said as he raised the white porcelain saucer with a band of gold decoration around the edge and took a sip from the white cup, an identical gold decoration around the rim. 'Yes, just right. I'll have to come here again.'

Sir Charles picked up his device. 'Let's see what the time in Amman is. Two hours ahead.' He rang a number. 'Hello Granville. You're on duty? Right. You remember my request about the English chap that's a plasterer? Were you able to get in touch with him?'

'You like *knafeh*? Hello, I'm Granville.'

'Hello Granville, I'm Pete.'

'I know.'

'Oh?'

'You only come here for the *knafeh*,' Granville made a statement.

'Yes. You can't be in Amman without coming to Habidah.'

'You prefer this outlet?'

'Yes, like many who live in the city, it has to be the 1951 original. It's iconic.' He looked over the queue and the people siting on the low wall with plates in their hand. 'It's wonderfully busy almost all the time. You can't not come to buy this delicious dessert.'

'The pastry is so like vermicelli. It's one of my daughter's favourites.'

The two men stood to one side among a number of others, all eating their *knafeh*. Pete always enjoyed the differences when he travelled; the diverse way people interacted; the willingness to stop and talk; the apparently casual life he observed that locals appeared to live; of helping in a small way the souls traumatised, a sense of self-worth wrecked, their lives rendered into a indeterminate state of enforced passivity, passing through the country as refugees, whether temporary – for a few days or weeks – or long term, for years, for generations, seeing how they lived and managed to live.

'What do you want?' Pete decided to ask directly of the Englishman, standing in his casual but well made trousers and shirt, smart shoes, urbane manner with a good command of Arabic – he had noticed this when Granville placed his order. The people serving Granville also knew him well. The repartee was obvious. Granville took pleasure in the crunch of the vermicelli-like pastry as he bit into the whole, the goat cheese adding to the sense of luxury, the tastes mixed handsomely, rich and sweet.

'You're doing some work for the royal household?'

'Yes.'

'And you know Sir Charles Beresford?'

'I've met him on two occasions.' The question did not surprise Pete. He realised they would not send somebody to get in touch unless they wanted something.

'He rates you highly.'

'Nice. I'm flattered.' Pete did not do deference.

'There's a problem.'

'Oh yeah?' Pete looked Granville in the eye. 'No. Don't even ask.' The two men moved away from the crowd to reduce the possibility that their conversation could be overheard. 'I'm not a spy,' Pete continued, 'I'm here because of my skills. I like what I do and I want it to stay that way. Right?'

Granville had not been given any guidelines as how to approach Pete, other than he was in a position to pass on a message discreetly. Pete's tone of voice brooked no dissent. The matter was closed. An appeal to patriotism was not going to succeed. It might even cause derision.

'Well, thanks for being honest and telling me straight. I understand.'

'No hard feelings if I ever need help from the embassy?'

'Of course not. This didn't happen.'

'René Magritte might have taken a contrary view.'

'Possibly. He might have painted the possibility of something happening, but wanting it not to have happened.'

'That sounds like the beginning of a great painting.'

'By the way, you do a lot of good when you come over here.'

'Thanks. It's nice your daughter likes *knafeh*.'

'Yes, C, but he didn't want to get involved. He said he was just an ordinary chap and wanted to stay that way. My comments are informally on their way to you.'

'Thanks, Granville, that's appreciated. I understand his position. I'll pass him a note to thank him and ask him to accept my apologies.' He paused. 'Bravington-Hartley looked after that young lady from Beirut. Apparently she's in Jordan at present. He told me that she was interested in our overtures, but wasn't ready yet. Did he fill you in on her?'

Henry Bravington-Hartley enjoyed lunch in Hall at University College Oxford with a friend who had become an academic. He praised the woman Henry had introduced to the College, taking PPE. Henry walked to the Master's Lodgings, where he waited.

Fazia and her group of fellow students prepared to leave Hall after lunch. A porter entered and whispered into her ear. 'Yes, of course' she replied, and asked those with her to accept her apologies, because she was wanted elsewhere.

On entering the Master's Lodgings, she saw Henry waiting for her. He told her that there was somebody to see her. He asked if she wanted him to be with her. She agreed. He took her to a small sitting room. Two men in uniform stood up as they entered; a tall, slim flying officer of the Royal Air Force in service dress sporting a head of blond hair in his mid-twenties, and a sergeant, taller, a dominating physical presence enhanced with regular physical exercise in his early thirties, the insignia on his number 2 Service dress indicating that he was serving with the 2nd Battalion, The Rifles. Both displayed campaign ribbons, the sergeant with the Conspicuous Gallantry Cross. Henry effected the introductions. Fazia indicated that Henry was her mentor, and stood in for her father. The officer began, hesitantly. His Commanding Officer had detailed him to inform Fazia of the news. The sergeant looked at the flying officer. They shared their distress.

Halil had obtained permission to attend an evening of music at a teahouse with members of the National Army.

Fazia knew what he was going to say before he said it. She listened carefully. The bulk of the sergeant collapsed into a burble of sobs and tears. He fell to his knees. Fazia caught his torso into her arms, cradling him as if a mother would do to her son, caressing the back of his head as he sobbed uncontrollably into her lap.

The flying officer stumbled, painfully, recited what happened in short bursts with a voice on the edge of despair, doing his duty. A bomb had been placed outside a nearby building.

Over one hundred people had been killed and injured. Halil was among those that died.

He explained why the sergeant had accompanied him. Months before Halil was killed, the sergeant and his platoon had been on foot patrol, and a roadside bomb had hit and seriously injured two of his men. They had been caught in a desperate fire fight. Halil and a colleague, now serving with the Tactical Medical Wing of the Royal Air Force, had come out to rescue the injured. Under intense fire and with no thought to their safety, they gave immediate first aid to his men and managed to evacuate them as reinforcements enabled the soldiers to repel those attacking them. Both men survived, but their injuries were such that they were invalided out of the army. A deep attachment had formed between the members of the platoon and Halil and his colleague. It was a bond brought about through adversity and exposure to a near death experience. Halil's tour of duty had continued in Afghanistan after the regiment had returned to the UK.

Unknown to Fazia at this time, among the music and songs he had listened to was a Musammat by the poet Hasan Beg of Takht-r Waras of Hazarajat, beginning *Qadash harhar rokhash ahmar tanash sim o labash shekar* – in which the singer tells of her wonderful stature, rosy face and sugar lips; and a Kisawi played on the dambura and sung by Arbab Ghulam with a colleague playing the pip, *Har du cheshma-ye tur*ā *kadem zi*ā *rat* – telling of his pilgrimage into her eyes. She would later be told of how animated he became when hearing and understanding the meaning of these songs, and telling everybody about the woman he loved.

Henry stood watching and listening to the heartbreak unfold. He observed the intensity of the raw emotions of the men who knew what it was to be under fire, to be prepared for death.

Unknown to the sergeant, Fazia took comfort in his

distress. She wore the simple engagement ring Halil had given her before going on tour. She experienced a solace in nursing this man's body. Now she realized that not only was Halil a man who had loved her and had intended to be her husband, but also that he had courageously faced death in his role as a nurse to save life; that he meant so much more to many others – his family, friends and military comrades. He shared his life with others, and here was a hero at her feet that deeply felt the pain of his death.

Before he left, Henry wanted to ensure she was safe. He felt responsible for her. He made the Master aware of the news. It was time to say goodbye.

'Please, Sir...' Fazia began.

'Fazia, please call me Henry.'

'Yes, Henry. You know my father has always been close to the British. He had many years sailing the world with British sailors.'

'Yes.'

'He hated to see the forces of disruption rip apart our country.'

'I know. We both know Yemen is full of twists and turns. One of the issues is that many Houthis believe they are restoring Zaydi traditions and beliefs that were curbed after the 1962 revolution.'

'Yes, and the religious puritanicals make the political mix even more complex. But war is so devastating. My fear is for the women and children of my country. I want to help.'

'In what way?'

'I will work with the British if it helps me achieve something positive. I want to be of use to my country and my sisters as best I can.'

'You do understand that the British have been, and can be, a devious, unpleasant and deadly partner?'

'Yes, but I begin to understand that the men in my own

part of the world are just as destructive. The British have provided me with sanctuary, and I will not forget that. I am going to take a Master's degree in history next. I have another scholarship. I want to know about the reality that was the past as it affects us in the present.'

Henry had observed her change of clothing. She had forsaken her wish to look chic western. She was never to be without a scarf.

'Yes, C, I've met her. She's very intelligent. I've been told by her tutors that she's going to get a very good degree.'

'Splendid. It's time to approach her. I've got a favour to ask. This is highly delicate. Let our ambassador know, and any senior people on a need to know basis. Here's the request. Tell her this is informal. I'd rather she concentrated on her education and perhaps work towards a senior position for her country one day, but right now she might be able to help an ally out.' Sir Charles outlined what he needed.

'Right Bruce, it's all set up. Our people will work with yours. We can leave it to them.'

'Thanks, Charles. I owe you big time.'

*

Michael Cocke boarded the 07:40 flight from Paris Charles de Gaulle airport. The aircraft landed at 13:10 in Istanbul Atatürk airport. Upon his arrival, his contact met him.

*

The ambassador to France, Ivan Vasilievich Shuysky looked at Colonel Zinovy Khodzhaminasov. A samovar had been put on a table in his office with cups and saucers, a plate of sugar cubes, gingerbread biscuits and chocolates, together with the garnishes – lemon, honey, jam, and marmalade. He motioned Colonel Khodzhaminasov to sit, and asked for his preference.

'Zinovy,' he referred to Colonel Khodzhaminasov by his first name, 'tell me all.' They were friends from university days.

Colonel Zinovy Khodzhaminasov began. 'It looks like a number of developments here in Paris might affect the plans for "istrebitel sputnikov", Ivan Vasilievich.'

'That is important, Zinovy. Please go on.'

'We have dealt with Jean-Frédéric Esparbès de Lussan. He was the head of Security Intelligence for the Direction Générale de la Sécurité Extérieure. He ordered the execution of one of his own officers, a woman named Stéphanie Beauharnais.'

'Really? How interesting. She is head of the Strategy Directorate. Did she survive?'

'Yes, she killed the hit man and the driver.'

'She must be good.'

'Yes.'

'So,' the ambassador sat back a little in his chair, 'tell me the significance of this dead Frenchman for us.'

'We were cultivating him, Ivan Vasilievich. He was not an official agent. We tried to make him commit to us, but he seemed to prefer to play other games. The Frenchman had passed a number of helpful documents on to us recently. However, the DGSE had a suspicion about him, and the Director requested one of their more experienced officers, Monsieur François Duhamel, to investigate. We were aware of this inquiry, and I gave Captain Milyukov the task of following him. Unfortunately, with the connivance of British spies, he successfully evaded Captain Milyukov.'

'That was unfortunate.'

'Yes, I thought so at the time. But in retrospect, I now realise that it was helpful to us. We had more freedom to approach the French officer that has been killed. We obtained more information from him. He was part of a group to overthrow the French liberal establishment. They authorized him to cooperate with us.'

'нет худа без добра – in every bad situation there is an element of good. Very helpful.'

'Yes, very useful. There is an unfortunate problem, though.'

'Go on.'

'De Lussan had duplicitous relations with an outsider that specializes in obtaining and selling state secrets relating to technology. His name is Michael Cocke. He seems to be English, but we are attempting to find out more. Two of my men were watching de Lussan, and followed him to a meeting with Cocke. They asked for instructions, and I authorized them to wait for him in his flat. He had begun to challenge us. His arrogance was becoming dangerous. Once he had been dispatched, our officers found some disturbing documents.'

Ivan Vasilievich Shuysky straightened himself in his chair and leaned forward, his elbows on the table in front of him.

'What did they find?'

'They found some original documents relating to the problems of our most recent work on our hypersonic missiles. They were very well hidden. It took them a little time to find them. The documents have the markings of the Roscosmos State Corporation for Space Activities, and may have come from the Central Research Institute of Machine-Building.' Colonel Khodzhaminasov handed over a plain brown envelope.

'This is serious. Thank you, Zinovy. What about this man Cocke?'

'We are working on this as we speak,' Colonel Khodzhaminasov answered. 'We do not know if Cocke gave the Roscosmos documents to de Lussan. It is possible that somebody attending the satellite conference handed them over to the Frenchman.'

The ambassador asked, 'Zinovy are you happy to liaise with our officers from the embassy on the ground here in Paris?'

'Yes, Ivan Vasilievich. I think we need to single out all of those at the conference whom we have authorized to attend, and to identify any others that are linked in any way to this man Cocke, especially the subcontractors of big corporations. The documents we found at de Lussan's flat will have been passed to him via third parties. Those responsible for the leak will want to distance themselves from any suspicion.'

'Agreed. The American document has proved to be very useful. We now have a list of the double agents working for the enemy. Some of them are our people working to penetrate the CIA, but some are clearly traitors. We have to be careful. We do not want to alert the Americans to our officers who have infiltrated the CIA. Interestingly, it's a printed document of an electronic version. It will be very helpful to find out how he obtained it. Did your men find his computer or Smartphone?'

'Yes, and the device he was issued with by the DGSE.'

'That is helpful. Have you sent them for investigation?'

'Yes.'

'They might contain more of our secrets, Zinovy. It will be interesting to know what our technical people find.'

*

Sir Charles Beresford sat at the breakfast table in the Tapestry dining room with John de Welles, the 18th Marquess of Welles and British ambassador to France, a title he acquired whilst in post on the death of an uncle. They were chuckling after a witty comment had been shared. A waitress knocked and entered with a basket of pastries.

'Oh, thank you, Rose, that is appreciated.' As she left, he explained. 'When Cecilia came over, she wanted a petit pain au chocolat, but not just anything bought at the nearest bakery. It had to be Elizabeth David's recipe, the one you make. She had a tête-à-tête with the pastry chef, and because she is so enchantingly persuasive, we now have them on request. As you can imagine, they go down very well with visitors – especially with our French grandees.'

'Tremendous. I'm glad Cecilia has managed to endear herself indirectly with some of the influential people that your entertain.' He took a bite into the perfectly round petit pain au chocolat that he picked up off his plate. It was still warm enough for the chocolate to be slightly liquid. The mix of the milk dough, rose water wash and chocolate gave a most satisfying feel in the mouth. 'Delicious, John. I'll have to congratulate your pastry chef. They are far more elegant than the ones I make.'

'Good, I'm sure she'll be pleased. You're off today?'

'Yes, but it's looking as if it'll be later this afternoon or evening. I've got to attend a briefing on events that occurred last night and how to deal with them.'

'Anything I need to know?'

'Not yet, but you never know.'

'Indeed. Life is full of surprises.'

'Right, John, I'll be off. I'll give you a call later.'

Jane Arkwright, the petit Senior Advisor for Defence and International Security, stood up when Sir Charles entered the secure room, her attentive dark brown eyes looked directly at him, her hair a natural pixie cut above a high forehead.

'Hello Jane, good to see you.'

'Good morning, C, it's good to see you. Coffee?'

'No, thank you, I've just finished breakfast with the ambassador. Do you mind getting straight to the update?'

'Not at all, C.' Charles Beresford always appreciated her efficiency. 'This is the present situation. We've found out where Cocke lives. It's a small, nondescript first-floor maisonette covered in pebble dash at the end of the Central Line in

Hainault. It's a few minutes from the underground station in a cul de sac. Our people are there now. They've found a server and all the usual paraphernalia you'd expect from somebody with a good knowledge of by-passing the typical controls and making himself virtually invisible.'

'Good. Have they been able to break into his system?'

'Not yet, they're working on it. He formed a completely innocuous background some time ago. He got a job in a mid-sized tech company under his assumed name, and he's been there ever since. At least he's on the payroll. In fact he left some time ago, but they've paid him from the time when he left. I expect he manipulated the records, and they've never noticed. I'm guessing, but it's probably not the money he wanted from this job, but the security that he could travel on a passport under a different identity. The property is in the name of his alter ego.'

'So our systems never noticed him?'

'No. He's been very clever, and it's not that easy to achieve anonymity now, as we know. He left Paris on the first flight out to Istanbul this morning. The Turks want to speak to him.'

'That's not good. He'll have his laptop and Smartphone with him.'

'Yes. If the Turks decide to challenge him, they might get hold of what we want.'

'What do Katharine and Margaret think?'

'I've been in touch with them this morning. They helped the Turks out. One of their officers tried to kill Davis in Belgium. Katharine discussed things with her counterpart in Turkey last night, and they reached an amicable solution that has saved the Turks from embarrassment. We're aiming to get their cooperation regarding Cocke. They've agreed to let him enter the country without raising his suspicions. Our officers are presently making arrangements in Istanbul to seize his hardware.'

'Good. Keep me in the picture on that one. We'll have to give the Turks something to prevent them from apprehending him and the computers.'

'Yes. I've got nothing to offer at the moment.'

'All right, we'll have to play it carefully. Let me know what our people are planning to do once they've reported back. Any news on the French and Americans?'

Jane took a sip of coffee from her mug.

'Jean-Frédéric Esparbès de Lussan was found dead in his apartment last night. No doubt Monsieur Lavigne and François have been too busy to update you personally.'

'I expect so. If that's what's happened, they probably haven't had much sleep. This man de Lussan was their main suspect. Do we know who was responsible?'

'The Russians. He ordered the murder of his colleague, Stéphanie Beauharnais. She was on her way to meet her boyfriend. Owain Davis was watching Cocke, and saw him and de Lussan together in a café. He also noticed a couple of Russian G.U. agents. They made a telephone call and left the café.'

'What happened to Stéphanie Beauharnais?'

'She managed to hit both the contract killer and the driver. They were both dead on inspection.'

'Very good.'

'Yes, she did well. Anyway, the interesting bit is that two Russians sneaked into de Lussan's flat.'

'Oh? How do we know?'

'Owain Davis contacted Elizabeth Yearwood. They decided to stake his place out. The Russians left with a slim bag.'

'What about his computer?'

'No sign of it. I expect they took all of the devices they could find. No doubt Monsieur Lavigne will bring you up-to-date on that one if it's not too embarrassing for them.'

At this moment, Sir Charles's device rang.

'Excuse me, Jane. Hello François my friend. I've discovered I slept through an exciting night.'

'You have, Charles. We are facing a problem that I need you and Bruce to help me with. Can you speak?'

'Yes, go ahead.'

'Our man de Lussan was killed last night. We think the killers took his computer and Smartphone. Unfortunately, we didn't get there as quickly as we would have liked. They attempted to kill Stéphanie Beauharnais last night. That meant we didn't pay sufficient attention to de Lussan. When we got to his flat, there was nothing there.'

'Were you able to disable his devices?'

'No. The device issued to him by the Service had nothing on it because it was only used to communicate to the server. It didn't store anything. His personal Smartphone and computer have not been switched on to our knowledge. But we were able to trace the calls he made. We have arrested the person he rang to order the murder. He's cooperating. He's telling us everything he knows. We're arranging to arrest the main conspirators.'

'That is good news. How can we help?'

'Can we meet in the next hour?'

*

François looked out for Bruce and Charles as they reached the Hôtel Carnavalet. He managed to find three dilapidated folding bistro chairs. He placed them in the sunlight outside the line of shadow that bordered the courtyard garden, redesigned in the classical style, of curved box hedges and wide gravel paths.

'Bruce, Charles, thank you for coming. Apologies for asking you to come out, but I had to find neutral ground where we were unlikely to be overheard. They are refurbishing the museum, and I have a friend working here. You know about last nights' events?' Both nodded. 'Let me be candid, as you Anglo-Saxons say.'

'Sure, go ahead,' Bruce encouraged him.

'Right. First, Charles helped me with pinning de Lussan down. My report was finished, and we were going to have him arrested today. However, he made a bad judgment last night that could have lost us a very good officer. Fortunately, all is well and we have two dead men on our hands who are better no longer alive. We traced the phone call he made and arrested the person arranging the killing. He's led us to the other conspirators. We now have one of the more important people in custody, and he's talking as I speak. He is trying to use subterfuge, influence and disgusting arrogance to get himself free. He doesn't know it yet, but the decision-makers are not going to spare him or the others.'

'Sounds good to me,' Bruce offered.

'Yes, but there's more, and it involves both your countries. We found a network run by a man that sells secrets.'

'Cocke?' Sir Charles asked.

'Yes. You know him?'

'We are just beginning to. He's on his way to Istanbul.'

'How much do you know Charles?'

'At the moment, we know that he's been very clever. We're working out what to do now.'

François knew his friend sufficiently well not to press him for more information, and continued. 'We've discovered that he's been selling secrets to the Russians and Turks, among others. It's serious for you, Bruce.'

'How so?'

'He's found an American document that lists all of your double agents in Russia.' Bruce gave a deep breath. 'Oh, right. That's serious. Do you know if it's in their hands?'

'No.'

Sir Charles interrupted. 'François, I expect you have had to take people off projects because of this. I'm not surprised.'

'Yes. Let's speed this up. We need to focus on the problems and think about what to do to our mutual benefit.'

'Agreed. Let me start.'

'Yes, please go ahead, Charles.'

'I don't want Cocke. I'm happy for the Russians to dispose of him. We have something that might persuade them to hold off taking out the US double agents until Bruce can get his people out of danger.'

'That's good of you, Charles. What do you want of us?' Bruce asked.

'I want you to get this stuff about a British double agent finished today. Can you do it?'

'You bet! I think we know what the answer to that particular problem is, Charles. But I need to act fast on our Russian agents.'

'The satellite conference is running down before lunch?' Charles stated a question.

'Yes,' François answered.

'We've all got people there, but the Russians are there in force. Both they and the Chinese are looking for Cocke. We need to have this matter resolved today.'

'I don't know what your position is with the Chinese, Charles, but the documents we have recovered tell us that he has succeeded in undermining a number of French contracts dealing with satellite technology, and one Italian contract that they are working on for a country in the Levant. If it gets exposed, it will be very embarrassing. It might even see the fall of governments. We don't know if the data we've found is in the hands of others.'

'Let's work on the assumption that it isn't.' Sir Charles suggested. 'After all, once somebody has got this information, they usually like to reveal they've got it. In this case, it's information that's for sale.'

'You're right, Charles,' Bruce observed. 'Maybe we're lucky on this one.'

'Yes,' François was deep in thought. 'I need to get back to the crisis unfolding here, and you two need to move on with your agendas. Let me think about this. You and Bruce have probably got your matter resolved?'

'Probably,' Bruce offered.

'Right, you need the Russians to give you time to get your agents out of Russia?'

'Yes, if they know about the list.'

'I think they do, Bruce, because my technical people have uncovered links to known Russian penetration methods. I think you should work on the basis that their cover has been exposed.'

'You're most likely right, François.'

'Charles, you've got something about the Chinese. Does it affect us or the Americans?'

'No, but I want to finish it today.'

'I've been thinking.' François had to help Charles. Without evidence from the British, he would not have solved the investigation. It did not matter that his report was no longer as important as it was. The report remained an important foundation with which to pursue the enemies of the state. He felt obliged to help Charles resolve some of his apparent problems. 'How about a meeting of the "Sixty-three" club?'

'Sure,' Bruce said.

'When?' Charles asked.

'How about two hours from now? Why not get the Russians and Chinese in to solve this? The usual place is free. I can make the arrangements now. That gives you time to get the agents into the room.'

Bruce looked at Charles. 'What do you say? Heck, this is

really serious for us. I've got to demonstrate I did my best to act.'

'All right, let's go with your suggestion, François. Pressures are building on other matters.'

*

Bruce was driven back to his temporary office and Charles returned to the embassy. Time was short. Both men had to leave Paris that evening.

'Hi Bart,' Bruce began his conversation with the Deputy Director of the Central Intelligence Agency. 'Hi Bruce. How ya doing?' Bartholomew Ridens always had time to respect the formalities of social engagement. 'I'm fine, Bart. How's it going your end?'

'Tough, Bruce. Have you got an answer on the British double agent yet?'

'We're working on that right now. The head of the Secret Intelligence Services is in Paris, and we expect to crack it in the next hour or so. Does that ease the pressure?'

'OK, if that's a promise, then it'll help me shed a load. I've got to brief the Director on that in three hours. We need a result.'

'You'll have it, Bart. Promise.'

'Thanks, Bruce. What about the Amman thing? Was Sir Charles able to help on that one?'

'Sure thing. We got to the computer through a number of third parties. This meant they couldn't get a report back to you direct.'

'Anything on it?' Bartholomew Ridens asked anxiously.

'No, sweet clean, I'm told. There's a report on paper in the diplomatic bag on its way.'

'The computer's clean, but it doesn't mean somebody else has got copies of the documents downloaded.'

'Right. We don't know, Bart.'

'Well, it was big stuff. If hackers have it, they'll be only too keen to put it online.'

'Yes, Bart. That tells me it might still be with the attacker.'

'Do we know if they left any signs that might identify them?'

'I just got a quick response about whether files were on the computer, Bart. I expect that'll be in the report.'

'OK, thanks Bruce. Now, what about the report with our agents in Russia? Our people have been quietly contacting some of them. Do we know if the Russians have the documents?'

'Not yet, Bart, but Charles tells me they might have an answer for us on that one soon.'

'How soon? We've gotta act if the Russians know. We know what they do to traitors. This could be a serious compromise for us.'

'I know Bart. I can't do anything more on that until Charles gets back to me.'

'OK Bruce. I trust you. My phone's ready as soon as you ring.'

'I'll be right back to you, Bart.'

'Hello, Charles. I was just about to ring.'

'That's fortuitous, Katharine. I need some answers now. The pressure is on, especially from the Americans.'

'That's fine,' Katherine noted the urgency in his voice. 'I'll begin with Cocke, because everything hangs on him. We've broken his passwords.'

'Super. What's the consensus on what action to take?'

'We're decided. We came to the conclusion that we ought to close the websites down immediately and wipe his devices remotely.'

'Agreed. Has it been done yet?'

'No, we wanted your opinion. Hold on,' Katharine put the mouthpiece to one side, 'C has agreed. Do it now.' Katherine turned her head back to the mouthpiece. 'That's done, Charles. We won't succeed in cleaning his devices until he switches them on.'

'What about the plans for Istanbul?'

'The Turks have agreed to hand him over to the Russians. In return, we'll keep quiet on their plans over Syria and the Middle East. Now we know what they're planning, it makes life easier for us. It gives us a bit more influence with Turkey.'

'Good. That gives me a little bit to negotiate with. What about attempting to get hold of Cocke's devices?'

'That's organized. Our people have entrusted the work to our usual source. I anticipate that will succeed, as usual. If he doesn't switch on his devices, we must still get hold of them.'

'Bruce is anxious about the double agent farrago. Bartholomew needs an answer in the next two hours. Have we managed to resolve this one?'

'Yes,' Katherine was emphatic. 'Cocke was our man again. We found all of the financial files on his server. He sold the right to the information to a rival of the President, one Selby S. Pennewill. Reginald Winterbottom met with him in Washington DC recently – we've got to watch him carefully – I'll brief you when you get back. Bruce's helper gave us a copy of their conversation. Pennewill has distanced himself by using a chap in serious financial straits – one Frederick A. Starring – who's on the periphery of the charmed circle to make it appear that the files are available and were obtained by a British agent. The allegation it's a British double agent is just whispers without any evidence, but it's good enough to be taken seriously. I wanted to ask your opinion about how we deal with it. My suggestion is that we get the President's favourite news agency to publish, naming names. That way, because he believes their news, he'll accept there isn't a British double agent. It's really just a little sordid in-house argument between spoilt moneyed men.'

Charles looked at his watch. 'It's ten to the hour. If we get the news out in the next fifteen minutes through our usual anonymous channels, that'll give Bruce the opportunity to tell the Deputy Director what's going to happen. He'll get the credit for that.'

'Precisely. That's what I thought. It's ready to go.'

'Fine, press the button. Anything else?'

'We found out how he got into the Italian system, and I've been liaising with Italy on that one.'

'Have we got the plans?'

'Yes, Cocke had them all.'

'Do the Italians know we've got them?'

'Not as far as I know, just that we have found out how he broke into the computer.'

'Excellent. Let's leave it at that. I expect they'll be relieved enough.'

'Another thing, he's got some excellent stuff from China on their latest plans for "shāshǒujiàn" through a careless sub-contractor based in Paris.'

'That doesn't concern me at the moment. I've got a deal for the Chinese, which I expect they'll accept. Just in case, send me a list when we've finished.'

'Will do. Now for the Russians.'

'Oh yes?'

'That chap killed in Paris – de Lussan – has proved to be very useful. Cocke had administrator rights over both his computer and Smartphone. Cocke seems to have backed up both his devices onto his server before de Lussan was killed.'

'Really? How interesting.' The tenor of Sir Charles's voice expressed surprised interest.

'Yes. We know the Russians got into the flat. They probably killed him.'

'Yes, so I understand, Jane Arkwright briefed me at the embassy.'

'Good. She's very efficient. GCHQ noticed a great deal of activity in the Russian embassy last night. They've been lucky, because one of the G.U. people who went into de Lussan's flat boasted to a friend on his insecure Smartphone about finding the American document with the list of their Russian agents. Now we know the Russians have a copy. Luckily for the Americans, the G.U. officer was speaking to a fellow officer, so knowledge of the document has stayed within the G.U. You know, I find it difficult to believe that somebody listed all their double agents in Russia in this document in clear text. It's standard policy to split everything.'

'It's the present administration.'

'It must be.'

'We'll have to get used to it.'

'And so will the CIA.'

'Yes.'

'Anyway, we think the Russians probably seized the devices.'

'I know.'

'Oh, right. Well, both devices were switched on an hour ago. Luckily, we had the time to analyse what was on the computer. We found one directory that had all the incriminating files in one place. We took the opportunity to delete this particular file immediately.'

'I presume we haven't had the opportunity to do an exhaustive analysis of the files yet?'

'No, but we have a load of files from the Russians about their work on anti-satellite systems and their plans for future space defence.'

'It's obliging of them to let Cocke obtain copies. Is there anything in particular that will be helpful to me?'

'Yes. There's one file about the work they're doing with a

certain state in the Gulf. If they know we've got it, they'll think twice about rounding up the American double agents they know about and killing them quickly. This could be so serious for them that they'll lose all credibility for their present diplomacy in the area.'

'Can you send it to me?'

'I've put it on the shared drive. It'll be there for an hour, and then it'll be automatically removed, as usual. You can print it out locally.'

'Thanks. If they were happy to have killed de Lussan, they probably want Cocke as well. That helps me with the negotiations. One last thing.'

'Yes?'

'What about any of our secrets? Have you found any?'

'Not yet. We're looking.'

*

When the French woman approached her as the conference was ending, Captain Alexandra Milyukov did not know what to do. She rang Colonel Khodzhaminasov for advice. He was equally bewildered, and referred the matter to his superior. Unknown to both, the diplomacy of cooperation, the discussion of possible mutual concessions, and perhaps compromises, had already begun at the highest levels. Captain Milyukov was ordered to attend, but to be very careful, to report back for instructions if it was necessary, and to get to know any others that were invited. Major Zhuge Xiùyīng had the same concerns when approached by another member of the Direction Générale de la Sécurité Extérieure, and was given the same advice.

François Duhamel entered Le Grand Véfour in the rue de Beaujolais, at the top of the Jardin du Palais Royal, and was greeted by the Maître de Maison. 'Hello, François, the room is ready for you, and Guy and his staff have been able to put on a light afternoon tea for you, my good friend.'

'Thank you, Flavien, it is very much appreciated. We have Bruce and Sir Charles, as usual, and two other guests. They should be with us soon. Shall I go up?'

'Yes, please do.' The maître looked over to a waiter standing to one side. 'Nu'man, will you be so kind as to accompany Monsieur Duhamel to the salon?'

'Yes, Sir.' In one single elegant movement, the Syrian raised his right arm, moved his hand, palm facing François, and his long, elegant fingers, carefully choreographed, to indicate the way up to the salon.

'Thank you, Monsieur,' François acknowledged the actions of the young man in his late teens. They ascended the stairs.

François placed a book on the table. Covered in a clear protective cover, the slightly faded cover announced that it was written by Marcel Pagnol of the Académie Française, and entitled *Critique des Critiques*. Published by Nagel in 1949, it had a personal dedication dated 1963 to Michel Droit, editor of Figaro-Littéraire and a supporter of de Gaulle. It was number 63 of 100 copies published. He looked over the table in the salon on the first floor, set for five people. Cool in the intense lightness of the decor, with empire chairs in black leather and black wood lined in gold, the pale blue walls were covered with delicate white silk paper sculptures by Claudine Drai, protected under glass frames.

'Is there anything you would like, Sir?' The waiter stood slightly taller than François, slim – the slimness that accompanies hunger – his black eyes sparkling under gracefully arched eye brows, his mop of thick black wavy hair tamed by a barber neighbour to keep his appearance smart and professional in his attempt to make another life.

Just before François could reply, they heard a new arrival.

Bruce had entered. François thanked him and suggested he meet the newcomer. The waiter returned to the entrance foyer to meet Bruce, when Charles arrived. They greeted each other. François heard the conversation and returned to the entrance just as two vehicles stopped outside. The doorman opened the passenger doors of each in turn. The two guests had arrived, both looking awkward.

François took the initiative, introducing Bruce and Charles to Alexandra Milyukov and Zhuge Xiùyīng. Their discomfort was interrupted by a tall, well fed, formally dressed aristocrat of a man wearing a monocle in his left eye, who walked out of the dining room.

'I thought it was you, Beresford.'

Sir Charles turned to the sound. It had the familiar German aristocratic accent. After Charles had come down from Cambridge, he had entered Sandhurst before being commissioned into The Royal Dragoons. He served with them for two years in Northampton Barracks in Wolfenbuttel. It was here that he and fellow junior officers had been invited to join a fencing society. They had discovered that not everybody fenced by the rules. It was this man, von Pfuel, who had inflicted the injury, deliberately, on Sir Charles, now a thin shadow of a scar traced across his cheek, down to just under his jawbone. This fellow was not somebody Charles considered to be worthy of acknowledging. Sir Charles lowered his eyelids in contempt, and reacted with condescendingly hauteur by turning to thank the Maître de Maison for looking after them, and indicated to the ladies that they should follow him. Puzzled, and not realizing he was not welcome or that he had committed a faux pas, von Pfuel returned to the dining room. For Sir Charles, once such a matter was in the past, it was not necessary to revisit the memory. He did not need to be reminded. It was against the social conventions of his class for the German to do what he did.

François prepared the ground by asking everyone to be seated, and began the introductions. Bruce and Charles each sat one chair away from François, their guests sitting between the men.

'Forgive this unusual invitation, ladies,' François began, 'but occasionally, we have a meeting of the sixty-three club. This is an exclusive club. It was formed by young people at the beginning of their working lives because of a shared interest in countering ignorance, injustice, snobbery and envy.' He held up the book, 'Marcel Pagnol expresses a grievance against critics. He thinks they are jealous of the success of others, but those young people that formed this club thought that was a little too much – after all, good critics can help us avoid excessive self-confidence. We agreed that occasionally a critic does have a generosity of spirit. The membership of this club will decline as each of us,' he looked at Bruce and Charles, 'dies, although today we meet in the absence of our fourth member, Dame Katharine Neville.'

As he spoke, the waiter walked around the table, offering white tea, black tea and coffee. He placed milk, sugar, lemon, on the table, followed by plates of dainty cakes. Neither woman could resist the sight of such delicious shapes and colours laid before them, nor the endearing eyes of the waiter who coaxed each to try the delights prepared by the pastry chef. The men watched closely, and smoothed over any embarrassment by accepting delicacies themselves.

'We have invited you to a neutral place with great historical connections because some problems have emerged over the past few days that we think might be dealt with expeditiously and effectively. We encourage everyone to be candid. We are here to try to resolve problems, not create them.'

Captain Milyukov spoke. She was angry. 'How are we to trust either this or you? We are sitting here, as though we were at the United Nations Security Council. What do you think we will achieve? Why should we trust the imperialist Americans? The Americans lie and cheat all the time. They have the biggest empire. They took it in the nineteenth century, from the Indians and the Mexicans, and they have continually interfered with other countries ever since. They deliberately hide the truth, they lie and withhold facts when it suits the policies they want to pursue.'

'Well, Captain,' Bruce decided to offer an explanation, 'as François says, we have a rule in this club that we insist on people saying what they like, and what we say doesn't go beyond these four walls. So here's a thought. Yes, we Americans, that is those Americans that came before me, they manoeuvred to expand the country. Yes, they did lots of unkind things to many people, just like all empires, the British, French, Portuguese, Spanish, Dutch, Germans, Belgians to name a few. And you Russians have done the same, too. But right now, you and me, we're doing our duty in a world that's full of people that hate and who won't even try to understand the other. That's how I see it. Lots of things have gone wrong, and will continue to go wrong. For me, it's important to try and prevent the worst from happening.'

'But your software companies,' Major Zhuge Xiùyīng took the opportunity to enter the conversation, 'listen to the world's internet traffic, yet you do everything in your power to attack China.'

Sir Charles motioned the waiter over and whispered in his ear. He nodded and left the room.

'Sure, Major,' Bruce continued to respond, 'we need to know what's going on, just as you do. You have the *Xue Liang* rural surveillance program. We translate that as "Sharp Eyes." And you also have the urban "Skynet" and "Safe Cities" networks.'

'But you Americans have done it illegally. Your eminent professor, Alan Westin, exposed the hypocrisy in 1967. You lecture other countries on the rule of law, yet your own officers of law and order broke the law on surveillance for decades, and your judges did nothing to stop it. Why should we trust you?'

'Well, now, you seem to have a good understanding of my country,' Bruce approached the criticism by deflecting the main thrust of the comments, 'thank you for the education, Major, I really appreciate that. But you know we live in an imperfect world. We need to try and understand the other side. I'm not saying we're going to make big things come to pass here, but we can make little things happen.'

The waiter escorted Owain Davies into the room. He sat on a chair against a wall. He nodded to Sir Charles.

'What an interesting, and I may say, expected discussion,' François took the opportunity to intervene. He looked at his watch. Captain Milyukov and Major Xiùyīng looked at each other. 'Perhaps none of us around this table, if we looked objectively at the history of our own countries, would be pleased at everything our forebears did. Let us get on. Charles, you might wish to discuss the possibilities?'

Sir Charles adopted a studied unresponsiveness. 'Thank you, François.' At a nod from Sir Charles, Owain handed the envelope marked 'China' to Major Zhuge Xiùyīng.

'Major Zhuge Xiùyīng, please feel free to retire from the room to study the document enclosed in this envelope, and to let me know if the suggestion we make is acceptable to your superiors.' Mystified, Major Xiùyīng took the envelope and left the room, closing the door. The waiter asked if she wanted to walk to the garden. She agreed. He escorted her.

'Hello, Major. I have been expecting your telephone call,' Colonel Commandant Xú Delun confided.

'Yes, Sir.'

'We have had an indication that an offer was going to be made by the British.'

'Yes, Sir.'

'Have you the details?'

'Yes, Sir.'

'It is noisy your end, where are you?'

'It is a garden, Sir.'

'Oh, how nice.'

'The Director General of the British Secret Security Services has given me a folder, Sir. Inside is a document entitled "Shāshǒujiàn".' She listened to a slight involuntary intake of breath. She continued. 'It has the stamp of the Jiuquan Satellite Launch Centre, Sir. It is marked top secret, and it contains seal stamps.'

'Thank you, Major. You do not need to tell me any more.' Colonel Commandant Delun had been made aware this document was missing after a routine inspection of classified documents conducted by an inspection team. 'Have they told you what they want? Are they prepared to return this document?'

'Yes, Sir, they have left a note. I can retain this document on the proviso that we do not attack the British banking system as planned.'

'That is interesting. It appears to be a low price to pay. Stay on the line. Let me make a telephone call.'

'Yes Sir.' Major Zhuge Xiùyīng waited, holding her device, watching people stroll through the gardens. She looked up into the sky, admiring the clouds rushing across the horizon with a high and forceful wind.

'Major,' the voice of the Colonel Commandant rang out.

'Yes, Sir.'

'We agree. Inform them. There are many untied ends that we have to deal with, but our people are already working on another way to listen in. The game continues, and it has been decided to let this success of the British rest. Besides, we have some problems that we have to deal with in other European countries. A number of employees of our main IT company have been arrested. We will leave this alone.'

'Yes, Sir, thank you, Sir.'

'Thank you, Major. We will meet in the airport for our flight back to China tonight.'

After Major Xiùyīng left the room, Sir Charles passed the envelope marked 'Russia' to Captain Milyukov. 'I ask you to study the contents of this envelope. Please stay in the room. You will be surprised. That does not concern us. Once you have looked at it, we have a suggestion to make to you to discuss with your superiors.' Captain Milyukov opened the envelope. She removed the papers. They were marked Особой важности – 'Particularly Important'. 'As you will observe, the documents are classified to the equivalent to top secret in the US,' remarked Bruce. 'Yes,' Captain Milyukov replied in a less assured voice than she had previously used. The first document set out, in broad outline, the plans for dealing with certain powers in the Middle East; a second document provided a list of Russian officers of the SVR put in place in each of the countries, and a further document listed the double agents that Russian relied on in each country. Captain Milyukov was astounded.

'To save you asking, Captain Milyukov, we will get to the point without wasting time. You have a secret CIA list in your possession of people in Russia that are friendly to the United States. You probably call them traitors. We have given you a copy of a list of Russian spies across the Gulf that are intending to cause serious problems in the region, and you have a number of double agents working for you that we would call traitors. You will notice that the papers in your possession are merely print-outs. The actual file is electronic in form.' Bruce paused. 'This is our suggestion. You don't act on the information you have with our people in Russia for a month, and we won't act on your documents for a month.'

Captain Milyukov looked at Bruce, then at Sir Charles. She had never been put in such a position before with such powerful people in the world of spies and spying. Before she could respond, Sir Charles spoke. 'As Mr Waller has indicated, the papers you hold are in electronic form. As part of the agreement, the Turks will release to you the person that is responsible for hacking into your systems and obtaining these documents. You will be free to deal with him as you see fit.'

'What nationality is he?'

'As it happens, he is a citizen of the United Kingdom. Do you wish to make a telephone call?'

'I will, please excuse me.' The waiter, having returned with Major Xiùyīng, escorted Captain Milyukov to the garden.

Major Zhuge Xiùyīng sat down. She looked at Sir Charles. 'Yes, Sir, it is agreed.'

'Thank you, Major. Please enjoy the tea before we leave.'

Colonel Khodzhaminasov asked Captain Milyukov to wait as he made a call. He rang Colonel Rurik, the military attaché in Paris. 'Rostislavich, we have an interesting development.'

'Really? Go ahead.'

'You know the head of station for MI6 in Paris has been crawling over the satellite conference?'

'Yes, we have been watching her and the other agents.'

'It seems as if Sir Charles Beresford has not seen much of her because he is in Paris to help his French friend in the DGSE. Their other friend from the CIA has also been helping the French out.'

'I wondered what was happening. We did not have sufficient people to track them. The conference was deemed to be more important. That trio, when they are together, have made life difficult for us on occasions.'

'I know. This time they've offered us a deal.'

'Oh?'

He outlined the offer.

The military attaché thought they should accept. 'We can live with that. It's interesting that the British and Turks are willing to give up the person responsible for hacking into our systems. I wonder why.'

'Maybe they have finished with him, but we haven't.'

'I expect so. Perhaps they want us to do their dirty work. Anyway, I'll arrange a suitable end for him. It'll be a pleasure.'

Captain Milyukov returned shortly. 'My superiors accept your suggestions.' She was irritated.

'You don't like the decision?' Bruce watched her demeanour.

'No. You are all…'

Before she could finish what she intended to say, François interrupted her. 'Captain Milyukov, we appreciate you are exasperated with the message you have to give to us, but we live in a world where lives also matter. I sincerely hope that one day you will understand that although ideology is dangerous and misused by people in power, we are the practitioners of what is feasible. We must to work within our remit, and that is controlled by those with the lawful power.'

Bruce took the opportunity to try reconciliation tactics. 'You might know of the ancient Greek poet Archilochus. He wrote *the fox knows many things, but the hedgehog knows one big thing.* Isaiah Berlin, the Russian émigré, wrote a remarkable essay about Leo Tolstoy's philosophy of art and history described in his masterpiece *War and Peace*. He articulated an interesting division. The fox understands that she knows many things, but she can never clearly understand the world in which she lives. She accepts the limits of what she knows, and will pursue many unrelated and even contradictory ends. In contrast, the hedgehog never makes peace with the world. She is irreconcilable, rejects limitations, and lives her life with a single central vision.'

François decided to surprise Captain Milyukov. She did not like what Bruce was telling her. 'Major Milyukov,' he said with relish, 'I see you are surprised. Congratulations on your promotion. I am sure it is well deserved.'

'But...'

'The FSB cannot keep all of its secrets secret. What we are trying to say is that although pure objectivity is not attainable, we must be as objective as we can, and to consider alternatives, otherwise we risk limiting our judgment. Our countries rely on our professionalism, and that means we must see beyond our personal biases and prejudices. Have you read Жизнь и судьба – translated into English as *Life and Fate*, written by Vasily Grossman? By the look on your face, you are disdainful. We need to have a wider vision of the world. We should not be narrow in our approach, because others, who have to make decisions, rely on our judgments. It is for the politicians to consider our analysis. They can accept or disregard.'

Bruce saw that Major Milyukov was not remotely convinced. 'I know you don't believe this liberal stuff. You will say we start from a hatred of your country and China. That the US controls you. Maybe a lot of our people don't like Russia or the Chinese, but there are folks that think highly of you. Maybe US political policy is to control your countries. Whatever it is, we can't reconcile our positions, but it doesn't stop our agencies working together in our mutual interests occasionally, as Major Zhuge Xiùyīng has done.'

*

Sir Charles and Owain remained in the room. Sir Charles nodded to Owain. 'Thank you for arranging the envelopes, Davies, that was appreciated. We'll talk on the train. Apparently there aren't many passengers, so we have the luxury of a closed carriage. Will you kindly ask the driver to collect us?'

'Yes, Sir.' Owain descended the stairs to wait for the driver.

Sir Charles looked at the waiter as he cleared the table. 'What is your name, young man?'

'Nu'man, Sir.'

'That's an interesting name.'

'I am from Syria, Sir.'

'You have done an excellent job this afternoon, Nu'man. You have been very discreet. You know at least three languages'

'Yes, Sir, thank you, Sir. I had a long journey. You have to learn languages. I am learning French quickly.'

'Do you have family?'

'No, Sir. My immediate family were killed.' He related the fact as if it was a matter of routine. 'I have some distant relatives in refugee camps in Jordan.'

'I am sorry. The Jordanians have been hospitable.'

'They have, Sir, but they cannot do much for those that have had to leave their country.'

'That is true.'

'I am learning that our country and other countries in our region are pawns between imperial powers, from the Ottomans, to the French and British, and now the Americans, Russians, Turks, Iranians and Saudis. I am trying to learn more. Life is hard for many Arabs.'

'I wish you well. The layers of history are far from satisfactory. How old are you?'

Nu'man noticed Sir Charles placing his left hand on the table as he stood up, his heavy gold signet ring, worn through the ages of wear, prominent against the white linen of the tablecloth. The waiter remained stationery.

'Eighteen, Sir,' he said with the air and gravity of a mature man.

'Was there anything that you were able to bring with you?'

'No, Sir. I had music, but that is gone.'

'Can you explain?'

'I was learning the oud.'

'The oud is a beautiful instrument. I have some recordings of the late Munir Bashir.'

Nu'man's face expressed pleasure. 'His son, Omar, continues his father's legacy, Sir.'

'You have been trusted today, Nu'man. The Maître de Maison must think very highly of you. Your future is ahead of you, sadly without your family. I wish you well. *Inshallah.*'

'Thank you, Sir. They took pity on me when I asked for a job. I am in their debt for helping a refugee. But religion has no meaning for me.'

Sir Charles looked mystified; he was merely passing the time of day with a young man who had demonstrated his competence as a waiter. But such an apparently mundane civility was not the same for Nu'man, whose face was transformed. It was as if he had been drained of life. His stare was an image of nothingness, brought into sharp focus by the stark white silk paper sculpture attached to the wall behind his head. There was no meaning in his demeanour. He looked as hopeless and lost as he was when he came across the mutilated bodies of his family. Nu'man set his arms in the shape of their love. He lived with the patience of the vulnerable; living the life of the disconnected. 'When you are in need of assistance, you discover that some people will help you. The devout will also offer comfort. But many will only do so for a price. Sometimes the cost is money. At other times it is the defilement of the body. I have learnt how many pious men wanted to rape me.'

Sir Charles took a doily and wrote the title of a book: *Woman at Point Zero.* 'I don't know what to say. I cannot offer you anything that will alleviate the pain. I hope you will find this book by Nawal el Saadawi to be moving.'

'Thank you, Sir. The morning star has disappeared, and I

no longer have tears. I exist in the twilight. Maybe one day the skylark will come into view.'

Sir Charles looked him in the eye. He understood that Nu'man had yet to wake up from the nightmare into which he was forced. Nu'man met the look. He saw the steel grey eyes of a man that had witnessed operational failure, where good men and women were killed in the line of duty. He saw compassion in those eyes. Sir Charles understood. 'The mist will always be with you. I hope you will find truth and love one day.'

*

'You both look puzzled.' François stated as they left the restaurant. Both women looked at him. François continued. 'You also think that Sir Charles does not appear to have achieved very much.' The four stood outside under the porch in the entrance area.

Bruce provided the answer. 'Sun Tzu wrote that there are five classes of spy or secret agent. He called it divine manipulation of the strings when these are all at work, and nobody can discover how they operate. You – and we – have just experienced Sir Charles' most precious faculty. He had very little to barter. His hand was the weakest.'

François took up the strain of thought. 'He appeared to have nothing. Perhaps he doesn't have anything. We will never know. But he had something none of us had. Control. Each of us has something to our advantage, yet he appears to have nothing.'

Bruce continued. 'But don't underestimate him. We have known him for a long time. We have been friends for a long time. He has probably achieved more than all of us put together.'

Captain Alexandra Milyukov asked. 'More than the United States?'

'I expect so.'

Having been surprised by the mention of Sun Tzu, Major Zhuge Xiùyīng now understood. She smiled in admiration. 'He controlled the space in between.'

*

The drive to the Grand Tarabya in Haydar Aliyev Caddesi in the Sariyer district of Istanbul was longer and slower than usual. Michael Cocke's contact received a number of telephone calls along the journey. On reaching the sleek rectangular hotel, finished in 1964 and recently elegantly renovated by the architects Tabanlıoğlu, Cocke booked in to his apartment overlooking the upper Bosphorus. The curvature in line with the road was a wonderfully inspired aspect of the design by the architect, Kadri Erdoğan. The bright blue sky and contrasting colour of the water acted to diminish the size of the building, reducing its bulk.

Immediately he entered his room, the hotel telephone rang for him.

'Can you speak?'

'Hello, Sergey, I'm not sure. Let me go down to the coffee shop. I need a drink after my flight. I'll ring back.'

'Sure. We have something interesting.'

Michael Cocke left his bags unpacked, including the holdall in which he kept his laptop. Once he had left the room, the IT manager switched off the cameras and opened his door remotely, without leaving a record of the actions of the software code.

Cocke chose an outside seat, next to the road, enabling him to sit undisturbed and to watch the coming and going of patrons, waiters and waitresses. After a coffee had been brought to his table, he rang Sergey. The conversation led him to sign the bill with his room number and quickly retrace his steps to his apartment. He retrieved his black leather computer holdall and walked out to the reception area.

'You aren't a man.'

'You're correct. My name is Alev. I have discovered that when a person is faced with ambiguity, most people think of a man, not a woman. My parents gave me a romantic name. It means flame. It's a metaphor for passion in Ottoman divan poetry.'

Cocke was in a hurry, so reduced the light conversation to a single short response. 'Well, thank you Alev,' and then asked 'you are taking me to the boat?'

'Yes. Please follow me.' They took the brief walk to the marina. Cocke did not speak. 'Here we are,' said Alev, 'the crew will take you to your rendezvous.' Without another word, Cocke entered the waiting powerboat, an elegant Numarine 70 Flybridge.

Alev watched the wake produced by the engines as the captain sped out into the Black Sea. It reached a bigger yacht, sailing under the flag of the Russian Federation. Through her binoculars, it was clear that transferring him was not easy. Once he was on board the larger vessel, three tall heavily built men came on deck. He looked around him. This was a trap. In desperation, he threw his holdall overboard with a mighty, desperate swing. The men rushed to capture him. They wanted to prevent him from jumping into the water after his bag. The captain barked out an order. His assailants stripped him, and set about breaking each forearm, upper arm, femur and tibia. Two supported his dangling puppet like body, as the third took hold of his testicles and crushed them between the palms of his hands until there was nothing but blood and limp skin. Screams of intense pain wracked his body and contorted his face. They threw his carcass into the sea. He drowned slowly as the ebb and flow of the waves covered his bobbing head and mouth grasping for breath. A junior member of the crew appeared with a bucket and mop to clean the deck.

The captain of the powerboat waved his hand in salute, turned the boat and returned to the marina.

Alev directed her binoculars to the hotel. She nodded. Twenty feet under the water, two small explosions occurred. Neither was detectable on the surface. The first split open the obsolete laptop. The second, a fraction later, ripped the holdall open. The contents gradually fell into the depths. Ten minutes later, a diver left the yacht. He wrapped a weight around Cocke's corpse. Within hours, it lay on the seabed. He looked vainly for the holdall. Returning to the yacht, he reported his findings.

Alev made a call.

'Hello, Alev.'

'Hello C. It's complete.'

'Thanks for letting me know.'

Sir Charles Beresford looked into the distance, recalling the beginning of the second stanza of Charles Causley's poem 'Conversation in Gibraltar 1943'.

*

'Hey Bruce. I got ya an upgrade.'

'So I've discovered, Bart. You're a pal.'

'Thanks, Bruce, great work. It means we can begin to get our people out of Russia.'

'Yeah, we did good work as a team. Myra learnt a lot.'

'Sure did. Thanks, Bruce. I don't get what the Brits got out of all of this, though.'

'Nor me, but believe me, Bart, Charles wouldn't have been playing without something going his way. I reckon they cleaned up with Cocke before handing him over to the Russians.'

'OK, maybe. You know him well. Anyway, you'll be back in time for the next lot of hijinks. The impetuousness is wearing.'

'I know, but we've gotta work with it.'

'Sure. So long. Have a great flight and a nice weekend. See ya on Monday.'

Efficient as always, the crew looked after the passengers by serving them the meal shortly out of Paris. Sir Charles took the opportunity to discuss the events of the previous few days with Owain, complimenting him on handling the Turk and using diplomacy and tact where it was required. He hinted that he should consider his next moves within the Service. There was a need to pass on skills and knowledge to those beginning their career, and to use his expertise to run teams to develop and manage relationships. Sir Charles realised that Owain had noticed the book he had placed on the table, together with some files, after he had settled into the seat on the train. It was *Britain's Empire: Resistance, Repression and Revolt* by Richard Gott.

'The book.'

'Yes, Sir Charles.'

'It's interesting. It provides a more nuanced view of the empire.'

'I know, Sir Charles. I've read it. I'd say it was a strong corrective to what children are taught at school.'

He noticed the baronet wince slightly. Owain conjectured that Sir Charles was probably embarrassed about the ruthless blood-stained reality adopted by the British ruling elite to invade and take possession of other countries. He said no more.

'We have an hour left,' Sir Charles changed the topic of conversation, 'so what music have you on your device?'

'Well, Sir Charles, I'm a fan of William Lawes and his contemporaries, and I enjoy listening to Bill Evans.'

'And everything before and in-between, I hope. Very eclectic.'

'Yes, Sir Charles. I've recently discovered Anoushka Shankar.'

'Have you heard her play live?'

'Not yet, Sir.'

'Well, get organized. Life is short. We only get one opportunity, so begin soon.'

'I will, Sir.'

At this moment, Sir Charles's telephone rang. Owain Davies motioned that he would retreat further down the carriage. Sir Charles thanked him silently.

'Hello Katherine, how did Turkey go?'

'Perfect. Our team obtained his laptop and the Russians assume it's at the bottom of the Black Sea. I don't think they'll be too bothered about trying to recover it.'

'Agreed, although they have his Smartphone.'

'He probably kept things in compartments. I doubt if it has much of interest, although it might be a useful source of his contacts. Pity about the plans for the double agents in Russia.'

'Yes. I wanted to get one or two out and let the Russians deal with those that breached our trust in the most egregious manner. But when events change, we have to adapt.'

'Yes. Let's let the Americans and Russians dance around that issue and we can clean up after it's over.'

'Did Quinton's people succeed with the retina scan?'

'Yes, it worked a treat. We've uncovered a great deal of useful materials. Incidentally, we discovered Cocke was also using a freelance hacker who was based in Karlovasi, on Samos. The Greeks have charged him with a number of hacks.'

'Oh. Have we managed to keep his activities for Cocke out of the indictment?'

'Yes, the ambassador worked on it personally. They've got enough to imprison him for some time, so the work he did for Cocke does not matter that much. Anyway, have a good journey, we'll see you tomorrow.'

'Yes, pass on my thanks to the team. By the way, please let Margaret know that he's been rejected from a number of clubs. The news is in the latest issue of *Private Eye*. She will know to whom I refer.'

Charles then rang another number.

'Daddy, how lovely. Are you on your way back?'

'Yes Cecilia.'

'How did it go?'

'Oh, as usual.'

'You mean you won some and lost some?'

'Yes. I'm ringing because I want to buy an oud for a young Syrian in Paris. Do you know where I can get one?'

'I'll ask around. There must be somebody that sells them. Is she good?'

'I don't know how good he is, Cecilia. I only know he needs some help.'

'Oh, daddy, how I love you!'

Sir Charles Beresford replaced the book he was intending to continue reading into his bag. He sat back and placed his small headphones over his ears. He closed his eyes as the train sped through the countryside. He began to immerse himself in a recording of the Sonatas and Partitas by the great Johann Sebastian Bach, one of the most sublime pieces of music ever written for the solo violin.

'Well, Monsieur Duhamel, you achieved a great deal.'

'Thank you, Minister,' François looked into her eyes, 'but we might not have succeeded without the help of the British and Americans. At least we have dealt with the irritant in our midst and discovered the people involved in the clandestine attempt at overthrowing the status quo.'

'True. Your personal contacts proved to be of great use. We are in their debt. The uncovering of the anti-democratic group has been helpful. Our political leadership has been badly shaken. There are a few loose ends we have not resolved, though.'

'Do you know the Japanese artist Maruyama Ōkyo?'

'No.'

'He painted a two-fold screen for the tea ceremony. It's called *Cracked Ice: Patch of Ice Just Beginning to Form*. It comprises a series of lines of ink along a white paper surface with sprinkled mica. The screen is owned by the British Museum in London, but it is not on display, although it was lent to a number of museums in Japan in 2003 and 2004. Here, let me show you it.' He found the image on his hand-held device. 'See, it's a minimalist composition. There are only lines that we interpret as cracks in the ice covering a pond. The work is so simple. It's conceptual before European painters worked their way towards abstract art. I think of the world as a series of interconnected, but sometimes disparate, sets of facts and imaginings. The lines might be thick, so as to make the viewer imagine some parts of the ice are overlapping others because of the rise and fall in temperature. Also, you see that the lines leave the screen. We do not see an end to the pond – that is, if it is a pond. I always try to think of our job that way, although the pressure these people applied to undermine me has made the past few weeks difficult to remain calm and clear in thought. At times, it was difficult for me. But now it is over? I do not think we will find out everything.'

Eleanor de Beauchamp looked up from the screen. She was enjoying this moment, when he began to share his doubts with her. 'Indeed it is an amazing painting. My experience tells me that the more certain a person is, the least I trust them.'

'I agree. It will be interesting to see how things develop, Minister. By the way, Jacques de Lalaing and Stéphanie Beauharnais were engaged that evening.'

'So she experienced romance and terror in the same

evening, one after the other. She was very brave. We have recommended her for the Ordre national du Mérite. Sir Charles is quite a character.'

'He is. I am fond of him, but I am also fond of my other friends, Bruce and Katharine.'

'Please, call me Eleanor.'

'Thank you, Eleanor. One of my favourite restaurants is not far from your flat. May I take you to dinner?'

'Yes, that would be very agreeable, thank you. You can tell me more about Japanese aesthetics.'

*

The airline had spare seating in business class on the flight to Beijing, and Colonel Commandant Xú Delun encouraged those allocating seats to upgrade Major Zhuge Xiùyīng. This meant he could debrief her before the evening flight in a quiet area in the lounge.

'The American and Frenchman gave us a little lecture on objectivity.'

Colonel Commandant Xú Delun laughed. 'How amusing of them. I trust you listened attentively.'

Zhuge Xiùyīng was surprised by his reaction, and began to realise that there was a difference between being a junior officer that implements decisions, and the wider vision expected from those in more senior posts. 'Well, Sir, the Chief of the Secret Intelligence Service hardly said anything, although he was the one to give me the paper and the Russian officer an envelope.'

'The contemporary British ruling elite are an interesting example of failing to understand their new position in the world. They are arrogant and over-confident. Many of them do not realise that they are no longer a global power. They lost any moral authority they might have had when they joined the American invasion of Iraq in 2003. Behind the bluster and marketing rhetoric pushed on us by their embassy, there is nothing. In 1904, the Englishman Sir Halford Mackinder identified the end of what he called the Colombian era of European power. He was also astute enough to observe that China has a distinct advantage over Russia because of our extensive oceanic coastline. We control a substantial part of the Eurasian landmass, and that is why the Americans are taking so much interest in Asia – as they are in Africa, because we have been cultivating that continent for some time now. The British, once so dominant, have failed to realise that their strength now lies in staying close to their European part-ners. The little Englander mentality will cost them dear. The English liberals are no better. They do not know their own minds until reality strikes them with a calamity, then they regress to the right. But I expect Sir Charles Beresford knows all of this.'

'Is that why he offered so little in exchange for the document?'

'Possibly.'

'Do you think he will share the document with the Americans?'

'No. It's damaging for us to have mislaid it, but I expect the British keep some things from the Americans. I expect him to adopt the strategy of "actionlessness". It is possible that the man you identified in Singapore obtained more secrets that we would prefer. The British have discovered his hideaway. They gave him up to the Russians.' He looked closely at Zhuge Xiùyīng.

'But the British and French are not to be trusted. They destroyed the Yuan Ming Yuan – the Garden of Perfect Brightness. They claim they are civilized, but how could they do such a thing?'

'That is an interesting observation, Major. But what do you think the imperial court did to warrant such destruction?'

'It was a deliberate act of humiliation against our country.'

'That is partly true. The Yuan Ming Yuan represented the power of the ruler – an overwhelming physical presence with a divine purpose. But despite the aggression of the French and British in beginning the war, the emperor prevaricated over the peace. The point at which the victors lost their patience was when General Sengge Rinchin, the emperor's emissary, detained the members of the peace delegation. They were imprisoned and tortured. Some died. One does not treat members of a peace delegation in such a way.'

'Ah.'

'Yes. Might the reaction of the British and French be better understood in the light of this?'

'Yes, Sir, but one bad decision does not excuse another bad decision.'

'I agree. But this act, which we must bear in mind was directed against the emperor, and not the nation, had the desired effect. The imperial court capitulated and signed the peace treaty.'

'This is not in the history books, Sir.'

'No, it is not. Interestingly, European books do not cover this very well either. The facts are, perhaps not surprisingly, barely recorded. This makes me think of contemporary poetry. Do you know of Zang Di?'

'No Sir.'

'In 1984, he wrote a poem called 房屋与梅树 – 'Room and a Plum Tree'. Nobody is able to understand the clear intention of the poet. It is a little like the American poet T. S. Eliot, who took British nationality. Eliot was mystified by some of the lines in 'To a Skylark' by the English poet Percy Bysshe Shelly. In 'Room and a Plum Tree', nobody has explained the woman and the white doves. Obviously, each reader will have a different interpretation. My analysis of this poem is that we know the dove is emblematic of love, purity, peace, and also of spring. This is therefore significant. There is also the symbol of falling flowers, illustrating the ephemeral nature of life. Time passes, as does youth and beauty. My theory about the poem is based on contemporary events around the time and just before it is dated. In April and May 1984, President Reagan of the United States visited China, and on 19 December 1984 the United Kingdom signed the agreement to transfer Hong Kong to China. I think the references to coagulated blood and red hot intestines are intentional. Perhaps the author is saying that the pain is now in the past. Our country is rejuvenated. We are now continuing that work. We are the next generation. The future is in our hands now. We will not crumble to the Americans, like the Soviets.'

Zhuge Xiùyīng listened in silence, ensuring the Colonel understood that she was listening to him by facing him and nodding her head. She always listened carefully. One day she intended to be the one guiding others, and doing so with as much grace and erudition as she had witnessed over the past few days.

The ambassador, Ivan Vasilievich Shuysky, and Colonel Zinovy Khodzhaminasov stood up when the door opened and Alexandra Milyukov walked into the room. 'Congratulations, Major Milyukov, on your promotion' the ambassador said as he shook her hands, and indicated she and Colonel Khodzhaminasov should sit on the easy chairs. The ambassador remained in shirt and tie, waiting to put on his jacket when he left the office at the end of the day.

'Thank you, Sir, but you might be surprised to know that the French officer informed me of my promotion first.'

The tall, fit body of Ivan Shuysky visibly bounced with delight as he burst out laughing the moment a waiter entered the room with a tray supporting three wide-bowled champagne glasses and a bottle of 1995 Champagne by Krug.

'Major Milyukov, that is most amusing,' he looked at Colonel Khodzhaminasov, whose face also showed signs of mirth, 'you should be pleased it was the French that told you, and in such an old and superb restaurant. Zinovy, please pass on my thanks to Monsieur Duhamel when you have the opportunity.'

The two men nodded to each other. Alexandra was slightly perplexed, but the bond between these men was obvious, and what entertained them – as serious as she thought the issue might be – must illustrate their greater knowledge of the affairs of State, and what was deemed important and what not.

'Now,' the ambassador said as the waiter had filled the glasses three fifths full and handed each a glass before retiring, 'please do try this champagne. I am led to understand that you are at the beginning of your tasting career with this luscious invention. It is nectar indeed. I was told that this vintage is just beginning to be ready to drink. When we tried it, they said it was robust and marvellously rich. I agree; it is amazing.' He raised his glass, looked at each in the eye, and said, 'On your promotion, Alexandra Milyukov,' and they drank.

A silence followed.

'Well, Major, what is your opinion?'

'Stunning, Sir. This is most wonderful.'

'Good, I'm glad you like it. We are getting some cases sent to the Kremlin. Now, do tell me about the negotiations this afternoon.'

Alexandra Milyukov expressed her distaste at being lectured at by an American agent and French officer, being told to think about objectivity and hedgehogs and foxes, how she considered the US never stopped being untruthful, France full of effete pseudo intellectuals, and Britain just an empty shell of nothing that was of any importance, and getting angry at the bartering she had to do.

'You've had an interesting experience, Major. We all serve politicians, and politicians are generally not much concerned for truth. They're only interested in power and how they maintain that power. From our perspective we need to remember this. The Americans are fascinating. They have a legal-bureaucratic state, but it's big business that controls power through an oligarchical political system. American leaders are known to manipulate things their way. Until we had intercontinental ballistic missiles, the Americans thought they were safe. They have two massive oceans either side of the territory they have stolen. They have never had the numerous invasions we have suffered. White Americans used to watch people kill each other on television or in the cinema. War happened somewhere else for them; the oppression of native Americans and the lynching of black Americans was normal: it happened to others. Things changed, however, when we put missiles in Cuba. Before Cuba, they thought nothing of secretly putting nuclear missiles within miles of us in Turkey. Suddenly, white American civilians realised they were as vulnerable as everyone else, yet nobody gives us credit for ending that particular stand-off. Americans used to exaggerate external threats because they have never had to face aggression. Their fear is greater than the risks. All we want as a country is respect, but even now, they hate us.'

The ambassador removed the bottle from the ice bucket and filled their glasses. 'Zinovy, Major Milyukov is moving into an interesting job on her promotion. Perhaps you would like to give her a taste of the realpolitik.'

'Of course, Ivan Vasilievich. You will probably have realised that our techniques have changed. Gone are the days when we worried whether or not intelligence from a double agent was correct, or whether we should act on it. The British double agents of the 1950s and 1960s gave us materials that we never used. But we have begun to realise that when they were uncovered, this had an effect we did not fully appreciate at the time. Their defections and exposure created a paranoid dysfunction inside the British state. We have discovered that this is enough. It works. More recently, hacking American files have given us vast amounts of information. But even better, we now make the material public, and then the American media does the work for us, especially the media owned by right wing ideologues. We have moved from gathering secrets to conducting warfare through the use of information. We have not stopped. We continue to adapt. In the Middle East, we merely rent the problem. The Americans created it after their illegal invasion of Iraq and their failure to plan for the consequences of their actions, which has lead to the disintegration and chaos we now witness. That way, we can counter the Americans and their toadies without much effort.'

Alexandra Milyukov smiled and offered a comment. 'I understand. It is becoming very clear. Gorbachev was taken by the west, especially over the future of Germany. He cooperated, but that was weakness, and the west took advantage. The US secretary of state and the German chancellor assured him that NATO would not expand eastwards, but they never wrote the promise down.'

'Exactly, Major. The Americans think they can do what they like. They believe they are the greatest country on earth. They also assume they are a force for good – to make every nation into their own image. But then, when a country changes to be like them – maybe after the Americans have interfered in their elections or removed the legitimate government – they do not like the competition. That's why we work with countries like India. The Indians do not like being trampled over by the Americans, so we are happy to supply India with missile systems.'

'It is all about projecting our view of reality.'

'Yes, Major, you have it completely. The west has been doing it for too long. Now it's our turn. We control the narrative.'

'But Sir, we must be careful. We must never be angry, because anger poisons itself, and it is counterproductive.'

Ivan Vasilievich Shuysky knew this woman could go far. He had no doubt that her promotion was well deserved and would be beneficial. He and one or two others thought it necessary, at a senior level, to have somebody that recognizes that our lens is always crooked; to be familiar with our prejudices; to consider other points of view, and to listen and look at what is happening without preconception. He thought it was important for somebody to disagree. A consensus invariably means that nobody understands everything about the issue under discussion. That is how mistakes are made, because of the illusion that we understand the world and how it works. It is better to ensure it is safe to differ internally, rather than face unnecessary consequences. He hoped Alexandra Milyukov would succeed and influence a more pragmatic approach in the future.

The intercom buzzed on the ambassador's desk. He stood up and leaned over to press the controls.

'Yes.'

'You asked to be interrupted when the call came through, Excellency.'

'Yes, thank you. Put it through.'

The telephone rang. He picked it up. 'Yes, good .... excellent .... very good .... pity. Thanks.' He returned to his champagne and chair. 'You will be interested to know, Major, that the British and Turks between them delivered the Englishman to us. His corpse is now at the bottom of the Black Sea.'

Colonel Khodzhaminasov wanted to ask a question. 'Yes, I know what you want to ask, Zinovy, what about his devices. Apparently he threw the bag in which he carried his computer into the sea as soon as he realized what was happening. They managed to seize his Smartphone from the pocket of his jacket. They sent in a diver, but he couldn't find the bag. They recorded two minor tremors in the bridge, so they expect these were explosions. I assume the aim was to damage it in the case of an emergency.'

Colonel Khodzhaminasov offered his opinion. 'Maybe.'

'Yes, maybe. Perhaps the British switched his bag and replaced it with a dummy, then destroyed it to persuade us we had the actual device within our grasp.'

'That's the most likely explanation.'

Ivan Vasilievich Shuysky nodded. 'I agree, but our people are not concerned. The US Department of Defence is only just beginning to realise that the security of weapons systems is now controlled by software code, and even if the British have copies of some of our plans, it has been assessed that they will not share it with the Americans. The important thing is to have dealt with this particular double-dealing detestable little maggot.'

4

They Swept the Beach with Steel Blue and Diamond-Tipped Water

'You have done well, Major.' Zhuge Xiùyīng was standing in the office of the Commander, a Lieutenant General, of the Aerospace Systems Department of the People's Liberation Army Strategic Support Force. They were both in uniform.

'Thank you, Sir.'

'We are very proud of you.'

'Thank you, Sir.'

'Your loyalty to the Party and the country has been tested and found not wanting. I will be recommending you for another post that will lead to promotion.'

'Thank you, Sir.'

'There is one small thing.'

'Yes, Sir?'

'You do not appear to have had any male friends.'

'No, Sir.'

'You know, it is difficult to progress as a single person.'

'Thank you, Sir.'

'Having a stable home life is important to the Party.'

'Yes, Sir. I live a modest life.'

'We know you do. But there are other things in life to consider.'

'Yes, Sir.'

'There is a young man, a major, who is exceptional and, it is hoped, will go far. He is a model for the Party. I think it will be to your advantage to meet him. But he too will not go very far without, let us say, "fitting in".'

'Ah.'

'He also lives on his own. He does not have any female friends.'

'Ah.'

'I would like you to meet each other.'

'You are very kind, Sir.'

'Come.' The General led her to the garden. As they walked, Zhuge Xiùyīng took the opportunity to ask the general a question. 'May I ask a question, Sir?'

'Yes, of course.'

'General Yuan Ah is very knowledgeable about the English painter, Turner.'

'He is. In 1966, he was just out of university, having taken a degree in fine arts. The future was bright for him. He was well liked. He had excellent prospects. He respected the Chinese ancients. To him, art was everything. Then the world changed.'

'Yes, Sir.' Zhuge Xiùyīng only vaguely knew about the Great Proletarian Cultural Revolution.

'Now, as he begins to consider retirement, he is revisiting his past. A number of directors of art galleries are asking him to be involved with their institutions. He is highly respected. He uses the internet to do a lot of research. As you know, it can be a very good source of information.'

'Thank you, Sir.'

A young man in his mid-thirties came into view, dressed for the gymnasium, his well toned body at the peak of fitness. He sat on a marble bench. He got up and stood to attention when the General and Zhuge Xiùyīng arrived.

'It is a good day, Major Lài Rao.'

'Yes, Sir, so beautiful. The sun enhances the vision of colour.'

'You have just returned from exercise?'

'Yes, Sir.'

The general introduced the two young people. They shook hands and bowed to each other. He told the man about Zhuge Xiùyīng's exploits in Europe and work with the Australians. As the general took his departure, they both thanked him.

The youthful looking man invited Zhuge Xiùyīng to sit on the bench with him.

'It is nice to meet you.'

'Yes, it is nice to meet you, too.'

'You had a difficult experience.'

'Yes.'

'The general is proud of you.'

'Yes. He has said I am to be moved for possible promotion.'

'He has said the same to me.'

They sat in silence. He interrupted the quiet.

'The general offers advice.'

'Yes, he offers guidance.'

'He knows a great deal.'

'Yes.'

'He says promotion is problematic unless...' He could not finish the sentence.

'Yes, that is right. I would like to further my career.'

He looked directly into her eyes. 'One has to fit.'

'Yes.'

'I also want to be promoted. I want to ensure our country remains strong and stable. It needs me. Looking at you, I see that it also needs you.'

'The path can be demanding.' She offered an opening, sensing he had begun to understand her ambition very quickly.

'Yes, it is arduous. I have many men friends.'

'I have many female friends.'

'Ah.' He was silent again. He knew he had to continue. 'It is nice to be here with you.'

'Yes, I like being here with you, too.'

'You seem to be a nice person.'

'You also seem to be a pleasant person.'

'Would you like to meet my parents?'

'Yes, that will be kind. Would you like to meet my parents?'

'Yes, thank you, that would be good.'

'Is it possible...' This time she could not finish her thought.

'Do you mean is it possible to be together, and to be companions?'

'Yes,' she intuitively understood him. The unspoken was spoken. They could marry and remain single.

He smiled a smile of relief. She witnessed the relaxation of the fear of a secret. She also saw kindness in the way his face relaxed. They both knew what the other was trying to say, not having knowledge of the other, uncertain whether either could confide in the other. The first link of trust appeared in his smile. She lowered her head and turned towards him, her cheeks stretched in a beam of understanding. He looked at her.

'Do you like opera?'

'I have not been.'

'Would you like to try?'

'Yes, I would like that.'

He lit up. 'The Zhengyici Peking Opera Theatre are putting on one of the Mei Lanfang classics, *Taking Command of Troops* tonight. We shall go.'

They walked back towards the building together. On the first floor, the general was looking out of his window into the garden. They stopped. The man stood to attention, she followed and they both bowed to him. He nodded. Recently arrived, the political commissar, dressed in a dark blue suit, was watching, slightly to the side of the general. The general turned to him. 'These two are the best officers we have had for some years. They are both clever and loyal.'

'To the Party?'

'To the Party and the state. She has shown courage beyond duty. She is conscientious. I was informed this morning by the Central Military Commission that she is to be awarded the Medal of Performing a Vital Mission.'

'It looks as if they are together.'

'I have put them together.'

'Was there something wrong?'

'Their loyalty is unquestioned. They assiduously follow the Communiqué on the Current State of the Ideological Sphere from the Central Committee. They needed help. We will benefit from their intelligence in the future. They are both in the process of mastering what they do. They have a long journey before they reach the level of Wang Tianwen, the master puppet-maker from Xi'an. But unlike his puppets, they will learn to direct.'

'For the good of the state?'

'Of course. You will receive my report later this week. By the way, how is the work with the underwater internet cables? We should be able to match the Five Eyes in our ability to intercept soon.'

'The project is going well. More importantly, we are just beginning to exert control through leadership in the world. We will not let the unequal treaties return, even if we have to restrict the export of rare-earth metals the west so earnestly needs to sustain its dominance. We have learnt the lesson that the Americans forced on Japan in 1940, when they intensified the measures they put in place to restrict Japan economically. We need good people who will carry on the work.'

'Excellent. Our people have also done well with the technique of "living off the land", as the Americans call it. The major and his colleagues suggested we use technology tools that are already installed on systems. They are testing how to run simple scripts and shellcode directly in memory. If they can succeed, these methods create fewer new files, or, better still, they do not need files. That means there is less chance of being detected. If we can exploit these techniques successfully, we can be inside without being noticed.'

*

After arriving in Khabarovsk, they drove four hours along bumpy roads and forest tracks to the remote forest reserve of Durminskoye. He insisted on taking her to try and get a glimpse of the Siberian and Amur tigers. They were going to experience being inside the natural habitat of the wild cats, whether or not they caught a sight of them. It was a week in the forest, away from the town and city. Sharing a basic life with Alexander Batalov and his son Sergey, both of whom understood the wilds of their country. For him, he wanted to share the emotional resonance and cultural significance of place that he experienced when walking and tracking. He wanted to share the importance, power and meaning of the unique cultural space of a Russian forest with her. They enjoyed a *banya* and a meal before retiring to their log cabin. Previously, he had pushed the two beds together.

She had been amused the night before on noticing a discreet label in his trousers, sewn on the inside of the fly. It read, in capital letters, A PLACE OF EVERLASTING JOY. Made by an Italian company and bought in London, he had not noticed the label. When she pointed this out to him and they stopped laughing, they agreed the Italians had a great sense of humour.

Alexandra opened her eyes to the morning sun. She shifted her body, moving it over the motionless Zinovy, his head resting peacefully in the pillow. Lowering herself over his chest, stomach and pelvis, he woke to the bliss of her breasts resting against his body. He opened his eyes. They kissed intensely, passionately. He explored her back, buttocks and shoulders as she held his head.

'Zinovy,' she asked, 'you liked my mother?'

'My darling,' he replied, 'of course. She is very nice.' She propped herself on her hands. He continued, 'What you are doing, it's so wonderful. You are so vibrant, so independently forceful.'

'Are the bodies of men always so accommodating in the morning?'

'They have to be when they wake up to such a gorgeous woman as you. How much I love you Alexandra.'

She laughed. 'You are so beautifully handsome, your beard with its twenty-four hours growth is irresistible.' She rubbed her hands over his cheeks and chin. 'I love you too. Now, Zinovy Khodzhaminasov,' she began, seriously.

'Yes?' he responded.

'Are you, Zinovy Khodzhaminasov, going to marry me, Alexandra Milyukov?'

His hands reached up and behind the back of her head. He pulled her to him and kissed her deeply, fervently. She reciprocated with equal vigour.

'For all the world, I want to be with you for the rest of my life.'

*

Étienne arrived at London St Pancras on the last train of the day. He walked into the lower level after passing through passport control. He listened. A piano being played; a small group of people standing around, listening: the night players. The final bars of Erik Satie's *Nocturnes* sung through the noise and clamour of the railway station as the end of the day approached. He walked to the sound and stood slightly to the side and behind the performer. The last notes played into the distance. The pianist closed his eyes against the glare of the night light. The aficionados applauded lightly.

'Beautiful,' Étienne interrupted Owain.

Owain turned. 'Oh, how lovely to see you.'

'I was told you came here to play in the evenings.'

'Yes, but you didn't know I would be here tonight.'

'No. I hoped. Do you know his *Sonatine bureaucratique*?'

'Yes, it's a great piece. Every so often I think too much of work. It's sometimes best to stop and give it a rest.'

'Not thinking about work is quite a luxury. A lot of people don't understand how hard it is to be unemployed. I've been there, and I'm there now. The job with the German company has lost its appeal. What many people don't understand is that having a job is more than the salary. You also have social status, social relations, daily structure and ambitions. They all exert a strong influence on a person's happiness.'

Owain stood up.

'So you need a bed?'

'I need somebody in my life.'

Owain's face expressed his delight. Étienne looked so handsome and glamorous in his light grey polo neck sweater.

'Then come with me.'

They left to walk to Owain's home, waving to the remaining pianists and the hangers on. Étienne carried his modest rucksack on his back. They shortly arrived in Granville Square, reasonably intact since it was built in the 1840s.

'It's a nice place.'

'Thanks. I bought it when this area was unfashionable. My parents insisted. It was too big for me, but they knew it would be money well spent. I couldn't have done it without their help. It's out of my price range now. But there's a nice thing to the name of this square – it's named after Granville Sharp. He was one of the first campaigners to try and abolish the slave trade.'

'Cool. I like it.'

They continued their conversation as Owain led Étienne into the living room.

'Freedom might be black.'

'But equality is white.'

'And as the Jamaicans will say, we're both moonlight shades.'

'You straddle two worlds, that of the imperial overlord and one of its former colonies, and I was born subject to the colonial master.'

Both men recognized the insight the other had on the way their respective societies reacted to the tensions of the twenty-first century. They knew what it was to experience belonging and otherness, identity and difference. Étienne looked at the books on the table, Chester Himes *My Life of Absurdity* and *The Quality of Hurt*. Owain noticed. 'I'm not sure I would have liked him if I met him, but he might have been right when he wrote that the life of a black man was an absurdity. It's a danger being a mix.'

'Maybe in some countries.'

'Yes.'

Étienne scanned the room. 'You are very tidy.'

'I know, I can't help it.'

'It's endearing.' He looked at the postcard reproduction of the painting *Olympia* by Édouard Manet propped up on the book shelf.

'What do you see?' Owain asked.

'Two women, one of which is a maid holding the flowers.'

'Exactly. I don't ask many people that question, because I know they never see her.'

Étienne raised his eyebrows. 'You told me about Scotland on our walk over. Do you want to make that call?' Étienne's suggestion, framed as a question, expressed a decisiveness that Owain could not resist.

'Archibald, how are you?'

'I'm well, Owain, how good to hear your voice.'

'Archibald, that Abhainn Dearg. Do you still have it?'

'Of course, young man. It's awaiting a visit.'

'Well, how about in the next day or so? I've got a friend with me. We'd like to visit and do some of that walking you suggested.'

'Owain, there's a bed for you both. Come up. We'll go to my parent's cottage for a few days. I share it with my sister and her family. We'll do the walking and discuss poetry, art, music and politics.'

As Owain spoke, Étienne wandered around the room. A CD lay on a table, ... *and His Mother Called him Bill.* When Owain finished the telephone call, Étienne asked, 'You like Billy Strayhorn?'

'Of course. He was so brilliant. His music is wonderful.'

'I know.'

'It's Duke's piano solo at the end of the album that's so poignant: Lotus Blossom.'

'Yes, it's played straight from the heart, in remembrance.'

Owain led the way upstairs to the bedrooms. Étienne placed his rucksack down in the guest room. By the soft light of the bedside table lamp, he took Owain's left hand, raised it, and undid the cuff button. He then lifted Owain's right hand. Owain winced. 'You're bruised.' He held the hand tenderly.

'Yes, my fingers. I held on too tightly.'

'How?'

'The Turk in Belgium.'

'You got the better of him?'

'Yes.'

'Good.'

Étienne undid the cuff button. He then began to undo the buttons on his shirt.

'Owain.'

'Yes,' his breathing had changed in anticipation. He felt the warmth of Étienne's physical presence, so close.

'I've never met anyone like you.'

Étienne removed Owain's shirt, revealing a regularly exercised torso. 'You don't know what to do, do you?'

'No. I just...'

'Leave it to me.'

Owain closed his eyes and put his hands around Étienne's waist. Affection and tenderness enveloped the lovers. *Je t'aime,* Étienne slowly whispered. He took him into his arms and kissed him. Owain reciprocated.

The First Law of Fate is the second espionage novel in a trilogy. *The World's a Minefield* is the first of the series.

Lightning Source UK Ltd.
Milton Keynes UK
UKHW012334250620
365566UK00005B/1122